T0265710

Praise for Tony Harrington's first adventure:

BURYING THE LEDE

"LeValley draws on his own experience as a newspaper reporter to give the mystery an authentic feel. Fans of reporter sleuths…will be pleased."
— *Publishers Weekly*

"Suspense is handled adroitly. It bobs and weaves its way toward an exciting climax. While you'll definitely want to know what happens next, you'll savor the telling of this tale as much as you'll enjoy its revelations. Don't miss it. RECOMMENDED."
— *U.S. Review of Books*

"Nearly impossible to put down and more than satisfying in its surprising conclusion."
— *Midwest Book Review*

"This book is filled with suspense that begins in the courtroom, and keeps readers on edge through a reporter's emotional investigation of a double-homicide. Overall score: 9 of 10."
— *BookLife Prize*

"A mystery thriller that takes you on more twists and turns than an Iowa gravel road. Start the book with nothing else to do because you may not be able to put it down."
— **The Honorable Thomas Vilsack, former Governor of Iowa and Former U.S. Secretary of Agriculture**

"A pleasing blend of courtroom drama and an unsolved crime, all told through the eyes of a good, old-fashioned investigative reporter. An enjoyable read that kept me turning the pages."
— **John Shors, Bestselling Author of *Beneath a Marble Sky***

CRY GRAVE FROM AN UNKNOWN

CRY FROM AN UNKNOWN GRAVE

JOSEPH LEVALLEY

BookPress®
publishing

Published in Des Moines, Iowa, by:

Bookpress Publishing
P.O. Box 71532
Des Moines, IA 50325
www.BookpressPublishing.com

Publisher's Cataloging-in-Publication Data

Names: LeValley, Joseph Darl, author.
Title: Cry from an Unknown Grave : a Tony Harrington Novel / by Joseph LeValley.
Description: Des Moines, IA: Bookpress Publishing, 2020.
Identifiers: LCCN: 2020906617 | ISBN: 978-1-947305-10-6
Subjects: LCSH Human trafficking--Fiction. | Sex crimes--Fiction. | Murder--Fiction. | Journalism--Fiction. | Iowa--Fiction. | BISAC FICTION / Mystery & Detective / General
Classification: LCC PS3612.E92311 C 2020 | DDC 813.6-- dc23

First Edition

Printed in the United States of America

10 9 8 7 6 5 4 3 2 1

For our children:

Rachel, Christopher, Alex, Emma, Beth, and Luke,
who are cherished, as should be all children.

"These are the woes of Slaves;
They glare from the abyss;
They cry, from unknown graves..."

— *Henry Wadsworth Longfellow, from "The Witnesses"*

Chapter 1

Would today be the day he killed her? The girl couldn't help but wonder. He came to her nearly every day, seemingly powered by an insatiable lust for her. How many times had he taken her? How many different ways? She had lost track. She had been abused, injured, and humiliated in ways she couldn't have imagined only a few months earlier.

Before this nightmare began, she had little experience with men beyond a drunken father who never got out of his chair except to pee and a few male teachers who seemed too busy to even notice her at school. She hadn't known a man could do such things to a woman or *would* do such things to a girl still in her teens and half his age.

She had endured horror upon horror nearly every day since she had awoken and found her ankle padlocked to a steel cable anchored in a concrete wall. She was trapped in this...place. What was it? A basement? A storm shelter? She couldn't imagine the purpose for a room such as this, windowless, with a concreate floor and walls and a metal ceiling interrupted only by the door that swung up at the top

of the open wooden stairs. Unless, of course, this *was* its purpose—
to imprison and abuse girls, undetected by the eyes and ears of the
outside world.

And if that was the purpose—her heart nearly stopped at the
thought—it meant, undoubtedly, that others had come before her.
Others who had been raped and tortured by the beast who called
himself Justin.

The ordeal hadn't started with him. It had started with a young
man with a nice smile and soft hands. "Just call me Donny," he'd
said when he'd stopped his pickup truck and offered her a ride.

She knew it was risky to climb into the cab of the truck with a
stranger, but Donny had big, chocolate-brown eyes, wavy blond hair,
and dimples. The dimples attracted her and, to be honest, it was cold
walking on the road at night. The inside of the truck looked so warm
and comfortable, she couldn't say no.

"I'm Brittany," she said shyly. "Thanks for the lift." She didn't
want him to know she was running away from home. It seemed so
dumb when she thought about saying it out loud. She also worried
he wouldn't let her ride with him if he knew. Looking back, she
realized it had to have been obvious, when she was unable to name
a destination and was content to stay in the truck for as long as he
would allow.

Donny worked hard to put her at ease and succeeded. After a
couple of hours of driving, they pulled into an interstate highway
truck stop. He bought her waffles and a Pepsi and seemed genuinely
concerned about her. He asked why she was walking on the highway
alone, and eventually she told him everything. She was miserable at
home. Her dad was worthless to everyone except the owner of the
liquor store, and her mom was gone. One night, two years previously,
Brittany's mom had met a rodeo cowboy in a Kansas City bar.
They had spent the night together at the Best Western, and the next

morning, when the cowboy had asked her to go with him, she had gone.

Brittany had taken the phone call. With one call, her mother had tried to make everything okay, explaining why she had no choice but to go, why she couldn't handle life at home anymore. As if one final comment of, "You know I love you, baby," could make it all okay, could make her mom any less selfish.

As soon as the phone call had ended, Brittany had known her life had changed from bad to impossible. Now she was the one who had to worry about finding money to keep the lights on and the rent paid for their tiny two-bedroom apartment in Platte City, Missouri. Now she was the one who had to make up lies about her dad's "illness." Now she was the one who had to cook and clean and try to maintain some semblance of dignity in their existence. All of this on top of the pressures of school.

And so, after two years of trying, failing, and crying, Brittany had followed in her mother's footsteps and had walked out the door. It was her seventeenth birthday. She was certain she was old enough to do better on her own. She'd taken only what she could stuff into her school backpack: some clothes, a few toiletries, and her only friend—her smartphone. Less than an hour later, Donny had picked her up walking along the paved county road north of town.

Brittany knew now that Donny had put something in her food or drink at the truck stop, probably while she used the restroom. She barely remembered the end of the meal and was unconscious by the time Donny pulled the truck out of the parking lot. When she'd woken, she was in this dungeon, a single light bulb hanging from the ceiling to fend off the darkness, one double mattress on a wooden platform, and a toilet and sink on one wall.

She was left alone for the first full day. Locked in this cell that smelled of mildew and sweat, tethered like a lamb left as sacrifice for the lion, she was terrified beyond comprehension. She screamed until she was hoarse, then cried until she passed out from exhaustion. When she awoke again, she was hungry, hungrier than she could remember ever being. This deep hollowness, combined with the fear she was being left to starve to death, made her nearly wild with anxiety.

When she heard the door open and saw a man appear on the steps, she wept again, this time with a mixture of fear and relief. The man was huge—tall and wide and a little overweight, like some of the football players she had seen on TV. He was carrying a bag of food from McDonald's. The aroma washed over her like a dream, as if the meal were from the finest restaurant in the world. Disoriented, scared, and angry, she wanted to scream at him. She wanted to strike him. But overwhelmingly, she wanted to eat. He set the bag in the far corner of the room, just out of her reach. He smiled broadly, not with warmth or compassion, but with an ugly and ominous leer. His words stopped her cold.

"I'm Justin. I don't give a damn what your name is. You wanna eat, you gotta do something for me first. Take off your clothes. You heard me! Hurry up. I paid a lotta dough for you. Now you're gonna make it worth it."

Brittany remembered every detail of that first time, but hated dwelling on it. Justin had raped her. He was brutal and demanding. Pain, fear, shame, and hunger had overwhelmed her. Now they were her life. Day after day for... How long now? Weeks? Perhaps a couple of months.

Slowly, Brittany was becoming numb to it all. The horrors of her captivity were erasing nearly every part of the person she used to be. That teenage girl with dreams of finishing school, getting a job, meeting a nice boy—that girl was gone. She had been replaced by this creature who existed only to eat once a day and lie in a room waiting for the beast called Justin to arrive and seek his pleasure.

One corner of Brittany's mind remained aware enough, and smart enough, to know she would not survive this ordeal. For starters, she knew no one was looking for her. She had left her dad a note saying she was leaving and wouldn't be back. If he sobered up enough to read it, he wouldn't report her as a runaway because he wouldn't want the authorities coming to the apartment asking questions.

More importantly, neither Donny nor Justin had made attempts to hide their faces or disguise themselves. She knew what that meant. When Justin decided he didn't want her anymore, he wouldn't let her go. At some point, he would grow tired of her, kill her, and dispose of her as though she were a cockroach caught crawling on the floor of his bathroom. Knowing these men would get away with what they had done enraged her. Knowing they would do it again to another innocent girl filled her with despair. Knowing she could do nothing about it tested her sanity and caused her to withdraw further from reality.

Would today be the day he killed her? Brittany didn't know. She only knew she hoped it was.

Chapter 2

At 3 a.m., Tony Harrington's cell phone rattled him awake. He had been asleep for less than two hours, so he was groggier and testier than usual.

"Rich, this better be good," he mumbled, assuming it was Rich Davis from the Iowa Division of Criminal Investigation. Davis was a friend and an occasional source of late-night calls to alert Tony to breaking news.

However, a very different voice said, "Mr. Harrison?" It was a very small voice, obviously female. She sounded young.

"It's Harrington. Tony Harrington," he responded with more than a little irritation in his voice. "Who is this?"

"Well I, uh, well... Do I have to tell you that if I want to share something important?"

Tony turned and sat up, his feet hanging over the side of the bed. "I can't make you tell me your name, of course," he said. "But I sure would appreciate knowing who you are, especially if you have something to share with me for the newspaper. I can't write material based on information from an anonymous source, so—"

The girl cut him off. "But I don't care about the paper," she said abruptly.

"Then why, may I ask, are you getting a newspaper reporter out of bed at 3 a.m.?" Tony found himself wondering for the hundredth time whether it was smart to have his personal cell number listed on the website of the *Orney Town Crier*, where he worked as a reporter. It led to a lot of good news tips, but sometimes only led to a loss of sleep.

"Pleeease," the girl said, as though she were praying for divine intervention. "I need you to... I need someone to... Look, I just need help. Please!"

Tony realized she was crying and immediately changed his tone. "Okay, okay. I'm sorry. It's the middle of the night after a long day. Why don't you tell me why you called, then we'll decide where to go from there?"

"I called because I heard about you. I heard you weren't afraid of anybody. My friend told me you even took on politicians and killers and won. She said you were really nice, too. I thought maybe someone like that, someone brave and nice, could help."

Tony wanted to correct her. He wasn't so brave. He was afraid of many things, including the men he had helped to send to prison earlier that fall. But the girl was speaking quickly.

"I need to tell someone about the girls. I think they've killed some. I know they've hurt them. I can't call the police because they say the cops are part of it. When I heard about you, I thought maybe you were someone who would care...who would do something to stop them. I want to—"

It was Tony's turn to interrupt. "Hold on! Slow down. You mentioned a lot of 'theys' and 'thems' just now. I'm not following you. Please start at the beginning and try to stay calm. And what's this about killing? What girls are you talking about?"

"Well," she replied, "I'm not sure. I know what I saw, and I've heard about these others."

Tony's frustration was growing. "Okay, let's start with some simple questions, like what did you see, where were you, when was this, and who did it?"

She was sobbing now. "I don't know where we were. They never told us anything. Somewhere like Kansas or Nebraska or maybe Iowa."

Tony mentally groaned. As a reporter for one of the smallest daily newspapers in Iowa, he didn't have the time or the budget to pursue stories in other counties, let alone in other states. However, the girl's obvious agitation and the magnitude of the crimes she was describing kept him on the phone. Even if he couldn't pursue it, he could pass the information to Davis who would know who to call to initiate some kind of follow-up.

"Okay, but what did you see? And by the way, are you safe? Where are you calling from?"

"I think I'm safe for now." The girl sniffled, and Tony could imagine her wiping her eyes. "I'm hitching a ride with a truck driver. I think we just went over the Mississippi River, so maybe in Illinois? Is that right? She stopped to use the can at a rest stop. She's a she. Isn't that cool? The truck driver is a she. I'm using her cell phone. I watched her use it, so I memorized her access code. I think that's her coming out of the can, so I gotta go."

"Wait!" Tony stood and yelled into the phone. "I need something more—a lot more. I can't do anything with the little bit you've shared."

"Well," the girl said in a rush, "you can start with four girls I know. These men took them to motels and made them do stuff. You know..."

"You're talking about sex?" Tony said, wanting her to be clear so he would have something concrete to share with his boss as well as with Davis.

"Yes, yes, and other stuff," she replied hurriedly. "Three of the girls got beat up pretty good. I heard they buried one in the woods. They gave us drugs sometimes, too."

"Gave *us*?" Tony asked. "You're talking about you, too?"

"Yes, me too. I knew I shouldn't... Take the drugs, I mean. But it helped." She paused, then said, "You know, it didn't hurt so much. I wasn't so scared when I was high. I'm sorry." Another sob. "But I stopped when I realized I never would escape if I was constantly out of it or hooked on something. And here I am. I got away. Now I just want to get somewhere they can't ever find me, and I want someone else—someone like you—to make them stop doing these things."

"Please tell me your name," Tony practically begged.

"First name only," she said. "I'm Glenda. The other four are Emily, Shelly, Elaine, and Ashley. I heard about two other missing girls, too. I mean I heard these guys talking about them like, you know, like they knew *why* they were missing. One was Brittany and the other was Madison. I'm sorry. I gotta go."

"Please," Tony said. "Call me back as soon as you can."

There was no response. A glance at his phone showed the call had ended.

Tony knew it would be useless to try to sleep, so he pulled on his jeans and a navy V-neck sweater, brushed his teeth, and headed to the office.

***

The newsroom of the *Town Crier* was dark and quiet at 4 a.m. While today's world of web sites and social media postings kept all news media active twenty-four hours a day, a small daily paper like the *Crier* could get by with just one person monitoring the wire services and CNN through the night. That person was Evelyn Crowder, a former columnist who now worked from home. In his seven years at the *Crier*, Tony had seen her perhaps a dozen times and had only spoken to her once or twice. In addition to monitoring the news, her job was to determine what stories might be of interest to the residents of Orney, Iowa, and convert them to postings on the *Crier* web site. Because Evelyn worked remotely, Tony's solitude was complete.

As he flipped on a few ceiling lights and booted up his computer, he knew he had most of the next five hours to himself. The busy hours for a morning paper's staff were from noon to midnight. Even the early risers wouldn't wander in until 9 or 10 a.m.

He took a deep breath, settled into his chair, and looked around the empty newsroom. He loved this old building and loved the atmosphere of the newspaper. While he wasn't a morning person, he enjoyed the relative quiet, sharing the space with nothing more than the hum of computers and fluorescent lights in the background, and the aroma of a hundred years of ink, paper, rubber cement, and darkroom chemicals emanating from every surface. The modern tools of computerized pagination and offset printing had done nothing to diminish the ambiance. Tony could close his eyes and easily imagine the room full of manual typewriters, slapping away at cheap yellow paper, and someone yelling "copy," so a runner could take the draft to the copydesk for editing.

It all served as a constant reminder of the men and women who had come before him, devoting their lives to reporting the news and serving their community. Orney, Iowa, may not be a metropolis, but its size did not diminish the challenges or the rewards of the work, or the sacredness of the task.

Okay, Tony, enough philosophizing. Get to work. He turned to his keyboard and spent the first hour typing thorough notes about the telephone call. He wanted to remember every word. When satisfied, he emailed the document to his boss, Ben Smalley, the publisher and editor of the *Town Crier*.

Ben was a Pulitzer Prize-winning journalist who had worked for big dailies in places like Detroit and Baltimore, before surprising everyone who knew him by quitting his job and buying a tiny daily paper in a town of 15,000 people northwest of Des Moines, Iowa. Tony was probably the only person in Orney who knew Ben had done it because his former bosses had refused to publish an investigative report he had written involving organized crime and money laundering on the east coast. Ben had told Tony it was intolerable to work in a place where fear and greed, rather than a dedication to the truth, dictated news decisions. Ben's boyish idealism was just one of the many things Tony loved about him.

With his memo to the boss finished, Tony opened up a search engine and began looking into the basic facts regarding human trafficking in the U.S., which is what Glenda appeared to have been describing. What he learned was appalling. The year prior, the FBI had received nearly 500,000 reports of missing children. While most of these were "cleared" after the children were found, the cumulative total of cases remaining open over the past 20 years still numbered in the thousands. Tony couldn't believe his eyes. *Thousands* of children who had disappeared and had never been found? How was that possible? As he continued his search, the frightening, horrendous truth unfolded. Just one alarming fact in a list of hundreds was that more than 14,000 calls had been made to the National Human Trafficking Hotline in a single recent year, and nearly 5,000 of those had been determined to be cases of human trafficking.

As a longtime Iowa resident, and as a reporter, Tony's perception was that only a few missing children cases were reported in Iowa each year. He thought most cases ended with the child or teenager being found, with the occasional sensational exception occurring in which a teen was killed. Clearly Tony's perspective was wrong. Many more children were disappearing than he'd realized. Somehow, they were escaping the notice of most people, as well as the news media. He couldn't imagine how this was possible.

Tony was absorbed in reading online articles and statistics and didn't realize how much time had passed until he heard the door open and saw Ben walk into the back of the newsroom. It was 8:40 a.m. A young-looking fifty-something, Ben was tall and lean. This morning, he sported khakis, a green Polo shirt, deck shoes, and a jacket with a round Detroit Tigers logo emblazoned across the left breast.

He strolled over to Tony's desk, smiling. "You're here early. After Freed's party last night, I figured you'd sleep in today."

"Yeah, that's what I figured, too," Tony responded, thinking that the party at Nathan Freed's estate seemed like a year ago. "I got a phone call at three this morning. Take a look at the report I sent you, then let's talk about it."

"Okay," Ben said, nodding. "Let me get the coffee pot going, and I'll read it first thing." Ben knew Tony was strictly a diet soda man, so he wisely discouraged him from making coffee, even when Tony was first into the office.

Twenty minutes later, Tony saw Ben waving at him from behind the glass wall of his office in the corner. Tony gathered up some printouts from the research he had been doing and walked into Ben's ten-by-ten "private" office, closing the door before sitting down.

"Well that was quite a call you got," Ben said. "I suppose you're as baffled as I am about what to do now."

Tony nodded but said, "I'll call Rich Davis, of course. I think the DCI needs to hear about this. But he's going to be as frustrated as we are. This Glenda person gave me enough to paint a picture of a pretty horrific situation. Girls being drugged, molested, injured, maybe even killed. But then, when you look at my notes, you realize she never really told me anything. I have no full names, no specific dates, not a license plate number or even any certainty about where these things happened. Even the name Glenda sounds like she made it up."

"More like the name of a great aunt, not a teenage girl," Ben agreed, leaning back in his chair and frowning.

"Any thoughts at all?" Tony asked.

"Well a couple of things," Ben said. "First, you shouldn't be surprised to get a call like this. There probably will be others. After all the publicity you received around the events of the past couple of years, all kinds of people are going to reach out to you. Some will have legitimate leads on potential stories, and some will be total nut-cases wanting to convince you an alien invasion force is living in their neighbor's attic. And some, like this one, will be hard— perhaps impossible—to determine one way or the other. What do you think, Tony? Could this all be some kind of prank? Could she have been delusional?"

Tony shook his head, saying, "Anything is possible, but she sounded to me like a young girl on the run who was genuinely upset —smart, but very scared." Tony passed the stack of print-outs across the desk. "My brief research this morning also gives some credence to her story. In just a few hours, I learned the enormity of the problem of human trafficking and the exploitation of not only girls, but boys too. I was shocked to learn that it's very prevalent in the Midwest, including in Iowa."

"I am, of course, aware of the issue," Ben said. "If this had come up when I was on the East Coast, I wouldn't have been surprised; but I have to say, I never expected to be hearing about it here."

Tony continued, "I also learned it comes in many forms. People think it's all about illegal immigrants—girls shipped in from Asia or South America—but that's actually a small percentage of the trafficking cases. Most often, these are American kids, coerced into sex by someone they know. It might be someone they met online or in a place like a shopping mall or a concert venue, or it might be someone they've known for years. A young girl, for example, might believe herself to be in a loving relationship with a man or even a boy from school, then, after giving in to sex with him, she is urged or forced to have sex with others. These kids often feel they 'owe' it to the people who have befriended them. The predators frequently seek out the most vulnerable young people. There are countless cases of runaways or kids who are struggling in school being seduced into these relationships. Once they've been talked or forced into sex with multiple partners, they lose all sense of self-esteem and don't believe they can return to a normal childhood existence. So it just continues. Perhaps worst of all, the younger they are, the more money they make for the predators. Twelve-year-old girls are often rented out to clients five or ten times a day."

Saying it out loud made Tony's revulsion even greater. He could feel the bile in his stomach roiling. He swallowed hard and shared one more revelation. "And Ben, according to a couple of those articles, another frequent scenario is family members forcing children to provide sex for buyers."

"Yes," Ben said grimly, "I've heard."

"Can you imagine? Older siblings, parents, and even grandparents have been known to force young children to do these things."

"Dear God," was all Ben said.

"Trafficking is too nice a word for this," Tony said. "This is human slavery, plain and simple. These people treat other human beings as property, to be abused and sometimes tortured in exchange for money from their clients. As others have said in those articles, slavery may have been abolished in America, but it hasn't been eliminated."

"Well then," Ben said, thumbing through the first few sheets of paper, "we have to do all we can to help this girl who called, and the other girls, too. Talk to Rich and see what he thinks we could or should do. Then come back and see me."

Tony stood, nodded, and turned to go. He stopped himself, realizing he never wanted to fall into the trap of taking for granted how lucky he was to have a boss like Ben. He turned and said, "You and I both know this could take a lot of time and maybe even a lot of money to pursue. I appreciate your support."

Ben normally might have smiled his acknowledgement, but Tony could see he was looking at some of the statistics from the National Center for Missing and Exploited Children. The look on Ben's face was a mix of horror and determination. Without looking up, he said, "Even if we never find Glenda or one of those other girls, her call has made us more aware of the problem. Our job is to make others aware, as well. There's a story in this, no matter what happens. So get your ass out there and find the best story you can."

Tony fought the urge to salute and strode back to his desk.

Chapter 3

After Tony had gone, Ben spent a long time reading the print-outs of specific cases of girls and boys being trapped—sometimes abducted, but more often seduced, then coerced—into a life of prostitution, drug addiction, and abuse. He had been vaguely aware of the issue, but had not realized the magnitude of the problem, neither in numbers nor in the extent of the horrors inflicted upon the children. Tony was right—this was the worst kind of human slavery. As his disgust and dismay grew, so did his anxiety about pursuing the story.

More specifically, Ben was concerned about Tony. His young reporter had been through a tremendous ordeal during the past two years, covering a double homicide, a related suicide, and a host of other crimes perpetrated by powerful people. More to the point, the girl Tony had loved had been killed, and Tony himself had been threatened, held captive, and shot at. Considering Tony was still grieving Lisa and recovering from his own traumas, asking him to tackle a subject as gruesome as human trafficking seemed risky.

On a whim, Ben picked up his cell phone, scrolled for a

number, and dialed.

"Nathan Freed," said the deep voice of Lisa's dad, a longtime Orney attorney.

"Mr. Freed, I'm glad I caught you. This is Ben Smalley at the *Crier*. Do you have a minute?"

"Of course, Ben, and call me Nate. I thought I made that clear at the party last night. Is this newspaper business or something else?"

"Well, I'm calling about Tony, so it's a little of both."

"Oh," Freed said, sounding surprised. "Everything's okay, I hope?"

"Yes, yes, but I wanted to run something by you, confidentially." Ben then explained his anxiety about having Tony investigate the trafficking story. He shared some of what he had learned about the issues involved and what Tony might face as he pursued it.

Ben said, "I know I have no right to bring you into this, but you know Tony better than anyone. Do you think he's ready to take this on?" Ben paused, then said, "Wait, before you answer, I'm realizing how inappropriate it was to call and ask you this. I'm sorry."

"Don't be sorry," Freed said quickly. "I appreciate your concern for Tony, and I certainly share your affection for him. Because of that, the selfish part of me wants to say drop it. Keep him out of danger, from both his own demons and the evils he may face from the perpetrators of these crimes. On the other hand, I know Tony needs the challenge. He's not going to get over what happened in the past if it remains the biggest thing that ever happens to him. Does that make sense?"

It certainly did. Ben knew Tony was too talented and too aggressive to spend the next two years, or ten, or twenty, covering city council meetings and traffic accidents, and reminiscing about the big story he covered when he was young.

Freed continued, "More to the point, Tony needs to be busy.

Not just busy with everyday tasks but with something that really engages his heart and mind. I hate thinking of him sitting and dwelling on what happened before. So, if it was my call, and clearly it's not, I would tell him to go for it." He chuckled. "I'm glad, by the way, that it's *not* my call. I wouldn't want the responsibility of having to make these types of decisions."

"Yeah, thanks," Ben said dryly, then realized he was sounding sarcastic. "No, I mean really, thanks. You've been helpful."

"Well, not very," Freed replied. "Keep me posted on what you decide, and please let me know if you need anything at all."

Ben promised he would and rang off. He was mad at himself for having made the call, mostly because he knew it was a waste of time. He knew Tony would follow the story with or without his blessing. After receiving the call from Glenda, and learning what he had about the issues involved, Tony would pursue this relentlessly until he learned the truth. He had seen it before. He had come to expect it. And it still scared the shit out of him.

***

Tony and Agent Davis agreed to meet at 11 a.m. in the Quincy County Sheriff's Department, where the DCI kept a local office. Davis figured if the information was important, his partner, Agent Dan Rooney, and Sheriff George Mackey might as well hear it, too. The Sheriff's Department was located in the west wing of the jointly-occupied Law Enforcement Center, just five blocks west of the *Crier* building, on the edge of downtown Orney. The east wing housed the Orney police and fire departments, and the center of the building contained the small county jail and the dispatch center. The residents of Quincy County were proud of this collaborative and efficient approach to law enforcement facilities and considered it a model for other counties to follow.

The meeting room was windowless and undecorated, with one long table, eight chairs, and a video screen at the end opposite the door. It reminded Tony of the basement of the Legion Hall where locals went to play poker on Friday nights. All that was missing was the Budweiser and the cigar smoke.

Sheriff Mackey was in uniform, but Davis was surprisingly casual in khakis, a plaid shirt, and a quilted vest. Rooney looked as expected for someone who worked undercover a lot, with his bushy red hair uncombed, and wearing jeans and an Arizona State sweatshirt.

Tony was glad his own attire, the jeans and sweater, weren't out of place. He handed out copies of his notes around the table. As he presented the facts, his first and biggest surprise regarding their reactions was that the other men in the room were not overly confounded by what they heard. Davis and Rooney said the DCI was well aware human trafficking, particularly for the purposes of forcing young boys and girls to provide sex for money, was a huge problem. Even Sheriff Mackey, normally as uncooperative in sharing information as a reformatted hard drive, acknowledged the topic was being discussed more and more at law enforcement meetings and in professional journals.

Tony thought of the sheriff as someone who would re-read his 20-year-old *Playboys* before picking up a professional journal, but he kept the thought to himself.

When the four had finished examining Tony's notes and other information, Davis and Rooney asked a few follow-up questions. Then Davis said, "If this call is for real, then Glenda is a remarkable girl. The experts will tell you that after being coerced into this so-called life, most young people suffer enormous mental health problems and withdraw into themselves. They trust no one, especially not strangers.

The fact she reached out to Tony is a rare exception. Again, if it's real, it may give us an opportunity to break one of these human trafficking rings."

He paused, then held out his hand. "Tony, unlock your cell phone and give it to me."

In some circumstances, Tony might refuse such a request without a warrant, but he knew what Davis wanted. Once the phone was active, Tony opened the recent call list and handed it to the agent so he could write down the number of the phone Glenda had used when she called.

Davis then woke up his own cell, dialed, and instructed the person at the other end of the call to have the number traced to its owner and, if possible, to learn the current location of the phone.

"That's gonna take a little while," Davis said, closing his phone and handing back Tony's. "Obviously, it's the best lead we have, so let's hope it gets us somewhere. In the meantime, let's take a look at the other information."

Tony didn't think there was anything else concrete enough to mention. Davis surprised him when he said, "Let's talk about Glenda's friend who knows you."

Tony sat up straighter in his chair. "Huh?"

Davis plowed ahead. "Think carefully about what Glenda said. Her friend didn't just tell her you were brave, which anyone could surmise from the news coverage last year. That person would be wrong, of course, but the mistake is understandable under the circumstances." Davis grinned at him. "However, Glenda's friend also said you were *nice*. Where did she get that if she doesn't know you, or at least know someone who knows you? Even your interview in *Rolling Stone* didn't depict you as nice. It was positive, but it was focused on your involvement in solving multiple murders from the previous year. Nice just didn't come up."

Tony nodded his understanding of what Davis was saying. It seemed thin, but he was glad to have something to ponder while they waited for more solid information.

"Even if we're wrong, let's assume Glenda's friend has some kind of connection to you. Who do you know in middle school or high school who might have crossed paths with someone in Glenda's situation?"

"Well, uh, no one I can think of off the top of my head," Tony said, truly baffled. "I don't cover the schools for the paper, and my only sibling is in graduate school in Chicago, so I just don't know anyone in that age group."

"Sure you do, Tony." Davis persisted. "Maybe it's a waitress or a counter clerk at a fast food restaurant. Maybe it's someone from church, or the son or daughter of a friend. I want you to give this some real thought."

Tony promised he would, and Davis moved on.

"Secondly, let's talk about the geography. Here we really have to do some speculating, but I think we can at least put some borders on the area we have to consider. Glenda said she was in a semi that had recently crossed the Mississippi. She thought they were in Illinois. That makes sense, considering she indicated she might be traveling from Kansas or Nebraska.

"It's not a certainty, but Interstate 80 is the most likely route they're taking. Probably seventy percent of the semis going from Iowa to Illinois are on I-80. And Glenda mentioned a rest stop, which also indicates an interstate highway. She could have meant a truck stop, but for now, let's take her at her word. Now think about the timing. She probably has been in the truck for less than a day. Not many semi drivers are going to let a hitchhiker, especially an underage one, stay with them while they're sleeping. So let's assume she was picked up yesterday afternoon. If the semi driver is operating at 3 a.m., she can't have started before that, at least not legally. So let's map this out."

Davis got out of his seat and turned to a white board on the wall. He scribbled a rough outline of Iowa and indicated each of the contiguous states. As he drew, he said, "If Glenda was right that she was in Kansas or Nebraska when some of these horrors were inflicted on her, and if she escaped in northern Kansas or southeastern Nebraska, and if she found a ride on a highway north, maybe I-35 or U.S. 71, and crossed into Iowa and caught a ride going east on I-80, the timing works out about right to place her in western Illinois at three this morning."

The others in the room nodded, but without enthusiasm. Davis continued. "I know that's a lot of ifs, and she could have started in Minnesota or Missouri, or even South Dakota, but if you go much farther west, you get into mountains. We have to hope she's smart enough to know Kansas looks different than western Colorado or Wyoming."

Tony's appreciation of his friend grew as Davis spoke. Tony certainly understood all this could be wrong, but there was a logic to it, and again, it gave them a place to start.

"To say all this more simply," Davis said, "She thinks she was in Kansas, Nebraska, or Iowa. Considering she's headed east in a semi, she's probably right. We should assume she escaped from somewhere in southwest Iowa, northern Kansas or eastern Nebraska. It's still a very big circle, since we can't be sure how long she's been on the run, but I'm willing to bet it's not for long. Finding a phone to make a call is not that hard these days, so why would she wait more than a few hours to contact Tony?"

The four men looked at each other and nodded again. There was a glimmer of relief in the room simply because they felt they had made some progress. It wasn't much, but it was better than banging their heads on the conference table. *Just barely better*, Tony thought gloomily.

Davis summarized. "So the plan is first to find Glenda, if we can. Let's hope the phone number puts us on her trail, or that she calls Tony again. Secondly, we find the friend who knows Tony or knows someone who knows Tony. And, lastly, we alert the authorities in a dozen counties or so, within the geographic circle we've painted, to be on the lookout for girls in distress. Truck stops and rest stops are popular places for these creeps—the traffickers I mean—to find johns and sell their 'merchandise,' so maybe the authorities down there can get a couple of people in plainclothes to do some trolling.

"Speaking of rest stops, let's check to see if Illinois has security cameras monitoring their interstate stops. If they do, that could be a huge help. Once the cell phone pinpoints the location of the call, we might get lucky and catch the driver or the truck on video."

He set down the marker and checked his fingers for dry erase ink. As he moved toward the door, he turned back and said, "Oh, by the way, Dan, why don't you spend some time today on the database of children reported missing from those three states? See if there's been a spike in activity or any reports that seem to be related in any way to what Glenda said. Obviously, if you find any first names of missing girls who match those on Glenda's list, we should take a close look at those."

Dan nodded, and the meeting began to break up.

"Tony, hold up a minute." The voice was Sheriff Mackey's. Tony tried to hide his reaction—surprise? anxiety?—as he turned back to the table in response.

After the others had left the room, Mackey said, "Here. I grabbed this for you." He slid a piece of paper across the table to Tony.

"It's an application for a permit to carry a concealed weapon,"

Mackey explained.

Tony was completely dumbfounded and a little miffed. He pushed the paper back toward the sheriff and protested. "There's no way I could..."

Mackey interrupted. "I know you probably haven't considered it, but I think you should. You have a knack for finding the worst sociopaths and criminals in our midst. And you obviously are interested in chasing these people." Tony tried to resume his protest, but Mackey held up a hand. "Okay, okay, let's give you the benefit of the doubt and say your interest is only in pursuing news stories. Unfortunately, experience has shown me, even if it hasn't shown you, your destination too often happens to be a cesspool full of murderous thugs."

Tony was shaking his head, but Mackey raised his voice. "You were almost killed last year. Twice! Now you're talking about finding people who make millions of dollars a year forcing innocent children to have sex with strangers multiple times a day. Think about that. Think about the kind of people who do such things. Do you know what the average life expectancy is of one of these children dragged into this so-called life? Seven years! Do you think you're immune to the dangers these kids face? Take the application. If you don't fill it out today, at least think about it."

With reluctance, Tony retrieved the form, folded it, and put it in the pocket of his slacks. "Okay, Sheriff, I'll think about it, but I don't love the idea. In fact, I've never liked guns, and I don't believe anyone should have the right to carry a concealed weapon."

"Of course you don't, you little liberal prick," the sheriff said with a scowl, just barely masking a smirk. "But if you find yourself face-to-face with one of these monsters, you're gonna be glad you did this."

Tony was astonished the sheriff cared enough about him to

have even thought of it. He thanked Mackey, but as he left, he knew he would never complete the application. In his mind, the only thing worse than being killed would be to kill someone else.

Chapter 4

Tony was leaning back in the chair at his office computer, eyes closed, as he tried to imagine what young boy or girl would know him well enough to describe him to Glenda as "nice." He was drawing a complete blank and was almost relieved when a voice broke in.

"Am I interrupting anything important?"

He opened his eyes and found himself looking up at the smiling face of Madeline Mueller, a fellow reporter at the *Crier*. Tony realized she was making an attempt at a joke, since it must have seemed he was napping in his chair.

"No," Tony said, smiling back. "I was just trying to answer a question in my mind, and failing."

"Have you had lunch?" Madeline asked, showing a surprising lack of interest in whatever question Tony may have been pondering. "It's later than usual for lunch, but I know you were at Mackey's office for a meeting, and I thought maybe you were like me, still needing to eat something."

"Actually, yes. Now that you mention it, I'm starving. Are you headed someplace special?"

"Nope, just down to Willie's for a burger," she said. "I thought it would be nice to have some company."

Tony didn't know Madeline well, even though they had worked together for nearly four years. Tony had always thought of her as a short-timer at the *Crier*. As far as he knew, she had no ties to Orney, but she was a good reporter and talented writer, so he assumed she was here as a stepping stone to someplace bigger. With four years of good work on her resume, he was sure she would be moving on soon. Maybe that's what she wanted to tell him today.

***

At 1:30 in the afternoon, finding a booth at Willie's was no problem. In fact, except for two local shopkeepers sitting at the counter eating pieces of Erma's homemade pie, Tony and Madeline were the only customers.

As promised, Madeline ordered a cheeseburger, plus a side salad. Tony asked for the hot beef sandwich. Both had diet sodas.

Once the drinks were delivered and they were relatively alone, Madeline spoke first. "Tony, I never told you how sorry I am about what happened to Lisa."

Tony tried to wave her off, but she continued. "After her death, you seemed so distant. Clearly you were grieving deeply. Then with everything that followed, it just seemed like a whirlwind."

"It was a crazy time," Tony agreed. "You certainly don't need to feel sorry about it."

"Well I am, at least a little." Madeline paused, apparently contemplating what to say next. "I didn't know her well, but she seemed lovely, and you two certainly seemed happy."

Tony mumbled an acknowledgement, and Madeline moved on.

"I also never told you how impressed I was... I am... with the work you did. You and Ben were incredible. You earned that Pulitzer and all the other recognition you received.

"Thanks, Madeline. I appreciate the compliment, but everyone at the *Crier* made it possible, you included."

Madeline smiled and surprised Tony when she said, "Okay, that's total bullshit, but it's nice of you to say." Tony grinned back, and Madeline said, "I wanted you to know that I also resented the hell out of it through most of the past two years."

Tony stopped smiling and leaned back, looking at her anew.

She said, "I hope I don't sound petty, but I need to be honest. Imagine yourself if the roles were reversed, with me taking on murderers and politicians and uncovering the story of the year, maybe of the decade, while you stayed behind and covered the school board election."

It embarrassed Tony to admit he hadn't thought about it, and he said so.

"The point of all this," Madeline went on, "is that I want you to know both of these feelings can exist simultaneously. Intellectually, I can appreciate you, while emotionally, I resent your success. Does that make sense?"

"Yes," Tony nodded. "It makes complete sense, and I'm grateful to you for sharing these things. But I have to wonder, why now? Is there something more?"

"Two things," she replied. "The scary part is that it'll be easy for you to think they're related. But I'm telling you they are *not*, and I expect you to believe me."

"Of course I'll believe you, no matter what this is about. Everything I know about you tells me you'll be straight with me. In fact, this very conversation is strong evidence of that."

"Okay then," Madeline said. She paused the conversation while

tonight. Lunch is on you."

Tony was once again open-mouthed as he watched her go out the door. *Holy shit*, he thought. *I guess I'd better go home and clean up my house.*

***

The sex was, indeed, great. Madeline arrived precisely at seven. Tony was ready with a bottle of Beringer White Zinfandel chilled, a couple of candles burning in the living room, and a collection of Jimmy Buffet ballads playing on the stereo. He had on an old pair of Dockers, loafers, and a maroon t-shirt. His rented two-bedroom bungalow in the long-established middle-class neighborhood wasn't sparkling clean, but at least it was picked up and looked presentable.

Madeline looked stunning. Petite, at just five feet, five inches tall, she looked taller in her high-top boots with heels. She wore a leather skirt and a tube top, with a white cotton button-down shirt over the top. *Sexy, but not slutty*, Tony mused. *She put some thought into this.* Madeline's dark, curly hair just reached her shoulders. She wore only a touch of makeup to accent her brown eyes.

Tony poured the wine, and they sat together on the couch. Tony couldn't deny he was aroused, even if he was unsure of the wisdom of her visit and fighting back a growing sense of betraying Lisa. They looked at each other awkwardly, then looked away. They turned back to face each other and almost simultaneously burst out laughing.

"I, uh... Oh, boy..."

"No, don't talk. How about you let me just..." Madeline suddenly set down her wine glass, put an arm behind his head, and swung her leg over his lap, lifting herself up on her knees so she was straddling him. She leaned down and kissed him hard. It only took a moment for Tony to abandon any reluctance and respond. He pulled her face back into his and kissed her gently while his other hand slid up under the cotton shirt and explored the small, soft mounds under the tube top.

After a few minutes, with their breathing intensifying, Madeline took Tony's roving hand and coaxed it up her leg beneath her skirt, under which she was wearing nothing.

Well, maybe a little slutty, Tony thought with a suppressed smile as his fingers found the intended spot. Madeline moaned as he touched her. He pulled back both hands, slid them beneath her buttocks, and stood up. She locked her legs behind his back and her arms behind his head. He carried her into his bedroom and kicked the door shut.

***

It seemed like hours before they were finished and quietly entwined on sweaty sheets, with Tony staring at the ceiling fan. He wondered what would happen next. Would she spend the night? Would she kiss him on the cheek and walk out the door? Would the clock strike midnight and turn her into a pumpkin? He leaned over and looked at the clock beside the bed, and burst out laughing.

"What?" Madeline asked.

"It's 9:45. I was sure half the night was gone."

Madeline chuckled. "Well, when you don't have to take the girl to dinner and a movie, you can get started a lot earlier."

That made Tony laugh again. "Hey, speaking of dinner, are you hungry? We can have Panucci's deliver a pizza."

"That sounds great. You call and I'll go in the bathroom and try to make myself look human again."

"You look fine just like that," Tony said as he watched her climb out of bed and walk naked through the door.

When the pizza arrived, they were sitting at the small table in Tony's kitchen, drinking wine and eating small salads Tony had thrown together.

The talk was light, as Tony described his childhood, growing up first in Chicago and later in Iowa City with an Italian stay-at-home mother and a father who was a famous author and screenwriter, now a professor at the University of Iowa.

"I've been incredibly fortunate," he said. "My parents and sister are great. I loved growing up in Chicago and was surprised to find I really liked going to high school and college in Iowa City. Of course, it probably helped that my folks love to travel. I've seen a lot of this country, and of course, we made regular trips to Italy to visit my mom's family."

"Oh, of course, Italy," Madeline said with more than a hint of sarcasm. Then more seriously, "It really does sound ideal, Tony. My life hasn't been as exciting as yours, but I have no complaints."

She said she grew up in Toledo, Ohio, where her father was an insurance broker. "I know that sounds boring, but he was very successful. He had his own agency and catered to all the CEOs and other bigwigs in the city. He ended up with more than twenty people working for him. He worked too hard, and ate too much, and a few years ago, had the heart attack his doctor had warned him about."

"I'm sorry," Tony said, feeling a pang of sympathy. "Did he survive? Is he okay?"

"Well, yes, he survived. But after bypass surgery and additional warnings from the cardiologist, he retired from his business. Two of his agents bought him out, and now he mostly plays golf or goes sailing on Lake Michigan."

"That sounds like a nice life," Tony said.

"Yeah..." She hesitated. "It's nice, but he's not the same. He's lost some of his spark. It's almost as if he's resigned himself to passing the time, waiting to die."

Tony began to respond with reassurances he had neither the background nor expertise to express, when Madeline cut him off and moved on.

She said, "Mom, on the other hand, is irrepressible. She runs a boutique in one of the wealthy western suburbs. Retail's tough these days, with internet shopping and all. But she's determined to keep the shop alive. She's constantly changing the inventory, making sure the latest fashions are on display and coming up with creative ideas for new experiences in the store."

Madeline clearly was proud of her mom, and Tony said so.

"You bet I am. She's a force of nature. For example, last year for Halloween she hosted a costume party. When people got there, she had a couple of movie characters in the store. Not just people dressed as characters, but the actual people who played the parts in the movies. One was from *Star Trek*, another from *The Hobbit*. They weren't the big stars, but everyone knew they were the real thing, so of course they made the party a huge success."

Tony had to admit Madeline's mom sounded pretty cool.

"So you come from two parents who were very driven. I can see where today's lunch conversation came from," Tony said.

"Yeah, about that. Tell me about the story we're chasing."

Tony had known she would ask and was prepared to discuss it. He grabbed copies off the kitchen counter of his memo to Ben and the internet research from that morning and handed them to her. "Read my memo first. It's brief. The rest is just background information."

Madeline read, the alarm growing on her face. When she finished Tony's summary, without looking up, she asked, "You think this is real?" She was already scanning the other documents.

"I do," Tony said. "But even if I were skeptical, how can we not at least try to make sure?"

He then described his discussion with Ben and the subsequent meeting with Mackey and the DCI agents, including the plan Rich Davis had outlined. He did not mention the sheriff's plea that he apply for a concealed weapon permit.

"This is horrifying. Unbelievable!" Madeline was shaking her head as she began reading one account of an Iowa girl whose new "boyfriend" had taken her on vacation to Las Vegas. When they arrived, there were men waiting for her in the hotel suite. She was held for two weeks against her will, while her boyfriend collected big money from men who used her for their pleasure. When they finally let her go, they threatened to kill her and her entire family if she ever told anyone. That didn't stop her from going to the police. When they were ineffective in doing anything about it, she took her story to the *Las Vegas Sun*, which was the source of the article Madeline now was reading. The publicity hadn't helped, either. None of the men involved had been apprehended, according to the follow-up article which was next in the stack.

"How is it possible these guys got away with this?" Madeline wondered aloud. "You would think everyone from hotel security to the FBI would be all over it."

"Hard to fathom, I know," Tony agreed. "Maybe the cops out there really are in on the deal, like Glenda's captors claimed. Maybe they're just incompetent. Or maybe in a state where prostitution is legal, they just don't make sex crimes a priority. I honestly don't know."

"God, it's horrible, but thank you, Tony, for sharing all of it. I'll go in early tomorrow and talk to Ben. Then I'll continue digging for information about the topic, and start organizing it into a reference file we can access as we need it."

"Wow, that's outstanding," Tony said, and meant it. "Thanks. And," he felt himself blush again, "thank you for tonight. It really was..." He couldn't find the perfect word, so he settled for, "great."

"And you only cried a little, just there at the end."

"I did not!" Tony objected, and Madeline giggled. *She has a nice laugh*, Tony thought. They stood and pushed their chairs away from the table. She walked over to him and kissed him lightly.

"I see in this report that you've been up since 3 a.m. I know Freed's party was last night, so you must be surviving on a couple hours' sleep. I should let you get some rest."

She turned to go, but he pulled her back to him. "I wouldn't mind doing this again," he said with a grin, then leaned down and kissed her.

She looked up at him, then left without another word.

Tony was pretty sure he wouldn't be able to sleep, but thirty seconds after climbing back into bed, he was out and dreaming... of Lisa.

Chapter 5

Tony woke once again to the sound of his cell phone. He groaned and rolled over, sunlight assaulting his eyelids. *Well, at least it's not 3 a.m.*, he thought as he pushed the green "Answer" button.

"Harrington."

"Tony, it's Rich. Time to get your ass out of bed."

Tony glanced at the clock. It was 9:30.

"I'm forced to agree," he grunted. "What's up?"

"We're getting some results back. I'm sorry to say what we've learned so far is troubling."

Cradling the phone under his chin, Tony pulled on his slacks. "Troubling how?" he asked.

"The phone Glenda used to call you was an unregistered pre-paid cell."

"Why would a truck driver be carrying a burner phone?"

"That's the question Dan and I have been pondering for the past hour. It could be innocent, you know. The driver lost her primary phone or doesn't like to take an expensive phone on the road or something."

"Yeah, sure," Tony grunted, well aware of all the other sinister things it also could imply.

"I know what you're thinking, but let's not assume too much too soon," Davis said. "The good news is we've got a location on the call. As we suspected, it was made from the area that includes the rest stop on I-80, about twelve miles west of Morris, Illinois. The Chicago office of the FBI is going over the videos now. It shouldn't take long to know if we have something, since the call and Glenda's comments pinpoint pretty precisely when we should see a female driver returning from the restroom to her truck."

"The FBI?" Tony voiced it as a question but knew the answer even before Davis spoke.

"We had to call them, now that this involves multiple states. And the evidence is mounting that Glenda was telling the truth. It was important to bring them in quickly."

"There's more?"

"Yes," Davis answered. "Dan found matches in the databases to the girls' first names."

"Really?" This got Tony's attention, and he stopped dressing to ask, "How many?"

"Every one," Davis said tersely. "Dan said it was like watching the PowerBall machine dropping each of your numbers into the tray in order. When you look at the data from all three states, girls with those names—Glenda, Shelly, Elaine, Ashley, Emily, Brittany, and Madison—all are in the active case files of girls reported missing from that area we defined yesterday."

"Holy shit!" Tony said, sinking back onto his bed. "I can't believe it."

"As you know, those are pretty common names. It could be coincidence, but I would say the odds are about ten thousand to one against it. I think your friend Glenda has put us on the trail of something pretty ominous. And speaking of Glenda, you might as well know..." Davis was struggling, but Tony urged him to continue. He said, "The full name of the missing girl is Glenda Putsch. She was reported missing three months ago from her grandmother's farm outside of Clarinda, Iowa. She's fourteen years old."

"Fourteen? Did I hear you right? *Fourteen?* Dear God, that poor girl. Those poor girls," Tony said, as much to himself as to Davis. Then louder, he said, "So what do we do next?"

"Vandergaard has assigned this to me and Rooney officially," Davis replied, referring to his boss and the director of the DCI, "and the FBI guys in Chicago have agreed to put me on a team being assembled to look into it, so I guess I'm headed to Illinois to try to find this truck driver and hopefully Glenda."

"Can I join you?" Tony asked.

"Sorry, Tony. You know if it was just me, I would agree in an instant. Unfortunately, the feds aren't going to allow a civilian on the inside. I'll do all I can to keep you posted about our progress."

"One way or the other, I'm going to be out there," Tony said firmly. "I'll talk to Ben this morning, but I'm guessing he'll authorize it. Describe me to your federal pals so they don't shoot me by mistake."

"Will do, but once I describe the newspaper reporter who's nosing around their case, they may still shoot you. It just won't be by mistake."

Tony managed a brief smile, then asked Davis about the follow-up needing to be done in southwest Iowa and the adjoining states. Davis said Rooney and Sheriff Mackey had agreed to work with the FBI in Kansas City to try to uncover some thread to pull there. Now that they suspected these particular cases of missing girls were connected in some way, they hoped a closer look would lead to some clue about the perpetrators.

Having run out of immediate news to discuss, the two men grew quiet for a moment. Davis broke the silence first. "You be careful out there. Seriously. You get any hint that you're getting close, you call me immediately. Understand?"

"I do, and I will. You watch your back, too. I don't want to lose you. It takes too damn long to develop a source as good as you."

Davis chuckled. "Thanks. The depth of your affection is touching."

They grew quiet again. Both men knew the truth of their friendship, but no more was said about it. Tony thanked Davis for the call and hung up. He needed to pack.

***

When Tony walked into the *Crier* newsroom, Madeline was behind the glass in Ben's office. He walked over and tapped on the door frame.

"If you're talking about our trafficking story, can I join you? I have news." Both nodded, and Tony settled into the one remaining chair.

Ben said, "Madeline's asking to be assigned to the story, and I was just telling her I'm not sure I can spare both of you. Someone has to report on the news around here. Last I heard, we were a local daily."

"I know we're asking a lot, but I think you should say yes," Tony said.

Ben's eyebrows went up at the reference to "we," but he stayed quiet so Tony could explain. Tony described what he had learned from Davis that morning. When he finished, he summarized his thoughts.

"You can see this story is developing rapidly in two places. I think I should go to Illinois, and you should send Madeline to Kansas City."

Madeline sat up on the front edge of her seat, flushed with excitement. "Please, Ben, let me do this. I need a chance to show you and everyone that I'm ready for this kind of work. If Rooney will let me go with him, I'll do that. Otherwise, I'll drive down on my own and nose around. At the very least, if the FBI or DCI breaks something, you'll have a reporter on the scene to scoop the other media."

"That all sounds great to the investigative reporter in me," Ben acknowledged, "but do we have any inkling there's an Orney connection in any of this, beyond one long-distance call to Tony?"

"No," Tony had to admit, "except Davis' speculation that one of the girls knows me somehow. Of course, that seems like dust in the wind, considering it's based on one fleeting comment. Despite that, the fact is the DCI and the feds got onto this case because of a call to the *Crier*. If they end up rescuing girls or arresting bad guys, or both, and it all started here, that has to be worth something to the people in Orney."

"Okay, okay, I give," Ben said, holding up his hands in surrender. "But you each have one week. Then I want you back here." Tony smiled, and Madeline practically leapt out of her seat.

"And your expenses are limited to a hundred bucks a day, each, so choose your motels wisely."

"We will," the two reporters said in unison. As they turned to go, Ben stopped them with, "Hey, be careful. Stay in touch with me and with your DCI contacts every day. For God's sake, let's not add any more names to the missing persons list."

As they walked back to their desks, Madeline whispered to Tony, "Thank you. That's the nicest thing anyone has ever done for me."

"Don't thank me," Tony whispered back. "You're the best person we have to do what's needed." He stopped, took her arm, and turned her to face him. "Please hear what Ben said, and be careful. I couldn't live with myself if something happened to you."

Madeline found herself hoping Tony was saying she was important to him, but realized it was more likely a reference to Lisa. Tony still blamed himself for her death, and it made perfect sense he wouldn't want another one on his conscience. She watched him as he gathered some supplies from his desk, bagged up his laptop computer and headed out the door. She longed to follow him out and embrace him before he left, but knew the newsroom gossip would be out of control before she got back from the parking lot. *Be safe, my friend*, she thought, then picked up the phone to call Dan Rooney.

***

The conversation with Rooney was short and definitive. "Hell no," he said flatly. He went on to give all the reasons it was a bad idea for Madeline to go with him to KC, on top of the fact it was prohibited by DCI rules and was never allowed by the FBI. It boiled down to Rooney's belief it was too dangerous. He stopped short of saying it was too dangerous for a *girl*, which Madeline appreciated, but her disappointment was acute.

"Can I at least call you while I'm down there?" she asked. "Please don't freeze me out. You wouldn't have this lead if it wasn't for the *Crier*."

"I can't stop you from calling, but I also can't promise I'll be able to share much," Rooney said. "And you can call me from Orney. You don't have to be down there to follow this story."

The hell with him, Madeline thought after the call ended. *I know as much as he does at this point. Maybe I'll just show him and his*

FBI pals who's the better investigator. She followed Tony's lead in giving some thought to the supplies she would need. When her shoulder bag was full, she took one look around the newsroom, waved at Ben, and headed out the door.

***

Tony was packed and ready to go. The lights were out, the computer and TV were unplugged, the doors and windows were locked, and the trash was out by the alley. It was then he had an idea. He picked up his phone and told Siri, "Call Doug Tenney."

Doug was Tony's best friend and a reporter for the rival news outlet in town, the local radio station. Normally a reporter would never consider letting a rival in on a story as potentially big as this one, but Tony trusted Doug completely. When he reached him on his cell, Tony put the question to him, "Care to join me for a week's vacation in western Illinois?"

"What, you lose a contest or something?"

Tony grinned and said, "Nope. I'm a winner actually. I've been assigned another terrible story of corruption and human suffering. So I immediately thought of you."

Doug snorted. "I'm too flattered for words."

"Well that would be a first."

Doug chuckled and then asked, "Are you serious, I mean, that you want me to ditch work for a week and take a road trip with you?"

"I know it's asking a lot, but..."

"Are you kidding?" Doug yelped. "I have almost two months of vacation built up and nowhere to go! I'd *pay* you to let me come along. When do we leave?"

"Umm, that's the thing," Tony said sheepishly. "I kinda need to go right now."

"You mean now-now? Boy, you do enjoy making a mess of my life Tone-man. Obviously, I can't leave until my shift is over, but if you can wait a couple of hours, I'll talk to my boss."

"I can do that," Tony said, seriously happy at the prospect of company on the trip. "Let me know if you run into any obstacles. Otherwise, I'll just wait for you here."

"Okie-dokie," Doug said, and hung up.

With at least two hours to kill, Tony decided to plug in his electric keyboard and play a few tunes. The Yamaha Clavinova was an exceptional piece of technology as well as a beautiful musical instrument. He was able to afford it only because his famous father, Charles Harrington, who wrote under the name C.A. Harker, had set up a trust for Tony and his sister, Rita. Each received a stipend every year to supplement their incomes. It made it possible for Tony to stay at a small daily paper like the *Crier*, and still live in a house by himself, and buy things like a Clavinova and his Ford Explorer SUV.

As Tony pounded out a couple of Springsteen tunes, something began scratching around in the back of his brain, like a mouse foraging in the pantry. He moved on to "Here Comes the Sun" by the Beatles, "Don't Know Why," by Nora Jones, and the theme song from Beauty and the Beast. There were stacks of music books on the shelf next to the piano, but Tony always preferred to play from memory when he could. Play from memory...

Oh my God, he thought. *I might know the girl who knows me.*

He suddenly was reminded of a conversation he'd had the previous spring with a girl at the high school. Before he owned the Clavinova, Tony would go to the high school after hours and play the piano in the choir room of the Music Department. Staff members at the school knew him and were very accommodating, as long as no one needed the room.

Late one afternoon, the building had been deserted, and Tony had assumed he was alone as he played. After a few minutes, however, he had noticed a young girl, perhaps a ninth or tenth-grader, peeking around the corner, watching and listening.

Tony smiled and assured her it was okay to come in. "I don't mind an audience," he said, "if you can stand to hear me play."

"I like it," the girl said quietly, looking at the floor. She set down her books and positioned herself fifteen or twenty feet away on the choir risers. She was plainly dressed. Not quite shabbily, but clearly not a fashion queen either. Her blonde hair was long and straight, with bangs over her eyes. She suffered from teenage acne, and kept her hair in front of her shoulders, covering much of her face as she turned to one side to listen. Tony noticed she was rail thin. At one point between songs, she expressed her surprise at his ability to play without music. He explained to her he preferred it that way, but admitted it limited his repertoire.

After that initial encounter, the girl had come by a few more times while Tony was playing, stopping to listen for a few minutes, sharing a few words of small talk, and moving on. By that time, Tony's fame was growing. The Pulitzer Prize had been announced, and he'd been front page news in the *Town Crier* more times than he could count. He hadn't thought about the fact the girl would have known who he was, beyond just a stranger who liked to play the piano. She might have thought of him as brave and nice, Tony thought, trying to convince himself it was logic talking, and not just his ego.

Sitting at his Clavinova and thinking about the girl, Tony became more and more convinced. He activated his cell and called Ben.

"Hey boss, how would you like to get an assignment from one of your reporters?"

Ben chuckled, "Oh, sure. You win some prizes, and now you

think you can order me around. What's up?"

Tony shared his newest insight. "I know this is probably a complete wild goose chase," he said, "but there was something odd about her. She never was able to look me in the eye, and she always kept her distance. I wondered at the time if she had a tough home life. Now I'm wondering if there was something more."

"So do you have a name of this wild goose?"

"I knew you'd ask, but unfortunately, the answer is no. However, I'm pretty sure people at the school will know who you mean when you ask about her. Start with the choir director, Sal Pederman. He saw her there on the risers listening more than once. If anyone at the school resists talking to you, let me know, and I'll ask Rich to put an agent on it to open them up."

Ben laughed, "Okay, Tony. Trust me, I know how to proceed if I'm having trouble getting the information I need. I won a Pulitzer too, you know. Two, in fact."

Tony was red-faced and said so. "I'm sorry."

"It's okay, Tony. Enthusiasm is good. And thanks for the call. I actually look forward to having an angle to pursue."

As Tony hung up, his cell phone rang again. The number looked familiar, but he wasn't sure who it was.

"Yes?" he said, forgoing his usual phone greeting.

"Uh, is Frank there?" a husky male voice asked.

"No-o-o," Tony replied. "Who's calling, please?"

"I'm looking for Frank Jones. Is this his phone?"

"No, I'm sorry, it's not."

"Did I get a wrong number? Are you a friend of Frank's? May I ask your name?"

"I'm Tony Harrington, and I'm sorry, I don't know anyone named Frank."

"Harrington, huh? Well, thanks anyway." The call ended and

Tony shook his head. He was mildly annoyed with himself for giving his name without finding out who was calling. *Why should that bother me?*

He went to his recent calls list to see if he could figure out why the number looked familiar. He spotted it almost instantly.

"Oh my God," he said aloud. It was the phone from which Glenda had called him.

Tony quickly dialed Davis' number. He answered on the first ring.

"You can't have found trouble already. Are you even out of Iowa yet?" Davis prodded.

"Actually, I may have. Found trouble, I mean. I'm so stupid. I think I just fell for the oldest trick in the book. Someone just called my cell. They didn't give a name, but they asked who I was, and I told them."

"Yeah, so?"

"The call came from the truck driver's burner phone!" Tony practically shouted. "It was a man, not a woman, and he was calling my phone number to find out who Glenda called yesterday morning. I'd bet my life on it!"

Davis was quiet for several moments. He wanted to assure Tony that he was probably wrong, but couldn't. "Okay, don't beat yourself up over what you told him. Just be glad he called using the same phone. It means it's still on and our FBI friends will be able locate it. This could be an important break. The perp probably assumed Glenda had called home, or a teenage friend. He didn't think about the risk of using the phone because he didn't know she'd called a journalist."

Tony was pacing, trying to process what this could mean, both to Glenda and to him.

"Remember, Tony, it's all speculation. Our truck driver could be innocent, and her husband might have simply picked the wrong number off a call list."

Tony didn't buy it. He knew what had happened. He also knew it would take the caller less than five minutes on the internet to learn all about him, his employer, and even his family. He groaned at the thought of having to warn everyone again, after what they had all been through a couple of years before. His anxiety also went up when he thought of Glenda. *Now that they know she called me, what will they do? If they don't have her already, they'll probably intensify their search for her. And if they do have her...* Tony couldn't think about the dire possibilities, but, if he was right, he did wonder why the man had the truck driver's phone. *Had he followed and caught Glenda, and then taken the phone from the driver? Had he hurt or killed her? Or was the driver a part of the trafficking ring in some way? Over-the-road trucks were a common location for prostitution, so it wasn't too much of a stretch to imagine...*

Fortunately, at that moment, Doug knocked on the back door. Tony turned off the Clavinova and walked through the kitchen to answer it, the phone still at his ear.

"Sorry, I forgot it was locked," he said to Doug. Then, into the phone, he said, "I gotta run. Let me know if the FBI gets anything."

Doug ignored the phone and responded to Tony's apology. "No problem. You ready?"

"Yep. Just let me grab my bags and double-check that everything's turned off." Tony called over his shoulder from the hallway. "You're early."

"Yeah, the boss wasn't too thrilled about the short notice, but he said things are slow today, so I could go ahead and leave."

"You're not in trouble, are you?

"Nah, it's fine. It's good for him to be reminded once in a while how much he needs me."

"Well, yeah, no one can read my stories from the *Crier* over the air quite the way you can," Tony said with a smirk on his face. He was mostly joking, but he knew Doug occasionally did just that. He had heard him do it on the radio and, on more than one occasion, actually had seen him in the studio, reading from the newspaper clipped on a stand in front of him, or from the *Crier*'s website. Of course, Doug did credit the *Crier* for the stories... usually.

Doug came back with his usual response to Tony's teasing. "As I've said before, you should thank me. If I didn't broadcast your stories, no one would ever hear about them."

"You sure you want to do this?" Tony asked.

"I think so." Doug smiled broadly. "Though it occurs to me you haven't said exactly what we're doing yet. I assume it must be bad, since you don't want me to know anything until it's too late to turn back."

Tony maneuvered the SUV out of the driveway, down the alley, and into the street. "You don't know how right you are," he said, and began to tell it all to his best friend.

Chapter 6

By the time they stopped in Iowa City to top off the tank, grab a bite to eat, and say a quick hello to his parents, Tony had finished telling the tale and answering Doug's questions. It was nearly 6 p.m., and Tony wanted to keep moving, but he couldn't drive within minutes of his parents' home and not stop. If his mother found out, she would never forgive him. He strictly admonished Doug to back up his story that the two of them were just taking a few days off to go to Chicago.

The visit was perfect. Tony's folks were at home and glad to see him and his longtime friend. They caught up over some strawberry gelato, and after an hour and a few quick hugs they were on their way.

Tony's dad followed them out to the street. As Tony pushed the button to unlock the doors, Charles said, "So you want to tell me the rest of it?"

Tony should have known he wouldn't be able to hide the truth from his dad. "Actually, Dad, I do want to tell you about it. I just don't have much time right now. The short version is, we're following up on a tip about human trafficking. We believe there are some young girls in serious trouble. The DCI and the FBI are on it, but one of the girls reached out to me. So once again, I find myself right in the middle of the story."

"Anything I can do to help?"

Tony loved his father beyond words at that moment. How great it was to have a dad who didn't discourage him or argue with him or even worse, beg him to stay out of it.

"There is, frankly. I want you and Mom to be extra careful for the next few days. There are some very bad people who probably know this girl called me. They know who I am, which means they know who you are. I think the chances of them coming after you are very slim, but if you knew some of the things they're reported to have done... Well, there's just no way to know for sure."

"I appreciate the heads-up, Tony." Charles hugged his son, then held him at arm's length and said, "You be damn careful out there." Then he turned and was gone.

"Nice job keeping our true purpose a secret," Doug said from the passenger seat.

"Bite me," Tony replied, and started his SUV.

***

It was dusk as they passed by the Quad Cities and crossed the Mississippi River bridge into Illinois. They were only a few miles east of the river when Tony's cell rang.

"Hey, Rich. We're in Illinois. I brought Doug Tenney with me. Where are you?"

"I'm in Morris," Davis said. "We've got a team of five agents assembled here. We've agreed to bring you up to speed on a couple of things."

"I'm all ears."

"First of all, the second call you received from that burner phone originated back in Iowa. Whoever called you was in LeClaire at the time." Tony knew LeClaire was a small town just north of I-80 on the Iowa side of the Mississippi. He and Doug had gone past that exit less than half an hour ago. "About twenty minutes after the call, the phone dropped off the grid. I'm guessing someone looked you up, had an 'oh shit' moment, and killed the phone."

"Doug and I aren't far from there. Think we should go back?"

"That's your call, but we have the local cop, the Sheriff's Department, and the state troopers on the case. They're canvassing to see if anyone has seen the truck or the girl. Last I heard, they were even searching trash cans and garbage bins to see if they could find the phone. It's a small town. If it's there, they'll find it."

"If our perps are smart, and they probably are, they just chucked the phone over the wall into the river. No one's going to find it there."

"Probably right," Davis agreed. "The second thing is, we got a picture of the truck. It's a white Kenworth cab. The camera didn't catch a good look at the driver's face, but we've estimated she's about five-eight and pretty heavy, maybe 220 or so. She was wearing a baseball cap, but you can see a ponytail out the back, down to about her shoulder blades. Hard to tell in the dark, but we think dirty blonde or maybe even gray."

Before Tony could ask, Davis added, "The scary part is, we haven't been able to trace the truck. It appears the DOT labels on the side, as well as the license plates, were fake."

"What the...?" Tony was dumbfounded. He'd never encountered fake license plates in his crime reporting.

"Either fake or stolen," Davis said, "Unless she has a magic wand that can turn a cement truck in Orange City, Iowa into an over-the-road semi in Illinois. No stolen plates have been reported, so we think they created these plates with random numbers."

It occurred to Tony to ask, "Did this truck have a trailer on it?"

"Yes," Davis said. "In the video it's clear it's hauling a standard, fully-enclosed box trailer."

"That's great," Tony said sourly. "In other words, she could be moving anything in there."

"Once again, Tony, keep your imagination in check. Let's deal with what we know."

"I assume you have an APB out on the truck."

"Of course," Davis said, a hint of irritation leaking into his voice. "But she's had time to get it to Chicago. There are thousands of places it could be parked. If they've changed the plates and markings on the doors, it might as well have been melted into a lump of steel for the sculpture park. We'll never find it. The FBI has people looking at traffic cams and other video feeds, trying to see if we can get more info on where it went, but don't hold your breath."

"So what now?"

"Well, I would pray Glenda calls you again. That's why the FBI agreed to let me share these things. I told them you probably wouldn't cooperate—that is, you might not tell us when she calls—if we didn't keep you in the loop."

"You told them..."

"Hang on," Davis said quickly. Tony could hear shuffling at the other end of the line. "You and I know that's not true, but a little fib to pry them open can't hurt, can it?"

"No, as long as you haven't increased the chances of them taking a shot at me," Tony said, glancing at Doug and smiling to indicate it was a joke.

"Just keep your cell phone handy and answer every call," Davis said slowly, emphasizing every word.

"Of course, I will. Thanks, Rich. I'll call you when we get to Morris."

"Make it Chicago," Davis said. "We're wrapping up here and headed back to the city on the assumption that Glenda's ride kept going east."

Tony closed the phone and filled Doug in on the conversation.

***

A couple of hours later, Tony saw the signs for the rest stop the FBI had pinpointed as the location of Glenda's call. He exited and pulled the Ford into a parking space.

Doug asked, "You doing anything special, or just checking it out?"

Tony didn't answer. He climbed out of the vehicle and breathed in the night air. It was hard to believe the call had come to him less than two days ago. It seemed like a month had passed. He motioned to Doug to follow and walked over to the section marked for semi-trucks. It was after 11 p.m., so the spots were filling with truckers bedding down for their required hours of sleep.

Tony turned in a wide circle. "She was right here, Doug. Scared, with just a few minutes alone, and she used that precious time to call me. She didn't even ask for help for herself. She thought she was free. She just wanted me to help the other girls she had met and heard about."

Tony realized a tear was inching down his cheek. He wiped it away and swore. "Damn these bastards. We are going to find her, and we are going to find them."

Tony knew there was nothing he and Doug could accomplish at the rest stop. Rich and his FBI peers would have checked the lot and the restroom for any evidence. Tony simply sighed and strode back to the SUV with Doug in his wake. In seconds, they were back on the highway, headed east.

It was nearly 1 a.m. when they pulled into the lot of a Hilton Garden Inn at the Bolingbrook exit off I-55, just west of Chicago. Neither man said much as they prepared for bed, crawled under the covers of their respective queen-sized beds, and struggled to find sleep.

***

Madeline also was having trouble getting to sleep. She was stretched out in a similar bed, this one in a Fairfield Inn off I-35, north of Kansas City. She had been there for hours, pondering different courses of action. Tony had texted her the information about Glenda's grandmother's farm back in Iowa. She had then called Rooney and convinced him to share some of the basic facts from the other active cases. Rooney didn't like helping her, and repeated that she shouldn't be there at all. However, much of the information could be found on the various missing persons websites or from media coverage of the disappearances, so he gave in to Madeline's argument that all he was doing was saving her a lot of time and trouble.

Now she had the names, locations, and dates related to the missing persons reports for five of the girls: Glenda Putsch, Elaine Gruver, Emily Reitz, Shelly Blaine, and Brittany Powell. Where to go from here? All of these families must be wrung out by now, answering questions for the police, the news media, and now the FBI.

On the other hand, she couldn't just sit in a motel room waiting for the authorities to spoon-feed her their progress, or lack of it. Rooney was right. She could do that from her desk in Orney. So she resolved to take a stab at talking to a couple of the families to see if she could pick up on anything the others had missed. If she was going to prove how good she was, she was going to have to get out in the field and find something.

In poring over the information, she decided to begin with Brittany Powell, mostly because Powell's home in Platte City, Missouri, was less than 30 miles from her motel. With that settled, Madeline felt some of the tension seep away, and eventually, she fell into a deep sleep.

***

At 5:42 a.m., Tony's cell phone clattered on the nightstand between the two motel beds. He was instantly awake. Grabbing the phone and punching the answer button, he said, "This is Tony."

"Mr. Harrisso... I mean, Mr. Harrington?" The voice was tiny, almost a whisper.

"Glenda, is that you?"

"I have to hurry," she whispered. "The man I'm with is in the bathroom. He made a call before he went in there, so I grabbed his phone before it shut off."

Tony marveled at the intelligence and courage of the young girl as he said, "I understand. Where are you?"

"I'm so dumb," she said, quietly but no longer a whisper. Tony was afraid she was going to start to cry.

"It's okay, Glenda. We can worry about that later. Just tell me what you know. Let me ask you again. Do you know where you are?"

There was a pause as she took a second to think. "It's a Super 8 motel. I know that because it's printed on the soap wrapper in the bathroom. We have to be near Chicago because I saw lots of tall buildings out the windows of the truck before we stopped. I thought it would be cool to see Chicago, but then Mavis pulled into this motel parking lot and there were men waiting. Waiting for me. Mavis was helping them. I just couldn't believe it. I'm so dumb. Mavis? Is that a made-up name for a trucker or what?"

Tony was thinking furiously. *How could he find out where, exactly, they had her?* "Glenda, don't worry about that. Just help me find you. I'm in Chicago. There are a lot of good people looking for you. We're going to help you."

"Really?" She sniffled.

"Tell me exactly where you saw the buildings out the window, and how long before you stopped. Were they right in front of you, off to one side, or what?"

"They were in front and to the left," she replied, back in whisper mode. "I remember 'cause I had to look past Mavis as she drove. I'd never seen so many big buildings."

"Good, good. And when was this?"

"Right before we stopped. We got off the interstate, and the motel was right there. We just made a couple of turns."

"Can you guess how far away the downtown buildings were— the tall buildings in Chicago?" Tony knew this was a hopeless question for someone who was unlikely to have a sense of the scale of a 100-story skyscraper, but any indication was better than nothing. As she answered, Tony started kicking the bed, to ensure Doug was awake. He stirred and sat up. Tony covered the phone and said, "Call Rich Davis. Tell him Glenda's on my line right now." He refocused on his phone as Glenda spoke.

"They're not real close, I don't think... I don't know how to describe it. Umm, you know I could still see the tops of the buildings without leaning toward the window."

So she's southwest of the city, close enough to see the skyline but far enough away that she could see entire buildings from her seat. "Good. You're doing great. Now tell me who's with you. Who's in the bathroom? Is it one of the men who took you from Mavis?"

"No this is just some john," she said. "He's really old, like 40 or maybe even 50. I think they called him, and he came here just to have sex with me. When he was done, he picked up his pants from the floor, took his phone out, and made a call. I think he was leaving a message for someone. Maybe his office? He made up a story about his car breaking down. I think he's going to be late for something this morning. Then he just dropped the phone on the bed and went into the bathroom."

Tony reeled as he heard this fourteen-year-old girl talking so matter-of-factly about having a "john" in her room. He fought hard to stay on task.

"So these are the men who held you before? The ones who made you have sex with them and others? The ones who hurt you and gave you drugs? Is that right? And they're still nearby?" Tony knew he had to slow down and not overwhelm her with so many questions, but he was desperate to understand where she was and what situation she faced.

"Yeah, I think the bad guys are in another room. Bad guys. Did you hear that? I don't know what to call them, but 'bad guys' isn't bad enough. They might be in the room next door. That's what they've done before. They told the john not to leave me alone. They're gonna be pissed if they find out he left me with a phone."

Tony knew she was right, but was grateful she had been able to call.

"Do you know a room number? What room you're in?" he asked.

"Not for sure. It's the first floor by the end of the hall. They brought me in the side door from the parking lot. Wait, let me look at the phone by the bed. Sometimes the phone... Shit. I gotta go."

The phone went silent.

"Dammit," Tony said, looking up at Doug. "Do you have Rich on the line?"

"Yeah," Doug said hoarsely, handing Tony the phone. "Here."

Davis didn't wait for Tony to greet him. He said, "We're on it. You'll recall we had a tracer on your phone. As soon as it rang, the FBI techs were tracing the location of the caller. This is good, Tony. She's alive, and she's in the area. I'll call you back as soon as I have something."

Tony ended the call, handed Doug's phone back to him, and headed for the bathroom. He was going to be dressed and ready when Davis called with an update.

It took forty minutes for Davis to call him back. To Tony, it seemed like a lifetime. He answered the phone and had it to his ear before the first ring ended.

Davis said, "She was right. It's a Super 8 on the southwest side of Chicago. It's one of the smaller suburbs and doesn't have a big police force, but they should be able to get a black-and-white over there soon. A couple of us from the SOT are gearing up to head that way as soon as we can."

Tony knew that SOT meant the Special Operations Team that had been assembled for this case.

Davis continued. "You can join us there later. Don't go charging in there before we're at the scene and ready, but we'll want you there to help put Glenda at ease." Davis gave him the address. Tony thanked him and ended the call.

Tony immediately entered the address into the maps app on his phone.

"Holy Mother of God," he said, causing Doug to stick his head out of the bathroom. Through a toothpaste-filled mouth, he gurgled, "What?"

"This address. This motel where Glenda's being held. It's two blocks from here." Tony jumped up, grabbed his jacket, and headed for the door.

"Hey, where're you going?" Doug spit out his toothpaste.

"I can't just sit here knowing a teenage girl is being forced to perform sex with strangers in a motel two blocks from here—a teenage girl who has called me twice to ask for my help."

"Okay, okay." Doug said. "Just take a deep breath so I can catch up. I'm coming with you."

***

They decided to walk, thinking their car would attract attention. As soon as they neared the curb, they could see the Super 8 sign across the street and a couple of blocks to the southwest.

It was now past 6:30 a.m. Tony hoped it was a time when early risers would be getting up, grabbing coffee in the lobby, and checking out. The arrival of two strangers might not be too noticeable.

Tony practically jogged the entire distance. Doug, who was heavier and not in great shape, was huffing as he struggled to keep up. To his credit, he didn't complain. As they neared the building, Tony noted there was a small swimming pool on one end. If Glenda was right about being near the exit at the end of the building facing the parking lot, it was at the opposite end from the pool. Tony's pulse raced at the thought they had narrowed their search to perhaps four motel rooms. "Try to look like we belong here," he said quietly.

He and Doug walked through the front door and right past the front desk clerk to the central hallway that stretched out in both directions, left and right. As far as Tony could tell, the clerk hadn't even looked up from her desk. He knew they needed to go left, the direction away from the pool.

It was hard to look casual as they slowed their pace and listened for sounds that would give away the location of either Glenda or the monsters who were holding her. When they were two-thirds of the way down the hall, a door suddenly opened on the right. It was the second room from the end. A man in a gray suit stepped out. He looked to be in his mid-fifties, tall, distinguished, with bushy eyebrows and hair that had turned a color matching his suit. He stopped in front of the room next to the one he had just exited. He was about to knock, but hesitated when he saw Tony and Doug.

Tony knew he was leaping to conclusions, but it seemed obvious to him that this was Glenda's john and he was about to tell the men next door he was done with her. In a fit of rage, desperation, and, if he was forced to admit it, stupidity, Tony walked right up to the man. The man was startled and clearly uncomfortable as Tony came close enough to smell his cologne.

"Don't knock on that door. Don't raise your voice, and keep your hands where we can see them," Tony said very quietly, grabbing the man's right arm.

The man tried to pull away and looked at the closed door as if he was about to shout an alarm. Then he seemed to think better of it. He said in a whisper, "Take your hands off me. Who do you think you are?"

"We're with an FBI task force," Tony hissed, choosing his words carefully. It wasn't exactly a lie. "Come with us to the parking lot. If you alert the men inside this room, this could get very ugly. If you cooperate, we might be able to minimize this incident and keep the media out of it. But if you raise an alarm and those men start shooting, then there won't be any controlling this."

At the mention of the media, the man turned white and practically rushed out the exit door, with Tony and Doug in tow. Tony knew he had guessed right. This was someone who would do anything to keep his name out of the papers.

The man made a beeline for his Lexus sedan, parked in the far row of the side parking lot. Tony and Doug stayed with him and made it clear they weren't going to allow him to leave. Not yet.

"Did you hurt her?" Tony asked.

"Who?" the man said, looking like he might start crying.

Tony grabbed the man's silk tie, pushed his fist toward the man's throat, and banged his head back on the roof of the Lexus. "Listen, you son of a bitch, there will be no more of that. Tell me the truth, or I swear I will kill you right now, before the rest of our team gets here." His fist was still wrapped around the man's tie and their faces were just inches apart. "Did. You. Hurt. Her?" Tony tried hard to sound as tough and as sinister as he felt.

"No, of course not," the man said. "We made love, that's all. Then I left. I swear."

"Made love? Made LOVE? Is that what you call it when you force yourself on a fourteen-year-old girl?" Tony was yelling now and Doug was standing to one side, glancing at the motel building and urging him to settle down.

"Fourteen?" the man in the suit squeaked. No! They told me she was eighteen. I swear!"

"But I'll bet you knew better," Tony spat back at him. "You saw her. You knew she was young. You didn't want to know the truth, did you? *Did* you!"

"Please," the man said. "I have to get out of here. I have a wife. I have a job. I have kids, for God's sake. I can't be caught here."

"Listen to yourself, you worthless piece of... of..." Tony couldn't think of a word vile enough. "Worried about your kids. What if that was your daughter in there? Did you ever think of that? Did you ever think about this girl's parents? The hell they're going through?"

The man began sobbing and slid down the side of the car to the ground. "Please. Please help me," he cried.

"Give me the room key," Tony demanded.

The man hesitated, but reached in the vest pocket of his suit and withdrew the key. Tony grabbed it and turned to Doug. "I'm going to get her. You stay here with Mr. Upstanding Citizen. If he tries to leave, shoot him."

"With pleasure," Doug said, smiling at the thought as well as at the fantasy Tony had spun so effortlessly. "Just be careful in there."

Tony jogged back across the lot, and used the key to re-enter the hallway door. He quickly stepped to the door of the room the man had exited, slid the key in and out of the electronic lock, and stepped in. He saw a young woman curled up in the sheets, hugging a pillow and crying quietly. At the sound of Tony's entry, she turned to face him. Her face registered surprise, then confusion.

"Who you?" she asked. Her accent was Hispanic, and she had raven black hair and light brown skin.

"Glenda?" Tony asked.

"Glenda? No. No Glenda."

Tony's heart sank. He had made a perfect three-point shot, but in the wrong basket. Maybe in the wrong gymnasium. "What's your name?"

"Camila. Who you?"

Tony let the door close behind him and approached the bed.

"My name is Tony Harrington. I am here looking for Glenda. She's a young girl being held by some very bad men. Do you know Glenda? Do you know these men?"

"Sí. I know. Glenda is *agradable*... uh, how you say? Nice, yes?"

"Yes, Glenda is very nice," Tony said. He looked into Camila's eyes and asked, "Is Glenda here?"

"Sí. I think. Last night they put in room with gray suit. When he finish her, he come here. Then Señor Al, they call Big Al, he go to her." Camila gestured toward her room's door.

"Across the hall?" Tony asked, struggling to control his anger. "In that room?"

"Sí. I think."

"Are you like Glenda? I mean, are you being forced to do these things? Are you a..." Tony struggled to remember the Spanish word and was reaching for the translation app on his phone when he remembered, "...a *prisionero*, a captive?"

"Ummm, Sí. Before. Now?" She shrugged. "Is all I know. What else I do?"

"How many are here? How many girls like you and Glenda are here now, in this motel?"

Another shrug. "Me. Her. Maybe more. I never sure."

"What about the people holding you? I mean the men holding Glenda and other girls. How many are here now?"

"Maybe two," Camila said. "Big Al is one. I think Freddy also here. Am I in trouble? Are you ICE? Police?"

"No," Tony said. "I am not police, and you're not in trouble. I want to help you. The police are coming, but we have to get you and Glenda out of here so you don't get hurt."

At that moment, there was a pounding on the door. A low, raspy voice said through the wood, "You're past your time. Get your ass out of there."

Tony called back toward the door, "We just finished. I'm getting dressed."

There was no response and Tony hoped the man had retreated to his room.

"Will he be waiting outside?" he asked Camila.

Another shrug. "Maybe no. Men pay Big Al first. Sometimes no talk when they go."

Tony said, "Camila, I have to ask you, do you want to leave? Do you want to get away from these men and find another way to live? I'll take you with me if you want, but it may be dangerous getting away from here, and I can't make you go."

"Some men not so nice. No *tiene el condón*. Nothing to protect." She pointed at her abdomen. "Many times I scare, sometimes hurt. But where I go?"

"I don't have answers for you today, but I promise I'll do everything I can to help you, if you come with me." Tony had no idea what he might be getting into. He only knew he wanted to help these girls get away from "Big Al" and "Freddy," whoever they were, and everyone like them.

Camila nodded, stood, and walked to the closet to get her clothes. She seemed unembarrassed to be naked in front of him, but he was embarrassed to take her in. He turned his back to her, but not before noticing she seemed more a young woman than a little girl. He could understand why men desired her, but this thought—the idea that even he could think such a thing—only served to make him more depressed and angry. Desire was the reason organizations like these even existed. Desire and evil.

Her clothes were simple: blue jeans, a pullover jersey with a Houston Texans logo, and waist-length windbreaker. She had no other possessions in the room, so she was ready.

"Okay," Tony said. "When we step out the door, you turn right and go out the exit into the parking lot. At the back of the lot, you'll see gray suit with another man. They should be next to a silver Lexus, a big expensive car. You know Lexus?"

She nodded, but fear creeped back into her eyes. "Gray suit? His car? Why? Why I trust you?"

Tony gently placed his hands on her shoulders. "Camila, I know I'm just another stranger, but please believe me, I'm not like these bastards. I want to help you. I *only* want to help you. Okay?"

Camila nodded. "Okay."

Tony put some urgency back into his voice. "When you leave the room, don't let anything or anyone stop you. Run if you can. When you get to the car, tell the other man to wait for Glenda. The man's name is Doug. Tell him to wait for Glenda, but not for me if I'm not with her. Tell him when he has you and Glenda and gray suit, he should get in the car and get away from here. Can you remember that?"

She nodded again and asked, "What you do?"

"I'm not sure what's going to happen," Tony said. "Once I find Glenda, hopefully I'll come with her to the car, but I can't be sure."

Camila took a deep breath, leaned up and kissed him on the cheek, and said, "Okay. We go."

Tony pulled open the door and looked both ways down the hallway as Camila followed him out of the room. Tony pointed to the right and said through clenched teeth, "Go, go, go." She went.

He could see her through the glass of the exit door heading straight for the Lexus. He turned and faced the motel room door directly across the hall from Camila's. He knocked lightly three times.

He tried to be patient as he waited for a response. Finally, the raspy voice of the man said, "Who is it?" Tony said, "Mavis sent me. She said I could find some nice, uh, entertainment here?"

"Yeah?" The door opened a crack. Tony could see the safety chain was latched. "You a cop?"

Tony laughed nervously and said, "No. I just want a little fun. Mavis said she dropped a young girl here. I like my entertainment young. Is this the right place or not?"

"Maybe," the man said, lowering his voice. "It's five hundred. Cash only."

Tony tried to look shocked, rather than simply mad as hell. "Come on, man! Across town, I can get a BJ for fifty bucks."

"Two hundred for a full hour. Pay in advance. Take it or leave it. I would take it if I were you. She's a really great piece of ass."

It took every ounce of control Tony could muster not to lash out at the door. His fists were clenched to knuckle-white, but he spoke calmly. "Deal."

The man closed the door and re-opened it without the chain. "The cash?"

Tony was glad he had stopped at an ATM before beginning this trip. He fished ten twenties out of his wallet and handed them over. The man opened the door wide, stepped out of the room, and motioned with his head that Tony should go in. "She's all yours."

Tony stepped into the darkened room. He stood for a moment so his eyes could adjust, expecting to hear the door close behind him. He heard the click but also could sense something else. As he started to turn, he realized the man had stayed in the room with him. He caught the movement of something out of the corner of his eye and ducked forward.

The butt of the gun coming down toward his head didn't hit its mark, but did scrape down the back of his skull, landing at the base of his neck. Tony screamed in pain and fell forward. The man followed, with a kick to Tony's side. Tony writhed in pain, curled up on the floor. When he managed to open his eyes and look up, the barrel of a revolver was staring back at him. The voice behind it growled, "I know who you are, Harrington. I looked you up online. Do you think we're completely stupid? Why are you here, anyway? What in the hell do you want?"

Tony could barely breathe. "Glenda," he said, his voice barely a squeak. "I want Glenda."

"Well you got her, pal. Now go join her." The gun motioned

him further into the room, and the man's foot kicked against his buttocks.

Tony crawled on all fours past the bathroom door and into the room. The TV set was on the left, and the two double beds were on the right. He lifted his head far enough to see there was a girl in the first bed. Her hands appeared to be tied behind her back, and she had a gag in her mouth. Her short, blonde hair looked greasy, and one side of her face was distorted by a big, purple bruise. She was naked except for the sheets she had managed to pull up with her feet to cover the lower part of her body. Her face was streaked with tears and her eyes wide with pain or fear, or both.

"What have you done to her?" Tony asked between gasps for breath.

"We've just been teaching this little bitch a few lessons about staying away from phones," the man sneered, "not that it's any of your business. Get up on the bed." He motioned to the empty bed next to Glenda's.

As Tony managed to stand, the man took another swing toward his head with his gun hand. This time, Tony was expecting it. Instead of leaning away, which would have been the natural reaction and probably would have earned him a broken jaw or a broken nose at least, Tony leaned in, grabbing the man's shirt and pulling their bodies close. The result was that the gun missed him completely, the arm wrapping around his back. The man's bicep caught the side of Tony's head, which didn't feel good, but left him able to respond. He wrapped his arms around the wiry man's body, twisting and pushing back simultaneously.

The movement took the man off his feet and down onto the nightstand between the beds. A loud crash erupted as the lamp on the table shattered. Then an even louder sound, which Tony realized was a scream coming from the man himself.

The raw shriek of pain was quickly replaced with the man's screams of anger. The gun fell from the man's hand as he flailed, trying to stand and trying to reach behind his back simultaneously. He failed at both. The man shrieked again, and Tony realized blood was dripping onto the floor from the man's back. A portion of the lamp had impaled him as he'd fallen. Tony staggered back, grabbed the handgun off the bed, and threw it into the far corner of the room. Then he approached the girl. He climbed up onto the bed to avoid the kicking feet of the screaming man.

"Glenda?" A vigorous nod. "Tony," he said, pointing to himself as he panted, trying to catch his breath. "I'm so sorry I didn't get here sooner."

Tony saw Glenda's eyes widen even further. She nodded again, then started to weep.

"Help me, you son of a bitch!" the man next to him screamed as he continued to fight to stand.

"I don't think so," Tony said quietly, never taking his eyes from Glenda as he removed the gag and untied her hands.

She threw her arms around him tightly and spoke through her sobs, "Thank you. Thank you."

"No, Glenda, thank you. Your bravery got me here. Now we have to go."

He helped her up and took her to the closet, assuming her clothes would be there as Camila's had been. But it was empty.

"They took my clothes," Glenda said. "They said one way to keep me from running away was to make sure I stayed naked."

"It's okay," Tony said. "We'll manage."

He pulled a clean sheet off the other, unused, bed and helped Glenda wrap herself into it. "Let's go," he said. They headed for the door.

"I'll kill you!" the man called after them, twisting hard,

screaming in pain, and finally crashing to the floor.

"He will, too," Glenda said, holding Tony back from the door. "You should get his gun. Freddy is still out there, and Freddy's the mean one."

"I hate guns," Tony said.

"Please," Glenda pleaded. Tony could see she needed the reassurance. He also could see the wisdom of not leaving it with Big Al, so he walked back to the corner of the room and retrieved it. He put his free arm around Glenda and said again, "Let's go."

Tony was glad to see the hallway was empty. He had no desire to bump into Freddy and wasn't too crazy about being seen escorting a teenage girl, dressed only in a sheet, out of a motel. However, as soon as they stepped through the exit, onto the sidewalk outside, Tony felt something hard press up against his temple.

"Stop right there." The voice was soft, almost feminine, but clearly that of a man, presumably Freddy. Tony turned to see he was short, overweight, and balding, with a neatly clipped goatee around his mouth. The man held a big, silver automatic pistol pointed at Tony's head.

"Hey, that's not necessary," Tony said.

"Shut the hell up," the man snarled. "Let go of the girl and get back inside."

"I don't have a key," Tony lied.

The man used his free hand to dig into his olive-green work pants and pull out a key. He looked down for a moment as he fumbled with it, and Tony took advantage of the brief distraction. He swung his right arm up while pushing Glenda down with his left. Big Al's revolver was still in Tony's right hand. It struck Freddy across the face.

The man stumbled back, tripped over a concrete parking stop, and fell hard on the asphalt. He yelped in pain or surprise—Tony hoped it was pain—but held onto his gun. As he began to raise it up off the pavement, Tony leaped forward and stomped down on his forearm with all his weight. The man screamed and let go of the gun. Tony kicked it away, then stooped down to help Glenda up.

The man was clambering to his feet, and Tony yelled at Glenda to run. At the same instant, two uniformed police officers popped up from behind a parked car and yelled, "Freeze! Drop your weapons! Hands above your heads!" Tony immediately dropped the revolver and held his hands high. Freddy stood and held his hands up, as well. Glenda stopped running, but kept her hands tightly clenched to the sheet around her body.

From there, it was just like the movies – up against the building, hands behind their backs, handcuffs, and into the back seats of a couple of squad cars. Tony didn't care. Glenda and Camila were safe, and that was all that mattered.

There was a flurry of communications as the officers called for backup. When Tony told them they would find a kidnapper in room 122 in need of medical help, they also called for an ambulance and a forensics team.

Over the next 40 minutes, Tony lost track of how many questions he answered and for how many people. He noticed Doug was sharing a similar experience. Across the parking lot, several police officers were interviewing him while Gray Suit sat, locked in the back seat of another patrol car.

Tony was very grateful when he spotted Rich Davis and another man getting out of a sedan, flashing their credentials and crossing the crime scene tape to join them. Davis pulled open the back door of the squad car, squinted at the two "suspects" handcuffed in the back, and said, "Tony Harrington, you are the biggest dumbass on the planet." He slammed the door and walked away.

Tony smiled. He couldn't really argue the point.

Chapter 7

Two hours later, Tony, Doug, Davis, and an FBI agent named Will Cunningham were debriefing in one of the small meeting rooms at the Hilton Garden Inn. They decided it would be more functional than using a motel room, and more private than sitting in the coffee shop or a restaurant. The Hilton manager, clearly relieved that the criminal activity had been in someone else's motel, had been happy to provide the meeting room for free.

Tony was struggling to placate Davis, who was beyond angry at Tony's irrational decision to enter the motel before the authorities arrived. Davis pointed out Tony had been unarmed, with no decent intelligence about what he would find inside. "And," Davis growled, unwilling to let it go, "you dragged your best friend in there with you. You both could have been killed. Christ, Tony, I thought you were smarter than this. I wouldn't have given you the location if I'd known you'd be this foolish."

"Rich," Tony said, with more than a little pleading in his voice. "I've said twenty times I'm sorry, and I've explained to you I couldn't bear the thought that a little girl could be subjected to another round of abuse while I just sat outside and waited. Maybe it was stupid... Okay, it *was* stupid. But I had to do it. There's nothing else I can tell you."

Agent Cunningham's strong, clear voice interrupted the argument. "Maybe it's time we move on." Davis glowered at him but nodded.

When the agents were finished with their questions, Tony had a few of his own. He asked about the two perpetrators and learned the first one, the one believed to be called Big Al, was in surgery at a trauma center in Chicago. The only medical report anyone had so far was from the EMTs who had taken him in the ambulance. They noted he appeared to have lost a lot of blood and may have spine damage where shards from the lamp had pierced his back.

"We should have a report from surgery later this afternoon, and some kind of prognosis tomorrow. In the meantime, there's an officer assigned to him. He's not going anywhere. We got his full name and rap sheet from his prints. He's Albert T. Ivers. At the very least, we've got him on a charge of carrying a deadly weapon as a convicted felon."

Davis continued, "The second perp is Frederick Kershaw, AKA 'Freddy.' You'll love this. He claims he was an innocent bystander and you pulled a gun on him. Of course, the testimony of the girls, as well as that of your friend Mr. Tenney, who witnessed the whole incident in the parking lot, will make Kershaw's claim laughable."

Doug piped in, saying, "Hey Tone-man. I can be convinced to save your butt once again. Let me see... Have I mentioned I could use season tickets to the Hawkeyes next year? Whatcha say?"

Davis and Tony grinned, but the FBI agent didn't look amused. "Let's not joke about bribery and tampering with testimony, Mr. Tenney."

Doug's smile disappeared. "Yes, sir," he said.

"And what about gray suit?" Tony asked, trying to get the conversation back on track.

Cunningham looked back a couple of pages in his note pad and said, "Mr. model citizen is Franklin Everly, Jr. I'm guessing dad won't be quite as proud in the future to share a name with junior as he might have been in the past. He's been charged with soliciting for prostitution and statutory rape. He'll be out on bail before the day is over, but his nightmare is just beginning. He's a CPA with one of the big Chicago firms. When they learn what's happened, I'm guessing they won't just fire him. They'll break all his pencils and put his calculator through the shredder."

"Whatever troubles he faces, they're not big enough," Tony grumbled. "Most importantly, what about the girls? Where are they? *How* are they?"

Davis said, "They've been taken to the local community hospital. They need to go through the rape protocol." He could tell Tony was going to push back, so he held up his hand and said, "It has to be done Tony. It may seem silly after weeks or months of abuse, but if you want to put these guys away, we have to hope we can capture their semen in the girls and find other evidence of abuse."

"Well you can start with the giant bruise that used to be half of Glenda's face," Tony said, shaking his head.

"That's it exactly," Davis replied. "We all saw that. Now it has to be properly documented by the medical people. They also need to check them for other injuries, diseases, or any other issues." He continued, "When they're done at the hospital, they'll have a chance to shower and get dressed properly. Then they'll be turned over to social services to sort out their personal situations."

"Wait," Tony said. "What do you mean by 'other issues'?"

Davis looked away and Cunningham said bluntly, "We'll be

checking for illegal substances in their systems and other signs of drug abuse."

"You do realize these girls are victims, not criminals, right?" Tony asked, his voice rising along with his pulse.

"I know what the situation appears to be," Cunningham said. "I also know there are laws we have to obey and procedures we have to follow. We're doing this by the book. The tests could corroborate their descriptions of abuse, as well as be an indication of any illegal activity on their part. If the girls are innocent, they'll be fine."

"Good grief." Tony turned to Davis, "Have we rescued these girls from kidnappers and rapists just to have them thrown into the law enforcement system as if they were the criminals?"

"I know, Tony, and I agree. Let's not jump to conclusions. I promise you I'll stay on top of it and try to head off any overzealous prosecutions."

"I can't believe this," Tony muttered. "Are you done with us?"

"There's a technician coming over from the crime scene at the Super 8 to get Mr. Tenney's fingerprints. We already have yours on file," Cunningham said, nodding toward Tony. "Once that's done, you're free to go."

As the men stood, Cunningham added, "For the record, gentlemen, I agree with Agent Davis. This stunt you pulled at the Super 8 was about as foolish and misguided as any I've ever seen."

Tony didn't want another fight, so he kept quiet.

"But good job."

Tony looked up to see if he had heard right. Cunningham was smiling. "If you tell anyone I said this, I'll deny it, but it took balls to go in there to get those girls out. It could have ended very badly, but it didn't. So I say good job." He tipped an imaginary hat and walked out of the room.

Tony and Doug looked at each other, then looked at Rich Davis who said, "I stand corrected. Agent Cunningham may be the biggest dumbass on the planet."

***

Tony's first call was to Ben at the *Crier*. It was midmorning, so he was in his office and answered his cell immediately. Tony filled him in on everything, then asked him for another favor.

"Would you call Nathan Freed and tell him about these girls? I'm terrified they're going to get swept up into the law enforcement and social services mess in Cook County. I don't want the cure to be worse than the disease, not after everything these kids have been through. Maybe Freed has an attorney friend in Illinois who'd be willing to represent them pro bono, or at least keep an eye on their cases."

"Good idea," Ben said. He then reminded Tony he had a story to file, or at least the facts for a story. Once again, the reporter had been in the middle of dramatic events. Ben expected to see all the details of it in his email in time for him to mold into an article for the next day's front page. Both men knew from experience that Tony wouldn't write anything beyond the facts, in note form. When Tony was directly involved in the story, Ben believed it best that he, as editor, actually write the account that would appear in print.

"And get me some art if you can. No photos of the girls, obviously, but get shots of the motel and maybe the local police officers who were first on the scene."

Tony acknowledged the assignments and was about to end the call when Ben said, "One more thing. I talked to a couple of people at the high school this morning. I'm pretty sure the girl who used to listen to you playing the piano is a sophomore named Trina Aston. She lives in town with her dad. She's an only child. Apparently, her mom died a few years ago. Growing up without a mom or siblings could explain a lot about her shy behavior. That's all I could get without raising a lot of questions about why I was asking."

Tony understood and thanked his boss for the follow-up.

His next call was to Madeline. He caught her in her car on the way to Platte City, Missouri, wherever that was. He filled her in on the rescue and said he was hoping to get her some additional information from Glenda, if they ever let him talk to her again.

"Nice job, Tony," Madeline said, then explained she was going to Platte City because she wanted to interview the father of one of the missing girls. "According to her file, the mom left home a few years ago. The dad reported Brittany missing a couple of weeks ago," Madeline said. "I don't expect to get anything from him that the police don't already have, but I need to start somewhere."

Tony agreed, wished her luck, and said he would call her as soon as he'd had a chance to interview Glenda.

Madeline thanked him and ended the call.

***

Madeline hit the End Call button so hard she knocked her phone off the center console of her car and onto the floor in front of the passenger seat. *That effing Harrington, she thought. He jumps in the car, drives to a city with millions of people, and ends up next door to a gang of rapists and two girls waiting to be rescued. He gets in a fight with professional criminals and he's fine, but one of them is in the hospital. Un-effing-believable.* Once again, she was filled with admiration and resentment. This time, the resentment was winning.

With her phone out of reach, Madeline used the OnStar system in her compact Chevy to direct her to the small apartment building in Platte City. Rooney's information said Vince Powell, Brittany's father, was a part-time laborer, hiring out to farms in the summer, the local grain elevator at harvest time, and homeowners for fix-it projects in the winter. In other words, it was anyone's guess whether he would be home before noon on a Wednesday.

She felt lucky when the first-floor apartment door opened shortly after she knocked.

"Can I help you?" The man who answered was tall and broad-shouldered, with wavy hair combed straight back. The broken blood vessels in his cheeks and nose, coupled with the bloodshot eyes, screamed "heavy drinker" at her. She was immediately uneasy about going inside the apartment.

"Miss?"

"Oh, sorry," Madeline said. "I'm Madeline Mueller. I was wondering if I could talk to you."

"I'll talk to anyone who can help me," the man said. He didn't sound or smell intoxicated. "Can you help me? Are you with the police?"

"No, I'm a newspaper reporter. I'm looking into the disappearances of several young women, including your daughter."

"You with the *Kansas City Star*? I ask 'cause someone was here already."

Madeline laughed out loud and said, "No, I'm from the polar opposite of the *Kansas City Star*. I'm from a tiny daily paper up in Iowa. If I could have a few minutes of your time, I'd be happy to explain."

"Of course," the man said, opening the door wider. "You'll have to excuse the mess. I've been painting the apartment. I want it to look good when Brittany comes home."

Madeline assured him it was fine and followed him inside.

As they sat at the kitchen table and shared their respective stories, Madeline grew more and more at ease. Powell seemed glad to see her and anxious to share whatever he could to be helpful. He also was impressed that Madeline had come so far to see him and that her employer would support the effort.

As lunchtime neared, Powell said, "I don't have much to offer, but if you're hungry, I can make tuna sandwiches." Madeline accepted, and their conversation continued.

"You know my name is Vince, right? Know how I got that name? My dad was a farmer, but he loved football. He played some until the war took him to Korea. I was born a few years after he got back. He named me after Vince Lombardi, convinced I was going to be one of the greats." Powell shook his head. "Boy, he couldn't have been more wrong."

Madeline tried to think of something to say to refute the comment, but Powell didn't give her the chance. "The fact is, young lady, I'm just about the poorest excuse for a man you'll ever know. No, hear me out. I spent most of my adult life full of booze. It's cost me more jobs than I can count and it cost me my wife. She got sick of it and left. Instead of learning a lesson, I just drowned myself in an ocean of Jack Daniels. Eventually, it cost me my baby girl."

Madeline knew the answer to her next question, but wanted to encourage him to continue, so she asked, "So she left on her own, is that right?"

"Yep. She left a note for me on this very table and walked out the door. I was too drunk to notice for two days. When I realized she was gone, I finally pulled it together. I threw out every ounce of alcohol I had in this place. It just about killed me, but I did it. I haven't had a drop to drink since." His voice grew quiet, and it sounded as if he was talking more to himself than to her. "It's been hell, but I'm hanging in there." He looked up at her, "Can you imagine how hard it is stay sober when you're out of your mind with worry? God help me..."

Powell's face dropped into his hands, and he wept. Madeline had no idea what to do or say. She reached out and touched his forearm and said, "I'm sure she'll be okay, Vince. She hasn't been gone very long, and a lot of people are looking for her."

Powell looked up and heaved a sigh. "You are so wrong, miss. So very, very wrong."

Madeline was baffled at what he could mean, and by the certainty with which he said it, but she held her tongue.

Powell looked her in the eyes for a long time and finally said, "Hell with it. I have to tell somebody. It might as well be you."

"Tell me what?"

"I've lied to people," Powell said. He suddenly stood up, knocking over his chair and bellowed, "I lied to everybody!" After a moment, he noticed Madeline's widened eyes and calmed a little. He grabbed his chair, set it upright, and sat again. "Write this down. You're the first one to hear it, and the cops need to know this."

Madeline was already writing furiously, so Powell continued, "Brittany didn't leave the note the week before last. I told everybody that because I was ashamed. I was ashamed at how long it took me to realize she was gone. Then I was ashamed to call the police because I didn't want people coming in here and seeing how we lived. I thought she might come back. I swear I thought she'd be back any day. So I told people she had been staying home to help me with the apartment-painting. I told them she was here until less than two weeks ago. How could I be such an ass?"

Madeline looked up from her notebook and prodded a little. "So when did she really leave?"

"More than two months ago. She's been gone nine weeks as of yesterday. Dear God, she's not coming home, is she?" Powell was sobbing again, and Madeline was on the verge of tears herself.

"I don't know," she said, "but you're right about one thing, Vince. It's important the authorities know the truth. It could impact where and how they look for her."

"I know," he said through his tears. "You tell them. Please. You tell them."

"I will," Madeline assured him. "Is there anything else? Anything at all that could be helpful?"

Powell assured her there wasn't, but said he would call her if he thought of anything, or if he heard from Brittany.

"I'll call you, too, if I hear anything," Madeline promised. "Hang in there. It's going to be okay."

As Madeline walked out to her car, she prayed she was right but feared she was not.

She got in the car, planning to stop for gas, then head west into Kansas to the home of Shelly Blaine. Before she'd driven two blocks, she had Rooney on the phone. "You aren't going to believe this," she told him, then shared what she had learned from Vince Powell.

"Well I'll be a frog on fire," Rooney said, sharing one of his favorite expressions of surprise. "I'll get the word out to everyone. Good job, Ms. Mueller." Madeline smiled at the compliment as she ended the call.

Her phone rang before she had a chance to set it down. It was Ben.

"Hey boss. I was just about to call you. I had a fascinating interview with one of the girls' dads just now."

"I'll look forward to reading about it," Ben said, "but I need to give you some news and an assignment."

Ben sounded tense, so Madeline simply asked, "What's up?"

He said, "Rich Davis just called me. They've found a girl's body buried in the woods near the Raccoon River."

"*Our* Raccoon River?" Madeline asked in amazement, knowing if it was the one she was referencing, it had to be north and west of Des Moines, which put it somewhere near the place she currently called home.

"Yes," Ben said. "It's less than thirty miles from Orney. We don't know yet if it's related to these human trafficking cases, but the early reports are that she appears to be in her middle teens and has signs of physical abuse. She apparently was killed by a blow to the head, according to Davis. In any case, I don't need to tell you that this is a big story. I want you to head up here and cover it."

"I'm on it," Madeline said. "I'm less than four hours away. I'll be there with some daylight left. If they'll let me get close, I'll be able to see the scene, talk to a couple of people, and be back in the newsroom in time to have an article ready for tomorrow morning. Do you need art from me?"

"No. I sent Billy over there as soon as I heard. I couldn't be sure you'd be back here by dark."

"That's good," Madeline said, knowing that Ben was referencing Billy Campbell, the *Crier*'s young new photographer. Billy was talented and ambitious. He tolerated his assignments to photograph merchandise and other mundane subjects for advertising clients, but relished the opportunity to photograph hard news. "He'll give you much better pics than I could get with my phone anyway. Can you get me the names and contact information of whoever's running this?"

"Actually, the body's buried right in the northwest corner of Quincy County, so this landed in Sheriff Mackey's lap. That means, of course, that Davis and Rooney will be pulled back here to work this for the DCI."

Madeline wondered if Rooney had known about it when she called him. It would be irritating as hell to think he had held out on her after she had recovered a valuable piece of information for him. Knowing it didn't really matter beyond informing her about Rooney's approach to collaboration. She put it out of her mind. The good news was she knew all the players already. That would streamline her efforts to get information considerably. "Anything else?" she asked her boss.

"No, except to remind you to be careful. Whoever killed her is out there somewhere. It could be anyone. So keep your eyes and ears open."

"I promise. And Ben, thanks," Madeline said. They both knew she was saying thanks for giving her the assignment and not waiting for Tony to get back or assigning it to one of the people in the newsroom who didn't normally cover breaking news. Any member of the staff would have been willing to do it, and one or two might have leapt at the chance.

Three hours and fifty minutes after the phone call ended, Madeline was parked next to a Sheriff's Department cruiser in a small gravel parking lot built for people bringing boats to the river. Extending away from the parking lot was a concrete boat launch carved through the trees and stretching down to the water. A deputy sheriff stationed in the lot had pointed through the trees when she had asked about the burial site, so Madeline had gone back to her car to change into Levi's and walking shoes. She had gone to Missouri prepared for this, but she hadn't expected to be heading into the woods thirty miles from home.

"Do not cross the crime scene tape," the deputy barked at her back as she strode through tall grass and into the first line of trees. She followed the path of broken underbrush and had no trouble finding the scene, where seven men and women were gathered, taking pictures, sifting through dirt, and doing all the other grisly tasks involved in getting a victim's body and grave to speak to them.

Sheriff Mackey spotted her and broke away from the others to join her at the perimeter. Without much fanfare, he covered the basics for her.

A man had been walking through the woods along the river

with his dog. The man said he had been scouting locations for deer blinds for the hunting season later in the fall. His dog had gotten all "twitchy," the hunter's word, not the sheriff's, and had started digging at the underbrush. The man said he had been able to see immediately that the ground had been disturbed then covered by brush pulled up from other places. He had watched enough television to know what it all could mean, so he had called 911 right away.

"Except for dumb luck, we might not have found this grave for months," the sheriff said. "Maybe never. As it is, the medical examiner is saying the girl might have been here only two or three days. That's a huge break for us, both in our ability to identify her and to find someone who might have seen something important."

The sheriff continued, "That's why I'm telling you this. We need everyone who lives around here, or who has been anywhere near here between Sunday night and yesterday, to call and tell us if they saw anything. Please, tell your readers I mean *anything*. What cars, trucks, or boats did they see here? What people have come and gone? Tell them not to limit their reports to strangers. We want to know everyone who has been anywhere near here."

Madeline was nodding as she wrote. She looked up to ask, "You mentioned the break in identifying her. Did she have any I.D. on her?"

"No, nothing official. We're disappointed but not surprised. Any killer who goes to this much trouble to hide a body also makes sure he disposes of the victim's purse or wallet. However..."

Madeline looked up again, and the sheriff asked her, "Can we go off the record here?"

"I'd rather not," she replied, "but if you think it's important, then yes."

"I do," the sheriff said. "I normally wouldn't show you this, but I know you've been in Missouri looking into these cases of missing girls. I wondered if this would mean anything to you? I know it's a long shot, but maybe someone you interviewed mentioned it."

Madeline didn't disclose she only had questioned one person before being called back to Iowa. She simply nodded and looked on with interest as the sheriff held out a gold necklace. It appeared to be a simple heart on an inexpensive gold chain. "We're thinking the killer left this on her because he or she didn't realize it's a locket."

His big fingers found the catch, and the heart opened into two halves. On the right was a tiny black-and-white photograph of a woman. It didn't look antique. It could be the girl herself, or perhaps the girl's mother.

"It's not the dead girl," Mackey said as if he could read her mind. "We're guessing it's the mother."

Madeline noticed something was etched in the metal on the left side of the locket. In the shade of the trees, it was too dark to read it, so Madeline got out her phone and turned on the flashlight function. What jumped out at her nearly caused her to faint. "No, no, no," she said, backing away from little golden heart as if it was a deadly snake poised to strike.

Mackey looked concerned and reached out to grab her arm and steady her.

"Madeline?"

"Please no," was all she said.

The inscription inside the locket said *Brittany*.

***

The sheriff was less sure than Madeline that this was the same Brittany whose home Madeline had visited earlier the same day. However, it only took a couple of hours to confirm it. The photo from the locket was sent electronically to the Platte City Police. Officers there carried an enlargement to the Powell apartment and confirmed with Vince Powell that it was a picture of his ex-wife. Powell also confirmed that Brittany carried the picture in a gold heart-shaped locket she wore everywhere. Based on these findings, the officers showed Powell a photograph of the victim, taken at the scene and sent to them. Powell confirmed it was Brittany.

When Mackey received the information, Madeline was back in the newsroom writing her story. Mackey called Madeline with the news. Because the victim's father had already been notified, there was no point in delaying the release of everything they knew. Upon hearing the news, Madeline burst into tears, fought hard to get control of herself, and apologized to Mackey.

"I'm sorry, Sheriff. This isn't very professional of me," she sobbed. "But I was just there. I told him everything would be okay. This is so awful. He must be suffering beyond..."

Mackey said, "The officers reported that Powell took it hard but is functional. He's going to stay with a sister in Kansas City tonight." Mackey sounded as gruff as ever, but Madeline could hear the sadness in his voice as well.

"Oh, the poor man," was all Madeline could think to say.

.

Chapter 8

The Thursday edition of the *Crier* would be unusual, with the front page split right down the middle, allowing each of the major stories to occupy half the page. A photo of the Illinois motel with a police car and the Cook County Forensics Team van parked in front would accompany Ben's story, to be written from Tony's notes and descriptions.

They had discussed at length how much to share about Tony's altercations with the men. In the end, they opted to include the fact that it had happened, but not to go overboard in sharing blow-by-blow details. Tony had urged the downplaying of his role. He'd had his fill of the spotlight and did not want a reputation with his peers, or with law enforcement, of being some kind of vigilante. He also did not look forward to weeks of ribbing from his friends and others in town.

Madeline's story would include a photo of Brittany Powell's burial site, taken from just outside the police tape barrier. The sheriff, the medical examiner, and others could be seen in the photo, working the site, much as Madeline had found them when she had arrived at the scene. The story would also include the girl's most recent high school yearbook photograph. The image of the smiling teenager somehow put an exclamation point on the magnitude of the tragedy.

Tony's contributions to the discussion and to Ben's article were done by telephone. Doug joined in the conversation via speakerphone to determine how he would handle the news with his boss and radio station. Ben certainly understood that Doug needed to file a story. He was equally sure he didn't want the radio station to scoop the *Crier* by half a day. In the end, they agreed the *Crier* would put the story up on its website at midnight, six hours or more before most local residents would see the printed version of the paper. The radio station also would wait until midnight to begin sharing the news. That way, most people would get the news in the morning from one or both of the two sources.

Doug kept to himself the fact he wouldn't upload his recorded story to the station until 11:59 p.m. This would avoid any potential fight with his boss, who would want to air it immediately if he heard it, and would ensure Doug lived up to his end of the agreement. He would text the night DJ to watch for it in the audio inbox. By the time Guy loaded the story and got it on the air, it would be after the midnight network news for sure.

Ben wasn't pleased that the radio station had the story at all, but he had long ago accepted Tony and Doug's friendship as a fact of life. If he wanted to keep Tony in Orney, and he did, then he had to live with the fact that Tony's best friend worked for the competition. Like tonight, they always collaborated on solutions whenever the friendship resulted in conflicts of news coverage, deadlines, and publication timetables. It wasn't ideal, but they made it work. In addition, Ben recognized the important role Doug often played when Tony got into stressful or dangerous situations. *The successful outcome at the motel in Illinois was a perfect example,* Ben thought. *If Doug hadn't been there, everything would have occurred differently. Tony may not have been able to rescue the girls before the police arrived. If the situation had escalated into an armed standoff, who knows what might have happened?* Ben set all these thoughts aside as he sat at the computer and began composing the article for the paper using the information Tony had given him.

***

Tony and Doug didn't head back to Iowa right away. Tony needed to get the pictures Ben had requested. While he headed back to the Super 8 to do that, Doug headed to their room at the Hilton Garden to outline and record his story for broadcast.

When Tony was finished taking and emailing photographs, he drove to the local hospital to talk to Glenda. He expected he would have to fight the hospital bureaucracy to get in to see her since he had no official standing in law enforcement and was not a member of her family. He was right. To the hospital's credit, the front desk staff either hadn't been told about their young patient or knew the protocol well for rape victims, especially those who were underage. They didn't just refuse Tony a room number, they refused to acknowledge Glenda was a patient at all. Tony was unsure what to do next. He couldn't wander the halls of a 200-bed medical center looking for her, and he couldn't just sit outside waiting. He wouldn't know which exit to watch, and even if he spotted her leaving, by that time, she'd be in the care of social workers who would be loath to let him speak with her.

As he stood in the lobby debating his next move, the elevator doors opened and Agent Cunningham strode out, heading for the front door.

Tony hailed him.

"Mr. Harrington, you certainly get around," the FBI agent said. "I can guess why you're here, and you must know I can't help you. I really shouldn't even talk to you."

"Sir, we're off the record for now. I promise. Your guess is probably right, but you know that Glenda called me, right? Twice. I led you to her. Is it too much to ask to have a few minutes to talk with her?"

"That may seem logical in your world," the agent said, trying to sound understanding. "But in my world, we don't let news reporters inside, especially when dealing with minors."

Tony quickly decided to take another approach. He said, "Maybe I can help you. The fact you're leaving already tells me Glenda didn't have much to say. Maybe she'll tell me things she wouldn't tell you."

Cunningham seemed intrigued by that thought, so Tony added, "And if she expresses to anyone that she'd rather not talk to me, I swear I'll leave immediately and not bother her again."

In the end, Cunningham agreed to give him access on the condition that he accompany Tony to the room and see for himself that Glenda was okay with Tony's visit, and after garnering Tony's promise he would share with authorities whatever he learned.

They went back up the elevator to the 6th floor. With the help of Cunningham and his badge, Tony soon found himself sitting at Glenda's side in a hospital room, with a suspicious nurse watching him from the hallway, through an observation window.

"Hi, Mr. Harrington," Glenda said, trying to smile through swollen lips. She shifted in her bed and pulled the sheets up to cover the gap in her hospital gown. "I guess you've seen enough of my skin already."

He blushed. "I'm just glad you're okay, and please, call me

Tony. Those men are in jail, and you're in good hands now. And by the way, if you get asked about an attorney, tell the authorities yes, you have one. His name is Nathan Freed. Can you remember that name? His practice is in Iowa, but he's making arrangements for someone from Illinois to look after your interests."

"But I can't..."

"Don't worry about it," Tony said. "He has more money than God, so he won't be charging you anything."

"Thanks Tony. That's... That's awesome, really. Everything you've done is really nice. But...

"But what? You can tell me."

"Well, it's just that I don't feel safe. Those two creeps at the motel were horrible, but they were just two guys. I know there are others. What if they want me back? What if they won't leave me alone? What if they think I talked to the cops, and they kill me or my family like they promised?" She wiped a tear from the eye that wasn't swollen.

"Glenda, please don't worry about those things. The FBI is on this now. With your help, everyone in this evil organization is going to be rounded up and put away. You stay strong and take care of yourself, and trust the cops to do their jobs."

"I'd like to help them. I would," she said. "But I don't know anything. I never saw anyone but Big Al and Freddy. Whenever they did business with their boss, it was over the phone or when they were away from us."

"I'm not here to push you," Tony reassured her. "Just to encourage you to think about it. You were with them a long time. Something you saw or overheard could end up being very helpful. And maybe you could identify a john or two. If the FBI can find a few of them, they may be able to get some tidbit that will lead back to the bad guys."

"I'll think about it. I promise."

Tony debated with himself about asking the next question, and decided to proceed. "One other thing, Glenda. Are you able to tell me why you described me as nice?"

The question clearly threw her. "Huh?"

"The first time you called me, you said a friend told you I was nice. I've been wondering who told you that. I think it might have been a girl from Orney High School who used to watch me play piano. A girl named Trina Aston. Is that right?"

Glenda seemed surprised that Tony knew the name. She slowly nodded and sighed, "Yes. Trina. That poor girl. She's not strong like me, Tony. She shouldn't be doing this. It's so awful. At least I made my own mistakes that put me in this situation. Trina, she... she... Let's just say she's a true victim."

"Trust me, Glenda, you're all victims. No child—not you, not this Trina, and not anyone you've seen abused—deserves what's happening, whether you've made mistakes or not."

"I understand that, Tony. I try hard not to blame myself. But in Trina's case, it's so much worse."

"How can that be? Can you tell me what you mean?"

Glenda was quiet a long time, clearly debating how much to share. Suddenly she asked, "This isn't for an article in the newspaper, is it? I mean, Trina was right, you're nice, but I can't tell you things that might be in the paper."

Tony was horrified she had to ask. "Glenda, I swear, I just want to help. I will never write anything that will cause harm to you or any of the kids who have suffered from these A-holes' abuses. So please, tell me about Trina."

Glenda nodded, making up her mind, "You're right that Trina's a high school student from Orney. We were together for only one night. Some rich guy arranged to have her brought in for a three-way with me. The guy was two hours late, so Trina and I had a lot of time to talk."

At the reference to a three-way, Tony winced and had to bite his tongue.

Glenda continued, "I said her situation is worse because she told me her dad brought her to the motel."

"Her *dad*?" Tony squawked.

"Yeah, she's one of those weekenders. You know, she goes to school and lives at home, but then her dad forces her to do tricks on weekends, and sometimes in the evenings."

"But her own father? He knows what he's doing when he brings her to you?"

"Yes, Tony," Glenda smiled ruefully. "You're not just nice. You're pretty clueless, too, aren't you?" It wasn't a real question.

Tony said, "I've read about family members forcing girls into sex, but hearing it's happening in Orney is… it's just..." He stopped, at a loss for words.

"Trina doesn't want to do this. Her dad makes her, you know, for the money. She said if she tries to resist, her dad forces himself on her, which is worse. It started with him when she was really young. Then he got the bright idea that he could make a lot of money renting her out."

Tony felt sick and just stared at Glenda as she continued. "Trina said her mom died when she was young. Her dad started coming to her room late at night not long after that. The poor thing was grieving the loss of her mom, and she had to deal with that," Glenda added, shaking her head. "So you see what I mean? It would be so much worse to be forced into this by your own dad, the person who's supposed to love and protect you. Trina seemed just so... so defeated. If your own family doesn't love you and sees you as nothing more than a piece of meat to be sold to anyone who wants sex, how can you feel anything positive about yourself?"

Tony ached. He wanted to scream. He wanted to hit something... someone. He managed his next question in little more than a croak. "Is there more? Anything else you can tell me?"

"Well," Glenda replied, "only that Trina wants out."

That seemed like a given to Tony. Glenda must have sensed his puzzlement at her comment and continued, "That's not always true. I've met girls who were abused when they were young like that. After suffering for a while, they become resigned to it. They don't know any other life and can't imagine themselves living in a way you think of as normal. In Trina's case, she never has lost the desire to get out. She hates her father for what he's done, and she longs to be an ordinary high school student."

Somehow Tony could see that. Remembering the shy girl sitting on the choir room risers, he could imagine her just wanting to be someone else. At that moment, Tony decided he had to help her do that. He wasn't sure how, but he would find a way to get her out.

***

The long drive back to Iowa was a quiet one. Each man mostly slept while the other took his turn driving. Even with minimal stops, they didn't arrive in Orney until well after midnight. Tony dropped Doug at his car, still parked on the street. He tried to thank his friend, but Doug waived it off. "Don't say it, Tony. I wouldn't call this fun, but it certainly was exciting. And who knew I would get a great story out of it? I'm glad you called, and I hope you'll call me again when you need me. G'night."

Tony gave Doug a quick hug and said, "You know it goes both ways, right? If you ever need me, I'll be there." Doug acknowledged him with a nod and was gone.

Tony drove his Explorer around to the alley to access the parking space behind his bungalow. He climbed out of the SUV, grabbed his bag from the back seat, and walked up to the carport which he used more as a covered patio and protection from the weather for the side door of the house. To his astonishment, Madeline was sitting cross-legged on the concrete, in the dark, with her back up against the door. She was wearing an old Mickey Mouse sweatshirt, blue jeans, and canvas walking shoes.

"Hey," Tony said. "You okay?"

She didn't reply. He helped her up, and she grabbed him, pulling him to her until her face was pressed into his chest and her arms were wrapped tightly around his back.

"Okay, dumb question," Tony said, reciprocating by putting his arms around her and squeezing equally hard. "I'm really sorry. Today must have been horrible for you. Come on inside, and I'll pour you a glass of wine or make you coffee or whatever you want."

They went through the aluminum door and up the three steps into the kitchen. Madeline sat at the table, just staring into space. Tony opted for the wine, thinking it would be hard enough to sleep without another shot of caffeine.

After pouring two glasses and setting them on the table, he settled into the seat across from her. He was smart enough not to push, so he sat quietly as she took a sip, then another. Finally, she asked the unanswerable question, "How can such evil exist in the world? How could anyone do these things to children and then kill them? Brittany was so young. She had her whole life ahead of her."

Tears rolled down Madeline's cheeks, and she made no effort to wipe them away. Tony was debating whether to respond when she continued, "I'm not sure I can do this, Tony. I don't know if I can get this close to human suffering and keep my sanity. What's the point, anyway? The police don't want us around. No one reads newspapers anymore. Even if they catch Brittany's killer, there'll be a dozen more creeps waiting in line to take his place."

"Madeline, you're right on every point," Tony said, "but you've only mentioned one side of the coin. Yes, there's evil in the world. There always has been and always will be. Yes, it's frustrating to seek the Hydra, to find it and cut off its head, only to watch helplessly as it grows three more. But consider the alternative. The alternative is to not chase the Hydra and let it feed on the innocent unchecked. The alternative is not to care. In my mind, that is the greater evil. Apathy is the greater death. Our job is to make sure others know about these evils—to share the hard truth so people can feel the pain of this the way we do, so they have the opportunity to rise up against the beast."

Tony reached across the table and took her hands into his. "I can't tell you what you should or shouldn't do with your life. I can only tell you two things tonight. First, you're good at this. You're a fine writer, but more importantly, you have good instincts. And," he said almost as an afterthought, "you proved yesterday that you're good at getting information from people—information that others couldn't get. The other thing I know is that you shouldn't make any life-changing decisions tonight, and probably not for a few days. Brittany's death was a huge blow. And for that, I'm glad."

Madeline looked up as he said this, and he explained, "We don't ever want to be the kind of people who stop caring about the victims. Let's hope we never get used to it. But as I learned when Lisa was killed, we do have to find a way to set it aside and move on."

Madeline pulled his right hand closer and kissed his knuckles. "Thanks," she said, then got up and walked out the side door into the dark.

Tony watched her go, fighting off tears of his own. *If only it were as easy to do as it is to say*, he thought. *She's right to wonder if we can keep this up.*

***

Madeline walked briskly to the front of the house. She had parked her Chevy at the curb. She climbed in, started the car, and pulled into the street. At the end of the block, she stopped, pounded on the steering wheel, and yelled at the stars, "How does he do that? I'm a wreck, and he pulls a thoughtful, heartwarming speech out of his ass!" She calmed herself and resumed the drive back to her apartment, while thoughts of Brittany, Vince Powell, Ben, Rooney, and Tony swirled in her head. *Tony. Tony, the man who can do it all. Tony, you creep, I hate you,* she thought. Then, *No, I don't hate you. I... I don't have a clue what I think about anything.*

In the end, she took his advice. She had another glass of wine, fought hard to put the events of the past two days out of her mind, and fell asleep.

Town Crier

Two Kidnapping Victims Rescued

Ben Smalley, Editor

CHICAGO, Illinois – Thanks to a tip received by the *Orney Town Crier*, a 14-year-old Iowa girl and a 17-year-old girl originally from Honduras were rescued from a motel room near I-55 west of Chicago on Wednesday. The two told police they had been

Girl's Body Found Buried in Quincy County

Madeline Mueller, Staff Writer

HANDOVER, Iowa – The body of 17-year-old Brittany Powell, of Platte City, Mo., was found buried in the woods near the Raccoon River in northwest Quincy County on Wednesday morning, according to held for more than two months by men who physically and sexually abused them and forced them to have sex with strangers.

The girls were found through a collaborative effort of the Iowa Division of Criminal Investigation, the FBI, and staff from the *Orney Town Crier* and KKAR Radio. Authorities became aware of the girls' plight when the Iowa girl reached out to *Town Crier* Reporter Tony Harrington by cell phone.

Harrington and KKAR reporter Doug Tenney were the first people on the scene Wednesday morning, after the girls' location had been identified by the FBI, as a result of tracking the source of a second cell phone call to Harrington.

Harrington and Tenney were instrumental in rescuing the girls and helping police capture two men suspected of kidnapping, rape, assault, and human trafficking. A third man was arrested at the scene on charges of soliciting · for prostitution and statutory rape.

Because of the nature of the crimes against them and their ages, the names of the girls are not being released. They were treated...

Quincy County Sheriff George Mackey.

The grave was found by a man and his dog who were hiking in the woods. Quincy County Medical Examiner Dr. Lance Torgesen said the girl died of an apparent blow to the head with a blunt instrument. He said the body appeared to have been buried only two or three days prior to being found.

Sheriff Mackey said, "Except for dumb luck, we might not have found this grave for months, maybe never."

He said the fact the girl was found soon after her apparent murder "is a huge break for us, both in our ability to identify her and to find someone who might have seen someone or something important."

The sheriff is asking everyone who lives near the boat launch south of Handover, or who has been anywhere near there between Sunday night and Wednesday morning, to call and report...

Chapter 9

At 10 a.m., Tony was at his desk in the newsroom, scribbling notes on a yellow legal pad. He was listing options for the next steps in pursuing Brittany's killer, and for finding more of the men and women who had forced Glenda and Camila into slavery. He was also making notes for Ben, sharing thoughts about potential sidebar stories on human trafficking and key points to make in any future editorials on the subject.

At 10:18 a.m., his desk phone rang. Out of habit, he glanced at the digital display. It read only, "Unknown Caller." Tony barely noticed. It was relatively common for people calling the newsroom to block their numbers. If they were calling to share a news tip or make a complaint, or even to point out a typo in that morning's paper, they often wanted to remain anonymous.

"This is Tony Harrington. How can I help you?"

A smooth, male voice replied, "How interesting that you put it that way. I could simply tell you and hang up, but I fear that wouldn't get the job done."

"Excuse me?" Tony said, "I'm not following you. Who's calling, please?"

"The problem is, Tony," the caller said, "you *are* following me. That's why I'm calling. It has to stop."

Tony sat up straight in his chair. He turned on his cell phone so he could record the conversation, and he waved furiously at Ben to come join him at his desk.

"I'm sorry," Tony said, "but I can't stop following you if I don't know who you are. Please don't talk in riddles. What's this about?"

"If you like it straightforward, that's fine with me," the caller said. He sounded adult, with a strong baritone voice, like a late-night DJ playing obscure blues tunes. "You chased Glenda to Illinois and your co-worker chased Brittany to Missouri and back. Now Glenda's free and Brittany's dead, so I'm guessing you're chasing me. Am I right?"

"Well," Tony said, with an edge of self-righteousness, "if you had something to do with the despicable things done to these girls, then yes, I would say you're right."

Tony's hands were trembling, and he had to prop his elbow against the surface of his desk to steady the phone. Ben was at his side, hearing half the conversation well, and catching enough of the other half to realize what was happening. He pulled his cell from his pocket and stepped away a few paces to call Rich Davis.

"It just won't do, Tony," the voice continued. "You need to let it drop. Think about it reasonably. Glenda called you, and you felt you needed to respond. Now she's safe, and your job is done. Let it go at that. What I do is fulfill a basic human need. If you catch me, it won't change anything. Men and women will still pay men and women for the opportunity to partake in their various fantasies."

"That may be," Tony replied curtly. "But meanwhile, you'll be rotting in jail, perhaps fulfilling your fellow convicts' fantasies."

"I knew you would react like this," the man sighed. "Young zealots like you are so predictable. Maybe you think you're still avenging Lisa's death. Is that it?

"You son of a bitch!" Tony shouted, causing everyone in the newsroom to look up. He paused and forced himself into a false calm. "You think you're so smart, but all you're doing is making me more determined."

"Well then, *Mister* Harrington," the man said with a sneer. "Try this on for size. If you don't stand down, you're going to find yourself at a lot more funerals. I hear you admire your boss. Ben, right? We'll start with him. And maybe that co-worker, Madeline. She's pretty good-looking, so I may have to let a few clients enjoy her for a while before I cut her heart out."

Tony couldn't believe his ears. He wanted to scream, but he couldn't give the man the satisfaction. He just sat there, clenching the phone, not knowing what to say.

The caller continued, "And then, for good measure, we're going to take Rita. She's beautiful, Tony. And so talented. We'll enjoy seeing what those fingers can do for some clients, just before we cut them off and mail them to you!"

Tony exploded at the reference to his sister, who was a pianist and cello player in graduate school at the University of Chicago.

"You bastard! How dare you say something like that!"

"Calm down, Tony. It's in your power to save all these people. All you have to do is walk away, and convince your two-bit editor and his laughable little newspaper to do the same. You only get one warning, Tony. If we see or hear of you again, the killing starts. We're very good at this, and we have eyes everywhere, so get over yourself and just let. It. Go."

The line went dead. Tony went numb. He dropped the phone and collapsed forward onto the desk.

***

At noon, Tony, Madeline, Ben, Rich Davis, and Dan Rooney were crowded together in Ben's office. Ben had wanted time for Tony to calm himself, so had set the meeting up for ninety minutes after the call had ended.

"My God, what am I going to do?" Tony groaned.

"Easy, pal," Davis said. "You're not in this alone. Before we talk about next steps, let's get everyone up to date on where we are. First of all, thanks, Ben, for calling while Tony still was on the phone. I tried to rush a trace, but it didn't get very far. All we know is that the call originated from the 207 area code."

"Where in the hell is that?" Tony asked.

"Maine, but I doubt that's where the call actually originated."

Tony shook his head in confusion.

Davis continued, "They probably routed it through a phone system on the east coast. The bad news is the caller knew how to prevent us from tracing the call. The good news is that this tells us a lot about him and his organization."

"How so?" Ben asked.

"Put simply, it tells us this guy is no fly-by-night operator. He's sophisticated enough to know how to avoid detection, so it's not some amateur who's decided to try his hand at abusing girls. Also, think about all the information he shared with Tony. Mr. X clearly was trying to scare him by showing him how much he knew about his co-workers and his family. We all know everything he said can be found online, or on social media, but the fact he had done his homework tells us he's smart and thorough, and he understands human nature enough to know what would get to Tony."

"Yeah, no kidding," Tony muttered.

"Next on the list," Davis said, "we've notified Tony's parents, as well as Rita. We have also talked to University Security at her school and to the Chicago PD. Our FBI friends in Chicago have also been alerted."

"Is all this sharing wise?" Tony asked. "He said he has people everywhere. Aren't we at risk of triggering the very thing we're trying to prevent?"

"Perhaps," Davis said, "so maybe we should've started with this question. Is the *Crier* going to back off and leave the rest of this story alone?" He looked at Ben, then Tony, then Madeline. The three of them looked at each other.

"This is my call," Ben said. "The buck stops with me. Considering my employees and their loved ones have been threatened, I have to take their feelings into account. But the final call is mine. My starting position is the same as it was nearly three years ago when Tony and I discussed the murders in Orney. That is, I can't ask my reporters to put themselves at risk, but I plan to pursue the story on my own, with or without them." He looked at Tony first, then rested his gaze on Madeline. "If either of you have objections, I expect you to be completely honest with me and speak up now."

Madeline spoke first. "I think Tony's opinion matters more than mine, since the call came to him. But I'm jumping in here because I don't want the threats to me to put anyone off the story. I'm in. I want the *Crier* to push this as if we were *The New York Times*, and I want to be right in the middle of it. Let the bastards come after me. They'll be sorry they did."

Tony started to respond, but Madeline interrupted to add, "Before you tell me I don't know what I'm saying, please hear this: I *do*. I saw Brittany's body when they lifted her out of that hole in the ground. I'm terrified of something like that happening to me. But I'm equally terrified of it happening to *anybody*. If we don't help track down these people and stop them, how will we live with ourselves? We didn't ask for this, but now we have no choice."

Tony smiled and said, "Hey, nice speech, but..."

Madeline thought, *Oh my God, I'm turning into Tony.*

Tony continued, "I don't believe you fully understand the risks. Despite that, you said the most important thing. We don't have a choice. So we're all in. Now what?"

Davis said, "That's my point. I knew you wouldn't back down. Of course, the DCI and the FBI aren't going to let it go, either. So knowing the hunt will continue, we're obligated to alert everyone and do all we can to protect those who've been threatened."

"Okay," Tony said. "I get it."

"Next, thanks to Madeline, we know Brittany had been missing for nine weeks, not two. That means she probably was held by this guy, or these people, somewhere remote. It's possible she was in a motel or a brothel, but based on the physical abuse she suffered and the length of time involved, I'm guessing she was in a more secure spot, like someone's barn or a basement out in the middle of nowhere. We've distributed this information to every law enforcement agency we can find between Kansas City and Quincy County. Maybe someone has seen something hinky that will tip us off about a personal hell hole."

"Now that she's dead, won't that be harder to spot?" Madeline asked.

Davis looked uncomfortable and cleared his throat. Rooney surprised everyone when he spoke first. "Think about it," he said softly. "Whoever had her for nine weeks isn't just going to stop. He either has, or soon will have, another girl or girls to be used for his pleasure."

"Oh God, of course," Madeline said, her face noticeably paler.

"We'll jump aggressively on any new reports of missing girls, naturally," Davis said. "And maybe we'll get lucky with an observant deputy sheriff or something. By the way, my personal opinion is that we're talking about someplace in or close to Quincy County." He noticed raised eyebrows around the room and explained. "It's unlikely Brittany's killer drove her very far to be buried. If she was alive in his car, he wouldn't have wanted her to be seen in the condition she was in. If she was dead, well, no one wants to drive very far with a dead body in the trunk. It's most likely she was driven from Missouri to Iowa in the beginning, shortly after she fell into their hands, and was held here and killed here, and buried reasonably close to where that happened. Remember, the killer didn't think the grave would be found."

"I'll talk to Mackey as soon as we're done here," Rooney said. "He can get the word out to his crew as well as the sheriffs in nearby counties."

Ben looked at his reporters and asked, "What's next for us?"

Tony said, "I was writing down some thoughts about that very question when this swine called me. Let me grab my notes."

"Wait," Madeline said. "I'm pretty sure Tony's next steps don't include the one I'm going to suggest." Before she even finished laying out her plan, Ben said no. Davis said absolutely not. Tony said she was full of crap.

Davis assumed it was settled, and the conversation moved on to other avenues they could pursue. After another thirty minutes, the discussion waned, and the meeting drew to a close.

As they left Ben's office, Madeline came up beside Tony in the newsroom. "I'm doing this," she said. "Whether you help me or not."

***

At two o'clock that afternoon, Tony walked into the Quincy County Sheriff's Department and asked to speak to Sheriff Mackey.

When they were in Mackey's office with the door closed, Tony reached into his jacket pocket and pulled out a sheet of paper, which he handed to the sheriff.

"Is this what I think it is?" Mackey asked.

"Yes. It's the completed application for a permit to carry a concealed weapon. I need it approved today."

"I'm sorry, Tony, but the rules require a three-day waiting period and a background check."

"When did you hand me the form?"

"Three days ago."

"I dated it that day. That takes care of that. Do you know me?"

"Of course, but..."

"Do I have a criminal history?"

"Not that I've been able to prove," the sheriff said, grinning.

"Okay, we're good. Give me the permit now, please."

The sheriff looked at him for a long moment. "You planning to kill somebody?"

"No, sheriff. I swear. I'm just trying to protect myself and the people I care about."

"Okay. First of all, Iowa requires you to take a firearms course. I know you went through the course last year because I read your feature story about it. Did you get a Certificate of Completion?"

Tony nodded. "I'm sure I still have it somewhere. I didn't exactly treasure it, but I save everything."

"Well, I hope you do, 'cause I'm gonna need it. Secondly, I don't issue the final permit. I just do the paperwork and background check for the State of Iowa. You'll have to pick up the actual permit in Des Moines. But I have friends in Public Safety there, so let me see what I can do. Give me ten minutes. I'll call you and let you know when it'll be ready."

"Thanks." Tony turned to go.

"Tony!" the sheriff barked. Tony stopped and turned to face him. "Do *not* make me regret this."

Tony didn't respond except to nod and walk out the door.

***

In the end, it wasn't a deputy sheriff who spotted something "hinky." It was Maggie Weir, a longtime waitress and daytime manager at the Pizza Hut in Orney. She was refilling the salad bar during the noontime rush when she overheard Justin Langly turn down a piece of pizza, telling his friend who worked at the local grain cooperative, "I'll stick with salad. I've been on a diet for weeks, and I haven't fallen off the wagon once. I'm sure as hell not gonna start with pizza from this place."

The comment irritated Maggie, who was proud of the food she served, but it also puzzled her. At least three times a week, she saw Langly at the drive-through window of the burger place next door. It seemed unlikely to her that he was being faithful to his diet if he was buying burgers every other day. She knew he was getting sacks full of food because, if she had to admit it, she kept a close eye on the sales going out the drive-up window at their competition. She didn't mean to be nosy. She just couldn't help but watch when people chose that junk food over her thick-crust, sausage-and-mushroom delight.

She had grown to resent Langly after seeing him at the drive-through so many times. He couldn't be dieting. Yet it seemed like such a silly thing to lie about. *Why would he do that? Maybe he has a kid. No, that's crazy. That big lug is single for a reason. Him getting a woman pregnant?* No, that scandal would not have escaped the attention of Maggie Weir.

Maybe he just has guests at home, she mused. *Yeah, guests he hates.* She chuckled to herself and moved on, concentrating on filling the croutons bowl, picking the stray leaves of lettuce out of the ice, and getting the poppyseed dressing drips out of the ranch dressing in the neighboring cask.

Chapter 10

Tony's stomach churned as he stood on the second floor of the mega sporting goods store in Des Moines. He was surrounded by guns. Walls covered in guns, cabinets full of guns, and people examining guns. It depressed him to see the enormity of the time, effort, and money spent by so many people in so many different companies, to design and manufacture machines whose primary purpose was to kill people. Tony tried not to scowl at the young man buying a huge military-looking weapon. He glanced at the promotional sign above the spot where it had come off the wall. "Fires 200 rounds/min.; Bursts of 400 rounds/min!"

Good Lord. What guy in his twenties needs to shoot anything at that rate? Tony wondered, *and who in their right mind would sell him a weapon that could do it?*

Tony dialed back his thoughts. Probably a room full of guns and gun lovers was not the place to begin a debate about America's firearms laws. He also recognized the absurdity of wanting to voice an objection to guns when he was in the store to buy one.

It was Friday morning, and Tony had risen early and driven the 90 miles to Des Moines to make his purchase. He knew he would find a good selection at the big store, and he figured his chances of being seen by someone who knew him were pretty slim on a weekday morning that far from home. Lastly, as Sheriff Mackey had noted, Tony had needed to come to Des Moines anyway to retrieve his Permit to Carry from the Iowa Department of Public Safety. He had just come from there.

"Can I help you, sir?" Tony's thoughts were interrupted by an older gentleman, tall, a little overweight but comfortably so, and gray-haired. *He looks like my grandfather.*

"Uh, well... yes," Tony stammered. "I'm here to buy a handgun. I have to admit, it's a first time for me, and I'm a bit overwhelmed."

"No problem. I understand completely." The clerk smiled warmly. "I'll be happy to help. Let's begin with a few questions, if you don't mind. If I understand your needs a little better, I can point you to the right weapon easily enough."

Tony nodded. He was as ready as he was ever going to feel.

"First question, do you know you need a permit to buy a handgun in Iowa? Or if you have a PAC, that'll take care of it."

"Yes," Tony said, reaching into his pocket. "I have that one covered."

The clerk took his permit and read it carefully.

"Ah, Sheriff Mackey's name is referenced, I see. Good man, that George. I've sold him a couple of hunting rifles over the years."

"Yes," Tony agreed. "Quincy County is lucky to have him."

"Well, this appears to be in order. I noticed it's a permit for concealed carry. Are you planning to carry the weapon when you wear street clothes, or only when you're wearing outdoor gear like hiking clothes, or will you just keep it locked in the trunk of a car, or what?"

Tony wasn't sure how to answer. "Well, I'm buying it for protection, just in case I get into a situation where I need it. So I'm not really sure under what circumstances that might happen. I hope it never does happen," he added quickly.

"Of course, of course. I understand. To get us started, let's assume you want something pretty portable, not too heavy, and able to fit comfortably into a jacket pocket."

"That sounds right."

The conversation continued, and Tony grew more amazed with each question. The range of options was unbelievable. Did he want a revolver or an automatic? What type of finish on the metal? Did he want grips in metal, wood, or plastic? Did he want hammer fire or striker fire? Single action or double action? How much trigger pressure?

Tony, of course, had no answers and continually put the questions back onto the clerk with responses like, "What would you choose? What do you think is best for someone like me?"

The clerk then examined Tony's hands.

"You're young, with no sign of arthritis, so we don't need to restrict ourselves to guns with low-pressure triggers. Also, your hands are average in size, so we don't need to worry about your ability to use a smaller gun with ease."

Tony must have looked puzzled because the clerk added, "You wouldn't believe some of the men we get in here with big, fleshy fingers who can't use a smaller gun. They can get it to fire, of course, but they can't manipulate the features well enough to be comfortable with it."

"Maybe we'll keep the news about my small hands just between us," Tony quipped. The clerk laughed loudly—too loudly— telling Tony he'd heard that joke a few too many times.

The clerk asked the inevitable question about budget. Tony

didn't want to say it was no concern, so he said, "I want a good-quality weapon that is completely reliable. If I need to spend a little more for it, that's okay." The clerk beamed his approval.

In the end, Tony settled on a Walther PK380. It was designed to be a concealed weapon, small, lightweight, and easy to use. It was described in one review as "designed for shooters not trying to be John Wayne or Bruce Willis." That sounded good to Tony. The gun also required a reasonable amount of pressure on the trigger to fire. He didn't want a gun that fired too easily, knowing that if he ever had to take it in his hand, he would be nervous as hell. He didn't want a twitch to cost him a toe, or worse.

Tony and the clerk had another discussion about ammunition. The clerk recommended hollow-point bullets.

"It's clear to me, sir, that you don't intend to ever fire this weapon unless you have to. It stands to reason then, if you're shooting, it's because you're in immediate jeopardy. In that situation, you want some stopping power. Unless you're a very good aim and intend to put a bullet in someone's eye, a smaller weapon like this may not stop a big man determined to assault you. Hollow-point bullets increase the stopping power and just may save your life."

Tony mumbled his agreement. He was feeling exhausted and disgusted by the entire experience. He assumed he would buy one box of ammunition. After all, he hoped he would never need any bullets. If he did, he hoped even more fervently it would only be one.

However, the clerk reminded Tony that he would want to practice with the gun. "The worst thing you can do is own a weapon you're not competent to use," the clerk said. "I strongly recommend you buy at least two boxes of bullets, and exhaust one of them at a firing range or some other safe place."

Tony knew the man was paid to sell more stuff, but he also saw the wisdom in the advice. After more than two hours in the store,

Tony walked out with the Walther, the bullets, a soft leather holster and a carrying case, and several hundred fewer dollars in his bank account.

***

Saturday morning was crisp and cool. Tony dressed in his "outdoor gear," or as close as he could come to it. He wasn't a hunter, and he hadn't been camping since he was sixteen, but he pulled on blue jeans, a long-sleeved t-shirt, and an Iowa Hawkeyes sweatshirt. He chose the sweatshirt because he was headed for the woods and he thought the yellow color would make it less likely he would be mistaken for a turkey or a deer or whatever people were hunting at the moment. He didn't have hiking boots, so he settled for his Reeboks. *I'm not going mountain climbing, he thought. I'm just taking a walk in the woods.* He pulled on a windbreaker so he would have pockets in which to carry the gun and bullets. He chuckled to himself. *I'll have to remember to take off the jacket, or the bright yellow sweatshirt will be no help at all.*

He drove his Explorer out of the north side of town, and headed west toward the Raccoon River Valley. He parked in one of the many lots designed to serve Iowa's bike trail system, and walked into the timberland on the trail. He kept to the left edge, where he could easily step off the path if a cyclist approached. After walking about half a mile, he turned off the path and clambered down a hillside into a ravine. Tony occasionally rode his bike on the trail, and knew the ravine was there. At the bottom, he resumed walking, this time in a direction away from the bike trail.

After perhaps a mile and three turns down the ravine's path, Tony figured he was far enough away that he could fire the gun without scaring the hell out of a passing cyclist. He had chosen the ravine for practice to ensure any errant shots had nowhere to go but into the dirt and tree roots that now blocked his sight lines in every direction.

He took the gun from his right pocket and the bullets from his left. He slid the magazine out of the butt and loaded eight rounds— Hey, he was learning the lingo!—into it. He remembered what Rich Davis had told him once about the agent's difficulty in passing the timing test for reloading his weapon. So Tony unloaded and reloaded the magazine several times until he felt confident he could do it smoothly, if not quickly.

Once reloaded, Tony held the gun away from his body, with the nose pointed at a 45-degree angle to the ground. He switched off the safety, added a second hand to the gun in a stance he had seen a thousand times on television cop shows, and pulled the trigger. The sensation was electrifying, nearly overwhelming.

"My God," Tony muttered, remembering the sensation from when he had taken the firearms course. "No wonder people get hooked on this. It feels like you're holding the power of an earthquake in your hands." He raised the gun a little higher and fired two more rounds into the dirt. The Walther reviews had promised minimal recoil from this model, and Tony was glad he had opted for it. *If this is minimal recoil, I would hate to fire one of those huge mothers I saw in the store.*

An hour later, Tony had expended all the bullets in the one box he had brought with him. He had aimed at dozens of targets in the form of trees, tree roots, clumps of dirt, and anything else he could find that wasn't breathing and wouldn't ricochet a bullet fragment back at him. By the end, he had managed to hit a couple of targets now and then, but not consistently. *In other words, I suck at this. I hope the sight of this gun scares away any attackers, because my chances of hitting one with a bullet are slim.*

His right arm ached, and he was glad he was done. *Not good, but good enough*, he thought, as he walked back to his SUV, packed the gun into its case, stashed that in the rear storage compartment, and headed for home.

***

Once again, Madeline was waiting at the side door when Tony arrived home.

"I'm going to have to get you a key, or at least a lawn chair," he quipped.

"Nah, the ground's good. Besides, this is more coincidence than routine."

"So what's up?"

She looked at him and then away, saying, "I'm headed back to Missouri. I thought you might like to go along."

Tony was surprised. It must have shown on his face because she quickly added, "We still have three days left on the week Ben gave us. I told him I'm going back to interview more of the families of these girls to see if we can get any more leads on these guys. But you know why I'm really going."

Tony unlocked the door, and she followed him up the three stairs to the kitchen. He turned to her and said, "Madeline, you can't do what you suggested before. You cannot put yourself out there as bait. In the first place, it's probably a waste of time. In the second place, if it works, the risk is simply too high. These guys have been getting away with this because they know how to make girls disappear. I can't let you be another of those victims."

"I've already made it clear that it's not up to you." Madeline's voice was firm to the point of sounding belligerent. "I'm doing this. I am going to find these assholes. You can be there with me to help, or I can do it on my own. It's up to you."

"Jeez, Madeline. Please."

"I'm sorry, Tony, but that's the way it is. We're leaving after lunch. You're still buying."

Tony shook his head, turned, and went into the bedroom to pack a bag. There was no way he was going to let Madeline do what she was suggesting, but he realized the only way to stop her was to go along and try to find other avenues to pursue that would keep her satisfied. Maybe if they were making some progress, he could convince her to stay out of harm's way.

They grabbed sandwiches from a shop on fast food row near the highway south of town and ate in the SUV. Tony had convinced Madeline that they should take the Explorer, saying they would have more room, and wouldn't have to worry if their travels took them to places cars didn't normally travel.

It was a beautiful October Saturday, with trees starting to share their fall colors and farmers beginning the harvest. Despite the dark nature of their task ahead, it was hard to not be upbeat. Especially, Tony had to admit, since it felt good to have a smart, talented, and attractive woman in the seat next to him. At 2:30, Tony turned on WHO Radio in Des Moines, and they listened to the Iowa Hawkeyes football team take on the Indiana Hoosiers in Bloomington. They arrived at the Fairfield Inn north of Kansas City before the game was over, but they didn't obsess about hearing the end. The signal had faded until an irritating level of static blanketed the announcers. In addition, Tony and Madeline needed to stretch after the three-hour drive, and the Hawkeyes had a comfortable lead. If they won, Tony didn't need to hear the end. If they lost, he didn't want to.

Tony had wondered several times during the drive what the motel arrangements would be when they arrived. He didn't quite know how to bring it up. He didn't want to presume too much, based on their one night together, but he also didn't want to blow it if there was a chance to spend another night with her. He hoped she would settle the issue without him needing to ask. She did.

When they entered the motel lobby, Madeline walked up to the desk and said, "We're the Muellers. We're checking in. We have a reservation." Tony stayed back and watched in wonder as the desk clerk nodded and said, "I have you down for one room, king-sized bed, for three nights. Two keys, I presume?"

As they walked down the hall to their room, Madeline waved the plastic room key in front of Tony and said, "You okay with this?" "Better than okay," he said, feeling his face flush.

Madeline unlocked the door, and Tony followed her inside. Ten minutes later they were naked, exploring every inch of the king-sized bed.

Later, as they relaxed, with Madeline's head lying on Tony's chest, she giggled, "This feels naughty when Ben is paying for the room."

"Just because Ben is paying?" Tony laughed, squeezing her bare breast.

She turned her head to look at him, more serious than he expected. "Actually, yes. Only because of that. Otherwise, it somehow feels just right. I like you, and it's not like you're my boss or anything. As far as I know, there are no rules about co-workers dating."

"Well, I doubt if Ben would love the idea, but I agree he's not going to give us any grief if he finds out. And I agree, being with you feels right. Except for my inherent Catholic guilt related to anything sexual, I don't have any regrets."

Madeline smiled, "Just to be clear I don't feel guilty about *this* at all." She cupped her hand over him, stroking lightly until he was hard again.

"Oh, you shouldn't have done that," Tony groaned.

"Sure, I should," she said, as she rolled over on top of him and placed her lips against his.

***

They had pizza delivered to the room, a local brand that wasn't bad but wasn't going to win any awards, either. When Madeline came out of the bathroom after a shower, Tony found himself genuinely admiring, again, her natural beauty. Her dark hair and eyes accentuated her pale skin. Coupled with her slender, athletic body, high cheekbones, and petite features, she looked terrific. She dressed for bed in loose-fitting cotton running shorts and a white silk, short-sleeved pajama top. She left three buttons undone, which had the effect of making Tony hunger to see more, despite the fact he'd seen plenty in the past couple of hours.

Tony quickly turned out the light. He knew they both needed rest, and he didn't want to embarrass himself by trying for another round of passion and failing. He felt her climb under the covers and slide over next to him.

"Thank you, Tony," she whispered.

"No, thank *you*," he said with a chuckle.

"I'm serious, and I don't mean for the sex. Thank you for being here. I'm scared out of my wits, and I'm coming unglued with each new horror this story throws at us. I don't think I could do this without you."

"You're welcome," he said. *But what will you think tomorrow when I tell you there's no way you're putting yourself out there as bait for these animals?*

Chapter 11

When Tony awoke, the room was mostly dark, but bright sunshine illuminated the edges of the blackout shade on the window. He rolled over and glanced at his watch. It was 10:15 a.m.

"Holy crap!" He swung his feet out of bed, then turned and saw he was alone in it. "Madeline?" His stomach started to churn. "Madeline!"

No answer.

Tony got up, pulled on his jeans, and swept the shade to the side, allowing sunlight to fill the room. He spotted a note on the desk next to the television set. It read, "Don't panic. Went to find some 'errant girl' appropriate clothes, get a bad haircut, and grab something to eat. I'll be back soon."

Tony sighed in relief and smiled. *She knows me well.*

***

With the help of Google, Madeline had no trouble finding a

shopping mall on the north side of the city. Like all shopping malls, it had stores that catered to teenage girls. She did her best to pick out clothes that a rebellious, free-spirited teen would wear. From the clothing store, she walked across the hallway and down three storefronts to the "This Do's for You" hair salon.

She had no trouble getting right in, which wasn't a great testament to the quality of the stylists. Her directions to the young woman with the scissors were short and simple: "Cut it off and make it unruly. I want to look like I live at home with a mom who doesn't love me but insists on doing my hair."

The stylist looked a little disheveled herself, so didn't seem to have any trouble understanding what Madeline meant. Thirty minutes later, Madeline left the salon looking like she had cut her hair herself, with grass clippers and a salad bowl. She was utterly torn. She had achieved just the look she wanted but was pretty sure Tony would hate it, and that bothered her. It bothered her a lot, which was a surprise.

As she walked out into the parking lot, she heard a car start off to her right. It barely registered. Engine noise was expected in a lot full of vehicles. However, as she neared Tony's Ford, a big, older-model Buick sedan pulled up between her and her vehicle. Madeline was instantly wary.

"Miss, can you help me?" an older man asked. He looked harmless enough, so Madeline stepped up to the car window to ask how she could help. As she stooped down, she saw the man had his pants unzipped. She froze as he grabbed her blouse, smacking her forehead against the top of the window frame.

"You see," the man said with a sneer. "I have this hard-on, and I need some relief. Get in the car."

Madeline screamed and tried to pull away, but the man's grip was tight.

"I said get in the car," he barked. Then Madeline saw he held a gun in his right hand. "Now!"

Madeline still struggled. Gun or not, she was not getting in his car. The man's arm moved out as Madeline pulled, then he yanked her back, driving her head into the door frame once again.

She yelped in pain and started to cry. "Please...," she squeaked as she struggled against his grip.

At that moment, there was an enormous boom—the sound of a gunshot, but not from inside the car. It came from behind her.

"Police! Freeze!" a man's voice shouted.

The man in the car suddenly shoved Madeline back, causing her to stumble and fall to the asphalt. The Buick then roared away, tires squealing and heading out toward the six-lane thoroughfare next to the mall.

The plainclothes policeman ran up to Madeline and knelt down beside her. "Are you okay, miss?"

Madeline yelled through her tears, "He's getting away. He has a gun. Stop him!"

"I'm sorry, miss, but my car is two aisles over. I couldn't get to it in time. I'm off duty. I always carry my gun, but I don't have my radio."

"We can take mine," Madeline said, scrambling to her feet.

The policeman looked at her ruefully and just nodded toward the street. The Buick was gone, lost in the flow of hundreds of cars. They hadn't even seen which direction it had turned out of the lot.

"I'm sorry," the man said. "I got part of the license number, but that's all. The most important thing is that you're okay."

"I am, thanks to you." She rubbed her forehead and fought back more tears. "He pointed a gun right in my face. I... I didn't know I could feel so terrified. It felt like my legs were melting under me."

"It's completely understandable. I tell you what, let's get a cup of coffee and I'll take your statement. Then as soon as I get back to the station, I can get an APB out on the car, with a description of the guy. You can describe him, I hope?"

"Yes, of course," Madeline said, composing herself. She knew Tony would be worried, maybe even mad, if she got back to the Fairfield much later, but she couldn't just refuse to tell the police what she knew. *What if the guy in the Buick was part of the gang of human traffickers they were seeking?*

"Okay, one cup."

"Great," the policeman said.

When they reached his car, she noted it was a Dodge Charger.

He seemed to know it wasn't what she'd expected. He explained, "It's my personal car. I like to go fast. Don't tell my friends on the traffic detail." He chuckled. "Oh, and here's my badge. You wouldn't want to jump into just any stranger's car." He reached in his coat and flipped open a leather wallet with the detective's shield inside. Madeline barely glanced at it as she walked to the passenger door.

They climbed in, and Madeline took a moment to study him behind the wheel. He was a great-looking guy, blond, wavy hair, nice clothes, clean-shaven, tall and slender. She guessed he was in his mid-thirties.

"I'm Madeline," she said, reaching over the center console of the car with her hand.

He laughed and shook it. "I'm sorry, I should have introduced myself back there when I first stopped. I'm Donald Frayer, the Third. A little pretentious, I know." His broad smile revealed two pronounced dimples. "Just call me Donny."

***

Rita Harrington was trying to concentrate. She was playing Bach's wonderful Cello Suite No. 1 in G Major. The expectation was that her playing would reflect her entire mind, heart, and soul. It didn't. Her professor and her tutor were listening intently, but were clearly not happy. Neither was she.

"Rita, stop."

She took her hands off her cello, feeling her face grow red.

Professor McMillan said, "You're attacking the strings as if they've offended you in some way. Clearly something is wrong. Your normal warmth and depth are completely absent today. Perhaps we should call it a day and hope tomorrow will be better."

"I can do this. You know I can. Let me start again."

"You are correct. I know you can," the professor said softly, nodding. "We all do. But no, not today. I think your time would be better spent getting some rest and clearing your mind. Thank you, dear. You're dismissed."

Rita stood, nodded curtly, and carried her cello and bow out of the room. Once in the hall, her embarrassment and anger nearly overwhelmed her. *Dismissed?* She wanted to scream. In twenty years of pursuing her career in music, she had never been sent from a room before she was finished. She felt like a twelve-year-old beginner rather than a graduate student preparing for an audition with the Chicago Symphony Orchestra. She carefully packed her cello into its case, stowed it on the locked wire shelf in the Music Department hall, and walked out of the building into the cool October afternoon.

"Damn you, Tony!" she said to the empty sidewalk as she stomped toward her apartment five blocks away. Rita loved and admired her brother, but not today. How was she supposed to perform at her best, after getting the call from Rich Davis warning her that someone had threatened her—her specifically—with the most gruesome kinds of threats? She brooded. *Hell, how am I supposed to function at all? For two days, all I've done is look over my shoulder.* She was having trouble eating and was sleeping very little. *Of course I suck! It's not McMillan's fault.*

Despite the fact she was peeved at Tony, she knew in her heart it wasn't his fault either. Still, his job had dragged their family through so much already. And now this.

Rita had never thought of herself as a coward. She lived alone and braved the city of Chicago every day with no problems. She knew how to be careful, and as a result, she almost never felt at risk or uneasy. Then Davis's call flipped some kind of switch in her head. The idea of being taken against her will and raped, perhaps repeatedly, simply made her weak in the knees. She couldn't stop thinking about it. Somehow, she had to cope, but she hadn't figured out how to do it so far.

There's a perfect example, Rita thought, glancing to her right. *Normally I'd look at that guy standing in the bus stop and think, hmmm, he's pretty cute. I wonder if he's single? I wonder if he's straight? I wonder if he likes women who like music? Now I look at him and have to wonder, is he watching me? If he is, why? Does he like the way I look, or is he after me? I mean, look at him, he is watching me. He's not very good at hiding it.*

Suddenly Rita was rushing away from the bus stop, her heart racing and nearly bursting with the desire to get inside her apartment with the dead bolt locked.

"Dammit, Tony! Look at what you've done to me!" Her outcry didn't slow her pace until she was inside the three-story brownstone she had called home for two years. With the apartment door closed behind her, she collapsed on the couch, exhausted and fighting back tears.

***

Tony was irritated. It was nearly noon, and Madeline still hadn't returned from her shopping spree. He hadn't come all the way to Kansas City to sit in a room at the Fairfield Inn and watch the Browns battle the Bengals on NFL Sunday TV. He dialed again, but she still didn't answer her cell. The unanswered phone made Tony uneasy, but he pushed his concerns to the back of his mind and focused on the game. He was sure she would be back soon.

At 1:10 p.m., he tried again. After the third ring, a man's voice said, "Hello? Who is calling please?"

Tony was baffled. Had he been calling a wrong number? No. He knew Madeline's number, and he had it programmed into his phone.

"I'm sorry, what? Tony stammered. "Who is this?"

"Excuse me sir, but this is Officer Finsk from the Kansas City Police Department. Who am I speaking with, please?"

Tony went rigid. "This is Tony Harrington. Who are you again? Why are you answering Madeline's phone? What happened? Is she okay?" The words exploded out of Tony like buckshot from a twelve-gauge.

"Slow down, Mr. Harrington. We're not sure anything has happened."

"Then why..."

The officer cut him off and continued, "I'm in the parking lot of a shopping mall in north Kansas City. Are you in the area, Mr. Harrington?"

"Yes, yes." Tony was aching for the officer to stop asking questions and tell him about Madeline. "I'm at the Fairfield Inn on I-35, probably not far from you."

"Do you own a black Ford Explorer with Iowa plates?"

"Yes!" Tony snapped. "Where is Madeline?"

"We haven't encountered anyone named Madeline. I assume

from your questions that this is her phone I answered?"

"Yes!" Tony was to the point of wanting to hit something. "Where did you find it? What has happened?"

"We were dispatched to the parking lot because someone called 911 and reported a gunshot. When we arrived, a husband and wife told us they had witnessed a young woman having an argument or some kind of difficulty with a man in a big sedan. The gunshot apparently came from a second man. They said the big sedan roared off and the young woman left with the second man in a black sports car."

"Left with him as in what? You mean taken? Forced into his car?" Tony asked. He was having trouble breathing.

"No, nothing like that. The couple said she appeared to be friendly with him and climbed into the passenger seat of her own accord. We thought perhaps the second man was a friend."

Tony was baffled. Could it have been Madeline? Did she know anyone in KC? If it wasn't her, then where was she?

The officer added, "As we stood here, we heard a cell phone ringing repeatedly nearby. It was in your Ford, which wasn't locked. We wondered if the cell phone had any connection to the girl, so we decided to answer it. Do you think the woman reported to us in the parking lot incident could be this Madeline that you know?"

"I have no idea," Tony said. "I can't imagine why she would leave her cell in an unlocked vehicle, but I also can't imagine her leaving with someone without calling me."

"Can you give me Madeline's full name and a description, please?"

Tony did. The officer murmured something Tony couldn't hear, probably to a partner from the patrol car. Then speaking to Tony again, the officer said, "Your description sounds similar, but the girl in the parking lot was described as a teenager. The couple was sure, and based on their description of her clothes and hair, my best guess is that they're right."

This did not put Tony's mind at ease. He would have smiled if he hadn't been so terrified.

"I think it probably is Madeline," Tony sighed. "It's a little hard to explain, officer, but she went to the mall specifically to buy clothes to make her look young." Tony groaned inwardly as he realized how that sounded. He started to explain, but the officer cut him off.

"Is Madeline staying at the same hotel as you?" Tony said she was. Then the cop asked, "What's the nature of your relationship?"

"We're co-workers," Tony said. "We both write for a small newspaper up in Iowa. She's not my girlfriend, exactly, but we are... close." Tony didn't wait for another question. He said, "Officer, there's something else." Tony could sense the tension on the phone immediately.

"Yes?"

"Madeline and I were recently threatened by a man we believe to be involved in human trafficking. There's no reason to think this incident is related, but please, take this seriously and help me find her quickly."

"We take all reports of gunshots seriously, Mr. Harrington."

"I'm sure you do," Tony said, "and I meant no offense. But this man, we believe he's responsible for multiple kidnappings and at least one murder."

"Okay, I hear you. I will call it in to my shift commander as I drive over to pick you up. I'll also get word out about the sports car. Meanwhile, let's all hope for the best. She probably got help from a good Samaritan and didn't realize she left her phone behind. She could show up any minute."

***

Madeline was enjoying her conversation with Donny. They had driven across the six-lane street to a Starbucks. It was busy but not crowded at noon on a Sunday. They sat at a corner table in relative privacy. Donny seemed very competent as he wrote down the details she shared about her encounter with the nut case in the parking lot. Then, when he confessed he had just made detective two weeks ago, she found him utterly adorable. Just a rookie trying to do the right thing. He also was handsome and funny. When they finished the official report, the conversation turned casual. Madeline found she didn't want it to end. She felt a little guilty, thinking of Tony back in the motel waiting for her. She tried to pull out her cell phone to check the time and realized she didn't have it.

"Oh crap," she said.

"Problems?" Donny asked.

"I must have left my cell in the car when I went into the mall. I have a friend waiting for me. He's gonna be unhappy that I haven't called."

"He?" Donny smiled, his blue eyes sparkling. Madeline blinked. She was sure his eyes had actually sparkled. And those dimples...

Donny continued, "I hope it's not a boyfriend, or a husband. I'm enjoying myself very much, and I'd hate to think you're already taken."

"No, no," Madeline said, a bit too quickly. "We just work together. But I am going to have to go. Can you take me back to my car?"

"Of course. To serve and protect is our motto, you know," he said, sitting up straight and saluting, making her laugh. "I guess today I get to do both for you."

"I've enjoyed this too," she said, "really I have. You have my phone number on the report we just finished. I hope you'll call sometime."

They stood. Donny put a hand behind her neck and pulled her close, whispering in her ear, "I promise I will."

He smells terrific, Madeline thought. *I didn't know police officers could afford Armani scents.* The feel of his warm breath on her ear enhanced the effect. *Down, girl. You've got a great guy waiting for you already.* She thought about her claim to Tony that she wasn't a slut and grinned.

"What?" Donny asked, as they turned and walked out of the coffee shop.

"Nothing," she said. "I'm fine now, thanks to you."

***

After using the remote to unlock his car, Donny's cell buzzed. "Do you mind if I look at this?" he asked. Madeline said she didn't and climbed into the passenger seat. Donny closed her door and stayed outside as he opened the text he had been sent. Noting who it was from, he stepped several paces away from his car to look at it. The text included two photographs, each labeled with a name: Tony Harrington and Madeline Mueller. Donny's eyebrows went up as his cell phone rang. It was the boss.

"Hey."

"Did you get the text I just sent?" the old man's silky baritone asked.

"Did I ever."

"What does that mean.?

"It means I think I have this woman sitting in my car right now."

"You're serious? What do you mean 'you think'?"

"Well," Donny said, "she looks like this picture, only with

shorter hair in a really terrible cut. She looks older in the picture somehow. What's the story on these two?"

"I got a call from a friend in Orney, Iowa. He said two of that town's newspaper reporters were down there snooping around. The guy, this Harrington, is the one who screwed up our operation in Illinois. The cops found that girl's body near where he's based, you know, and now he and his co-worker and everybody else is focused in on these missing girls. Keep an eye out and be careful."

"Shit, Ray, we spend every day avoiding the police, the state troopers, the FBI, and everybody else in the world, why would a couple of hick reporters bother us?"

"Get your head out of your ass, Donny," the man said. "You just told me this woman is sitting in your car. I'd say she's on to you."

"You would be wrong," Donny said, clearly irritated. "Hank and I pulled the flasher-rescue bit on her. She thinks I'm a police detective, and I'm pretty sure she wants to do me without any of the usual encouragements."

"Just don't get cocky. We avoid all those cops you mentioned because we're careful. Every day. Every minute. Don't forget it."

"Okay, I get it. So what do I do with this bitch in my car? I was planning to put her out and send her into the pipeline. There's a big demand for the petite ones, as you know."

"No, I wouldn't," the man said. "Taking a reporter is going to bring a lot more media heat. If you're sure she doesn't know who or what you really are, let her go for now. She'll be easy enough to find if we decide we need to take her later."

"Ten-four, boss." Donny ended the call and walked back to the Charger.

As he climbed in, he smiled at Madeline and said, "Next stop, shopping mall parking lot."

At the motel, the two police officers put Tony through the wringer. They asked to see the room he and Madeline were sharing. Then they asked to go through her things. Then through his. Tony didn't like it, but he understood. Whenever a girl went missing, those closest to her were the first and primary suspects. In this situation, Tony couldn't have expected them to act any other way. He was very glad his gun was in its case and locked in the storage compartment in the back of his SUV.

By the time they were finished, it was pretty clear the police knew he and Madeline had made love on the bed. Beyond that, they hadn't found anything interesting. They were smart enough to check Tony's phone, confirming he had indeed called her multiple times, and looking to see if he had called anyone else.

Finally, Tony said, "Guys, I'm glad you're being thorough. After all, I'm the one who asked you to take this seriously. But can we get back to my car, please? I can't stand the thought that she might be getting farther away with each passing minute."

The officers pointed out there was nothing Tony could do but wait to see if the police got a line on the Charger. Where he waited didn't matter.

"Even if I'm checking the mall stores or driving around in circles, I'll feel better than I do just sitting here watching you examine the labels in my shirts."

The officers relented and finally headed to their cruiser with Tony right behind.

As they neared the Explorer in the mall parking lot, Tony's jaw dropped. "My God. There she is!"

Madeline was leaning into the front passenger door of the SUV, clearly searching the floor for something.

The cruiser pulled to a stop, and Tony hopped out. Madeline glanced up and stood, astonishment on her face. "Tony, what are you doing here? How did you..."

Her question was cut off by his arms wrapping around her and pulling her in tight.

"Madeline, what the hell? I was *so* scared," Tony said breathlessly into the hair at the top of her head. "Where have you been?"

He backed off so she could reply, and she noticed the two police officers behind him.

"You called the police? Really? I know I was late, but..."

"No," Tony interrupted. "I called you. The police just answered your phone. They had a report of a gunshot in the parking lot, and witnesses said the man with the gun took you in his car. I thought... I thought..." He couldn't say it.

"Oh, Tony, I'm so sorry. The man with the gun was an off-duty police detective. He was helping me after this other guy attacked me."

This got the officers' attention. They insisted Madeline go back and start at the beginning. She did, telling them everything, except of course the part about having the hots for the young detective.

Officer Finsk then surprised her when he said, "Miss, I think you're mistaken. No police detective on our force would leave the scene after discharging his weapon. There's an entire protocol involved in locking down the scene, waiting for a response team, filling out reports... You know, all that bureaucratic stuff. Firing a police weapon inside the city is serious business. This young detective, uh, Frayer, you said? He's in a lot of trouble if he did what you described."

Just then, the second officer came back from the police cruiser, where he had made a call on his radio. He said, "I just finished talking with the shift commander. She confirmed that the Kansas City

PD does not have a detective name Frayer. No one named Donald at all. She's going to check with some of the suburban departments, but she's guessing this man was a phony."

Finsk asked, "Miss, did he show you any identification?"

Madeline was instantly red-faced. "Yes, he flashed a badge, but I barely looked at it. I mean, he had a gun and he used it to rescue me. It never occurred to me to question who he was. He was very polite and professional." *And handsome and charming and, well, hot,* she thought, fuming at herself for her stupidity.

Tony was surprised and angry she had been so naïve, but he kept quiet. He could tell she was embarrassed, and it would serve no purpose to pile on.

Finsk didn't have such qualms, and proceeded to lecture her about getting into a car with an armed man, without being certain who he was.

"I know. I *know!*" Madeline said. "Can we just move on? What's next here?"

Finsk removed his hat and ran his hand from his forehead back through his thinning hair. "I suppose we'll keep the alert out on the car. I'd kinda like to know what this guy was up to. Does he just get his jollies playing cop, rescuing the damsel in distress?"

"Somehow I doubt it's that simple," Tony said. "He went to a lot of trouble to get to know her. Think about that report she helped him write. He now knows her phone number, address, and a lot of other information."

Madeline groaned. "What a dipshit I am." Her disappointment in herself was compounded by the thought that the man she found so charming, so attractive, might be some kind of mental case, pervert, or worse.

Finsk said, "At the moment, the only crimes he committed were firing a gun within the city limits and impersonating a police officer.

They're both misdemeanors and not likely to get the boys on patrol too revved up about catching him. Especially since, according to Madeline, she never actually saw him fire the weapon."

At that moment, a tall, lanky boy with red hair and freckles came jogging up to the officers. Out of breath and excited, he tried to explain himself. "Officer, there's a dent on the hood of my dad's pickup truck."

Finsk and his partner looked at him quizzically.

The boy said, between breaths, "I think it was caused by a bullet. There's a lead slug on the ground next to the front tire. I do some hunting with my dad. I know what a slug looks like after it's been fired. I didn't touch it because, well, you know, I watch TV. I was going to call 911, but then I saw you guys were right here."

The officers convinced the boy to slow down, assured him they were impressed with how observant he was, and agreed to have a look. They all followed the boy across the lot.

The second officer brought the police cruiser to the site and got out wearing latex gloves and carrying a camera. He documented the dent and the position of the bullet, and took down the boy's information. Tony assumed this was all primarily for show, or perhaps for an insurance claim, but he was impressed as he watched the officer carefully follow police procedures. That included retrieving the bullet and placing it in an evidence bag.

Tony assumed the officers knew what he was about to say, but he said it anyway to make certain. "It wouldn't hurt to have your ballistics team take a look at that slug. It's in great shape. It was probably fired into the air, and the dent resulted from the fall back to earth. If that gun has been involved in any crimes, you might get a hit."

"Yes, Mr. Harrington," Finsk said. "I'll alert Gary Sinese that he can retire, now that you're on the job."

Tony thought the sarcasm a bit much, but he let it go.

"I think we're about finished. We have your numbers if we need anything more. And miss, please call us if this Donny person calls you or if you see him anywhere again. It would be nice to get to the bottom of this."

Chapter 12

"What is wrong with me?" Madeline asked again as she and Tony snacked on egg rolls and sodas in the mall food court.

"Stop beating yourself up," Tony said. "The way it all happened, anyone would have done the same."

Madeline shook her head and sulked. She lowered her eyes to the cheap food spread before them on paper wrappers.

"Rather than dwell on what you did or didn't do, I'd like to talk about what *he* did."

"How so?" she asked without looking up. She played with a French fry, dragging it through a pool of ketchup.

Tony didn't know any way to ask this politely, so he simply said, "Do you think they could have been working together?"

"Who?"

"Donny and the first guy. The old man with his rod sticking out of his pants."

Madeline reacted negatively, as if to say "of course not," but then paused to consider. "I suppose it's possible. I don't think so, but, obviously without the first guy, there would be no distress from which to rescue the damsel."

A look of dread spread across Madeline's face. "God, if that's true... If they're working together, that makes this whole thing a lot more sinister, doesn't it? It's not some guy with a hero complex playing Robin Hood. Now it's an orchestrated plot to get a girl into a stranger's car, and into a mindset of trusting him, admiring him."

"Maybe even desiring him," Tony said.

Madeline was jolted into looking up and saw Tony had a big smile. He said, "I could hear it in your voice when you described him. You..."

"Shut up, you dick. He was cute. I noticed. End of story."

"Whatever you say." Tony still was smiling.

Madeline wasn't. "Seriously, Tony, what if this is them? You know, the guys who are snatching girls in Missouri and Iowa? Even if it isn't them, what if it's others like them? I can't... I can't stand the thought that I was in his car. I was *nice* to him. Jesus, will I ever be able to trust anyone again?"

In a classic Tony move, he reached across the table and gripped her hand. She waited for the thoughtful, compassionate words of wisdom, but none came. Tony just looked at her for a long time, squeezing her fingers tightly. She was grateful.

Finally, he retrieved his hand and said, "You're scared. I get that. But whatever you are feeling couldn't compare to the terror I felt when I thought you were gone. And no, this isn't some Lisa flashback or 'Oh my, I can't lose another woman' crap. Madeline, I was so scared I was going to lose *you*. I didn't know I could be that scared of anything."

He's done it again, Madeline thought, feeling herself begin to smile. *Just the right words at the right time, but this time I think I like it.*

She stood and walked around the table to stand beside his chair. She looked down and said, "Come on. Let's go. I think it's time for bed."

Tony looked at his watch. It was 4:30 in the afternoon. *I could learn to like working assignments out of town.* He smiled up at her and said, "If you insist, I guess I have no choice."

As they walked out to the car, Tony took Madeline's hand. He said, "By the way, have I told you how hot you look with your hair chopped up and wearing clothes from 'Forever 15'?"

"Shut up, you dick," Madeline said sharply, then laughed.

***

As Tony and Madeline climbed into the Explorer, they were oblivious to the man standing just inside the nearby department store. He stood behind two sets of glass doors, where he was invisible from the outside, but could see the couple clearly in the late afternoon sunshine.

Laugh it up, young lady, Donny thought, as he stared at the two of them. *I'll look forward to watching a few clients wipe that smile off your face. Maybe we'll feature you in one of our specials and let three or four of them have you at once.*

He never used the girls himself. He had no trouble getting dates and getting laid when he wanted. And the risk was too great. If something went awry, a girl escaped or had to be killed, he didn't want his DNA found inside her. *But for you, Madeline Mueller, I just might make an exception.* The thought aroused him, and he turned back into the mall so no one would notice him staring. *Careful,* he reminded himself. *Always very careful.*

***

Monday morning arrived, but without the sun. It was a little before eight when Tony pulled back the room curtains to confirm it was raining. Not a hard rain—more of a cold drizzle. When Madeline rolled over and saw the scene outside, she groaned.

"Well, look at the bright side," Tony said. "The rain will keep the farmers out of the fields. A couple of the missing girls are from farm families. This will be a good day to talk to them."

"That's a good point, but I'd still opt for sunshine."

They decided to stay together for the duration of the trip. After Sunday's scare, they had agreed to take no unnecessary chances. "We haven't even interviewed all the families yet," Tony noted. "It's too risky to go back out there, at least until we've exhausted every other avenue."

Madeline accepted the logic, at least for now. She climbed out of bed and headed for the shower. As soon as she spotted herself in the mirror, she groaned and grabbed the mop on top her head, "Did I do this to my hair for no reason? Kill me now." Tony smiled, knowing she would look fine by the time she finished messing with it.

He was right. It was short and a little boyish with its blunt cut, but it looked good on her when she stepped out of the bathroom thirty minutes later.

Tony drove, and Madeline served as navigator. She suggested they head west across the Missouri River into Kansas, then turn north. The Blaine family farm was about thirty minutes west of Leavenworth, just a couple of miles off Highway 92. Shelly had been missing from there for more than three years.

"We'll be going against the traffic coming into the city," Madeline said. "I bet we can be there in an hour or so."

They drove through a Burger King to grab breakfast sandwiches, then headed west. When she finished her orange juice, Madeline said, "Why did he let me go?"

"Huh?"

"Donny. If he was part of an orchestrated effort to kidnap me, why did he let me go?"

Tony was tempted to make a smart remark about her haircut but stopped himself in time. It was a legitimate and serious question.

"I don't know. Maybe something you said over coffee scared him off. Maybe he liked you and decided to find someone else."

"Hmm... You know," she said, "as we got in the car, he took a text and a call on his cell phone. I wonder if something was said that convinced him to stand down."

"Could be." Tony nodded. "Whatever it was, I'm really, really glad he brought you back to the shopping mall."

"Not half as glad as I am," Madeline said with a shudder.

Guided by Google Maps and the rural address provided by the police reports, they had no trouble finding the farm. They turned into a long, wide lane bordered on each side first by ditches and later, white painted fences.

"Someone here cares a lot about this farm," Tony noted. "It takes a lot of work and money to keep a painted wooden fence looking good for that much distance. This lane must be a quarter-mile long."

Past the fence on the right was pasture. A large number of cows were grazing. Tony wasn't much of an expert on farm animals, but they appeared to be dairy cows. On the left was a barren field. Tony surmised it recently had been harvested. It could have been corn, but he wasn't sure. He knew even less about plant stubble than he did about cows.

They could see an attractive, two-story brick home, set on a large lot covered in healthy bluegrass. It had a three-stall garage attached by a foyer. To the left, on the far side of a big, open area, sat a large, white barn, traditional in its peaked-roof design, and a second metal building, as big as the barn but modern with huge sliding doors. He also spotted three large grain bins with the Sukup logo on them.

Made in Iowa, Tony thought, with a tinge of pride.

They had planned to stop at the house but spotted a man moving around inside one of the open doors to the metal building. Tony drove across the farmyard and stopped on the concrete pad in front of the building. The drizzle had stopped, and the sun was peeking through the clouds.

The man, wearing blue jeans and a green John Deere windbreaker, stepped out of the building, wiping his hands on a rag. Tony could see two large, green tractors inside the building. One was a late-model four-wheel-drive. Tony refrained from whistling, but was tempted. He didn't know what it cost, but he knew it was a lot. *Also made in Iowa*, he thought, smiling.

"Can I hep ya?" the man asked in a heavy drawl as Tony and Madeline climbed out of the SUV. The man was tall, perhaps two or three inches taller than Tony, and lean. He had the weathered face and hands Tony expected to see on a farmer. He had a full head of hair, straight and cut short above the ears. The salt-and-pepper color made it hard to discern his age. He could have been 40 or 60.

"We apologize for bothering you," Tony said, sounding as pleasant and contrite as possible. "My name is Tony Harrington, and this is my co-worker, Madeline Mueller. We're newspaper reporters from Iowa."

"Y'all here 'bout the tractor pull or the threshin' contest over in McCouth or somethin'?

Madeline put on her best smile and said, "No, actually, we'd like to talk to someone about Shelly Blaine. Are you Mr. Blaine?"

"Oh that," he said, and seemed to deflate. Tony was amazed at the transformation. At the mention of Shelly's name, the man had gone from a proud and hardworking farmer to a wounded puppy. His shoulders sagged and he stared at the ground.

"Yep, I'm Irwin Blaine. Why the hell ya comin' 'round now? My girl's gone missin' for more 'n three years."

"Yes, we know," Madeline said. "We're looking into the disappearances of several girls from this area over the past few years. We're genuinely sorry if this re-opens some difficult wounds for you, but we'd really appreciate learning more about her. If you'd rather not talk about it, perhaps there's someone else...?"

"Nah." He spat on the ground to his right. "Ain't no one here but me. The missus died when Shelly was three. Nearly kilt me, that did. Then, when Shelly left, I didn't know what the hell... Well, I can tell ya, I came this close to climbing up on the bin over there and jumpin' off with a rope 'round my neck."

"Sir, if you prefer, we can..." Tony started, but the man interrupted.

"Nah, settle yer britches, young man. I should be grateful there's anyone in this here world gives a shit 'bout my baby. Let's walk up to the house. I'll pour us some Folger's and y'all can ask yer questions."

Seated in the kitchen with this widower and grieving father, Tony didn't have the heart to reveal that he didn't drink coffee, so he let Blaine serve it. He played with the coffee mug, letting it warm his hands. Madeline immediately picked hers up and took in the aroma, so Tony began the questioning.

What they learned from Blaine was troubling and saddening, but not surprising. He said he had tried to be a good father and mother to Shelly, and thought he had succeeded for the first several years. "Me and that girl did everythang together. She loved ridin' on the Deere and helpin' with the cows. I was careful not to keep her tied to the farm though. I made sure she got to school and stuff. I even took her to Brownie Scouts, and to swim lessons in the summer. I tried to be Santa Claus and the Easter Bunny, even the Tooth Fairy, and sometimes on days when I just wanted to crawl in a hole and cry. But I did good. I did! Then, as she got a little older, well, y'know, what the hell do I know about girl-stuff, see what I'm sayin'?"

Tony and Madeline could easily imagine how hard it would be for a single dad to deal with a girl's passage into her teens, going through puberty and all that came with it.

"We always got on fine," Blaine said, shaking his head, "but those last couple years, it wasn't the same. She was always in her room with the door shut. Or stayin' with friends in town. Or findin' somethin' to do to keep from havin' to talk to me. Least that's how it felt." A tear inched down his cheek.

"What kind of things did she like to do?" Madeline asked, just to keep the conversation moving.

"Well, she spent way too much time on that damn computer. I can tell ya that. I told the cops more'n once that I blame that thing."

Tony and Madeline glanced at each other. Tony asked, "Did the police examine her browser history? Did they learn what she did on the computer, what sites she liked to visit?"

"Oh, yeah, they looked at it, but I ain't sure they gave it much mind. They was too busy diggin' into my life."

Tony and Madeline weren't surprised, but must have looked like they were, because Blaine smiled and said, "Ya ain't much for reportin' if ya don't even know who the prime suspect was. My girl's gone and they were all over me. Like I would ever hurt one hair on her head!" His anger was evident.

Tony said, "Sadly, Mr. Blaine, we do know it. The authorities' actions are maddening but understandable. Based on experience, the cops know that family members or boyfriends are most often to blame when something unfortunate befalls a young woman. Which reminds me, did she have a boyfriend?"

"Not that I ever met nor heard 'bout. But who knows? She was only fourteen when she disappeared. She'd a known I'd be askin' after him if she'd a told me she had a boyfriend at that age."

Blaine went on to explain that Shelly probably had run away from home. He hated to think she would, but that's how it looked to him. She had told him she was going to a friend's house after school and would be staying overnight. It was a Friday night, and that was something she had done before, so Blaine hadn't thought much of it. However, on Saturday, she hadn't called for him to come pick her up. Blaine had called the friend's mother and had learned Shelly had never been there.

"That's the last any of us ever heard of her," he said. "She was just gone. Of course, my first thing was to get hoppin' mad. I figgered she was with a boy or maybe gettin' drunk with some friends or somethin'. Never occurred to me she'd run away. When I hadn't heard from her by Sunday, I called the sheriff. Thought he was a friend. Hell, I voted for the bastard. Some good it did me. He still looks at me, y'know, funny-like, when he sees me. You don't think I had anything to do with Shelly disappearin', do ya?"

"No, Mr. Blaine, we don't," Madeline said. "If you don't mind me asking, could we see her room? Do you still keep some of her things in there?"

"Of course, on both counts," the man said, and unfolded his too-long body out of the too-short chair. "Follow me."

They did. He took them upstairs to a room at the back of the house, facing a grove of trees to the north. The room was large and well-furnished, with a queen-sized, four-poster bed, matching nightstand, and dresser. The décor was tasteful, if a little girlish for someone Shelly's age. My Little Pony sheets peeked out from beneath an off-white comforter on the bed. As often was the case when teenagers went missing, the room had been left intact.

"She comes back, I don't want her thinkin' I ever gave up on her," Blaine said. "Look through her room if it's gonna help you find her. Take pictures, whatever you want. You wanna look at the computer, the passwords are on a card in the right drawer. I made her keep 'em where I could find 'em so I could check now and then on what she was doin'. Now if you'll excuse me, I got work to do." He left them.

"Smart dad," Tony said, and pulled out the desk chair to sit at the built-in computer nook. "I think I will have a look at this, since he offered."

As Tony booted up the machine and started opening files and programs, Madeline proceeded to search through the girl's things. She had no idea what she was hoping to find. The police would have done all of this at least once, probably multiple times.

Madeline did note that some things were missing. There was no backpack or shoulder bag for her schoolbooks. There was no purse. There were a few pairs of dress shoes, but no casual shoes or boots. There were enough empty hangers in the closet to indicate missing clothes.

Madeline could easily assemble the mental picture. A girl, planning to run away, packing all the clothes she could fit into a backpack and perhaps a large purse. The girl would think, *Leave the dress shoes, but take the comfy shoes for the walk.* If she owned boots, take those. Take a few pieces of jewelry, some other personal items, and of course her smartphone. She made a mental note to ask Blaine about all of this. Had the police taken some of it, or were these things already missing at the time he'd first realized Shelly had gone?

As she looked through the dresser drawers, she came across nearly half a drawer filled with swimsuits—Blaine had mentioned swimming lessons—then a label caught her eye. She pulled a black, one-piece suit out of the jumble.

"Tony, look at this," Madeline said. Tony got up and walked over to join her at the dresser. She said, "This is a Karla Colletto swimsuit."

"Yes...?"

"Well, in the first place, look at the design. No fourteen-year-old would normally wear a suit with the cut in front open down to the navel."

She held it up in front of her, and Tony said, "Ah, I see what you mean. That would be risqué, even for a babe like you."

"Tony, please," she responded testily. "More importantly, this suit probably cost three hundred dollars. With these designer ties on the sides, it might be more than that. I don't own a Colletto swimsuit because I can't afford one. How did this end up in Shelly's drawer? You couldn't buy one of these in Leavenworth, and maybe not even in Kansas City. I've only seen Colletto suits in Nieman Marcus. Nowadays you could find one of these online, but four years ago? I doubt it."

Tony's face revealed that he understood what she was saying. Assuming Irwin Blaine, the conservative Kansas farmer, didn't buy this sexy and ultra-expensive suit for his daughter, who did? One more thing to double-check with Blaine.

Madeline took a photo of the suit with her phone, then a close-up of the label. She continued digging with renewed interest while Tony returned to the computer.

He didn't find much in the documents or photos folders. Shelly had either been extremely careful or as innocent as one would hope a fourteen-year-old would be. She did, however, have a Facebook account. There had been no new postings from Shelly since her disappearance, but her frequent posts prior to that told Tony a lot about her life. He saw her in pictures on the farm, usually with a baby animal, and in pictures at school. He saw numerous selfies and group photos, often with friends at a school sporting event or at the mall, presumably in Leavenworth.

Tony remembered her photo from the official police report, but the shots posted to Facebook made Shelly come to life. His heart ached at the thought of what might have happened to her. He also found pictures of her at the swimming pool. She seemed to have no qualms about being photographed in her swimsuit. The pictures confirmed she had several, both one-piece suits and bikinis. Then, buried deep in an album she had labeled "Summer Fun," Tony found a picture of her in the black, low-cut swimsuit.

"Oh, my God," Tony said out loud. Madeline scurried over to see what he had found. He pointed at the picture. Shelly was standing on a beach in the sunshine. Waves could be seen on the water behind her, with trees in the distant background. "Look at this," Tony said, moving his finger to the bottom of the photo where the caption was. Madeline gasped as she read, "At the lake with Donny!"

"That effing pig," Madeline said, seething, wanting to scream but not wanting to alarm Mr. Blaine.

"Do you think...?"

"Oh, absolutely," Madeline said. "It's him. He stalks girls, he seduces them, they disappear. I met him. I *liked* him. He was charming and sexy and attentive. A lonely fourteen-year-old girl meets this twenty-something guy with a warm smile and a great car, he sweeps her off her feet. Maybe she meets him online. Maybe he rescues her in a damn parking lot!" She paused to compose herself. "Yes, this is our Donny. I have no doubt he's capable of exactly what we're dreading."

Tony expanded the photo on the screen. "Look at this," he said, pointing to the bow of a speedboat in the background. "It looks like a boat anchored offshore. I wonder if our friend owns one?" The background was not in clear focus, but Tony went to his iPhone, pulled up Facebook, found Shelly's page, and saved the photo to his phone. He then went into the photos function and texted the picture to Rich Davis, with a request the agent have the lab try to identify any numbers on the boat.

Davis called him moments later, and Tony explained what they believed they had found.

"You two are something else," Davis said. "I'll get right on this and get back to you."

Tony and Madeline finished nosing around and returned to the kitchen. A note on the table told them Blaine had returned to the machine shed.

They found Blaine changing an oil filter on the smaller tractor.

"Found nothin', right?" he said, as he unboxed the new filter.

"Not exactly," Tony replied, causing Blaine to drop what he was doing and walk up to face him.

"What? Ya think ya did?"

Tony and Madeline walked him through what they had and had not found. Madeline asked about the things she perceived were missing from the room, and Blaine confirmed they had been gone from the beginning. The police hadn't kept anything as far as he knew. She then asked if Shelly had been employed or had access to money for expensive things. The answer to both questions was no.

"What y'all gettin' at?" Blaine asked.

Tony pulled it up on his phone. "Have you seen this photo before?"

Blaine grabbed the phone and said, "Christ! What's she wearing? She looks like... like..."

Madeline reached up and put her hand on his shoulder. "We're sorry, Mr. Blaine, really. But this could be an important clue. That suit she's wearing was expensive, which means she probably received it as a gift from this man she mentions in the caption. We've encountered a predator named Donny before. If she knew him, this could put us on her trail."

"I'm sorry," Blaine said, beginning to cry. "My baby. Oh Shelly, what were you doing?"

"Sir," Tony interjected, "do you recognize the lake? Do you have any idea where she might have gone with this Donny the summer before she left?"

Blaine swallowed, took a deep breath, and said, "Let me look again." After several moments, he said, "It coulda' been a lot of places. A beach and some trees don't tell me much. But she never was far from home. This had to be a day trip, which means it's prolly Perry Lake. It's not far. 'Bout thirty minutes or so west." Two more deep breaths and he asked, "You think there's a chance? You thinkin' you'll find Shelly?"

"I have to be honest," Tony said. "After this much time, it's a long shot. But I can promise you we're going to try."

Blaine nodded slowly. Madeline pulled on his arm, and he bent down. She kissed him on the cheek and whispered, "A lot of good people are helping us. Don't give up yet."

***

Back in the Explorer, they headed west on the gravel road, then jogged south until they came to Highway 16. They turned right and headed west. The highway jogged back and forth a little, taking them north through a couple of small towns. At the second one, they caught Highway 92 West and immediately started seeing signs for Perry Lake.

Madeline had the map open on her phone. "There's a state park on the west side of the lake. It has a boat launch. Let's start there."

It made sense to Tony, so he remained quiet as she directed him across a long bridge over the lake and back north to the park. They saw a sign for the beach, but Tony shook his head. "He wouldn't have brought her to a public beach at a state park. But as you said, if they were here, he would have used the boat launch. Then he would have taken her somewhere more secluded, to that place we saw in the picture. Despite the sexy swimsuit, she looked underage. He would have avoided being seen if possible. I think if we're going to find any leads, it will be at the boat launch."

It was Madeline's turn to agree with a nod. In short order, they entered a large parking lot near the water. The boat ramp and small dock were to the left. A shelter house was on the right. Only one other vehicle was in the lot. This didn't surprise Tony, knowing it was harvest season and just shy of noon on a school day, not to mention the weather was cool and rainy.

Tony glanced at the old Dodge pickup, then looked out toward the water. A lone figure sat on the dock in a folding chair, watching his fishing line bob quietly. Before Tony could take a step, his cell phone buzzed. It was Rich Davis calling.

"Hey," Tony said.

"I have something for you," Davis said. "It isn't much, but..."

"Whatever it is, we'll take it," Tony said, then mouthed to Madeline that it was Davis on the line.

"We couldn't get a number off the boat in your picture. Too little of the bow was showing. What we could get, however, were the first two letters: I-A."

"I-A?" Tony repeated. "You mean I-A as in Iowa?"

"That's right. The boat in the picture appears to have an Iowa number on the bow. Are you sure the picture was taken in Kansas?"

"Well, no," Tony acknowledged. "We're not sure about anything. But Irwin Blaine said his daughter didn't take an overnight trip anywhere that summer. He thinks it was a day excursion, probably to Perry Lake, which is where we are now."

"Okay," Davis said, sounding less than enthusiastic. "I hope you find something. Keep me posted." The call ended, and Tony told Madeline what he had learned. The two of them walked over to the dock. As they approached the man in the chair, Tony spoke quietly, trying to respect the man's attempts to attract fish. "Excuse me, sir. May we bother you for a moment.?"

"Guess ya already have. Heh, heh," the man chuckled. "Sure, pull up a seat. Heh, heh."

The man's chair was the only place to sit, except for the dock itself. Tony and Madeline smiled, trying to show they appreciated the joke.

"This may sound like an odd question from a stranger, but do you come here often?"

"Well, ya could say that. Heh, heh. Ya see that buoy out there, 'bout half way 'cross the narrow part of the lake?"

Tony nodded, and the man continued.

"The house I was born in used to sit below that very spot. Then, oh, 'bout forty years ago, the great State of Kansas and them Army Corps boys got together and decided to turn my farm, and about 11,000 other acres, into a lake. Don't that just beat all?"

Tony had no idea how to respond, but he needn't have worried. The man kept talking.

"They paid for the land, of course, so I mostly retired. I was forty-six years old, so I worked an odd job here and there, and I came here a lot to volunteer at the park. The State's always lookin' for help. I'm nearly ninety now." The man looked at Madeline. "But you'd never know it, would ya, sweet cakes? I bet you find me damned attractive. Heh, heh."

Madeline laughed. It was a soft, "you might be right" kind of laugh.

The man beamed. "Now, what can I do for you young folks on this dreary October day?"

Tony cleared his throat. "This is a long shot. Maybe as long as the odds of you pulling a swordfish out of that lake, but..." He pulled out his cell and opened the lake picture. "Do you happen to remember seeing this girl here? It would have been in the summer, more than three years ago."

The man looked at it and said, "Nope."

"Look closely, sir, please. This girl has been missing since this photo was taken. The picture's our only lead."

"Well, I might be able to help a little. Heh, heh."

Tony wondered if he had heard right. "You might?"

"Yep! Heh, heh. I ain't never seen the girl, least not dressed in that. Believe me, a man in his eighties still notices all that skin on a woman, although your girl there clearly ain't no woman."

"So how can you help?" Tony asked, exasperated.

"I know the boat."

"Holy shit! I mean, holy cow," Tony squeaked. "Sorry about the language."

"Don't bother me none, but you shouldn't oughta talk like that around the lady. Heh, heh."

"This could be very important. Can you tell me more about the boat?"

"That's a Chris Craft inboard ski boat, a real expensive one. You don't see boats like that on Perry Lake. This is mostly a fishin' lake. And you sure as hell don't see 'em with Iowa numbers. Sorry, miss." He looked at Madeline and said, "So yeah, I noticed it. This blond kid, he come here pretty regular-like for a couple of summers in a row, back 'round the time you're talkin'. The rule in Kansas is that you can use a boat with out-of-state tags for sixty days, but then you're s'posed to get a Kansas number. I thought 'bout turning him in, but I figured it wasn't hurtin' nothing. I also noticed he always had a woman with him. I hate causin' a hassle for a woman just tryin' to enjoy the lake."

"The same woman?" Tony asked.

This made the old man laugh until he coughed. "Sorry. Gettin' old is a bitch. Sorry, miss. No, this blond boy never had the same woman twice. Always had some pretty young thing on his arm. But you had to be quick to see 'em, 'cause he was quick to get the boat in the water and get away from here."

"Any idea where they went?"

"Well, an hour ago, I would of said no. The lake's got a hunnert'n sixty miles of shore line. There's a lot of little coves and beaches where a boy could show a girl a good time, if you know what I mean." Another glance at Madeline. "Forgive me."

"But now...?" Tony prodded.

"Now you showed me that photograph. I know every square inch of this lake. Open your map on that fancy phone of yours, and I'll show you exactly where the picture was taken."

He did. Madeline was careful to note the exact map coordinates so they could find it later. Tony then asked about the boat trailer and vehicle that towed it. The man confirmed they both had Iowa plates, but he'd never paid attention to the numbers. The vehicle was described as a big, silver, four-door pickup, like a Ford F-150 or a Chevy Silverado, the man said, expressing his regrets that he couldn't be sure which.

"Would you know him if you saw him again?" Tony asked.

"Well, maybe. I'm old, but my eyesight's pretty good. Course he was young, and it was four years ago. He could-a changed quite a bit since then."

Madeline shook her head, saying, "Based on the description

you've given us, I don't think he's changed much. I just saw him yesterday, and I would have described him the same way."

"Huh. So what's up with this guy? You thinkin' he had somethin' to do with this girl's disappearance?"

"We really don't know," Tony said. "But if she was with him the summer she disappeared, we sure would like to talk to him.

"Okay," the man said, turning back to his fishing rod and reel. "If I see him again, I'll tell him."

"No!" Tony and Madeline reacted simultaneously, causing the man to jump.

"I mean," Tony said more evenly, "if he is involved, and he finds out we've talked to you, you could be in some danger. If he hurt this nice young girl, and I do mean *if*, then I'm afraid he wouldn't hesitate to harm an elderly gentlemen who could lead the authorities to him."

"I get it," the man said. "I watch all three NCIS shows. I'll be careful."

Tony and Madeline gave him business cards with their contact information, and the old man promised to call if he thought of anything more.

**

Finding the secluded little beach wasn't easy. It was accessible primarily from the water. Tony and Madeline had to hike through some dense woods to get to it from road. As they stood in the sand, looking out across the water, they could see no landmarks, buildings or other points from which activity on the beach could be observed.

"He chose this spot carefully," Tony said. "I wonder how he found it?"

"I shudder to think of what happened here," Madeline said

without turning to face him. "She looks so happy in the picture, and she posted it on Facebook with an upbeat caption. Do you think it started here?"

"I doubt it. The seduction probably started a lot sooner, before he was able to convince her to come here. The picture posted on social media indicates she was still happy and excited at the time. The dark side of this, the coercion, if that's what happened, didn't come until later."

"But not much later," Madeline said, the sadness overtaking her voice. "Maybe six weeks later she packed a bag and left. Shelly Blaine, where are you now?"

She shifted her gaze from the water to Tony. "We have to find her, Tony. We *have* to."

***

Leaving Perry Lake, they decided it was time to go home. They had Blaine's permission to include him and Shelly in a newspaper article. That, combined with the information Tony had gotten from Glenda, provided plenty of material for a compelling article, maybe even a series, about human trafficking in Iowa and adjoining states. They also felt the need to return home to recharge and, if they were willing to admit it, feel safe again. There was no rational reason to feel safer in Orney, Iowa, than in Missouri or Kansas, but rational or not, the feeling was real.

This time, Madeline drove while Tony made phone calls. First to Rich Davis then to Ben Smalley, filling in both men on the basics of what they had done and the fact they were headed home. Tony also called his parents to check on them and Rita and to assure them he was fine. Then he offered to dial the phone for Madeline. He punched the numbers as she recited them and handed the phone to her so she could talk with her parents.

They arrived back in Orney at dinner time. They agreed to go to their respective homes to clean up and eat something then meet at the *Crier* offices to collaborate on articles for the following day.

Ben greeted them warmly and welcomed them back, but he asked them no questions about the details of what they had seen, heard, or done. Tony had learned this about Ben long ago. Ben was smart enough to know that a story is told best in its first telling. He insisted his reporters write first and verbalize their experiences later.

Tony and Madeline finished writing just before the late deadline. They hung around the newsroom for a while, catching up on mail and emails while Ben read and edited their drafts. At 11 p.m., he stepped out of his office and gave them a thumbs-up backed by a grim smile. "That's great work, you two. You make a good team. If you can stay awake long enough, I'll buy you a beer at the Iron Range."

Tony and Madeline looked at each other, shrugged, and nodded in agreement. They were profoundly saddened by what they had experienced, but they were equally proud of the work they had done. Tony was thinking, *I won't mind a bit if my boss takes me out to tell me how great I am.*

Madeline was thinking, *Hell, yes, I could use a beer.*

Town Crier

The Horrors of Human Trafficking
Town Crier Reporters Encounter Evil in the Midwest

Tony Harrington and Madeline Mueller, Staff Writers

ORNEY, Iowa – Human trafficking has many faces. In the past eight days, we have encountered many of those faces, ranging from criminals, to parents sick with worry about missing daughters, to two young girls held captive and repeatedly raped in Illinois motels and truck stops, to Brittany Powell, the 17-year-old girl whose lifeless body was found in Quincy County with telltale signs of similar physical and sexual abuse.

Sadly, there are others we met or learned about in just eight days. Countless others are on Iowa's and the nation's rolls of missing children. As *Town Crier* reporters, we feel indescribable sadness at the plight of these children. We are sharing our experiences here, in the first person, not to shock or offend you, but to help you understand the seriousness of the problem, as well as its scale.

We first learned of Shelly Blaine from police records of missing children in, or near, Iowa. We met Shelly's father, Irwin Blaine, on his farm west of Leavenworth, Kansas. There, we experienced first-hand...

Chapter 13

Tony tried to work as he watched Ben field a stream of visitors and answer numerous phone calls. The human trafficking articles had been published in Tuesday morning's *Crier,* and by 10 a.m. that day, Ben had talked to at least twenty community leaders, subscribers, and others who had strong opinions about the articles. The callers fell mostly into two predictable categories: those who appreciated the time, effort, and money the *Crier* had spent to bring such an important issue to light, and those who felt the subject matter was offensive and inappropriate for their community newspaper. Ben thanked them all for their input, even those who said they would be cancelling their subscriptions.

Tony eventually walked over to the glass enclosure, stuck his head in the door, and said, "I don't know how you stand it."

"Bah, this is nothing. When I was in Baltimore, we had two full-time people in the newsroom who did nothing but field complaints and requests for corrections or retractions. I would've been far more concerned had the story generated no reaction. This level of feedback is wonderful, Tony, really. It means you and Madeline wrote powerful prose for this morning's paper, and more importantly, it means people are reading it."

Tony smiled. "I have to admit, I like your perspective. By the way, as long as no one's waiting in line with a baseball bat, can I have a minute?"

"Of course! Sit. What's on your mind?"

"I've been thinking about things we could do to find the people responsible for these crimes, and maybe some of their victims too. Obviously, we hated Madeline's idea of putting herself out there as bait, and as it turned out, we were right to worry about that."

"Obviously," Ben said, nodding.

"But what about exploring the other side?"

"How so?"

"What if I went online looking for a teenage girl? You know, went shopping for sex? One thing the experts keep pointing out in articles and lectures is that the sex slavery business only exists because lots of people are willing to buy the product. It must be relatively easy to arrange to have sex with these girls. So I'm thinking I should do that—make the connection, I mean, not have sex with anyone." Tony suddenly was red-faced, and Ben laughed. "I knew what you meant, but I'm a little reluctant. Posing as a buyer might not be as dangerous as trying to become a victim, but it still has risks, especially since some of these perpetrators know who you are."

"I could disguise myself. And if it worked, I'd be on the inside, talking to one or more of the bastards involved, presumably making arrangements through him. I might be able to learn something from him or from one of the victims that would lead us to the actual leader of this enterprise."

"I have to admit, it seems likely you'd succeed in at least contacting them. As you say, there has to be an easy way to make this connection, or they wouldn't have any clients." Ben leaned back in his chair and ran his hand through his hair. Tony could tell he was warming to the idea.

Ben said. "We would have to set you up with a fake identity, of course, and somehow access the Internet in a way that couldn't be traced to you." Tony nodded as he thought through Ben's words. Ben continued, "We would want to bring Rich Davis and maybe the sheriff in on this. We don't want you getting arrested with an under-age girl in some unrelated sting operation. Can I help you, Billy?"

Tony turned and saw Billy Campbell, the photographer, standing in the doorway.

"No, Mr. Smalley. I just saw Tony talking with you, and I wondered if he's on the trail of something big again. I thought I'd wander over and see if he needs me for anything."

"Not at the moment, Billy, but thanks. I genuinely appreciate the initiative."

Billy nodded and sauntered back toward the darkroom entrance.

With a smile, Ben turned back to Tony. "You have to hand it to Billy, he's ambitious. I'd like to bottle some of that energy and serve it to a few of the staff in the advertising department."

Tony laughed.

Ben said, "I was about to tell you to go visit with Rich Davis to get his blessing and ask for his help with your idea, but look who just walked in the door."

Once again, Tony turned. Through the glass, he could see Davis, looking clean-cut and professional in a nicely-pressed tan suit. Davis stopped at Madeline's desk and said something. Madeline rose and followed him to Ben's office door.

"Is this personal, or can we join the party?" Davis asked.

"By all means, squeeze yourselves in here," Ben said. "We

were just talking about you."

"I'm anxious to know why, but perhaps I should go first. Because we certainly have been talking about you all."

Tony instantly was on high alert. He feared Davis was here to complain about the morning's articles or, God forbid, point out some error in the reporting. However, Davis began talking about something else altogether.

"When Tony called me yesterday afternoon, he told me about the beach they had found where this Donny character apparently had entertained Shelly for an afternoon three or more years ago. Tony mentioned, almost in passing, that he wondered how many other girls had been in that same spot. He said he might like to go back when he had more time and take a much closer look around, to see if evidence of other missing girls could be found."

Tony remembered saying this, but quickly corrected Davis. "Actually, it was Madeline who said it to me. I passed on the sentiment because it made sense, but it was her idea originally."

"Well, kudos to you, Madeline," Davis said sincerely. "I thought about it and decided you were right. We have a long list of missing girls, and now we have a suspected perpetrator and a witness who says the perp has visited the spot several times with different companions. So I called the Kansas Bureau of Criminal Investigation and convinced a"—he pulled his note pad from his pocket to look it up—"a Lt. Fairchild to send a couple of agents down there. On a whim, I suggested they take a cadaver dog."

The room grew very quiet. Everyone was both anxious and terrified to hear what was likely to come next.

Davis continued. "Yes, I'm afraid so. In less than an hour, the dog found a burial back in those thick woods. The tree roots apparently prevented these girls from being buried very deeply."

"Girls?" Madeline cried out. "Oh please, Rich, no. You're

saying you've found more than one dead girl?"

"I'm sorry," Davis said. "The dog has found two so far. There may be others, especially if they're much older sites or buried much deeper. Of course, there also may just be the two. These guys seem to be very good at what they do, so if they have killed other girls, they probably haven't gone back to any one site very often."

"For God's sake," Ben said, standing. "Has the world gone crazy? What in the hell is the matter with people? These are *children* we're talking about."

Tony was heartsick and concerned he might get physically ill. He was bent over in his chair, his head in his hands. He said to the floor, "Do you have any identifications? Any idea who these girls were?"

"Not yet," Davis replied. "We just found them this morning, and the bodies were badly decomposed. Initial reports from the site indicate they may have been there for two years or more."

Madeline's mind was exploding with just one thought, *Not Shelly. Not Shelly. Not Shelly.* She knew she was being ridiculous. Whoever the girls were, someone would be grieving them. However, Madeline couldn't bear the thought of Mr. Blaine going through what Mr. Powell was experiencing. She couldn't bear the thought of her words of encouragement to a second frantic father going to waste just like they had with the first. *If I'm being selfish, so be it. But please, God, not Shelly.*

✳✳✳

The next forty-eight hours were some of the most difficult Tony and the team had ever experienced. Waiting for news from Kansas about the girls' identities was agonizing. Having no other leads was infuriating. Even proceeding with the undercover "shopping expedition" was on hold while Ben made some necessary arrangements and Davis talked to his supervisor about setting up a team to monitor and protect Tony, if and when he made contact with the traffickers.

Tony and Madeline tried to stay busy, covering routine news events—traffic accidents, a Planning and Zoning Commission hearing, a fire in the school district's bus barn, and others that neither reporter would remember by this time next year. It wasn't easy to focus on the tasks at hand.

And then all hell broke loose.

It began with a phone call from Rich Davis.

"I have news," he said, not waiting for Tony to respond. "In the body of one of the girls found in Kansas, they recovered a slug from a .38 revolver. Coroner says it passed through her chest, probably through the heart, and lodged against a rib in her back. They found the slug in the rubble at the bottom of the grave."

No response.

"Tony, this bullet matches the one the officers recovered from the parking lot in the mall."

"*What?*" Tony lurched up in his chair as if an executioner had thrown the switch for the 20,000 volts. He must have cried out pretty loudly, because Madeline and Ben both were at his elbow before Davis spoke again. Tony pushed the speakerphone button on his cell as Davis said, "That's right. It appears the man who had coffee with Madeline was carrying the gun used to kill at least one of the girls we found buried."

Now the other three people in the newsroom were listening, too—the sports editor, the copy desk editor, and the photographer. Billy came closer, clearly not wanting to miss any details but also savvy enough to not crowd their space.

"Word about this is being shared with the Kansas City police and every other law enforcement agency in three states," Davis said. "There'll be a whole new level of intensity in the search for this scumbag and his Charger. Even his pickup truck from four years ago. Also, we're going to need Madeline to set up a time to come in and meet with our sketch artist, hopefully later today. She's the only person we know of who's seen this guy up close."

"Of course," Madeline said, still reeling at the thought she had sat with him. Hell, she had even touched him.

Davis said, "I can tell I'm on speakerphone. Tony, when you're free, call me privately, and we'll discuss next steps for the other idea you want to pursue."

Tony worried Ben would be offended at Davis' implication that he couldn't talk about the undercover operation in front of others at the *Crier*, but considering what was at stake, he couldn't fault Davis for being cautious.

When the call ended, it was Billy who spoke first. "Since I'm not as close to this case as the rest of you, let me be the one to suggest something."

The other three turned to face him.

"Madeline, agree to do the sketch on the condition that the final product is released to the *Crier* first. We should have that picture before the other media get it." Perhaps worried about pushback, Billy quickly added, "Hey, I'm just looking out for the *Crier*. The cops wouldn't be onto this ring of creeps if it wasn't for us... I mean, you. They won't have a sketch unless you give it to them. The least they can do is let us run it first."

"No." Ben's voice was firm and commanded the others' attention. They turned to look at him.

In a more normal tone, Ben said, "Billy, that's great thinking, and I admire you for it. I don't want my rejection of your idea to ever stop you from making similar comments in the future. However, in this case, these girls need all hands on deck as quickly as possible. Think about it. After all that's happened in the past few days—rescuing Glenda and Camila, arresting two men, finding Brittany Powell's body, and now finding these two—clearly, the heat is turning up on Donny and his pals. They could decide at any moment to pull the plug and run. That decision could have deadly consequences for any victims still in their control."

Ben took a deep breath. "I love being first. You all know it. Billy is right to suggest it. But my decision is final. We all must hope Madeline and the artist can come up with a good sketch, and we must hope the distribution of it leads us to these bastards. At the very least, if we can't catch them, maybe we can stop them from taking the next victim. Understood?" Nods all around. "Good."

Billy turned and left without a word. The others watched him go, then turned their attention to Madeline. "Good luck today," Tony said. "That's a lot of pressure on you."

"I'll be alright. I sat and stared into that face for more than an hour. They'll get a good sketch out of me."

Ben nodded his agreement and excused himself.

Once Tony and Madeline were alone, he knew what Madeline was going to ask even before she spoke.

"So," she said. "What does Rich want to talk with you about privately? What do you have up your sleeve?"

Tony knew it was hopeless to resist, so he told her. He expected an angry reaction, but Madeline's demeanor was more melancholic.

She said, shaking her head, "I thought I could expect more from you. This male prejudice thing is intolerable."

"Now, wait a minute..."

"No. You listen for a change. This is the epitome of the male double-standard. The suggestion that I go at risk is completely unacceptable to you, to Ben, to everyone. But when Tony wants to put his ass on the line, the *man* wants to take the risk, everyone thinks it's a reasonable thing to consider. That's sexism, pure and simple. And don't tell me it's because these bastards are abusing women. You told me yourself sexual slavery involves both boys and girls. I'm sure they could find someone who wants to screw even you."

"Ouch," Tony said, trying to smile.

"Dammit, Tony, I'm serious," she said. "Your life is probably more at risk than mine. They might want me alive to make them some money. When they realize who you really are, they're going to put one of those bullets in *your* heart before you can say 'freedom of the press.'"

"Okay, I get it. You're right. But the fact is, I've got Rich and the DCI agreeing to put a team around me so I can do this. They never would have agreed to do that with you. It doesn't make it right, but my God, let's fight the women's rights battle after we've put some of these people in prison. I mean, aren't we both fighting for the same thing, here?"

Madeline stared at him a long moment. Tony couldn't be sure if the argument was done or not. The FedEx delivery man settled the question for him.

"Excuse me," the man said, "Are you Tony Harrington?"

"I am," Tony said.

"Sign here, please."

Tony signed, and the man handed him a standard parcel box, about fourteen inches wide and three inches deep. Madeline looked at him quizzically, and Tony shrugged. He pulled the tab, tearing open the seal at one end. A small bundle wrapped in newspaper tumbled out onto his desk. *Yesterday's Chicago Tribune*, Tony noted to himself. He cut through some more tape, unrolled the newspaper and three things came out, a photograph, a note, and a plastic baggie containing a human finger.

"Oh no," Tony croaked. "Grab Ben again, and call Rich."

"Already on it," Madeline said. She jogged back to her desk, waving at Ben's office as she went.

Tony sat. Being careful not to touch it, he looked at the photo more closely.

"My God." It was a picture of Rita, walking across an open, grassy area. He was pretty sure he knew the spot where it had been taken. There was a grassy courtyard outside of the building where Rita took cello lessons and attended orchestra practices. It looked like she was walking away from the building, perhaps on her way home after rehearsal.

He turned his attention to the note, and his brow furrowed. The note said, "Your story in Tuesday's paper was very touching. It told me a lot about these poor, innocent girls and their families. It also told me you have ignored my warning. The gift I included isn't from Rita, but the next one will be, along with some other parts of this poor girl. Remember, Tony, this gift is because of you. This and future unnecessary suffering will be because of you. Let it go. Now. Today." It was signed in block letters: "RAY."

Tony leaned in to examine the sealed sandwich bag, what the note had referred to as a gift. "Dear God," Tony moaned again.

***

Once again, everyone was assembled in the Sheriff's Department conference room: Tony, Madeline, Ben, Rich Davis, Dan Rooney, Sheriff Mackey, and the sheriff's chief investigator, Daniel Bodke. Participating by telephone were Anna Tabors, the FBI special agent in charge of the team based in Chicago, and Special Agent Cunningham.

Tony was a wreck. The combination of the threat to Rita and

his guilt about the torture inflicted on some other innocent girl was more than he could bear. He barely heard the discussion in the room as the hurricane raging in his brain threatened to incapacitate him.

"Tony!" someone said, jarring him back to the room. He looked up but did not respond.

Rich Davis spoke again, "Tony, pay attention. Special Agent Tabors is trying to tell you something important."

Tony fought to focus, and he heard the voice from the speakerphone say, "Tony, you need to understand something. The girl did not lose her finger because of you. Hear me on this. Neither the call nor the package you got from Mr. X had anything to do with him wanting you to stand down."

This got Tony's attention, primarily because Tabors was making no sense.

"Think about it, Tony," the agent continued. "Once the two men were arrested in Illinois and the two girls were rescued, this man knew the state investigators and FBI were involved. He knew threatening a small-town newspaper reporter would have zero influence on our pursuit of this case."

"Then what's this about?" Tony asked.

"This guy is simply torturing you. He knew you couldn't or wouldn't stand down when he made the first call. In fact, if he's as smart as we think he is, he knew the call would make everyone more determined than ever. The same is true with the package he sent. Each of those three items is designed to create anxiety and fear."

"Yeah? Well, it's working," Tony said. The fear, in fact, was gnawing at his gut like a nest of termites in a lumberyard.

"The package is another demonstration of his sadistic nature," Tabors said. "He wanted to hurt the girl. He gets off on abusing girls, or he wouldn't be in this business. I'm guessing he's gleeful because he had a chance to terrorize two people with one sadistic act. We see this behavior in some sociopaths. They believe they're smarter, more clever than everyone who's searching for them, so they find elaborate ways to toy with us. Obviously, 'toy' is too soft a word for it, but you get my point, I hope."

Tony did, and appreciated Tabor's efforts to make him feel slightly less responsible. Beyond that, the conversation was a waste of time.

Davis seemed to read his mind. "Okay then," he said. "What do we do next?"

"Before we do anything, I'd like to make something clear," Tabors said. "We are not dealing with a typical ring of sex traffickers. As horrendous as everyone in this business is, the people in this particular operation are worse."

She had their attention as she continued, "The other FBI agents and I have been talking about this. We're seeing things with this group that are rare, maybe even unheard of, in the sex trafficking world."

"Such as?" Ben prompted.

"Such as selling their slaves to private individuals who apparently use them for sex, abuse them, and kill them. Such as murdering and burying girls themselves, when they're finished with them. As you have reported, many girls who are trapped in this life die young, but usually from drugs or suicide. Cold-blooded murder is relatively rare. And I've never heard of a trafficker calling up a newspaper reporter to threaten him and his family and co-workers, or shipping a body part to someone just to create terror and feed his sadistic nature. Lastly, have you noticed almost all the victims we've seen or heard about are white girls? This too is different from the norm. Statistically, a large percentage of trafficking victims are non-whites."

Tabors added, "And consider this. It appears Donny and Ray

and the rest of this bunch have been operating successfully for years in multiple states. All of these things combined create a picture of the most vile, dangerous group of traffickers we've ever encountered. We cannot underestimate what they're capable of."

They spent the next hour determining next steps, logistics, and assignments. It was agreed someone needed to go undercover as a buyer. Considering Tabors' warning, Davis and the sheriff suggested Dan Rooney do it. Rooney had undercover experience and was an agent with a gun and a permit to carry it. Others were agreeing when Tony interrupted to say no.

"I'm doing this. Period. Whether you support me or not, I'm going to find these bastards," Tony said. "I, too, have a gun and a permit to carry it, thanks to Sheriff Mackey's advice. I'm doing this."

A chorus of objections erupted, based primarily on Tony's status as a civilian and his obviously distressed mental state. The sheriff said, "We can't have you out there on some vendetta."

Davis said, "This was risky enough when we first discussed it. But look at yourself now, Tony, you..."

"Dammit!" Tony slammed his hand on the table. "This is *my* sister who's being threatened. This is *my* phone the bastard's calling. The package was addressed to *me*, Glenda called *me*. I am not gonna sit back now and hope for the best. I'm going out there, and that's it! I will appreciate it if you have my back while I do it."

Tabors was the first to respond. "Tony, we get it. The FBI can't condone this, but before I decide whether to actively derail you or stay out of your way, I have to know one thing."

Tony was taking deep breaths to calm himself.

"I have to know if you're going to keep your finger off the trigger of that gun," Tabors said. "Can you control yourself so we don't find ourselves forced to arrest and prosecute *you*?"

Tony didn't need to think about how to answer. "Agent Tabors, anyone who knows me knows I hate guns. That includes the one I own. I have practiced with it, so I know how to carry it safely. I will have it close by for self-defense, but I promise you, the last thing in the world I want is to use it."

Mackey spoke up, looking at Tabors. "I could deputize him, if that would make the Bureau feel better."

The response didn't come from Tabors. "No," Ben said firmly. "Tony is a reporter seeking a story. He's not an officer of the law. Besides, if he served as a deputy, that would further blur the lines of responsibility and liability. That probably would require getting the lawyers involved, which only raises our costs and slows us down. Tony reports to me. Let's just leave it that way."

"Okay," Mackey said, holding up his hands. "I was just trying to help."

As the sheriff spoke, there was a tap on the door. Deputy Bodke was closest, so he stepped out. He quickly returned, announcing, "Dr. Torgesen, the medical examiner, is here. He says he has something to show us."

Torgesen came in carrying a large black pouch under his arm, the type artists use to carry their paintings. He placed it flat on the table, unwound the ties, and slid out three large color photographs. At first glance, Tony couldn't tell what the images were. Everyone else in the room was equally puzzled.

"Thank you, everyone, for allowing me to interrupt," Torgesen said.

Sheriff Mackey said, "It's no problem, Lance. Whatcha got?"

"Well, it may not be helpful, but I'm convinced it's something. I was writing my final report on Miss Powers, and finally getting photos captioned and filed, and I saw these." He passed the photos around. "I'm sorry I only brought three. I didn't realize there would be so many of you here."

"So what are we lookin' at?" Mackey asked.

"These are photos of the skin underneath the dead girl's arms. I'm embarrassed I didn't see and report this sooner, but as you know, the poor girl was covered in cuts, scrapes, and contusions. I don't think I've ever seen a victim so badly abused prior to death."

Davis said, "Please, doctor..."

"Sorry, I should be more discreet. The point is, when you look closely, under her arms, you realize there are marks there that aren't random. I'll take that back a moment." He took the photo Mackey had been examining out of his hand. "Thank you. Now, if you will, look here, and here, and here. When viewed from the angle the girl's own eyes would have seen it from, these appear to be letters."

"Letters?" Tony said. "As in someone scratched letters into her skin? Like they branded her or something?"

"Well," the doctor said, "traffickers have been known to brand their victims. They do view them as property, you know. But no, that's not what this is at all. Based on the crudeness of the scratches, and the angle from which they were made, I believe the victim scratched these letters herself."

Everyone in the room was stunned. Madeline spoke first. "As in a message?"

"Well perhaps, but not a very helpful one, I fear."

Tony was mortified. "After everything she had been through, she mutilated herself?"

"Mutilated is a bit strong for scratches like these, but it would have been painful, yes. My best guess is that she took something with an edge on it that she had at her disposal—something her captors wouldn't have considered a threat, such as a broken pencil or pen, or even the plastic tip on a shoelace—and scratched at the skin on her sides, under her arms where it would be hidden from others."

"I," Tony read aloud from the photo of the girl's left side. "Is that what you see? The letter I?"

"I would agree," the doctor said.

"Well, what the hell does that mean?" Mackey asked no one in particular. "An Initial? Iowa maybe? A pronoun?"

"Wait, wait," the doctor urged. "There are more on the other side." He pointed to another of the photos. "The letters under her right arm would have been scratched using her left hand, obviously."

"J – U – S – T," Rich Davis read. "Is that all?"

"Yes, of that I'm sure. After I noticed these, I went over every photograph, covering every inch of her, and found nothing more."

"I just. What do you make of that?" Tony asked, looking at Davis. "I just what? Why would she go to all that trouble and pain to write the start of a message, but not anything pertinent?"

"She ran out of time?" Mackey pondered.

"But why write the pronoun and a modifier at all? Why not just a word or two of importance?"

Davis responded by simply stating the obvious, "I have no clue. The beginning of an unfinished message seems likely, but it could mean anything. Maybe it's in code. If not, she endured a lot to tell us nothing."

The doctor said, "I'm sorry it isn't more. I feel like I've let you down, but I thought you should see this at least."

"Of course, Lance," said the sheriff. "You were right to bring it here right away. Now we just have to put our heads together and try to understand what she was struggling to say."

Tony said, "I think we're missing something." He looked at the others in the room. "We media people probably aren't going to get copies of these pictures, but Sheriff Mackey or Davis, I think one of you should get a full set of the photos taken before the autopsy. Maybe putting these letters in context with her other wounds will tell us something."

Everyone agreed, and the medical examiner said he would make similar enlargements of them all and have them delivered to Mackey's office by the end of the day.

The meeting ended with a discussion of what should be publicized and what shouldn't. Everyone was uneasy about the *Crier* reporting on the severed finger. Tony worried that the publicity would in effect reward the sadistic bastard who had done it.

Ben shared that feeling. He also worried that the gruesome and unusual nature of it would bring an avalanche of national media down on Orney. He not only worried about the *Crier* being beaten by the resources and influence of bigger media outlets, but about national publicity chasing the perpetrators out of the region before they could be caught. Spurring the devils to run also carried serious risks for the girls. It was possible the captors, before they fled, would kill some or all of them to speed their travels and reduce their chances of being caught.

In the end, Ben made the call to hold off a day or two on everything except the sketch of Donny, reserving the right to publish something immediately if other media got wind of the latest developments.

"Daniel," the sherriff said, "you get the word out to everyone in this office and over at the medical examiner's that not one word of this is to be shared with anyone. Understand?" Deputy Bodke nodded and went out the door.

Rich Davis concluded the discussion with advice to everyone in the room. "Let's all go home and get some rest. It's been a trying day. We'll get an early start tomorrow, and hope a good night's sleep will help us make sense out of some of this. Tony, I'll come by your office at nine, and we'll get to work on your cover as a pervert."

The quip normally would have sparked humorous responses, or at least a few grins, but not today. There was no lighter side to be tapped among a group that had spent the day examining a severed finger and photos of an abused teenager. There was also no optimism that anyone would get any rest tonight.

Mackey sat down at the conference table and rubbed his face as everyone filed out of the room. Tony held back until the two of them were alone. The sheriff looked up.

"I need a favor, Sheriff," Tony said. He didn't wait for a response. "When those photos of Brittany arrive, would you drop them by my house?"

"What?" the sheriff replied grumpily. The request was ridiculous, and the young reporter should have known better than to ask the county sheriff to do his bidding.

"Sheriff, please. I just want to spend some time examining them before I go undercover. I may not have another chance for a few days. It's probably a waste of time, but I want to try. I promise you'll have them back first thing in the morning.

"You have an ego as big as my old man's barn. You know that?"

"That may be, but I'll be up late regardless. Might as well be doing something more valuable than playing video games."

"Alright, hot-shot. I'll bring 'em. Now get out of my department before I have you locked up for excessive self-importance." Tony left, glad to take the abuse if it meant he had a shot at solving the mystery locked in those photographs.

Chapter 14

Tony was spreading large color photographs across his kitchen table when he heard a knock at the side door. He wasn't surprised to see Madeline's face looking at him through the glass.

He pulled the door open as she opened the outer screen door. He wrapped his arms around her and asked, "Are you okay?"

"That's what I'm here to ask you. I was really worried about you today in that meeting."

"I'm getting through it," Tony said.

After a long pause, Madeline spoke. "So are we going to stand here in the doorway, letting bugs into your house, or are you going to invite me in?"

"Well, actually..." Tony wasn't sure how to discourage her.

"What? You're into something, I can tell. Or onto something. Don't think you can shut me out now."

Tony shook his head. "No. Relax. It's just that I have the color photos from Dr. Torgesen. Mackey loaned them to me for tonight. They're on the table in the kitchen. It's a pretty gruesome sight. Are you sure you want to come in?"

She frowned. "No, I'm not sure at all." She took a deep breath and exhaled. "But I'm here, so let's have a look."

Despite bracing themselves, it was difficult to look at something so repulsive.

"How can any human being do that to another?" Madeline asked.

"There's just no understanding it," Tony agreed.

They removed the photos of Brittany's face and put them back into the envelope, figuring—or perhaps just hoping—nothing in them would be relevant to the marks on her torso. Looking at the remaining photos was slightly easier.

They moved them around, viewed them from different angles, looked for partial letters or something else Torgesen might have missed, but they came up empty. Tony used a magnifying glass for a while and found it provided nothing but a headache. After nearly two hours, they gave up and retired to the couch.

Tony put Joe Cocker's "Respect Yourself" on the stereo, poured Madeline a glass of wine, and grabbed a Diet Dr. Pepper for himself. They sat together, Madeline's hand on his leg and his free arm behind her neck. They were quiet for a long time.

Tony broke the silence. "I called Rita when I got home."

"She okay?

"She says she is, but I can tell she's really scared."

"Can't say I blame her."

"Me neither. Even worse, I can tell she's really ticked off. She didn't say it, but she's angry with me, or maybe I should say with my career choice. Again, I can't blame her."

Madeline tried to console him. "She'll get over it. We just have to put an end to this, and she'll be fine."

"The problem was, I found myself stuck in an impossible

conversation. I know she would be supportive of me—of us—and would agree we're doing the right thing, if I shared with her the horrors these girls are experiencing. But then, if I gave her all the gory details..."

"You'd just scare her even more," Madeline finished for him. "You're right. It sucks big time."

"God, I just find myself going back and forth between wishing Glenda had never called me and being glad someone's finally making an effort to put a stop to this, or at least a small part of it."

"Despite everything, I'm still leaning toward the latter. And I'm not just glad *someone* is on this case. I'm glad that someone is us."

"That's probably B.S.," Tony said, "but I appreciate you saying it."

There was no more talk. There was no kissing or thoughts of sex. There were just two co-workers, friends, lovers, clutching each other for support and finally finding sleep on a living room couch.

***

At 3:06 a.m., Tony sat up suddenly, nearly knocking Madeline onto the floor. She scrambled up. "Tony, what? What's wrong?"

"My God," he said. "I figured it out."

"Figured what out? The scratches? You figured that out in your *sleep*?" Madeline didn't know whether to laugh, cry, or punch him in the face.

"Look," he said, getting up and nearly running into the kitchen. He turned on the light over the table, and fried their eyes. "Sorry, but look at this." He pulled the photograph of the Brittany's side, where the J-U-S-T letters could be seen. "She scratched these here, hoping the creep who was abusing her wouldn't notice, right?"

Madeline nodded. This much had been discussed in the

afternoon meeting at the Sheriff's Department.

"So think about where she *didn't* scratch."

Madeline looked puzzled and shrugged, indicating she didn't know where he was going with this.

"Take the extreme and work backward," Tony said. "A slender girl like her could have reached all the way to her hip and down her leg without too much trouble. But she didn't scratch letters into her hip or leg, right? Why? Because a man forcing himself on her might have noticed it."

Madeline wanted to say, "So what?" but she didn't want to slow him down.

"So where does she stop? Look. She quits scratching letters right above where the elbow would touch her side – right where her upper arm would end. Put yourself in her shoes. Wherever you mark your body, he might see it. So where do you have the best chance to conceal it? Under your arm. It's natural for your arm to be next to your body from the elbow to the shoulder, and possible to hold it there even when you're having sex. She stopped at the elbow because she feared discovery if she went any lower."

"Okay," Madeline said, "I'm with you so far."

"And what if she's left-handed?" Tony said, his excitement growing. She starts on the right side. She scratches J-U-S-T into her skin and realizes she's out of room, so then..."

"She finishes on the other side!" Madeline yelled. "Oh my God, she didn't write 'I JUST,' she wrote 'JUSTI'."

"Bingo," Tony said, beaming. "And that, my dear, is the beginning of something important."

"It could be a name. I've heard weirder names in Iowa than Justi."

"Could be, but the fact there's just one letter on the second side indicates she was interrupted. "I'm guessing she was writing Justin, or Justine, or maybe even Justice, as in someone's last name. We can't be sure it's her captor, but I'll bet it's a name of somebody involved in this. Let's pray it's a real name, and let's pray it leads us to him or her somehow."

Madeline stood back and shook her head in amazement.

"You really are something, Mr. Harrington. Now put those horrible pictures back into their pouch, and let's go to bed." Tony didn't argue.

***

The next day, Rich Davis and everyone else involved in the investigation expressed similar opinions to Madeline's. Once Tony had pointed it out, it seemed obvious Brittany had done exactly what Tony had surmised. Within an hour, they had confirmed with Mr. Powell that Brittany had been left-handed. They then put the name, or partial name, in the hands of all the different law enforcement agencies involved in looking for the ring of kidnappers, rapists, and murderers. State investigating agencies began cross-referencing the names, both as first and last names, with any vehicles matching the descriptions of the Dodge Charger or the silver pickup truck. They all knew this was a long shot, not just because the broad search parameters would turn up hundreds of names, but because the vehicles were believed to belong to Donny, and not a Justi or Justin or Justine, unless they were aliases for the same person.

"We have to try everything," Davis had said, in the ultimate example of stating the obvious.

The morning's *Crier* carried the sketch of Donny on the front page. Most of the daily newspapers in Iowa carried it as well, though no one else gave it front page treatment. It was shared by a couple of TV stations in smaller markets, but the Des Moines stations were hijacked by a major apartment building fire, and the news about a possible suspect with possible Iowa ties got bumped.

Madeline thought the sketch artist had done a good, if less than perfect, job of capturing Donny's looks. He looked older in the sketch —it was hard to capture his youthful charm—and maybe the cheekbones were a bit too pronounced, but overall it would work. There was a possibility it would generate some leads.

It did. By noon, Davis reported the DCI had received over 200 calls. "I hope it slows down," he said in a call to Tony. "Having too many leads is almost as bad as having none. Where callers are giving us full names, we're cross-checking those against registered vehicles. I can tell already we're going to have a big number of them who own silver pickups. This is Iowa; everyone drives a truck."

Davis hadn't come to the office as promised. Instead, he told Tony that a makeup expert from Des Moines was on her way there to work on altering his appearance.

"The DCI keeps makeup people on staff? No wonder you look so marvy," Tony said.

"No," Davis said flatly. "This woman comes from the Des Moines Community Playhouse, and she's really good, so listen to her. Let her help you."

A short time later, Ben called Tony into his office. "I have something for you," he said, holding out a laptop.

"You may know this, boss, but I already have one of those."

"Of course you do," Ben nodded. "But you're about to go online shopping for sex. I thought you might like to use an anonymous machine. I also figured you wouldn't want all the spam, pop-ups, and viruses infecting your machine once you start visiting those sites."

"Excellent points," Tony said. "Thanks."

"And this," Ben said, handing him a piece of paper, "Is a secure login you can use. It's an account the paper in Baltimore set up for investigative reporting and undercover work. I called my old boss and got permission for you to use it. So, to be clear, use this laptop when you go looking for illegal entertainment, and only do it from a public wi-fi access, such as an internet café or the public library. It's no guarantee Mr. X and his cronies won't spot you, but I think you'll be ninety-nine percent safe. There is so much of this activity online, it would be a miracle if they happened to spot a connection from Baltimore to Orney."

When Tony returned to his desk, Laurie was waiting for him. Laurie worked at the front desk of the *Crier*, serving as receptionist and classified advertising salesperson. Today her hair was tinted purple and pink. Between chews of her ever-present bubble gum, Laurie said, "There's a lady at the front desk asking for you. Says she's from Des Moines." Chew, chew. "Said you'd know what it's about."

"Yep, I do. Send her on back here please, and thanks."

***

Two hours later, Tony looked like a 50-year-old Wall Street banker. The transformation was incredible. He was sitting at his kitchen table. MaryAnn Baker, a hair stylist and part-time volunteer makeup artist from Des Moines, was standing behind him as they stared into the mirror together.

Tony's hair was gray, including his eyebrows. It was trimmed up above his ears and slicked down to hold a part on the side. He wore wire-rim glasses and a gray-brown moustache, trimmed neatly. MaryAnn had not added wrinkles, but had subtly accented the tiniest creases in his skin.

"I don't think I like you, MaryAnn," Tony commented as he shook his head. "I'm not ready to be old."

"Hey, I'm fifty-four," she said. "Trust me, that's not old. You're now looking just distinguished enough to be interesting and rich. You're gonna be very popular with the girls."

"A guy can always hope," Tony muttered.

A short time later, Madeline stopped by, knocking on the side door. She shrieked when Tony answered it.

"Holy crap. You scared me to death. I thought some stranger was in your house. You look... amazing."

"That's one word for it," Tony said.

MaryAnn smiled. "It appears this is going to work, so I'm going to remove it all now. We can't have anyone seeing you like this before it's needed. I'll be back before you leave for your assignment."

When he had been restored to twenty-eight, MaryAnn packed her bags. Tony thanked her and escorted her to the door. He then headed for the shower.

When he finished, Madeline was waiting in the kitchen. She closed an app and set down her phone.

"You ready for what's next?" he asked.

Madeline had asked to be with him when he went online looking to buy a good time with an underage girl. Tony had agreed, keeping his reservations to himself. They had decided to leave town, as an extra measure of protection from being detected by the wrong people.

They climbed into Tony's SUV and drove to nearby Viscount, Iowa, a town much smaller than Orney. Tony had a little history in Viscount from his previous run-in with killers. When they arrived in town, Tony turned right off of Main Street and made an immediate left into an alley.

"You appear to know where you're going," Madeline noted.

Tony nodded and turned into an empty parking lot behind a

metal-clad building.

"So where are we?" she asked.

"Viscount City Hall," Tony said, smiling. "I'm betting they have wi-fi, and because the taxpayers pay the bill, I'm guessing it's not password-protected."

He was right on both counts. In less than a minute, they were connected to the Internet and logged on to the secure service provided by the people in Baltimore. Tony began his search by looking at a couple of the major pornography sites that were readily available to anyone with a computer. The ads for telephone sex and live video sex were everywhere. There were ads for escort services, massage services, and "Click Here to Meet Girls Near You." It was all carefully worded to assure the viewer that all girls were eighteen years of age or older.

They agreed they should take the plunge and visit the "dark web." Tony had heard about it, but had never experienced it. He used some access protocols provided by the DCI and immediately was astonished at what he saw. Every conceivable type of human depravity was on display. After 40 minutes or so of searching, exploring, sampling, and rejecting various content, Tony was able to connect to a pimp named John, likely not his real name, who said he had "entertainment" available in Iowa.

In an exchange of messages, Tony said he was a sales manager for a chain of auto parts stores. He said his wife had died recently and he was ready to try some "alternative" types of physical encounters.

John didn't mince words. His next questions were simply, *How young?* and *Male or Female?*

Female, and young, Tony replied. *How young is available?*

Name it, came the reply. *Twelve is pretty common, but we can go younger if you're willing to pay for it.*

"Holy Mother of God," Tony said to Madeline. "This can't be real." To John, he wrote, *How much?*

John asked, *Are you a cop?*

No, Tony typed. *I'm in sales. I hate cops. They put my old man in prison. How about you? Can I trust you to protect me? I don't want to lose my job over a piece of ass.*

Madeline smacked him in the shoulder. "Do you have to be so crude?"

"Hey, these guys expect to be talking to a pervert. I'd say I'm being pretty mild."

John answered. *Two hundred to set up your account. Then two hundred an hour for teenagers, five hundred for ten to twelve, another thousand for anything younger than ten.*

Madeline gasped. Her face was white enough to be seen in the darkness of the alley parking lot. The questions and answers went back and forth until, after about twenty minutes, Tony was set up with an account, a password, and a cell phone number for his personal "agent" in Iowa, the person he should contact whenever he wanted to pay for another "visit."

Madeline said, "Can you ask him if he can connect you with Shelly? We can't forget, we have to find her."

"I'm sorry, but if I do that, he's gonna get suspicious. It would sound just like a parent, or a cop, looking for a missing girl. We need to take this one step at a time."

Madeline didn't argue, but she did look crestfallen.

Tony wrote, *All this talk is making me horny as hell. How soon can I do this?*

Response: *Bring the cash. Truck stop on I-35 north of Ames. Tomorrow night. 8 p.m. Pull your car to the far northeast corner of the lot and wait there. Tap your brake lights three times. Someone will come to your window and ask if you want a deluxe car wash.*

You say, 'Only if I can get a wax too.' Got it?

Got it, Tony typed. *I'll be there.*

One other thing. If it turns out you are a cop, or you're helping the cops, we cut off your dick, then we put you in the ground. Then we track down your family and kill them too. Understand?

No cops. Don't worry, I don't want them anywhere near this either.

I never worry. That was the last they heard from the contact. Tony logged off and closed the laptop.

"That," he said grimly, "was horrifyingly easy."

***

Donny was having trouble concentrating on the handball game and was losing badly. His competition, a short, balding man in silly-looking shorts and a "Best Grandpa Ever" t-shirt, was loving it.

"When you asked me for a game, I figured you'd clean my clock," the man said. "A young guy, as fit as you... I was sure I was toast. If you're just being nice and letting me win, well... that's okay. I appreciate it!" The man laughed and hit another fat serve, which Donny normally would have pounded down his throat. He hit it poorly, and the best grandpa ever scored on him easily.

"Sorry," Donny said. "My heart's not in this. I'm going to call it a night."

The man was clearly heartbroken as he watched Donny duck through the door in the back of the court and disappear down the hall.

Donny no longer looked like he did in the sketch that had appeared in the media that morning. He now had a goatee, dyed red, with hair to match and some new freckles. As Donny changed clothes in the West Side Health Club locker room—he couldn't risk a shower in a public place, in case his makeup ran—he thought about how stupid he and Ray had been. He wanted to pound his head against one of the expensive wooden lockers that surrounded him on three sides.

When he'd let Madeline go, he thought he'd fooled her. He had felt safe. He should have realized the gunshot in the parking lot would bring the cops, and that those cops would have led her to finding out he'd lied about being a detective. But later, Ray had heard from one of his inside sources that the bullet from the parking lot had been connected to the gun used to eliminate that Ashley chick—his gun. The result? The gun now was at the bottom of the Des Moines River, and Donny was compelled to look like Seth Green. *Less dorky than Seth Green, thank God,* he thought, but still, he hated the look. He loved his blond hair and clean-shaven dimples.

How in hell had they found those girls by the lake, anyhow? Donny wondered, his anger rising every time he thought about it. *Those two reporters, Madeline and her pal, led the cops right to the spot. But how? They're really getting to be a nuisance. No, these two are more than a nuisance; they're becoming a real threat. Despite Ray's caution about killing media ass-wipes, they have to be stopped.* Donny licked his lips. *And it's going to be fun drilling that bitch Madeline and making her suffer.*

***

Donny enjoyed making people suffer. He always had. When he was young, growing up in Independence, Missouri, he learned the pleasure that came from inflicting pain on his sister's cat. He was in elementary school when it started. His sister had gotten the cat when she was nine, so two years later, when Donny turned nine, he asked for a dog and was surprised and disappointed when his dad said no. His dad said dogs were too expensive and too much work and needed to be boarded whenever the family traveled. That last excuse made Donny fume. The family never went anywhere.

Donny sought his revenge by subjecting the cat to a wide assortment of painful encounters. He quickly learned he felt a rush of pleasure whenever the cat yowled in pain. He loved seeing how far he could go before he left a mark or anyone suspected the cat had been hurt. Sewing needles seemed especially effective. If the cat did suffer a residual effect, such as a limp for a few days or a spell of cowering under a chair in the den, Donny was never blamed. His dad would just yell, "I told you, that cat is psychotic!"

Whenever someone would ask Donny if he knew why the cat was limping or bleeding, he would flash his innocent look, a pained frown, and say something like, "Of course not, mother. It's Susie's cat. Ask her." This was one of the many ways Donny learned that his dimpled cheeks, wavy blond hair, and carefully crafted lies could keep him out of trouble. Most adults found it impossible to believe this adorable, well-mannered child could do whatever awful thing someone might be claiming he had done.

As Donny grew, so did his obsessions. He bullied younger school kids, intimidating them, occasionally punching them, and always leaving them humiliated. He loved finding ways to terrorize some pathetic dweeb who was three or four years younger than him. Donny was smart about it. He hated getting in trouble, so he always acted alone, and never in places where he could be seen. He also made sure his punches were delivered to places that wouldn't leave a mark, usually in the belly, leaving the kid on the sidewalk gasping for air.

Sex began creeping into his fantasies during puberty. When he was twelve, he began devising ways at home to watch his sister when she was bathing or changing clothes. Susie had never liked him and had always suspected him of being a creep, so their relationship was limited to grunts of acknowledgement and occasional arguments. She hated it, really *hated* it, when he walked in on her in the bathroom or went into her room when she was undressed, so of course he went out of his way to make those "mistakes" as often as possible. The more red-faced and angry Susie became, the bigger Donny's rush of pleasure.

Then, when he was fifteen, a girl who had grown up a couple of blocks away seduced him. She was just out of college and home for a visit before moving to Nashville to begin a career with a health care company based there. Her name was Loretta, and she had baby-sat for Donny and Susie a few times when all three of them were younger.

Donny was home alone one afternoon when Loretta knocked on the kitchen door and asked if she could come in. He said sure. She claimed she just wanted to say goodbye to her old friends before moving away, but as they talked, Donny could tell she was flirting with him. It made him feel awkward, but his desire to touch her pushed those thoughts into the background. She was tall and lanky, a former volleyball player. She was dressed in tiny shorts, making her legs look like they went up to her ribcage, and a beige cotton top with a wide neck, which allowed the right side of the collar to hang down past one shoulder.

After only a few minutes of small talk, she stepped in close and kissed him on the lips. Donny had kissed girls before, but this was different. There was a hunger in the way she held his face in her hands and pressed her lips to his, with her mouth open and tongue teasing. Without a word, she took him by the hand and led him to the den at the back of the house. Standing in the middle of the room, she undressed him, then slowly pulled off her own clothes. She pulled him to the floor, pushed him onto his back and mounted him, screwing him right on the furry rug in front of the fireplace. Donny had not known anything could feel so good. But beyond pure lust, there were no emotions involved at all. It didn't last long, and when they finished, Loretta grinned and said, "Thanks, Donny. Did you like that? I always hoped I'd be the one to get you first."

Then she pulled on her shorts and top and departed.

Donny was left lying on the floor, confused and embarrassed. Those feelings quickly grew into anger and humiliation, and to his surprise, a growing urge to do it again. It was a revelation to him that achieving climax didn't result in satisfaction or contentment. Within minutes, the desire was on him again. He wanted more.

That night, Donny walked the two blocks to Loretta's house. Her car wasn't there, so he sat in the shadows by the side of the house and waited. At 11:30 p.m., her Toyota pulled into the driveway. Donny walked up and was inside the passenger door before she turned off the engine.

"Jesus, Donny," Loretta said. "You scared the hell out of me! What are you doing?"

"I... I wanted to say... Yes, I liked it," he said. "Can we do it again?"

Loretta laughed out loud. "No, Donny. That was a one-time thing. It was nice, but don't misunderstand. I don't need a boyfriend. I sure don't need one who's eight years younger than me and just starting high school. Now please, head on home and let me get some sleep. I have a long drive ahead of me tomorrow."

Loretta's laugh really angered him, and looking at that bare skin on her shoulder and her legs, *my God, those legs*, had made him hard as a rock. "No," he said simply.

"Donny, get out of my car. You're being silly. I'm not going to have a scene with a teenage boy in my parents' driveway."

"No, you're not. You're going to have sex with me in your parents' driveway, whether you want to or not."

"I am not, you little jerk, now get out of here."

Donny smiled. It was not a pleasant smile. It was not a teenager's smile. "Loretta, get in the back seat and take off your clothes. If you don't, I'm going to walk up to that front door and start banging on it. When your dad answers, I'm gonna tell him what we did this afternoon. In fact, I'm going to tell him you made me do it, against my will. I don't know what your dad might do to you, but it probably won't be enough, so then I'm going to tell the cops. I'm smart enough to know that you having sex with me is against the law. Think about where that'll leave you. I'll be the poor kid who was taken advantage of, and you'll be the one going to jail."

"Oh, my God," Loretta said, sucking in air, trying to keep from passing out. "Oh, my God."

"Just get in the back seat, Loretta, and show me a few more tricks. Then tomorrow, you'll be gone and no one has to know."

Loretta was crying when she climbed over the seat and pulled her top over her head. Her tears aroused Donny even more. He pushed her onto her back and took her, as hard and as roughly as he could. The more she cried, the more pleasure he found in it. By the time he finished, he knew. *This* was what he wanted, what he craved. This was a feeling beyond the physical pleasure of sex. This was the ecstasy that came from being in charge, from being a king. Donny liked being a king.

***

Donny had no regrets. He had become a master at hiding his true self, occasionally enjoying a relatively normal relationship with a girl, but always finding ways to access that darker side of sex. Sometimes his partner was a paid companion, but just as often she was an unsuspecting victim taken by force.

Then, four years ago, he had met Ray. It was as if Ray had taken an ordinary foot soldier and molded him into a special forces commando. Ray had taught him how to make money—more money than he ever had imagined possible—by simply doing more of what he already loved to do. Ray had taught him additional ways to stay off the authorities' radar screens and new ways to find and seduce younger and younger victims. Now, every day of every year, Ray and Donny had dozens of girls, and half as many boys, in the hands of clients. He was making them suffer and being paid more than a million a year for it. This was the ideal life. This was what he was born to do. He was good at it. He was careful. He loved it.

Now two reporters from Iowa of all places were bringing trouble to his perfect life. It was time to deal with them.

Chapter 15

Ray was sitting in a banquet hall at the Westin Hotel in downtown Chicago. He had tuned out the speaker long ago. As a partner in a legitimate business, a firm specializing in marketing and development, he had agreed to attend the banquet. It was important for one of the partners in the firm to be visible at these charitable events, and it was Ray's turn in the queue, but his mind had been elsewhere all night. It hadn't helped that the meal—an intimate affair with six hundred of his closest friends—had consisted of the predictable chicken breast/salmon combo with green beans and a slice of cheesecake for dessert. Well, actually, the cheesecake had been good, but it was small consolation for giving a night of his life to this fundraising effort to cure the disease of the week.

Ray thought of the wasted night and the wasted money only in passing. He was preoccupied with thoughts about recent incursions by law enforcement and two pesky small-town reporters into his private business—that other business that didn't have offices in downtown Chicago and couldn't be found in the telephone directory.

He was reaching the same conclusion as Donny. The reporters had to be buried.

The rescue of the girls in Illinois and the arrest of the two dimwits at the motel had been irritating, but not particularly concerning. None of the four knew anything about the larger operation nor the names or locations of any of the other players in the organization. Ray had simply destroyed the burner phone he had used to communicate with Big Al and Freddy and had taken down the website they had used to attract clients to Glenda and that Hispanic girl, and that was that. Nothing could be traced back to him.

The incidents in Kansas and Iowa, however, were far more concerning. The authorities had now found three of the dead girls, two of whom had been killed by Donny. They also had the bullet match, which tied at least one body to Donny's gun. That female reporter had seen Donny, had talked with him, and had ridden in his car, and now the authorities and the news media had a sketch of him. Donny's disguise was good, but he couldn't keep it up forever. Ray realized he had to get him out of the picture, and quickly.

He disliked the thought of killing Donny. He had grown close to the young man and had worked hard to train him. Donny was the only person Ray ever had trusted enough to let in on the larger operation. Donny had even been allowed to see Ray's face once. Of course, Donny didn't know Ray's real name or anything about him, except that he was based somewhere near Chicago. But Donny knew all the contacts for all the teams. If the cops got to him and turned him, it would be disastrous. The entire operation would have to be shut down. Ray couldn't let that happen.

He noticed a different speaker had taken the stage. It was a woman. A young woman. *Hmm, she looks good in that strapless formal gown,* Ray thought. *She might bring...* Then he stopped himself. *You foolish old man. You have more important things to think about. You need a plan to eliminate these pests before they overtake your garden.*

***

Tony spent Saturday morning with Rich Davis and a room filled with agents and officers from the FBI, the DCI, and probably a couple of other three-letter agencies he didn't want to know about. Ben and Madeline were there as interested third parties. Sheriff Mackey was nearly relegated to the same status even though the group was meeting in his conference room.

Agent Tabors had driven over from Chicago. She took the lead in setting up the team around Tony. She wore the leadership role well, and Tony found himself impressed with her clear thinking and direct manner. She was tall and lanky, with dark skin and short-cropped, curly, black hair. She wore a blue blazer over a white blouse and gray skirt, and black flats. *Function over fashion*, Tony thought, something he'd learned to expect from the FBI.

Rich Davis played the role of mediator whenever disagreements erupted. The primary topic of contention was also the most fundamental: if Tony succeeded in meeting a girl who was being held against her will, should the team try to rescue her, or simply gather information? Even those who expressed opinions on one side of the question or the other were torn. Everyone understood that if they rescued her, they would have another Glenda/Camila situation. Removing a girl or two from a life of forced sex and other abuse would be the right thing to do from many perspectives, but almost certainly would result in no real progress in finding the people responsible for the larger sex trafficking organization. The girl was unlikely to know anything, and her handler or pimp probably would be as clueless as Big Al and Freddy had been. Chasing their phones and email accounts would produce nothing... again.

In the end, it was left up to Tony. If the girl seemed okay, and he could convince her to help him build a deeper relationship with the scumbags who "owned" her, he was empowered to try. If the girl he was with, or any child, seemed at risk of serious injury or worse in the near future, the team would descend on the motel and take everyone into custody. They would arrest Tony and treat him as an actual client in an effort to protect his cover.

The rest of the planning revolved around where and when the surveillance team would be positioned and how they would be hidden or disguised. They assumed Tony would be taken to the motel across the parking lot from the repair bays, restaurant, and convenience store that comprised the truck stop. Tony was glad to hear at least one agent would be inside the motel, masquerading as a service technician for the heating and cooling systems.

They knew Tony couldn't wear a wire or recording device. The pimps almost certainly would check for that, especially with a new client. They assumed Tony's cell phone would be taken from him, so they agreed he would leave it behind in the car. Any actual client could be expected to do the same. So they had to discuss how Tony would communicate with them.

Tabors said, "We can't be sure what room you'll be in until after you're inside. We're hoping one of our people will be able to see you go in or pick up something about where they're taking you on our remote mics. Try to say the room number out loud even if they don't. Once inside, all you need to know is the emergency signal, which is two knocks, a pause, and three rapid knocks."

"Knocks?" Tony was puzzled.

"We'll have remote, high-tech mics on the motel from every direction. Knock that signal on a window pane if you can, or loudly on the wall, and trust me, all hell will break loose immediately. If you realize they're on to you, or if you feel in jeopardy for any reason, use that signal. Understand? No unnecessary risks. A dead hero is still dead."

Tony blew the air out of his inflated cheeks. "Oh boy. I get it. I promise."

Agent Tabors had brought with her the materials Tony would need to confirm his alias: a driver's license, business cards, insurance cards and credit cards, all in the name of Mike Bradbury, age 52, from Ames, Iowa. All were handed to Tony in a well-worn leather wallet. Tabors said, "When they Google Mike Bradbury, they'll see a couple of dozen references to you and your business. You should be sure to do the same, so you know what we said about you."

"You people think of everything," Tony said as he slipped the wallet into his back pocket.

"We try," Tabors said, "but there are a million ways this can go wrong. For starters, make sure every item of clothing you wear is carefully checked. No laundry tags or receipts buried in pockets, no names written on labels, and no references to where your clothes were purchased. We don't want these thugs finding anything they can use to double-check your story, or cast doubt on it. And be sure to memorize the details on your documents. If they ask you your date of birth, and you have to stop and think about it for even a moment, you could be a dead man."

Tony swallowed and nodded his assurance that he would be ready.

Tabors had also brought a late-model Volvo station wagon for Tony to drive, also registered under the alias. "We thought someone in sales should drive an SUV or a station wagon. This is what we had available with enough miles on it to look legit. You should probably take the time to look through the glove box, center console, and rear storage area to familiarize yourself with the miscellaneous items 'you' have accumulated in the two years you've owned the car.

"One other thing," Tabors said, "Practice hearing your new name out loud. Maybe one of your co-workers here can help you." She said, nodding at Madeline and Ben. "The point is that if someone calls, 'Hey, Mike!' from somewhere, you have to react naturally."

Rich Davis concluded the session saying, "Okay, everyone. You have your assignments. Let's be in place and ready to go at our appointed times. We've got a civilian in the crosshairs tonight, so no screw-ups, understood?"

Nods all around.

"Tony, you need to head to the truck stop at about 6:30 to be there on time. Remember, your alter-ego is from Ames, so no comments tonight about how far you had to drive."

"This crap is complicated," Tony said. "Maybe I should just go as Tom Cruise. As you can see, without the disguise I already look just like him."

A few smiles broke through the tension. Davis said, "Very funny. Let's hope you're a better actor than you are a comedian."

***

Tony and Madeline were in the midst of preparing—memorizing facts and practicing Tony's new name—when a single knock sounded on the side door and Doug Tenney walked up into the kitchen.

"Hey guys," he said. Then he stopped in his tracks, noticing the grayish moustache Tony had donned to get used to wearing it. "Boy, Madeline, I didn't realize you had the hots for older men. No wonder I couldn't get you to look at me."

"Ha, ha," Madeline said dryly. "You should see him in his full get-up. He looks the part of Mike Bradbury, a salesman from Ames, and a pervert who likes young girls."

"Well, who doesn't?" Doug quipped. No one laughed. "Okay, sorry. That was a little tasteless, considering the subject matter at hand."

Tony nodded. "This is completely off the record, Doug. Not a word to anyone."

Tenney looked hurt. "Hey, Tone-man, this is Doug you're talking to."

"I know, but lives are at stake in this, so I had to say it. Don't get all bent out of shape."

Tony then explained what they were doing. Doug, of course, said he wanted to be there.

"Sorry, pal. Not this time. Believe me, Madeline wants to be there even more than you do, and the FBI said no to her too. I'll call you both as soon as it's over so you won't have to worry."

"Well, I will worry, you idiot," Doug said. "Remember, I was in Illinois. I saw what these bastards are capable of doing and how quickly they put a gun to your head. Don't tell me not to worry."

Tony just nodded.

Doug then smiled and said, "On the bright side, if you get your ass shot off, Madeline will have no one in town worth dating except me. Maybe she'll see the light."

Madeline picked up an empty plastic bottle from the kitchen table and hurled it at him. Doug and Tony both laughed, but it didn't last. The stress of the looming evening quickly found its way back into the room. Doug walked over to his friend and put his arms around him, squeezing tightly. "Do *not* get your ass shot off tonight," he hissed in Tony's ear. Then he turned and walked down the steps and out the door.

Tony wiped away a tear. Nothing more was said about Doug's visit as they resumed Tony's preparations.

***

As late afternoon approached, Tony's stomach growled loud enough for Madeline to hear it. She grinned and said, "You've done everything you can to be ready. Maybe we should grab some food before you get back into your makeup."

"Good idea. It occurs to me I haven't eaten anything today but a donut in the conference room."

Tony was about to suggest they split a pizza at Panucci's, his favorite restaurant, but Madeline spoke first. "How about Pizza Hut? I know it's not your favorite pizza, but it's still afternoon."

Tony looked at her, puzzled.

"Maggie will be there. She'll make sure your pizza is good; maybe better than good. And I really like the salad bar."

"Pizza Hut will be fine," Tony said, secretly wishing he had beaten her to the punch, or that Panucci's had a salad bar.

Maggie was, indeed, on duty. At that hour of the afternoon, Tony and Madeline were her only customers. Maggie treated them like royalty. Then, when she delivered the pizza, she pulled out a chair at their table and sat down.

"So how are you two lovebirds doing?" she asked, a big smile on her face.

"We're not lovebirds," Madeline said, dipping one edge of a bite of lettuce into a cup of Italian dressing.

"Oh, don't B.S. me," Maggie laughed. "I know everything that goes on in this town, and I happen to know the two of you have spent some late-night hours together. I'm not stupid. You're hooking up. So tell me, are you a couple now, or is this just friends with benefits?"

Tony shook his head, smiling, and said, "Maggie, you are a wonder. The *Crier* should hire *you* as an investigative reporter. Of course, then you'd put both Madeline and me out of jobs." In an effort to keep her from returning to the topic of his and Madeline's relationship, Tony added, "By the way, because you are remarkably well-informed, we should ask you about the girl whose body was found up in the northwest corner of the county. Have you heard any talk about it? Anything that would be helpful to us or the police?"

"Well, honey, I've heard lots of talk about it, but nothing that sounded like anybody knows anything. You know how people talk. They wanna believe they know something, but they don't. I've heard speculation about the killers that ranges from drug runners to spurned lovers to a coven of witches. It's all B.S."

"I figured," Tony said. "Just thought I should ask."

"Now I hear plenty of lies at these tables. Usually when a guy's trying to get his date into the sack. If I had a quarter for every time I heard a guy tell some girl he's in a loveless marriage and planning to leave his wife... Well, I wouldn't have to sell pizzas anymore."

Madeline and Tony both laughed at that. Maggie clearly was enjoying being the afternoon's entertainment, so she continued.

"'Course the biggest lies are about food. I love it when some overweight guy says 'I'll *just* have a large deep dish with extra pepperoni.' As if the word 'just' magically reduces the calories."

More smiles and more bites of food.

"And dieting! Half the people who come in here say they're on a diet. I'm not sure how they define their diets, but they seem to eat a lot of pizza. I have to tell you though, the one that really burned my butt the other day... That Langly kid was here, telling some co-worker how he's on a diet and hasn't fallen off the wagon once. What a crock of hooey."

"I take it he sneaks in to grab take-out when his friends aren't looking?" Tony prompted.

"Worse!" Maggie practically shouted. "After work every other day, he drives through that effing burger joint next door," she pointed a thumb toward the golden arches across the parking lot, "and buys bags full of food at the drive-through window. You know he's single, right? Dieting, my ass."

Tony teased her. "Ah-h-h...you don't like it when people frequent the Hamburgler's establishment. I'll have to remember to park on the other side of the building when I go there."

"Hey, if people wanna eat that crap, I don't care," Maggie said with a snort. "But every other day? Gimme a break."

The phone by the cash register rang, and Maggie hopped up. "Back to work. Don't you two lovebirds go and do anything I wouldn't do!" She chuckled and bent down to look at Madeline. "Course there ain't much I wouldn't do with Tony, if he'd have me."

Both smiled as they watched her go. Tony whispered, "I may have to come here more often. The food isn't my favorite, but the comedy show is excellent."

When they arrived back at Tony's house, MaryAnn was waiting. An hour later, a very distinguished-looking salesman came out of Tony's house, climbed into a Volvo parked at the curb in front, and drove away.

***

Tony arrived at the truck stop at precisely 8 p.m. He parked the Volvo exactly where he had been told to park it. He was careful to tap the brakes three times as he stopped. Within thirty seconds, a young man in jeans and an unmarked hooded sweatshirt walked up to the car window. As Tony lowered the window, the man asked, "Ya wanna deluxe car wash?"

"Only if I can get a wax too," Tony replied.

"You have the cash?"

"I do."

"This way," the sweatshirt said, and he began walking across the lot.

Tony scrambled out of the car, pushing the button on the fob to lock it as he hurried after the man. His stomach tightened into a knot almost immediately when he realized they weren't walking toward the motel.

The man stopped at the back of a large straight truck with a moving company logo painted on the side. Tony guessed it was a twenty-footer. The man knocked twice on the big metal doors at the back, and one immediately swung open. A second man leaned out. He appeared to be a little older, perhaps mid-30s, and had a boxer's build, tall and broad and muscular. He wore jeans and a ski vest over a flannel shirt. He had the kind of no-nonsense look Tony had seen on the faces of the bouncers outside Chicago nightclubs, whose primary jobs seemed to be keeping Iowa boys from coming inside.

"Pay me," the man inside the truck said.

"Hold on," Tony said, "I'm sorry, but I'm not going to hand a bunch of cash to a total stranger until I know I'm in the right place. I need to see the, uh, merchandise first. Please," he added, feeling silly on top of feeling terrified.

"Show me your I.D. first," the man said.

"Do I have to?" Tony put some whine in his voice, as he had been coached by Tabors. "I don't want anyone to know who I am. You can understand that, right?"

"Sure," the man said. "I can understand you don't want your wife to know you pay money to screw underage girls. Tough shit. This is how it works. If you want her..." The man pushed the swinging metal door open far enough that Tony could see a young blonde girl in the back of the truck, smiling at him. The man pulled the door back to its former narrow opening and said, "...we have to see your I.D. We have to know who you are. And tell us again you're not a cop."

"Oh, for Christ's sake, I'm not a cop," Tony said, sounding exasperated and handing over his driver's license.

The big man looked at it, then handed it to the younger man, saying, "You know what to do."

The younger man turned and walked away.

"Hey!" Tony said, "You can't take that."

The big man in the truck said, "You'll get it back when you're done. Now give me the cash, and I'll leave you alone with Emily for as long as your money allows."

***

Tony was alone with the girl in the back of the truck. The interior had been made to look inviting, in a cheap, bordello kind of way, with some kind of velvet-like drapes covering three walls, and a big four-poster bed at the back. There was a small table with bottles of water, under which was a shelf with various oils and a box of condoms.

The girl must have seen Tony eyeing the condoms. "Those are for you if you want them. I don't need them," she said sweetly.

Her blonde hair was long and straight. She had large, dark, oval-shaped eyes. A few freckles dotted the skin just below her cheek bones. Her nose was small and her smile wide over a pointed chin. Her body type was similar to Glenda's, slender, small-breasted. She was wearing a white top, just sheer enough to give the viewer a taste of what waited beneath, and white panties with some kind of colorful characters on them. She could have played an elfin princess in a fantasy movie.

She's just a kid, Tony thought. He knew he shouldn't be surprised, but seeing her here, like this, was heartbreaking.

"Wow, you're a good-looking man. What's your name?" she asked, patting her hand on the bed beside her. Tony walked up and stood next to the bed, staring down at her, sad and uncertain of what to do.

The girl continued. "I'm Emily. I've been looking forward to meeting you. John told me you're real nice. I've been aching for a man who's nice. Come on, sit. Tell me what you like."

Tony sat. "Uh, I'm not sure. This is my first time."

"Really? Oooh, I love that. I'm gonna make you so glad you came to see me." She reached over and stroked the side of Tony's face. "Would you like me to start with my hands? I'm really good with my hands."

Before he realized he was doing it, Tony's right hand flashed upward and grabbed her wrist, pulling it away from his face. "Don't!" he ordered.

"I'm sorry." The girl's confidence evaporated, and she drew back away from him. "Don't you like me? Please tell me you like me. If you don't like me, it can go bad for me. John won't be happy. I think you'll like me. Really, you will. Look..." She started to pull her top up over her head.

Tony reached out again, pulling her hands down to the sheets. "No." he said curtly, sounding like a schoolmaster. "Just wait."

The girl looked confused, even shocked, and Tony was afraid she was going to cry.

"I like you just fine," he said. "Just slow down and talk to me first."

"Oh, I understand," the girl smiled, her confidence back, as though a light switch had been turned back on. She crawled over to him, got up onto her knees, and put her arms around his shoulders. "You can tell me all about it, and I'll help you forget."

He could feel her breasts pressed into his arm. *Good grief,* he thought. *Stay focused. She's just a kid.* He pulled away and moved to the end of the bed. The girl collapsed like a marionette whose strings had been cut. She sat back on her feet and simply said, "What?"

"Just talk to me, please," Tony said. "Tell me something about yourself? What's your last name?"

Emily snorted. "Well for God's sake, you must know I can't tell you that."

"Okay, then tell me anything. How old are you?"

"Twelve," she said.

"Emily, let's be honest. I know John wants you to say you're twelve, but how old are you really?"

"Well, I used to be twelve," she pouted. "Men wanted me when I was twelve. They still want me. Except you, apparently." Her eyes got wide. "You're not a cop are you? Oh, God, you're a cop. Oh, God, John's going to... Do you know what happens when a girl talks to a cop?"

"Emily!" She stopped abruptly, and Tony said, "Listen to me carefully. I am not a cop. I swear. I'm just a guy who cares about other people and is curious how a beautiful girl like you ends up having sex with strangers in the back of a truck."

"Listen mister," she replied. "Cop or not, we can't talk about that. You're not the first guy to ask us girls how we got here. Plenty of guys take what they want from us first and talk second. Some of them get all gushy and act like they want to help, now that they've got their rocks off. Well I don't want your help, and I don't want what comes from John if I tell you anything. Do you know what he does to girls? Of course you don't. You're some do-gooder who can't imagine the damage a red-hot iron rod can do, or a pair of pliers."

Tony grimaced. Emily added, "You need to know that you have to have sex with me. Now. Tonight. It's a kind of test for new clients. If you don't, they'll think you're a cop. Even if they're wrong, they'll think you're a threat to them. They'll make you wish you had never been here. Or more likely that you'd never been born. Then they'll come back and do the same to me for 'failing' with you. Please, can we just do it? Then you go away and leave me alone."

"I'm sorry, Emily, I can't do that."

"Oh God, oh God," she started to cry and curled into a ball on the bed.

"Please don't cry," Tony said. "I really am going to help you."

She raised her head up, and suddenly uncurled and leapt at him. She threw a fist and caught his face, just below his left eye. A second fist, aimed at his groin, just missed. Tony lunged backward and allowed himself to fall off the bed onto the floor. The thin rug did little to ease the impact. He clamped his mouth shut to stifle a cry of pain as he scrambled to his feet.

"Emily, for God's sake, chill out."

She was back on her knees, still on the bed, red-faced and angry. "You son of a bitch! Don't tell me to chill out. You have no idea what you're doing. You're gonna get me killed. Is that what you want?"

Tony took a deep breath and spoke clearly and deliberately. "Emily, I do know what I'm doing. I also know that these bastards are going to kill you no matter what you do. In the past eight days, I have seen the bodies of three dead girls who were used and abused by these assholes and tossed away like yesterday's garbage."

Emily was crying again, shaking her head. "No, no, no. They like me. They do."

"You may be right," Tony said, "but at some point, you're going to get a disease, or get pregnant, or grow too old, or get hurt by someone in a way that makes you less valuable, and they'll get rid of you. I'm sorry to speak so harshly, but that's how it is. Now talk to me, and let me help you out of this mess. Let me help you get a real life back."

"You are such a pathetic jerk," she spat back at him. "What kind of life do you think is out there for me? Where am I supposed to go from here? Do you think my nice family with the big house in the suburbs wants a daughter back who slept with strange men and women every day for the past three years? You think I can just go back to seventh grade, as 15-year-old, and finish my essay on 'What I did on my summer vacation?' This is my *life*! When I do well, they treat me okay. And when I fail, like with you, I get the shit beat out of me. Please, please, just do me and go. Please." Tony was appalled to hear her begging for sex from him.

"We can fool them," he said. "Tell me a couple of the things we would have done. Tell me some things I would have seen... Do you have a tattoo or a piercing or anything they would have expected me to see? Look, I'll even take some of this oil and rub it on myself. Then, I'll jog in place while you talk. I'll work up a real sweat, I promise. You talk, and I swear I'll fool them. We'll both be okay."

Emily looked at him wide-eyed, then laughed, a deep laugh that erupted from her soul. Tony thought it might be the most beautiful sound he had ever heard, coming from someone so young and in such a hopeless, terrifying situation.

"You're out of your mind," she said, "but if it's the only way to get rid of you, then I give up. Start running. If I see real sweat, maybe I'll answer one question."

Tony started jogging in place. After a few minutes, Emily began talking, first to tell him what he needed to know about the unicorn tattooed on the inside of her left thigh, and about the tricks she had learned to make men finish quickly. "I get little extras from John if I get them out of here in less time than they paid for," she said.

She still refused to give her full name, but said she had lived in Overland Park, Kansas. Her life at home wasn't great because her mom and dad fought a lot. Her dad was successful, and everyone thought he was a great guy, but at home he could be mean and demanding. She was only twelve, so she had just started thinking about boys in that little girl way of giggling with her girlfriends about who likes whom. Then she discovered websites she could visit on the family computer or even on her smartphone—websites that showed girls and boys doing things with their clothes off. She was shocked by what she saw, and embarrassed, and intrigued, and before long, excited.

Her interest in older boys grew, and her interest in boys her own age diminished. "I mean, really, could I imagine kissing, or even talking to dorky little Bobby, who sat across from me in class, after seeing the boys in those videos?" So she went online looking for older boys who would talk to her and had no trouble finding them.

One asked to take her to a movie at the mall. She went to movies there all the time, so she knew she could get away with it. When she met him, he was gorgeous—tall and blond, with a great smile and dimples.

Tony's jogging slowed. He was out of breath and needed a break anyway. "Dimples?" he gasped.

"Yes," she said. "His name was Donny, and I thought he was the hottest guy I had ever seen."

"Donny."

"Yeah," she continued, not picking up on Tony's piercing stare. "He was a perfect gentleman, and treated me like I was special. I was *so* excited. He asked if he could buy me dinner at a nice restaurant. I practically flew out of the mall. Then when we got in his car, another boy sat up in the back seat. He reached his arm around the seat and held a knife to my throat. I started crying, but Donny didn't seem to notice. He was like, you know, a totally different person.

"They drove me into Kansas City to a huge apartment building. Some rich guy had an elevator that went right from the parking garage to his apartment. Can you imagine? I think the guy paid Donny five thousand dollars for my first time. He handcuffed me to this giant bed in a room with windows on two sides looking over the city." She hung her head. "Who would've guessed that Hell would have such a nice view? He must've raped me eight or nine times over the next six days. Then one day he called Donny, said he was done, and Donny and his friend came and got me. You can guess the rest. It's mostly been motels or semi-trucks with sleepers since then." She waved her arm around the room. "This truck is a new twist. I've only done it a couple of dozen times in here."

"A couple of dozen..." Tony shook his head, horrified by everything he was hearing. "Have you ever tried to escape?"

"No," she said flatly. "In the first place, Donny told me they have pictures and movies of what I did in that apartment with the rich guy. He said if I ever spoke a word, those movies and stuff would go on the Internet with my real name attached. I'd never be able to show my face anywhere again." She sniffled and added, "He said if I didn't cooperate, they would take my little sister, and she would get the same as me. She's two years younger than me. I just can't let that happen."

Tony started to reply, but Emily kept going, so quiet now that Tony had to strain to hear. "I've also heard the screams," she said. "Girls who've been caught trying to run away. The things John does to them... And it's the ones who mess up who get sold. I can't stand thinking about it." She looked up and smiled. "So I'm the good girl. I do whatever they say and do it the best I can, and I get along okay."

The word "sold" caught Tony's attention. He asked her to explain.

"Well, it's never happened to me, so I don't really know for sure," she said. "But the girls say if John or his boss or any one of these guys gets mad enough at you, they take you off the circuit and sell you to someone who wants a girl... You know, full-time. That might sound like a better life than this, but everyone knows it's not. It means you're probably handcuffed to a bed again, or locked in a basement and used until your new owner is done with you. Then *you're* done."

Tony waited to hear more. Emily said quietly, "The girls who get sold never come back. We can guess what happens to them. That's how those girls you mentioned ended up in graves." She was shaking.

Tony resumed his jog, hoping to take her mind off of that potential fate. "The guy in the high-rise apartment, did you ever hear his name?"

"No," she sighed. "He told me to call him 'big stud' or 'lover.' I wanted to puke every time he made me say it. He was so... gross. I mean, not gross like some of the slobs I've been with since then. But you know, it was my first time. I had imagined being with a Prince Charming like, well, you know, like Donny. This guy had great clothes and kept himself clean, but... He was fat. Not enormous, but chubby, you know, like the dad on *The Simpsons*."

Tony nodded and smiled at Emily, encouraging her to tell him more.

"He was smart," she said. "I suppose most rich guys are, but I heard him on the telephone a couple of times, and he was using a lot of big words I didn't understand."

"Can you remember any of them?" Tony asked hopefully

"Oh, man..." She paused to think. "I remember being so confused because at first I thought he owned a laundry, then I thought maybe he's a chef... Then I thought..."

Tony interrupted. "You've lost me. Can you explain what you just said?"

"Well, I heard him reference folding stuff, and I thought of a laundry."

"Folding stuff?"

"Yeah, you know, like how often he folded things. But then I heard him say 'pressure cooked' and I thought maybe he was a chef. I knew he wasn't, though, 'cause he was home too much for that. All his business seemed to be on the phone."

"Pressure cooked..." Tony mused.

"Yep. I know I heard that one right 'cause my mom has a pressure cooker. She warned me about staying away from it when it was hot." Madeline related a few other snippets of conversation, each more confusing than the last. Tony was not finding it helpful.

"Oh, one other thing you should know, he has a weird... mark," she said. "He has one of those purple splotches on his skin. It's below his neck and off to the side, like above where his heart would be if, you know, if he had one. You couldn't see it when he was dressed, but when he took off his shirt, it looked like someone had spilled ink on him. The shape reminded me of a ribbon, you know, like you would win at the fair, rounded on top with a couple square edges at the bottom."

"That's really good, Emily. That's very helpful."

Someone banged on the truck doors.

"You done," a voice asked, "or are you throwing some money in the pot?"

"Just finishing," Tony said. "Give us a minute."

He turned to Emily and held her face in his hands. "I admire your courage and your determination," he said. "Walking away from here will be the hardest thing I've ever done. If you want this to end tonight, I can take you with me. I swear you'll be safe."

"No!" she said, recoiling. "I can't, and I won't. Stop talking like that, or I swear I'll rat you out."

"Okay, okay, I'm sorry. But is there anything else you can tell me about Donny or John or any of the people you've met or places you've been or anything at all that will help me find the people leading this? Can you think of anything at all? Consider the other girls, like your little sister, who'll suffer the same fate if we don't stop them."

"I think about that every day," she said, tears welling up again. "I haven't seen Donny in over two years. I think he's just the magnet that gets stupid little girls like me to fall into the trap. These two guys, John and Sam... I mean, obviously, those aren't their real names. They get their orders over a cell phone. Where to have me and the other two girls, and at what time, and who to look for."

"The other two girls?"

"Yeah, Cindy and Marta. They're probably over in the motel. We've been together for a few months now. They're a lot like me. They're not gonna run or anything, so John and Sam have no trouble managing things for the three of us."

As Tony feared, she didn't know much more. She said the five of them moved around a lot. Often, she didn't know where they were. They travelled in a Chrysler minivan. "It should be in the parking lot at the motel. It's dark blue. Kinda old." The truck had just shown up at the motel a few days ago. She never saw who had delivered it there. She didn't know if they would be travelling in it now or if it was temporary.

Tony sighed. He was going to have to do something to get a lot closer to John or Sam, or they were going to have to close down this part of the operation. Talking to the victims clearly was not going to lead them to anything useful.

"Then there's the money guy," Emily piped up as Tony finished rubbing a minty-smelling oil inside his jeans.

Tony's eyes shot up. "The money guy?"

"Yeah, every Wednesday morning some guy comes around to

collect all the cash. John and Sam are collecting thousands and thousands of dollars every week. They can't exactly go deposit it in a bank, so some guy comes and gets it. They don't let us see him, but you know, after months and months of this, they slip up now and then."

"So you can describe him?"

"Sorta. I guess so," she said. "Mostly, he's just creepy. He tries to look normal, like a farmer or a truck driver, but you can tell he isn't. He wears work pants and a denim shirt, but they always look like they just came off a shelf or something. No one's ever done any real work in them. The guy's real skinny, has a big nose with a bump here," she pointed to the bridge of her nose, "and dark hair, including his eyebrows. His hair is kinda long, past his collar in the back. I swear, if I was making a movie about somebody evil, I would put him in it."

Tony was about to ask if she'd seen what he drives when she added, "And man, you should see the car he drives. It looks like something out of a spy movie. No truck driver ever got into a car that fancy." She smiled. "Before you ask, I don't know the license plate number, but I can tell you it's from Iowa. At least I think so. It had the right colors."

"Emily, you've done great," Tony said. "I'm gonna tell these guys I had a great time, and even give them a tip. Please be careful for the next few days. I promise you, I'll be back."

"Don't promise," she said. "Just go away and keep me out of trouble with John."

Tony knocked on the door and John pulled it open.

"Bout time," he said. "I think you owe me another two hundred."

Tony climbed down, smiled, and said, "It was worth it. That's a nice piece of ass in there. Here's three hundred. If you guys will be around for a few days, I'll be back."

Tony noticed a middle-aged man in casual clothes hanging back in the shadows and realized immediately this was somebody waiting for his turn with Emily. A huge pang of regret and anger surged through Tony, but he managed to keep the smile frozen to his face.

John looked at the extra C-note and grinned. He said, "Just call that cell number or go back online and place the order. We'll tell you where to find us. Here's your license, Mr. Bradbury. Have a good night."

Tony took the license, nodded, and strolled back to his car. *Tactful use of my name*, he thought. *He's making sure the client knows that he knows who he is. It's a neat form of intimidation, in case anyone had any thoughts of tipping off the police.*

***

At midnight, the entire group re-convened in Mackey's conference room. Tony related the events as vividly as he could recall. He had called Ben, Madeline, and Doug from his car to let them know he was okay. Each had peppered him with questions, but he had put them off. He wanted to tell it once, and first, to the assembled group. The other call he had made from the car was to Rich Davis, to urge him to get pictures and plate numbers for the truck, but also for the Chrysler minivan. Davis had assured him the truck and the men around it were already on film. They would go look for the minivan right away.

"Please be careful," Tony had urged him. "I promised Emily this wouldn't come back on her. They can't get wind of our team being there tonight."

In the conference room, Davis reported it hadn't taken long to identify Emily. He pulled the electronic file up on his laptop and spun it so Tony could see the screen. Davis said, "Emily Reitz, Overland Park, Kansas. Taken at age twelve. Missing for more than three years. Is that her?"

Tony looked at the little girl's picture. Tears filled his eyes as he nodded and said, "Yes. She looks older now, but that's her."

Davis also said the agents on the scene at the truck stop had found a dark blue minivan with Illinois license plates in the parking lot. The Illinois Bureau of Investigation was running the plate numbers as the group was meeting.

"I doubt it will lead us anywhere," Agent Tabors said. "Clearly the best thing Tony got tonight was the intel on the money guy. It's usually the money trail that leads us to the centers of these rings. We'll be ready to tag him on Wednesday. If we can track him back to a boss or, God willing, *the* boss, we could be celebrating a real victory in another week or so."

"She also confirmed it's the same group, and not some other random collection of rapists," Tony said. "Her description of Donny was spot on. This same bastard has been luring girls into the spider's web for years."

Davis mulled that over and said, haltingly, "That means you got very lucky, if that's the right word for it, when you made your first foray onto the dark web. Either that, or this particular group of traffickers is much bigger in Iowa than we realized."

As the group contemplated that, Davis added, "I wonder if Donny is the ringleader? If not, he must be closely connected to whoever is running this thing. We have every indication he's been at it for at least four years, maybe longer. He'd have to know a lot by now. We can't let up in our search for him."

"We've got his face in forty newspapers and in the hands of every officer in four states," Tabors said. "We'll find him."

"Don't forget," Tony said, "the guy's probably a millionaire from this enterprise. He'll have the resources to disappear, or at least replace his car and alter his looks."

"Excellent point," Davis said. "Dan, why don't you get the word out tomorrow and have people start talking to car dealers in the region? Maybe Donny has traded the Charger or the pickup truck to get himself into new wheels." Rooney looked doubtful, and Davis added, "I know he's smart, so this is a long shot, but we have to try."

***

At 1 a.m., the core group of Tony, Madeline, Ben, and Rich Davis found themselves sharing drinks at the Iron Range. In light of what he had been through, Tony agreed to have one beer—a Coors Light.

"Coors Light?" Davis had asked, feigning offense. "That's not beer. Surely you jest."

Tony stuck by his order, had one, then switched back to Diet Dr. Pepper.

Ben looked at the bottle and said, "I'm pretty sure they didn't stock that stuff here until after I hired you."

"Probably right," Tony nodded. "See what a positive influence I'm having on the community?"

The group chuckled and talked of other things, but Tony could not get Emily off his mind. He ached at the thought of what she had been through already and felt nauseating guilt for leaving her behind, knowing what awaited her. Suddenly, he said out loud, "We have to get her out of there."

Any conversation from the other three stopped, and they turned to look at him.

"I have an idea," he said.

"Oh, no," Davis and Madeline groaned in unison.

Tony ignored them. "Think about this rich guy in Kansas City. There can't be many people in KC rich enough to live in penthouse apartments with corner bedrooms overlooking the city and elevators that go straight from parking garages to their apartments. I think we can find this guy."

"That's probably true," Davis said, nodding, "and we should, considering he's guilty of kidnapping and rape. But how does that help us in the larger case?"

"Well..." Tony hesitated, then plunged forward. "Consider this: it's possible Rich Guy just goes online to arrange for twelve-year-old sexual companions, but I doubt it. Think about the risk of that. He couldn't be sure he wasn't talking to a police sting. He would also have to worry about being blackmailed by the traffickers once they knew who he was. He would need some other connection, some other way to reach the people who feed his depravity."

"So?"

"So," Tony said, "it's possible this guy knows somebody on the inside. Don't you see? He's able to do these horrible things because he knows somebody he trusts who can arrange it. We've already acknowledged these traffickers are millionaires. Isn't it possible Rich Guy in KC knows someone at the top of this organization? Maybe he even *is* the top of the organization."

The other three let that sink in. Davis finally spoke.

"Jeez, Tony, I think you've done it again. You might be wrong, but you've identified a lead we can't ignore. I'll make some calls tomorrow."

"No," Tony said firmly. "I'll go down there. Let me find him. Then I'll call you, and you can have the tech people start digging into his financials or whatever it is you folks do. You can make the arrest if you think it's the right time. But let me find him. That's regular legwork that anyone can do. It'll keep other investigators on the more direct paths, like searching for Donny and tracing the money guy.

Davis looked at him, shook his head, and said, "If you don't get killed doing this crap, I'm going to shoot you myself."

Tony smiled.

"Swear to me," Davis said. "I mean it, Tony, swear to me you will not approach this guy or do anything more than identify him before you call us in."

"I swear," Tony said, then got up to leave.

He and Madeline looked at each other, and Tony gave the tiniest shake of his head. He couldn't imagine being with a woman tonight, after where he had been and what he had seen. He just wanted to go home, wash off the filth, the scents, and especially the body oil, and get a good night's sleep.

Madeline seemed to understand and simply said, "G'night Tony. Sleep well."

The others called out their farewells and "good jobs" as he walked out into the cool October night.

***

Once he was settled into his bed, Tony dozed off more quickly than he'd expected. However, he was immediately immersed in nightmares every bit as terrifying and disgusting as he had feared. These were not like the realistic dreams he sometimes experienced, with a sequence of events he could understand. These nightmares were just a sea of images. Dead girls, grieving families, sleazy motel rooms, mutilated bodies, then, emerging out of the chaos, the back of a truck. He could hear screams as he ran to pull open the doors. Inside, a girl was giving pleasure to a man, using her hands, talking about her desires and her fears. The girl looked up and stared into

Tony's eyes. It was Lisa.

***

The next morning, as Tony was packing, Ben showed up at his door. This was a surprise since the *Crier* only published six days a week, Tuesday morning through Sunday morning. Sunday was the one day Ben could take off without worrying about what he should be doing at the paper. Tony found himself trying to remember if it was Ben's first visit to his home. He thought it was. "Hey, boss. Come in, come in. Coffee? Something else?"

"No, I'm good, thanks," Ben said as he crossed the threshold, Tony leading him toward the kitchen. "I just wanted to catch you for a minute before you left. Can we sit?"

"Sure, we can. Sit, sit." Tony was gushing, his nervousness showing.

Ben sat, looked up at Tony, and gestured toward the chair across from him. Tony pulled it away from the table and sat.

"Tony, you know how much I respect your work, how valuable you are to the *Crier*, and how much I value our relationship, right?"

Tony nodded, but thought, *Uh-oh.*

Ben continued. "So please, listen carefully. None of that has changed. However, I do need you to climb off your high horse."

The words hit Tony like sledgehammer to the face. He slunk back in the chair. "What do you mean?"

"Tony, you are much too caught up in the emotions of these tragedies you're trying to cover. You've stopped thinking and acting as a newspaper reporter, and have morphed into some kind of vigilante. I don't think it's too strong to say you're imagining yourself an avenging angel, or some kind of a storybook hero. At the very least, you're behaving as though you're the one who bought the *Town*

Crier." He held up his hand to keep Tony from responding. "Think about this trip you're taking to Kansas City. Did you come to me and ask for permission to go down there looking for this rich cretin? No. You announced to the group last night that you were doing it. You never even looked at me as you said it. Did you talk to me about getting a permit to carry a concealed weapon and buying a gun? No. Did you even stop to wonder if your boss would want one of his employees carrying a gun on the job? I doubt it."

Tony ached to respond in some way that would make it okay, but he knew Ben was right. He kept his head down and feared he might start crying.

"Tony, I'm here because I need you to get back on track," Ben said. Tony looked up at him as he continued. "I need you to do three things for me. First, I need you to fix firmly in your mind that your job is to report the news, not to rescue girls, not to arrest evil men, and not to solve the world's problems. Your job is to investigate and write, period. Secondly, I need you to remember you have a boss. You're a great reporter, and you have a great career ahead of you if you don't get yourself killed, but no editor will tolerate a reporter who's out there doing whatever he wants, without approvals and without filing news copy along the way. Lastly, I need you to remember who I am. I have thirty years of experience doing what you do, in a lot tougher and scarier places than Orney, Iowa. Draw on that experience. Let me help you." Ben paused to let his words sink in.

Tony stammered, "Ben, I... I am so sorry."

"No need to go there, Tony. I didn't come here for an apology. I came here to help you be successful. Don't let this chat grow in your head into some kind of devastating reprimand that preys on your thoughts. Just hear what I've said, commit yourself to the three things I asked, and go out there and find another kick-ass article for the front page. Okay? Are we clear?"

Tony nodded, and both men stood and faced each other.

"I swear, boss, we are clear. Sadly, I can't argue with anything you've said. I hope you know how much I admire and appreciate you. You're right that I've been acting like an ass. I'd try to use the subject matter and the experiences we're having as excuses, but I get it. There are no excuses. If I'm going to be as good as you someday, I have to learn to cover tough issues like these without going off half-cocked."

"Thanks, Tony. That's the response I hoped for and expected." Ben turned to go.

"By the way," Tony called after him. "Do you want me to get rid of the gun? Should I bring it to you?"

"Hell no," Ben said. "You're chasing killers. I want you to keep it nearby every minute."

The side door slammed, and he was gone. Tony was embarrassed and angry with himself, but the conversation had only increased his admiration of his boss and made him more determined to get a great story for the *Crier*.

***

Madeline was at her desk in the newsroom pondering what to do next. She didn't love working on a Sunday, but she knew she couldn't just take the day off. She wanted to go with Tony to Kansas City, but she couldn't figure out how to justify the request. She was also torn by the desire to be in Iowa on Wednesday, when the FBI and DCI connected with the money man in the trafficking organization. If something exciting happened, like an arrest or even a shoot-out, she didn't want to be down in KC. Just as she confirmed in her mind there was no option but to stay, her office telephone rang. She spouted her standard greeting. "*Town Crier*, this is Madeline

Mueller, how may I help you?"

"Hello, Madeline. This is Donny. You remember me, don't you? I'm the guy who rescued you in the parking lot in Kansas City."

Madeline could hardly speak. She started waving her arm for Ben, but realized he wasn't in. Billy had just come out of the darkroom. He saw the commotion and scooted over to stand by her desk. Madeline reached into her purse, pulled out her smartphone, hit the "Memos" app, and began recording.

"Yes, Donny, of course I remember. I could never forget you," she said tersely.

Donny laughed. "Oh, of course. You remember me so well, you helped the police put my picture in all those newspapers."

"Yes, I did," she replied. "I only regret that I was so stupid I didn't get your I.D. or license plate number."

"Trust me, Madeline. It wouldn't have helped," Donny chuckled.

"What do you want, Donny? You obviously know that I know what you are. Why would you call me?"

"What am I? Go ahead, tell me."

Donny's silky voice and relaxed manner were infuriating. The feeling was exacerbated by Madeline's knowledge that he was manipulating her emotions.

"Since you asked, I'm happy to tell you," she said. "You're a serial rapist and murderer. You're a psychopathic monster who needs to be locked away in a hole somewhere. You are evil incarnate, a piece of shit who soils whatever surface you occupy."

"Wow," he said, the mirth in his voice oozing through the phone line. "That was quite a description. Fortunately, I can tell you in all honesty, you're wrong. I am a businessman. Just a simple businessman. I've learned there is a huge demand for a product—a product I am particularly good at producing. I get paid a lot of money to produce that product. I never rape anyone, and I certainly never kill anyone. I'm just a... a recruiter," he said, with a self-satisfied punch to the title.

While Donny was talking, Madeline was furiously writing a note to Billy, instructing him to call Rich Davis, and to try to reach Ben on his cell phone. Billy nodded, took a few steps away from the desk, and dialed.

Madeline seethed into the phone, "You believe what you want, but I know what you are, and a jury will know what you are, then everyone will know what you are. Now why are you calling me?"

"Oh, Madeline, I'm disappointed you have to ask. I could tell when we had coffee that you were attracted to me. I rather liked you, too, despite the funky haircut. I thought we should get together."

Madeline wanted to scream at him that he was out of his mind, but she resisted, wondering if she should set up a meeting. Maybe it would be the best chance they would have to catch him. She was smart enough to know she should not agree too readily, so she said, "You can't be serious. You must think I'm even dumber than I acted in the parking lot that day."

Donny's tone changed. "Actually, Madeline, I do want to be serious for a minute. I've been in this game a long time, and I've seen too much. Now that the cops have my picture, I realize I'm in serious trouble. I want to make a deal. I want you to tell the FBI and whoever else needs to hear it that I'll turn myself in, and I'll give them everything they need to put a lot of important people away for life, if they'll give me immunity. If I can walk, they can have every-body else."

Madeline was stunned. *Could he really be serious?*

"I'm not sure I believe you," Madeline said. "Even if I did, I'm not sure I would support that deal, and I sure as hell can't speak for the authorities."

"I get that, Madeline. I do. But carry the message to them. I'll call you back tomorrow, same time, and you can let me know what they say."

"Why me? Can't you just talk to them directly?"

"I could, but I don't want to. I want you as my intermediary. I'll call you tomorrow."

And with that, he was gone.

Billy walked up to her desk, his phone to his ear. He said, "I couldn't get Rich. Dan Rooney is on the phone. He started a trace, but he doesn't think he got anything."

"Give me your phone," Madeline said, then related to Rooney what Donny had said.

"Well I'll be a frog on fire," Rooney said. "I didn't see that coming. Okay, I'll get on the horn to as many players as I can. This is gonna be a mess, you know, with all these different jurisdictions involved. Jeez, if we have to ask prosecutors from multiple counties in multiple states to say yea or nay to a deal... Jeez, this is gonna be a mess."

Madeline could tell Rooney was talking to himself more than to her.

He said, "Sit tight. We'll be in touch."

Ben walked into the newsroom a few minutes later. He came straight to her desk and suggested she and Billy join him in his office. Once seated, Madeline and Billy related what had just happened, then Madeline played the ad hoc recording. The sound quality was terrible, but it was possible to hear both sides of the conversation. Ben was as amazed as everyone else. He pushed his speakerphone button to get a dial tone and called Tony's cell. When Tony answered, they could hear the highway noise in the background. Ben asked Madeline and Billy to repeat for Tony what they had told him.

"Holy mother," Tony said. "Do you believe him?"

"I don't know," Madeline said. "I don't really know him at all. He's clearly been acting throughout both conversations. It's hard to believe the contrite Donny is any more real than the smug Donny or the hero Donny. Regardless, it doesn't matter what I think. My best guess is the prosecutors from the three states will meet by phone or Zoom this afternoon, and they'll put together some kind of offer. It might not be full immunity, but I think they'll want to tempt him with something generous."

Tony said, "Makes sense, if they can even find everyone fast enough to put a call together. I feel badly for you, Madeline, getting stuck in the middle of it."

"I don't mind. It will make a better story." She tried to sound upbeat, but she was dreading talking to Donny again.

Tony asked, "Madeline, or Ben, do you want me to come back there?"

Ben said, "No, Tony. There's nothing you can do here. Madeline has it covered. We'll be careful, and you do the same."

"Will do," Tony said, trying to think of a way to say something personal to Madeline without giving away too much to the others in the room. He quickly decided he would call Madeline separately later, and simply said, "Good luck."

In the end, Madeline was right. The prosecutors from nine different jurisdictions somehow managed to construct an offer for Donny that afternoon. It was lengthy and complex and filled with contingencies. For example, if Donny had personally been involved in raping any girls, the offer was less generous. The same was true, only more so, if the evidence indicated he had actually killed anyone.

Rich Davis and the local county attorney brought the written document to Madeline after dinner that evening. She was still in the newsroom. As they walked her through it, the pit in her stomach grew into a chasm. They really were offering to reduce the charges and sentences for a man who had lured, in all probability, dozens of girls —maybe hundreds—into a life of slavery, drug addiction, and sexual abuse. She understood the logic of it. Going easy on Donny could be justified if it led to the convictions of many others whose crimes were equally bad or worse. Just because she understood it didn't mean she had to like it.

Chapter 16

Tony arrived in Kansas City at lunch time. He went in search of a hotel downtown, and found a Hampton Inn that was affordable and seemed well-kept. He then went in search of Kansas City barbeque, which he believed to be the best in the world. He found one of the tiny hole-in-the-wall places where the aroma grabs and hog-ties your taste buds as soon as you walk in the door. The servers behind the counter were speckled with sauce, and their arms looked like they had been immersed in it.

They threw a rack of ribs, a ladle full of beans, and some fries onto his plate without comment, and turned to the next person waiting in line for a serving of heaven. When Tony finished eating, he was stuffed to the point of being in serious pain. *It was worth it*, he thought, smiling.

He drove back to his hotel and spent the afternoon searching the web for information about high-rise apartment buildings in the city. Of course, he also had to consider condos. He doubted if Emily really knew in which type of unit she had been held. Using the description Emily had provided—bedroom with windows on two sides high enough to look over the tops of other buildings, an underground garage, and at least one private elevator—Tony identified two buildings that fit all the criteria, and another five that could be added to the list if they had private elevators that simply weren't mentioned on their websites.

He didn't have much of a game plan, but thought he would start by driving past the buildings on the list and stopping to walk around the two he knew for certain had private elevators to penthouse suites. He didn't expect to see any neon signs announcing "Evil Bastard Lives Here" or anything else that would help, but he had to start somewhere. He also knew that six of the seven buildings had full-time door attendants. An attendant almost certainly would know more than anyone else about what went on inside his or her building. If he could get that person to talk to him, he might get a hint of something helpful.

Tony decided to start out on foot after realizing two of the buildings, including one of the two primary targets, were within ten blocks of his hotel. It was chilly, so he wore his quilted down jacket and black leather gloves. Underneath was his favorite V-neck sweater. Blue jeans and tennis shoes completed the college-boy-wannabe look.

The first building was older, and Tony immediately dismissed it. He knew his prejudices were at work, and he may have to come back to it, but he didn't believe the type of person he was looking for would live there. The building looked as though it were home to rich widows and other elderly people. Tony believed Rich Guy thought of himself as a player and would live in something that looked more hip, more like a bachelor pad. Or not, Tony thought grimly, knowing he really had no idea what the inside of the building and its units looked like, or for that matter what went on inside the head of someone who would imprison a twelve-year-old girl. Standing outside in the cold, he realized how daunting his task was and felt his enthusiasm waning. He put his head down and kept going.

The second building was exactly what Tony had envisioned as he had listened to Emily describe her ordeal—tall, modern, and elegant, with beautiful landscaping and an underground garage entry on one side. The penthouse was obvious, not only because it occupied the top floor, but because it had more windows and bigger balconies than the other floors. Tony wished he had asked Emily more questions about things that could be spotted from outside, such as the type of balcony or the shapes of the windows or the heights of the ceilings. He put building two down as a strong possibility.

He walked back to his hotel, got into his car, and drove to Country Club Plaza, the famous open-air mall in Kansas City that featured many upscale stores, restaurants, hotels, and apartments. When he arrived at the third building on his list, his heart sank. It was an equally strong contender, with all the same features as the second building he had observed downtown. He knew from his online research that this building had condos in it that sold for more than $1 million each. If the man was truly rich and wanted to get out of downtown, this would be a great area in which to live. Country Club Plaza also attracted a lot of tourists and out-of-town shoppers. Bringing strangers to his condo might be less noticed here.

Tony knew he was grasping at straws. He really had no better idea of where to look than before he had started. It was getting dark, and he decided to park and grab a drink at the steakhouse on the corner.

He sat at the bar, not wanting to take up a table in the dining room when he wasn't planning to eat. The bar was busy but well-staffed, so Tony struck up a conversation with the woman making drinks in front of him.

"I haven't been down here in a while. It looks like the Plaza is doing pretty well."

The blonde bartender was in her twenties and pretty, with a large chest to match her stocky frame. She looked like a softball player or weightlifter, fit but not lean. Tony thought she probably assumed he was flirting with her. She didn't seem to mind.

"Yep," she said. "This place is always crazy busy. Best job I ever had. The time goes fast, and if I talk nice to guys like you, I get giant tips." She winked at him. Tony hadn't seen a wink from a woman in a long time.

"Well, don't get your hopes up," he said with a laugh. "Most of your customers probably have money. I'm only here because I'm on my boss's expense account, and he doesn't reimburse for big tips, no matter how attractive the bartender is."

The comment drew another big smile and wink. She stepped away to use the blender, then returned to pour IPAs from the taps.

"Speaking of money," Tony said, "I noticed that penthouse on top of the building down the street. Whoever lives there must be loaded. I'll bet that place cost him a million bucks."

She glanced toward the window, in the right direction, but of course, she couldn't actually see it. "I wouldn't know what it cost, but I can tell you the old lady who lives there doesn't tip worth a damn."

"Really? An old lady?"

"Yeah, they say her husband was some kind of hot-shot financial broker back in the day. He died a long time ago, and she's lived up there alone ever since. She comes in here once a month or so with another woman, probably her daughter. She always picks up the check, but then she calculates a twelve percent tip, and that's it."

Tony laughed.

"I mean it!" The bartender continued to work as she spoke,

wiping down the bar with a wet towel. "She takes a pen and pad of paper out of her purse and does the calculation by hand. The waiters and I laugh about it, but the truth is, it's irritating as hell. Why is it the richest people are always the stingiest?"

"I wouldn't know, sadly," Tony quipped. "Is it universally true? There must be exceptions."

She grinned and said, "Well, sure. The exceptions are the men who want to get into my pants. Everett gave me twenty-dollar tips for seven-dollar drinks for months until he finally realized I wasn't going to go home with him."

"Everett?"

"Yeah. He's some kind of wheeler-dealer in the high-tech world. He has a penthouse even bigger than the one down the street. It's near here, but on the other side of the Plaza, up the hill. He thinks every woman should want to have sex in a place like that. Don't get me wrong, I wouldn't mind waking up in a luxury suite with a two-thousand-dollar bottle of champagne by the bed, a hot tub as big as my bathroom at home, and a private elevator, but I'd prefer it be with a man who's, you know, attractive."

Tony stared at her. The "private elevator" comment had jumped at him like a cobra strike. He tried to keep his expression neutral as he said, "Really, a private elevator? That sounds pretty cool. This guy must be a real dog if his money and his home haven't convinced you to give it a try."

"Well, I don't care about looks all that much," she said, a little defensively, "but he's just so obvious, you know? He's pushy and clearly just wants a female, any female, to do him. That's not for me."

"Everett, huh? I'll have to be careful not to come in here with him for dinner. I wouldn't want you putting me in the same category as him."

"Trust me, honey, you are the polar opposite of him." She

leaned up against the beer taps, the mounds in her blouse obscuring one of the labels, and said, "I've sent you all kinds of signals that I might be interested, and you've barely noticed. You're cute, but I can tell you're going to disappoint me."

Tony smiled, genuinely flattered. "I think you're lovely, Brenda," he said, reading the name from her tag, "and really fun to talk to. The problem is, I'm sorta seeing someone."

"Ah, just my luck," she said with a sigh. "I didn't see a ring, so I assumed you were fair game."

"No, sorry," he said. He tried to get back on track. "What is this building that's even nicer than the one I spotted when I parked? I might want to walk past there and see if any money falls from one of the balconies."

Brenda was instantly wary. Her tone shifted, and Tony realized she had been around enough to know when she was being played.

"I'm sorry. I probably said too much already. With my luck, you'll turn out to be some kind of con man or cat burglar or something. I shouldn't be gossiping about other people anyway. It's not like me, and it's not good for business."

Tony put on a wounded expression. "Brenda, believe me, I am an honest, upstanding citizen. You don't have to worry about what you share with me. I'm just a guy who's trying to make it big, like everyone else. Stories of the rich and famous—especially the rich— get my attention. I'd love to get Everett's full name so I could Google him and see how he makes all that money."

"Sorry, honey. I believe you, but I think I'll let you get any additional information from someone else. I want to have some self-respect left when my shift is over."

"No problem," Tony said. He offered a smile while his insides churned with frustration. He was dying to ask Brenda if Everett had a weird birthmark at the base of his neck, but couldn't imagine how to broach the subject without proving himself a liar.

"Hey," Brenda said suddenly and with a new upbeat tone, "I still won't tell you his name, but if you want to see what he looks like, I think that's him in the red Corvette at the stop light."

She nodded toward the front door, and Tony whipped around to look. A new, shiny Corvette was indeed waiting for the light to change.

Tony turned back to Brenda. "Are you serious?"

"Can't be sure," she said, "but I know he has a car like that. He pays the valet kids big bucks to leave it in front when he eats here. He doesn't want them driving it."

By the time she had finished speaking, Tony had pulled forty dollars from his wallet, slapped it on the bar, and headed out the door.

"Hey!" she called after him. "What the hell?"

Tony jogged down to the corner as the Corvette pulled away. He only caught a glimpse of the driver, but the impression left by the silhouette was that of a fleshy adult male. He pulled out his phone and took a picture of the back of the car as it moved down the block.

He immediately texted the picture to Rich Davis, with a caption. "I may have found him. Can you run this plate?"

A moment later, a thumbs-up emoji came back.

***

Thirty minutes later, Tony was back in his hotel room, asking Google all about Everett Caulder, age 48, of Kansas City, Missouri. It hadn't taken Davis long to provide the basics. Fortunately, Caulder was well known to the Internet. Numerous articles about his business successes appeared, some with his picture. Some pictures matched Emily's description. In others, Caulder was younger or appeared thinner. Tony could easily imagine a rich man making efforts to have newspapers and magazines use pictures of him that were taken when he was younger or were even doctored to make him look more attractive.

Caulder was an electrical engineer. He had founded a company that made component parts for computers, such as the transformers that converted 110-volt AC into useable levels of direct current. Eventually, his firm had become a major supplier of power systems for server farms. As companies like Facebook, Google, Apple, Microsoft, and others stored more and more data about and for people all over the world, and expanded into cloud-based services, their needs for gigantic server farms had grown exponentially, and were growing still. Caulder had caught that wave and now was considered one of the wealthiest men in the Midwest. In one article in *Forbes*, an industry expert estimated Caulder's personal wealth at nearly three billion dollars.

Tony whistled. That would buy a lot of condos and Corvettes. The information also made sense of what Emily had shared about the conversations she had overheard. Tony was no expert, but he knew enough about electronics to know that components were often "pressure tested." A quick online search revealed the term "folding frequencies" was also used, along with others Emily had mentioned.

This was the guy; Tony was sure of it. He was impressed with himself, at how quickly he had found him. Then, in thinking about it, he was forced to admit he hadn't done anything but strike up a conversation with a pretty barmaid. Dumb luck had found Everett Caulder, nothing else.

At 10 p.m., Tony climbed into bed and turned out the light. He knew he would have trouble going to sleep, but he was determined to try. Tomorrow could be a very big day, and he wanted to be rested and ready. He spent time in the dark pondering a variety of next steps and finally dozed off.

***

About the same time, Caulder was on the telephone with Ray. He was horny and frustrated, and now he was growing angry as Ray was telling him he couldn't have a girl for a while.

"What does a while mean?" Caulder asked, the irritation dripping from his tone.

"I'm not sure," Ray said. "I'm sorry, Mr. Caulder, but the authorities are snooping around, and we need to lie low for a short time."

"I know, I know. They got Donny's picture... Well, not his picture, but you know, that sketch in the papers. Well, fine. Use someone else. And do it now, 'cause I don't wanna lie low." Caulder sneered. "I want to deflower someone. Someone young and cute. That's your specialty, isn't it?"

"Yes," Ray replied tersely. He despised the thought of telling one of his best clients that the police had found one of the girls he had held captive and raped. Ray had gotten the call earlier in the evening from his source, telling him that the Harrington kid had found and talked to Emily. How that had happened, he didn't know. But the situation was becoming dire.

Caulder was still harping on the phone, and Ray finally barked, "Shut up!" The line went silent. Ray cursed to himself. He was sure no one had said a harsh word to Caulder in a long time.

"I'm sorry, Mr. Caulder, but you need to understand something. There's a newspaper reporter who's on this story and won't let go. He's in Kansas City right now, looking for you. So you need to stand down and lie low, like I said."

"Looking for me? Looking for *me?* Why you...You cocksucker! How could he be looking for me?"

"Don't come unglued," Ray said. "He's heard there's a rich guy in KC who's been a client. He's down there snooping around. He doesn't know your name or anything. We just want to be careful. Please."

Caulder was trying to relax but failing. KC was a big city, but not that big. If enough questions were asked in the right places, it was pretty easy to imagine his name coming up.

"Wait a minute," he said suddenly. "What's this prick look like?"

Ray described Tony and pointed out that Caulder could find his picture online in about two seconds. "Why do you ask?"

"Hang on," Caulder said, walking over to the coffee table. He picked up his Huawei MediaPad and typed Tony's name into the search engine. "Well, fuck me," he said to himself. Then to Ray, he barked, "Listen, you stupid ass. I saw this guy tonight. He came running out of a restaurant in Country Club Plaza as I drove by. I thought he was staring at my car, and didn't think much about it. A lot of guys stare at my car. But now... Jesus! This guy is on to me. You moron! You said no comebacks. I paid you a fortune to be sure there would be no comebacks!"

The news about Tony's behavior in KC was as disturbing to Ray as it was to Caulder. Could Harrington really be on to Caulder? If he was, that could end everything. Ray decided quickly and spoke just as fast.

"Okay, relax. We can handle this if we work together. Here's what we're going to do. If he shows up again, or if he contacts you in any way, you..." Ray described his plan quickly. It was simple and, if successful, permanent.

"This better work," Caulder said. "And it better be the end of our troubles. I'm sitting on top of the freakin' world here, and I'm not losing everything because you can't run a covert operation."

Ray's face flushed red as Caulder talked. He thought, *I*

want to kill this jerk. Unfortunately, I need him, at least for now. Maybe I will kill him, but later, after we've taken care of Mr. Tony Harrington.

Chapter 17

At 8 a.m., Tony's cell phone blared "Good Day Sunshine" by the Beatles. He was already up and dressed and answered it quickly. Seeing the display said "Rich Davis" Tony's greeting was, "Hey, it's not three in the morning. See? You *can* call at a normal hour if you just try."

"Very funny," Davis said. "So tell me about Everett Caulder. Why the interest?"

Tony explained his brief search and the lucky conversation that had pointed him toward Caulder.

"So this guy just happened to drive past when you were talking about him?"

"Well, I'd love to tell you my extraordinary investigative skills led me to him, but yeah, it was luck."

"Jeez, Tony, go buy a lottery ticket," Davis said. "You are unbelievable."

"Well, we don't know it's him, of course. All we really know is that he's the right body type and lives in the right kind of place.

We could be barking up the wrong tree."

Davis was quiet a moment, then he said, "No. Remember the telephone comments too. Emily's captor was in the electronics business. No, my gut tells me this is the guy."

"Mine too. Now I just have to make sure."

"Hold on, Tony. Remember your promise," Davis said quickly. "You don't do anything more until we do some research and get a team assembled."

"That would be fine with me," Tony said, "but do you have enough to go on? You know, to call out the troops and get a warrant and all?"

Davis hesitated. "Well..."

"That's what I thought. Give me another day to dig around and see what I can get. When I have enough for you to get a warrant, we should have no trouble getting what we need from his phone records or DNA from his bedroom or whatever."

"Dammit, Tony, you're taking too many risks. If you've seen him, he may have seen you. If he gets even a hint that you're looking at him, you could be in real trouble. Think of what he has at stake."

"Rich, I promise, I'll be careful. I'll just talk to a few more people who might know him, or know of him, and see what I turn up. Meanwhile, if you want to start getting people assembled and looking for a friendly judge, I'm all for that."

Davis finally conceded, but urged him to tread lightly and watch his back every minute.

"I promise," Tony said, ending the call.

In fact, there was only one person Tony wanted to talk to before the proverbial shit hit the fan: the door attendant. Tony was convinced the person who watched everyone come and go all day long, who monitored the security screens and received the mail, would be a wealth of information, not only for the investigation, but for the newspaper article that would follow. Tony wanted to get to him first, before he was spooked by a swarm of armed officers and agents and eventually national media.

The simple truth was, Tony couldn't stop. Every time he thought about Brittany or Shelly or Emily, he became obsessed with pressing forward.

Girls are being locked up and abused, forced into a life of slavery. Some are being killed! How can I not push hard?

Something about that last thought caused an itch at the back of his brain. *What is it about girls locked in cellars? What am I missing?* Then it hit him. He pulled his cell out of his pocket and called Ben.

"Hey, Tony. What's up?"

Tony laughed out loud. "I have another assignment for my boss." Ben joined in on the laughter, but Tony felt obligated to be clear. "Obviously, I'm joking. I have a very respectful request, or maybe just a suggestion. It's a complete long-shot, but we keep saying we want to look at everything."

"No need to explain, Tony. What've you got?"

"I've been thinking about Emily's comment, about some girls being sold to owners who hold them in basements. As we've discussed, if a person is holding another person captive in his or her home, there should be some clues about that. Somebody should notice when the guy—you know, the bad guy—is suddenly buying more supplies or food."

"Right," Ben said. "The DCI guys have told everyone to be watching for that. But when we're dealing with three states, where do you even begin to look?"

"Well, that's what hit me," Tony said. "Brittany's body was found in Quincy County. Our agent friends think she probably was held and killed near her burial spot."

"So we should be asking around here," Ben said, seeing where

Tony's logic was headed.

"Yes, and I'm calling because I know where you can start. Madeline and I ate at Pizza Hut on Saturday afternoon. Maggie, the day manager there, told us about someone named Langly who has been buying a lot of food at the drive-through next door, even though he's supposedly on a diet."

"Well, lots of people..." Ben started, but Tony cut him off.

"I know. I already said this is a long shot. But it can't hurt to take a closer look at him. He's single, he lives in the country and he's buying extra food. I think this could be worth our, uh, your time."

"I guess I can't argue with that," Ben said. I'll try to find out more about him in the next couple of days, while you're still nosing around in KC."

"Thanks, boss. I appreciate it. Now it's my turn to say 'be careful.' On the outside chance this guy is involved somehow, messing with him will be plenty dangerous."

"Tony-y-y..." Ben said in a warning tone.

"Sorry, boss. I'm doing it again, aren't I? Trying to tell the smarter, more experienced guy what to do. I'll shut up now and go to work."

After a continental breakfast in the hotel lobby, Tony headed over to the high-rise, which he had since learned was called "Caulder Place." *I could have saved someone the trouble of running the license plate number if I had just looked up the building name,* he thought.

He parked a block away and walked, giving him time to survey the building in the daylight. It was after 9 a.m. when he crossed an outdoor courtyard and went through the revolving doors into the lobby. The room was designed to impress, and it succeeded. The ceiling was thirty feet above his head and covered in tiny LED lights. The floors were stone, some kind of slate or rough granite. The front wall was all glass, and the back wall appeared to be walnut, stained dark.

As he had expected and hoped, only one person was there, behind a marble countertop. The man wore a blue uniform, looking more like a security guard than a traditional doorman. He was tall and solid, with thin hair turning gray at the edges. *Retired cop or military*, Tony assumed. *Probably bored to tears. Maybe he'll appreciate a chance to talk.*

"May I help you, sir?"

"Well, I hope so," Tony said, extending his hand and shaking the big man's calloused paw. "To be honest, I'm a newspaper reporter working on a story about Mr. Caulder. I know lots of stories have been done about him already, so I thought maybe you would be willing to tell me a little bit about him. You know, to give an up-close, personal side to the story."

"Well, sir, you know I shouldn't do that. I could get fired for talking about one of our residents, especially the one who owns the building."

"We don't have to use your name. Your involvement can be completely anonymous. Perhaps you could just share a few little tidbits?"

"You swear?" The guard pressed.

"I swear. I will never reveal you as a source."

"Okay, to be honest, I never liked that little jerk. I'd like to see someone knock him down a peg."

Tony's heart raced, and the guard glanced around. He said, "Let's get out of the front lobby. It's a little too public here."

The guard turned to his right, walked past the end of the counter, pushed open a door to allow Tony to enter the area behind it, then turned into a door on the other side that led to an office behind the wall. Tony followed. As soon as they were in the office with the door closed, the guard reached over and touched a button on the phone. A man's voice answered. "Yes?"

"Sorry to bother you, sir," the guard said, "but I believe I have Mr. Harrington here with me in the office."

Oh, shit, Tony thought, backing up a step. He stopped when the guard turned back to face him. The guard was holding a .357 automatic. Tony knew what it was, now that he was a handgun "expert."

"Bring him right up," the voice said, hanging up the phone.

Tony swallowed hard, trying to figure out where he had gone wrong and, more importantly, how to get out of the building immediately.

The guard waved the gun and said, "Turn around and put your hands behind your back."

"You can't... No, I..." Tony stammered.

"Just do it, dumbass," the guard said. "I'm just as happy bashing your head in with this," he waved the gun again, "and carrying you to the elevator over my shoulder. So do you want to be awake or in a coma when you meet Mr. Caulder? It's up to you."

Tony turned around and felt plastic handcuffs being pulled tight to his wrists. One mistake he had made was immediately apparent. It hadn't occurred to him that the doorman would be Caulder's employee and loyal to him. It should have been obvious, and Tony was angry with himself for not thinking it through.

The remaining question was tougher to crack. Based on the brief exchange on the office phone, it was obvious Caulder had expected him. *How is that possible? Was he tipped off? Did that barmaid, Brenda, tell him? She seemed worried I might be some kind of criminal. Or maybe it occurred to her that doing a favor for a billionaire might be advantageous. Or the Chicago guy, Ray, said he had inside sources. Is someone at the FBI or DCI tipping him off?*

Tony had to face the fact that the authorities might be compromised. *With the kind of money involved, and with officers and agents from three states getting updates, the leak could be anywhere.* Tony trusted Davis completely, but he wondered how many other people up the chain of command and across jurisdictions were getting information.

As the guard marched him into the service elevator from the inside hallway behind the office and hit the button for the penthouse, Tony realized all his musings could be moot. Considering what they had done to an innocent twelve-year-old girl, there would be no limits on what they would do to him if they felt it necessary.

The doors opened, and the guard shoved Tony into a storeroom, the fanciest storeroom Tony had ever seen. No, not a storeroom, a pantry. The service elevator led to the condo's huge walk-in pantry. Tony didn't have time to look around. The guard prodded him with the nose of the automatic, saying, "In there. Move it."

Tony walked into and through the kitchen. Double doors led into a huge great room with a vaulted ceiling. Caulder sat on a large leather chair angled toward the window. He was nursing a drink and enjoying the sunshine on his face.

"Welcome, Mr. Harrington. We've been expecting you."

"That's interesting," Tony replied, trying to sound brave. *Isn't that what all the super-spies do, when bound in handcuffs and facing the villain?* "I have to admit I wasn't expecting to meet you today."

"No worries," Caulder said. "You're not staying long. I just wanted a chance to see your face when you realized how stupid you are. Our mutual friend in Chicago, the one we lovingly call Ray, has given me very specific instructions about what to do with you. You won't die today. I think he has a special treat waiting for you first. But trust me, you will die. I guess I would be wasting my breath to tell you to stay the hell out of my business. You're gonna be staying out of everyone's business, forever, beginning very soon."

"Mr. Caulder, you may want to think about that." Tony was struggling to keep it together. "There are people who know I'm here."

"That may be," Caulder said, his tone indicating a total lack of concern. "But when they show up looking for you, I'll simply acknowledge you came by, tried to question my security guard, and left when he had integrity enough to refuse to talk. There will be zero evidence you ever came up here or that we ever had a talk."

Tony was at a loss. His mind swirled and his "fight or flight" instinct was dialed all the way to "flight." Unfortunately, the big man with the big gun standing behind him was not going to let that happen.

Caulder looked up at the guard from his drink. "Let's have one just for fun, then get him to his final destination."

Tony braced for it, but it didn't help. The guard spun him around and, in one motion, buried his right fist in Tony's stomach. Tony collapsed to the floor, needing to scream but unable to muster the air to do it. *Why is it always the stomach?*

The guard simply asked, "Again?"

"No, we're done here," Caulder said. "Get him out of here."

Tony saw the guard remove a syringe from his pocket and felt him plunge the needle into his neck. Then the room spun and faded into darkness.

Chapter 18

Madeline's office phone rang right on schedule Monday morning. Rich Davis, Dan Rooney, Ben, Billy, Sheriff Mackey, and Agent Tabors all were there. Tabors had brought a slightly more sophisticated recording device for the phone.

"Mueller," Madeline said simply.

"Madeline, please, tell me we're on a first-name basis," Donny's chipper voice said.

"Up yours, Donny. We have what you want. How do we get it to you?"

"Wonderful," he said. "I assume by 'we' you mean the FBI and DCI people gathered with you there this morning? No need to confirm or deny. I'm not stupid, and I know they're listening. It's good actually. Then they can all hear this at the same time. I want to meet with you, Madeline. No one else. We'll pick a public place in Des Moines, somewhere you'll be safe. You can even pick the spot if you want. But you leave your pals behind and come alone."

"Donny, you know that's not going to happen. You have years

of experience tricking girls into your various traps. I'm not going to fall for it, and even if I was willing, these 'pals' you mentioned aren't going to allow it."

"Sorry, Madeline, but that's the deal. I trust you to not be armed and to not attack me while I look at the offer. If it's acceptable, you can call your friends to come get me. If it's not, I'll at least have a chance to get away before they arrive. So, the bottom line is, if you want the names and details of an entire operation of sex traffickers and drug dealers operating in more than the four states you know about, then we do this my way. If you can't promise that, I'll just disappear. I have enough money to go very far away for a very long time."

Tabors held a note in front of her that read, "Promise him anything to get him there."

"Give me a minute," she said into the phone, then hit the hold button.

She turned to the men gathered by her desk. "He's not going to buy this. No way. I don't even understand why he's asking."

"You never know," Tabors said. "If he's desperate, he may want to believe it. And he's met you and thinks he can trust you. Give it a shot."

Madeline waited several moments, collected herself, and pressed the button to release the hold. "Okay, Donny. We've been talking about it, and I think I've convinced these gorillas to back off. They suggested we meet on Capitol Hill in Des Moines. The Legislature's not in session in October, so there won't be many people around, but it's public enough, and protected enough, that I'll be safe. Also, if you need to get away, there are roads leading away from there in every direction."

"Hmmm, you make a good case, Madeline. Excellent! I agree. Shall we say tonight at midnight?"

"Midnight?" Madeline was taken aback. Of course, that would make perfect sense from Donny's standpoint. The hour would reduce the number of people in the area to almost zero, and the darkness would provide another measure of cover if he had to run. She looked at Davis, then at the Tabors. Both men nodded in agreement.

"Midnight, on the east steps of the Iowa Capitol. I'll be there," she said curtly, then hung up the phone.

Tabors smiled and said, "That was pretty quick thinking for a media hack."

"Yeah, well, I don't want to do this at all. I'm trusting you people to have me covered every minute."

"We will," Tabors said. "This will be a full tactical operation. You'll never know we're there, but if he makes one wrong move, he'll find himself trying to reassemble pieces of his brain."

"Sniper?" Billy asked.

"That, and a lot more," Tabors said.

Ben said, "Madeline, you don't have to do this. Your job description does not include putting yourself at the center of a police operation."

She shook her head. "As I said before, I'm all in. We have to find and stop these people. I don't like it, but I have to do this."

Ben said he understood, adding, "I don't like it either, but I agree it may be the best chance we get." Everyone in the room seemed to pause and take a deep breath.

Ben broke the silence. "Okay, Madeline. You've done enough for now. Take the rest of the day off. You'll need to leave for Des Moines at nine or so, just to give yourself some margin in case you run into road construction or car trouble."

Sheriff Mackey spoke up for the first time. "I'm gonna assign a deputy to Miss Mueller for the rest of today, just to be sure she's safe until she gets to Des Moines."

"Thanks, Sheriff," Ben said. He turned to the others and said, "Rich, Agent Tabors, I trust you'll have everyone in place by 11, so if she gets there early, there's no risk."

Both agents nodded. Davis said, "Madeline, I'll position myself at the rest stop on I-35 near Ankeny. Pull in there as you head into Des Moines. You can drop off the deputy and then make sure I get on your tail as you leave. I'll follow you into Capitol Hill in case he's planning an ambush before you get to your destination."

Madeline shivered. The discussion of precautions only served to make her more anxious about the risks. She managed a weak smile as she said thanks to everyone, and headed out the door. Deputy Tim Jebron followed closely behind.

Madeline spoke to the deputy only enough to get his name and reiterate her appreciation. She was in no mood to talk. She was in a total funk. She didn't really want the afternoon off. She didn't know what she could do that would take her mind off of what was coming. She didn't really want to stay at work either. As she started her car and waited for the deputy to climb into the passenger seat, she took a deep breath and consciously acknowledged she was frightened. Deeply, completely scared to her core.

She also was confused. She knew Donny wouldn't walk into a trap like this, so what was he up to really? *We'll know soon enough, I guess*, she thought, as she decided to grab a burger and stop at the supercenter at the edge of town to pick up some groceries and other things for her apartment. *Too bad we don't have a gun shop in Orney. I wouldn't mind putting a bullet in Donny's brain myself. Maybe this nice officer will loan me his gun.* She knew she didn't mean it, but she didn't mind fantasizing about it.

***

When Madeline left the store, she immediately wished she had zipped up her jacket. Clouds had rolled in, and a stiff breeze from the northwest made the chilly October air feel downright cold. She threw the two plastic bags into the back seat, and climbed into the front. Deputy Jebron was with her every step of the way. He had apologized for not carrying her bags, but said he preferred to keep his hands free.

Madeline turned to him in the car and said, "No apology is necessary. You do whatever it takes to keep me safe."

The deputy simply nodded. Madeline started the car and headed home. The gloomy weather somehow seemed perfectly suited for the task she faced.

She pulled into the parking lot behind her apartment building, and saw leaves blowing across the surface. Madeline's thoughts were coming at her from all directions, another indication of her state of mind. She couldn't seem to stay focused on any one topic. The weather made her think of how fortunate she was to have an apartment with a garage, which made her think of her landlord, who was a stereotypical kindly old man, except he was lazy and never raked the leaves in the fall, which made her think of the fall foliage, which was going to be gone too quickly if the cold and the wind kept up, which made her think of the bike path through the timberland west of town, which made her think of exercise, which she hadn't been getting lately, which made her think of her bad haircut, which made her think of Donny again. *I feel like I'm playing mental Whack-a-Mole.*

She pulled into her garage, gathered the groceries from the back seat, walked through a vestibule into the apartment building, and climbed one flight of stairs to number 204.

Jebron said, "Let me get the door."

"Fine. The keys are in my right coat pocket."

He fished them out and unlocked the door, as she held the shopping bags. The deputy pushed the door open, reached around the jamb, and found the switch to turn on the ceiling light.

He said, "Okay, Ms. Mueller, after you." Madeline stepped inside, walking briskly toward the kitchen counter. The deputy followed more slowly, intending to secure the door before checking the apartment. As he turned, he only had time to register bewilderment before the man behind the door smashed the side of his skull with the butt of a handgun. Three things then happened rapidly, almost simultaneously. The deputy collapsed to the floor, his attacker kicked the door shut, and Madeline spun around. At the sight of the man she shrieked and dropped her bags.

Madeline managed to sputter, "What? Who? Get out of my house!"

The man raised a gun and pointed it at her face. He had short, red hair and a red goatee. "Shut up, Madeline," he said. "If you yell again, I will end your life."

Madeline began shaking. She could feel her knees weaken, and she was afraid she was going to pass out. The gun had a big, black tube on the end of the barrel. Madeline had watched enough TV to know this was a silencer. The man behind the gun was Donny.

"Why are you here?" she stammered, backing up against the counter.

Donny walked toward her. In his hand, the cannon with the black silencer glistened and never wavered. "Madeline, please. You're not stupid," he said. "You knew that setup in Des Moines couldn't be real. Certainly *I'm* not that stupid."

"Please, get out of my apartment," she whimpered. "You need to go. Agent Davis is on his way here now, and I don't want to get in the middle of a fight between the two of you."

Donny glanced at the deputy on the floor and smiled. It was

that wide, boyish, dimpled smile. What had once looked charming now looked demonic. "That was pretty quick, sweetheart," he said, "but as you can see, I'm not too worried about any heroes they send to protect you. I also happen to know that Agent Davis, and Agent Rooney, and Agent Tabors, and all your other pals are on their way to Des Moines right now to get ready for your, and my, grand appearances later tonight. Won't they be surprised when no one shows up?"

It was more of a statement than a question. Still shaking, Madeline slid down the side of the cabinet to the floor, realizing how easily they all had been fooled. Donny had set up the meeting only for the purpose of getting the cavalry out of town. He had been here all along, waiting to get her alone. She started to cry as she imagined the horrors she was about to endure. Through her tears, she whispered, "Please... Donny... Please go."

"I am going," he said, "as soon as it's dark. And you're coming with me. Now put these on." He dropped a pair of handcuffs onto the floor in front of her. "Behind your back, now, and don't make another sound. I'll gag you if I need to. I think you know I would actually enjoy that, so be thankful I'm being kind."

Madeline did as instructed, her heart sinking lower with each click of the ratchets on her wrists. While she did so, Donny backed up and kicked the deputy in the stomach. Jebron didn't react. Satisfied the deputy was out cold, or dead, Donny returned to Madeline. He grabbed the collar of her coat with his free hand and lifted her up off the floor. He spun her around to check and tighten the handcuffs, then turned her back to face him.

He stroked her face. "Yes, I'm going to enjoy this."

Madeline shuddered but held her tongue.

"I know you liked me when we talked in Kansas City. You're going to like me again when I take you, because if you don't, then I'm going to make you do some things you really won't want to do."

He laughed. "You should be flattered. I've recruited a lot of girls, a lot of beautiful girls, a lot of beautiful *young* girls, some of them virgins. But you're the first one I've had trouble getting off my mind. You're the first one I've really wanted to... you know, fuck."

He cupped her breast in his hand. "I really want to right now, but unfortunately, Ray made me promise to wait. He wants to be there to watch. He's coming to Iowa on another errand anyway, so he said it's no trouble to stop by and enjoy the party. Ray's funny that way. He thinks he's a businessman, but he's a true sadist. Maybe a bigger one than me. He gets his jollies by watching women suffer. Doesn't seem to be interested in getting laid himself. He just wants to see you scream. You might want to remember that when I'm riding you."

Madeline's sobs grew, and she fought the urge to curl up into a ball on the floor. She dared not move. Donny pushed the silenced gun barrel hard into her abdomen, just below her rib cage.

With his other hand, Donny squeezed her breast harder. "Ray won't know if we just touch each other, right? Why don't you touch me, down there, right now. I'll even say please. Please turn around and use your hand to give me just a little rub down there. I promise you'll like what you find."

Madeline spit in his face. She didn't think about it, she just reacted.

Donny reacted as well, stepping back and suddenly swinging the gun, striking her across her left cheek, knocking her to the floor. She screamed as she hit, then he was on top of her, pushing the barrel of the gun into her mouth. She was terrified beyond all comprehension.

"Shut. Up. You. Bitch." He spat out each word forcefully.

Madeline was crying and trying to turn her head away. The silencer was choking her, and her panic was causing her to lurch even harder. Donny backed off and pulled the gun away. As Madeline gasped for air, he slapped her hard across the face with the other hand.

"Enough!"

She fought to control her sobs. Her arm hurt where she had fallen on it, her head was throbbing in unison with the sting in her face, and her throat hurt like hell.

She looked up at the ogre who was straddling her and saw a distinct shift in his expression. A switch had flipped in his mind.

"Let's go," he said, standing up. "Dark or not, it's time to get out of here."

Madeline felt a glimmer of hope. If he took her outside in the daylight, there was a chance someone would see them. Maybe there was some hope of surviving this. That glimmer was quickly extinguished when she saw him take a plastic case from his jacket pocket and remove a syringe from it. Before she could speak a word of protest, he plunged it into her neck. In seconds, the world went black.

***

Donny found a roll of duct tape in a kitchen drawer and spent some time binding and gagging the deputy. He then took the officer's gun, radio, and cell phone. He found Madeline's phone as well, and checked the apartment to be sure it had no traditional phones. If the deputy woke up, Donny wanted to be certain the man had no chance to call for help.

Donny left Madeline's apartment and walked the three blocks to the convenience store lot where he'd parked a rented Chevrolet Impala. He drove back to Madeline's apartment and backed up to her garage door, then he let himself into the vestibule with her key and stopped in the garage to punch open the door before heading up the stairs to her apartment. He was loving the adrenaline rush that came with the risk of being caught and the euphoria of success, of getting away with another kidnapping.

Ray had promised him a bonus for this one, if he succeeded in taking her without being seen. Donny hadn't confessed that he would have paid Ray for this. He wanted, no, he *needed* to show this bitch who was smarter, who was in control. He suspected she would be a fighter, which would only make his success more delicious, and the sex more satisfying.

Of course, having an audience would be weird. But if it made her hate the experience even more, he might learn to like it.

Inside the apartment, Donny pulled the small dining table over to the side, exposing a tan, oval area rug. He dragged Madeline onto it, and rolled her up inside, like rolling a big pancake around a sausage. *Yes, you're my little pig in a blanket*, he thought gleefully. The purpose of the rug, of course, was to ensure no one saw a body being removed from the building. The risk was small anyway, but this would make his success certain.

After carefully wiping every surface he had touched in the apartment, he bent down, lifted the bundle from the floor, and threw it up over his right shoulder. He aligned it so she, and it, could bend toward the ground in the front and back. No one could see, nor ever would guess, a woman was inside.

He stepped into the hall, turned and pulled the door shut with his left hand tucked inside his coat sleeve, and walked down the hall to the stairs. When he reached the garage, he walked past Madeline's car to the open garage door and touched the fob in his pocket. The trunk lid of his rented sedan popped open. He had no trouble maneuvering the rug into the gaping cavity. He smiled as he pushed the lid shut. He never would buy a daddy's car like this, but he could appreciate some of its features, like plenty of trunk space to hold a victim.

He remembered to step back into the garage and close the door, wiping the button clean as he did so. Then he exited through the vestibule, climbed into the Chevy, and headed out of town. He was glad he didn't have far to go. The excitement was fine, but getting a kidnapping victim out of his trunk sooner rather than later would be a relief.

***

Ben Smalley walked into the Pizza Hut around 3 p.m. Monday. He had chosen a time when Maggie would be there but wouldn't be too busy to talk. He was partially right. Maggie was there, but she was fully engaged in an argument with the beer truck driver. Apparently, the restaurant had run out of beer the previous Saturday night, and Maggie was letting the young man know in no uncertain terms the extent of his idiocy for failing to leave the proper number of kegs in the storeroom, and the magnitude of the offense. Apparently, it carried the potential for capital punishment because Maggie was threatening to kill him.

When she saw Ben standing inside the door, Maggie brought it down a couple of notches, but she continued to berate the delivery man until she had elicited a dozen apologies and twice that number of assurances it wouldn't happen again. Then the young driver scurried out the back, and Maggie came over to Ben.

"Sorry you had to get in on that. You know these kids. If you don't beat them over the head with it, they don't hear you." With a gesture and a smile, she directed Ben to a nearby table. "What can I get you?"

"Just grab me a cola, and one for yourself if you have a minute to chat," Ben suggested. Maggie looked at him quizzically, nodded, and returned with two glasses.

"Okay, Mr. Smalley. I've got time. Now what does the big city newspaper man want with little ol' me?"

Ben smiled. "In the first place, I haven't been a big city guy for a long time now. Secondly, I'm here because I need your help."

He explained that Tony had shared what Maggie had told him about someone named Langly. "Tony asked me to look into it while he's out of town. I thought I would start by getting what you told Tony from you directly. You know, that horse's mouth thing."

Maggie looked baffled. "Look into what exactly? Langly's diet? His obsession with eating crappy food? What exactly did I tell Tony that would be of any interest to the newspaper? That fact he buys junk food he says isn't for him?" She paused for a moment, then shouted, "Oh my God! You think he's involved with that girl who was murdered! You think all that extra food was for her! Oh my God, well... I guess... Well, sure, I could see..."

"Whoa," Ben said firmly, taking her arms and pulling her deeper into her seat. "Maggie, stop. Langly is almost certainly an innocent young man. At least innocent of abusing and killing girls. We're just checking out every report like this we hear. It's just routine. I promise."

Maggie looked skeptical, and Ben continued. "Maggie, you have to promise me this goes no further. You and I can't be party to ruining a young man's reputation just because he eats food from the wrong restaurant."

"Of course, but..."

"But nothing," Ben said, even more strongly. "Now please, tell me what you told Tony. Give me every detail as best you can remember it. Don't embellish to make him look guilty, or to make him look innocent for that matter. Just give me the facts."

Maggie's face grew red. "Okay, Mr. *Big City* Editor," she snorted, "I'll tell you, but I don't know why you'd accuse me of embellishing anything. Ask Tony. He'll tell you I'm no gossip, and when I share a story or two, I always stick to the facts."

Ben immediately realized his mistake. He quickly said, "I

believe you. I do. I'm sorry if I offended you." He sighed, irritated with himself while simultaneously wondering if he would ever shed his east coast mantle and be seen as just another Orney resident.

Maggie visibly relaxed and took a gulp of her soft drink. She then shared what she had seen, and it was just as Tony had related it. Ben pressed her to try to remember details, such as dates or time periods when the purchases began and ended, if they had, or additional insights into what or how much was purchased. All he learned that Tony hadn't known was that Maggie hadn't seen Langly in the drive-through at all in the past ten days or so. When she told Tony he had been in "just the other day," it was actually the previous week, and it probably had been a few days before that when she'd seen him last at the drive-through window. "I work hard, though," she said. "I may not see him every time he's there."

"Of course," Ben said with nod, wanting to roll his eyes. The similar time frames of Langly's last visit to the drive-through and Brittany's death intrigued him, but he dared not say anything about that to Maggie. He didn't want to trigger another rant. Unfortunately, she was quick enough and suspicious enough that she might make the connection later.

He finished by asking about Langly's companions on the day he made the dieting comments, or on other days.

"Well, he was in here with a coworker from the co-op on the day he lied about his diet," she said. "But usually he hangs out with Ed Grimsman. You probably know Ed. He's a little older than Langly, but they started golfing together on Men's Nights at the country club a few years ago, and they've become good friends. I think Ed still works for Anderson Construction, building barns and other farm buildings. They'll put him on a house framing sometimes, when they get the work in town. Ed's okay. He's divorced, but everyone says it was her. She got bored with small town life and took off to California or somewhere. Anyway, Ed's a good sport. The guys love to tease him about his name, you know, the similarity to that guy Martin Short does, Ed Grimsley? They'll put on that weird voice when they talk to him. He's unfortunate enough to look a little like the Grimsley character, so it's kinda mean. They think they're real comedians, but of course it's completely stupid. Anyway, Ed never seems to mind. He's about the most easygoing guy I ever saw."

Ben was listening in amazement. Maggie seemed to know everything about everyone. He made a mental note to use her as a future source for the paper, and to never share anything personal in front of her. He was afraid she might go on forever, so he cut her off to say thanks, to tell her how helpful she had been, and to ask her again to not say a word about Langly to anyone.

"Not to worry," she said with a smile. "You know I wouldn't share anyone's secrets."

Ben left the restaurant with a growing sense of unease. Not only was he certain Maggie was a ticking time-bomb, but he was reminded of how difficult it was to investigate a local resident without setting off a torrent of reactions throughout the town. He felt hog-tied. He dared not go around asking about Langly, or he would irreparably damage the man, and he couldn't think of any excuse to actually go out to his acreage. Even if he did, what would he expect to find?

The only possible path was to talk to Langly's friend, Ed Grimsman. Of course, the fact he was Langly's friend made it unlikely Grimsman would share anything damaging, but very likely he would immediately call Langly and tell him Ben was asking about him.

Ben sighed and headed back to the newsroom. *Time to do some actual work while I think about this.*

Chapter 19

Justin Langly was watching pornographic movies on his home computer in his bedroom when he saw a silver Impala driving up the lane to his acreage. He quickly stood and fastened his belt. *It's about time.*

He walked out on the front porch and waved to the Impala's driver to go around the house to the back, then he walked back through the house and out the door onto a small porch facing the farm buildings. The man who got out of car was tall and handsome, with reddish hair and a neatly-trimmed goatee. *He looks like one of them contestants on The Bachelor,* Justin thought. *Jeez, I'll keep that thought to myself. Can't have people knowin' I watch The Bachelor.*

Justin stepped down onto the gravel and walked up to the car. "Hey, are you Donny?"

"Yes sir," the man said with a wide smile. "You must be Justin."

"Yep. Did you bring me a package?"

"Well, yes and no," Donny said.

"Whadda mean, no?" Justin snapped. He'd been asking for a

new girl for days, and Ray had promised him one was coming tonight.

"Relax," Donny said, the smile never leaving his face. "I've got a sweet little package here for you. The thing is, Ray has said neither one of us can do her until he gets here on Wednesday."

"Wednesday? Holy shit! I've been waiting for days. What's with you guys? I pay good money for your services, and now all this crap. What's so special about this one?"

"She's been making trouble for Ray, and for me. He said to tell you he wants to be here to... to orchestrate."

Justin had no idea what that meant and was tempted to tell Donny to go to hell. He wasn't going to pay good money just so he could pleasure himself in front of porn for another day and a half.

"I have a carrot and a stick for you," Donny said pleasantly.

"Huh?"

"The stick is this: if you touch her before Ray arrives, he takes her away with him and you never get another girl from us. But..." He held up a palm to stop Justin from reacting. "If you do what he asks and wait until Wednesday, you get this one for free."

Justin liked the sound of that.

"Okay, whatever. Let's have a look."

Donny popped the trunk open and lifted Madeline out, still wrapped in the rug. He carried the bundle as he followed Justin to the bomb shelter. Looking at the steep steps, he shrugged, set the rug on the ground, then dragged it down the steps behind him as he descended. He assumed the rug would protect the girl inside from any serious injury, or in reality, he didn't care whether it did or not.

Justin followed them down. He clicked on the sole light, then kicked the rug a few times, rolling it open on the floor. With the final rotation, Madeline's body sprawled out on the floor in front of them.

"She's not as young as I like 'em," he said immediately.

"Yes, but look at this body. She's as lean and taut as a gymnast. And look at how pretty she is." Donny reached down and turned Madeline's head so he could see her face clearly.

"Do I know this chick? She looks familiar."

"You've probably seen her around," Donny said, nodding. "This one's a local girl."

"Well, normally I'd make a stink about her age, but since she's free, I guess she'll do. God, I wish I could dig into that right now."

"Sorry, but you can't. However..." Donny paused for effect. "If you leave her down here without food until Wednesday, think about how hungry she'll be. She'll be begging you for it."

"Yeah, that would be good," Justin said, nodding and wiping saliva from the corner of his mouth.

Donny didn't share that he was going to have her first.

Justin asked, "So Ray's coming here, huh? That's never happened before."

"No surprise there. Ray doesn't like anyone to see him. But as I said, he insisted on being here for this one. She and her boyfriend have been causing some problems for him, and he wants to enjoy getting even. He said it was no trouble because he needed to come to Iowa anyway. He's got another little task on his calendar for Wednesday morning. He's got a goon who's been skimming, and he wants to have a little chat with him."

"Huh. With all the money he must make, I'm surprised he would notice."

"Oh, he notices everything," Donny said. "Trust me, you don't want to cross him."

"Hey, I don't wanna anyway. He's been a reliable source of the best pussy I've ever had. I hope he stays with it forever."

As they talked, Donny removed Madeline's handcuffs, and Justin fastened her ankle to the steel cable lying on the floor.

Donny commented about the ideal nature of the 1950s bomb shelter for Justin's current purposes, then said, "One other thing. There's someone else coming tonight."

"Someone else? Whadda you mean, like another girl?"

"Sorry, but no. The boyfriend. He's on his way here now."

"Won't he..."

Donny interrupted. "No. Relax. He'll be in the same shape as she is. You can use these cuffs to attach him to your anchor, where the cable is affixed to the wall. When Ray decides to get even, he knows how to create someone's worst nightmare. He's going to make the boyfriend watch while we take the girl apart piece by piece."

Justin's anxiety rose. The thought of an audience, the thought of other people in his shelter calling the shots. He didn't like it. *But then again, I don't have to pay for her... I guess if she's free, what the hell?*

***

It was shortly after sunset when another car drove up the lane and stopped behind the house. Another driver, another trunk, another limp body dragged down the stairs and fastened to the wall. The driver barely said five words to Justin. When he was certain Tony was secure, he simply nodded, walked up the stairs, and was gone.

Donny had left earlier, saying he would be back on Wednesday afternoon for the "party" and reminding Justin to keep his hands to himself until then.

Justin sat for a long time in the shelter, watching Madeline lying on the mattress, breathing in shallow spurts. He ached to have her but decided angering Donny, and more importantly Ray, would be unwise. He was no coward, but these guys were professionals.

He finally stood, took a deep breath, and walked up the stairs, closing and locking the steel hatch behind him.

***

Rich Davis looked at his watch. It was 9:30 p.m., and all units had checked in. Everyone was in place and ready. It would be a long wait, but being in place early reduced the chances Donny would see them. Davis shared Madeline's skepticism about the whole operation. He knew Donny could just be playing them. He could have made the call from Maui or Paris or Brazil. They had no way to know. They also had no choice but to follow through.

He decided to call Madeline and make sure she was doing okay and was on her way. Her cell phone rang through to voice mail. Immediately, he was on edge, hoping she just wasn't answering while she drove, but fearing something was wrong. *Why didn't I stay with her myself?*

Davis immediately called Tabors and told her Madeline wasn't answering her phone.

"Give me ten," she said. "I'll have somebody check her cell signal to see where she is."

Ten minutes later, Tabors called back. Davis knew immediately the night had plummeted into a disaster.

"Her phone's off the grid," Tabors said. "The battery's been removed, or it's been run over by a truck or something. There's no sign of her."

"Son of a bitch!" Davis yelled. "We've been had. Dear God, that bastard has her. Tabors, you hear me? He has her!"

"Settle down, Agent Davis. Screaming won't help. You may be right, but let's hope you're not. Get someone over to her place to check it out."

Davis hung up and dialed Sheriff Mackey's number, glad he

had convinced the sheriff to stay home and not join them in Des Moines. The sheriff answered on the first ring.

"You get him? Already?"

Davis said no and explained the situation. The sheriff was in his patrol car, red lights flashing, before Davis finished talking.

Fifteen minutes later, he called. Davis didn't speak, just let the sheriff confirm his worst nightmare.

"Her place was locked, so I busted in the door," the sheriff said. "It's bad, Rich. There's no way to sugar coat it. Deputy Jebron was on the floor, bound with tape, his head bashed in. Madeline's car is in the garage but there's no sign of her in the apartment."

"Oh, no..." Davis felt light-headed.

"Yeah, and worse. There are signs of a scuffle. Two bags of groceries are spilled out on the floor near the kitchen. I'd say she spent some time on the floor. Her purse is there and her keys are on the coffee table. And Rich..."

Davis almost couldn't stand to hear what would come next.

"The dining table has been moved. By the fading on the wood floor, I would say an area rug is missing."

It was immediately obvious to both men what had happened. It took every ounce of self-control Davis possessed to keep from vomiting. After a few deep breaths, he said, "No offense, Sheriff, but let me remind you not to touch anything. Especially her personal effects, like her purse. He may have rummaged in her purse or... or... dear Lord..."

"I know the drill, Agent," the sheriff said. "An ambulance is on the way for Tim, but other than getting him to the hospital, the scene will be just as he... as she left it when you get a team here."

"Thank you, Sheriff. I should have asked sooner, but is your deputy okay?"

"He's unconscious but his pulse is strong. You never know with head injuries, but we can hope he'll pull through."

"Well, yes, let's hope. Also, can you get some men talking to neighbors? Dammit, I hate being this far away."

"We'll get on it. Don't kill yourself trying to get back here. There won't be much you can do. Drive slow enough that you'll be able to notice the cars you pass. You might see him on the highway."

Get serious, Sheriff. It's dark. I won't see past the headlights. Even if I did, I can't know for sure who took her. And even if it was Donny, he'd be disguised, and I wouldn't know him anyway. "Dammit!"

He turned on his siren and the flashing lights hidden behind his front grill and roared out of the rest stop parking lot. He immediately called Tabors to tell her Madeline had almost certainly been taken. He suggested the FBI pull everyone off the operation at the Capitol. Then he drove like a maniac back to Orney.

***

It was nearly 11 p.m. when Davis arrived at Madeline's apartment. The neighborhood looked like Times Square, only with more flashing lights. Mackey had called in help from neighboring sheriff's departments and had more than twenty officers talking to everyone within a five-block radius of the apartment. So far, none of the residents had reported seeing anything.

One huge frustration was the large time frame involved. She could have been taken anytime between the time she'd left the *Crier* newsroom and the time she was scheduled to depart for Des Moines. Madeline's apartment was still sealed. The State Crime Lab van wouldn't arrive for another hour or so. They never moved as fast as Davis just had. He stood staring at the building, wondering where to start, when Ben Smalley walked up. He looked gray and unsteady on his feet.

"Ben, I am so sorry."

"Can it, Rich. It's even worse than you know."

"What?"

"They didn't call you while you were driving because they didn't want you any more reckless than you were already."

"What, dammit! What?"

Ben sagged and said, "Tony's gone too."

Davis felt like he'd been punched in the gut.

"Oh, God."

"When Mackey called me about Madeline, I naturally called Tony. You've probably noticed they've grown close. He didn't answer his cell. It turns out, his phone is off the grid as well. The Kansas City police checked his hotel room. They just called back and said there's no sign of him."

"How can this be happening?" Davis screeched. "It's like they're ahead of us at every step. Goddammit, if there's a leak, I will kill the person who did this."

"Please don't talk like that in front of me," Ben said. "I don't want to have to testify against you. Feel free to do it. Just don't tell me about it."

Davis' mind was shredded. *What to do? Which way to go? Where to start? Well, I'm here, so I start here.* He opened his trunk and retrieved latex gloves and booties. He turned to Ben.

"I'm going inside. When Rooney gets here, ask him to get a report from the sheriff about any results from the canvas, then come join me."

Smalley nodded.

Davis jogged up the stairs, ducked under the crime scene tape, pulled on the gloves and booties, and entered Madeline's apartment. It was just as Mackey had described it. Throw rug in front of the door bunched up unnaturally, coffee table pushed to the side with keys lying on it, and a purse, its contents, and groceries scattered across the floor. In short, all signals there had been a confrontation, accented by what he assumed was the deputy's blood smeared on the floor near the door.

He stepped over to the dining area and saw the spot Mackey had seen. The sheriff was exactly right. There had been an area rug on that spot, and now there was not. He looked closely at some of the obvious surfaces the intruder may have touched. It looked like the place had been wiped. The doorknob was the give-away. Even a fastidious housekeeper doesn't wipe a knob clean after using it to exit an apartment. The fact it was clean told Davis the intruder had been very careful.

He went back to the coffee table and knelt in front of it, peering closely at the bundle of keys. What appeared to be the apartment key was at an angle, facing him. He didn't touch it, but took a big breath and exhaled over it. A print was immediately visible. A big print, like a man's thumb.

"Well, maybe you're not the smartest guy on the planet," Davis said aloud.

"Of course not, cause I am." Rooney's voice was a welcome sound despite the inappropriate comment.

"Glad to hear it, smart guy. So tell me you got something from the neighbors," Davis said, looking up over his shoulder.

"I didn't, but I think Deputy Bodke may have."

Davis stood. "So tell me."

"He's good. Have you noticed that? For a sheriff's flunky, he's pretty good. Bodke was smart enough to ask himself where he would park if he were the perp, so his vehicle wouldn't be seen here by the neighbors, or by Madeline. He knew the convenience store is just three blocks away, so he went there first. He found a pimply-faced clerk who says a guy left a big Chevy rental in the lot for over two hours this afternoon."

"How'd he know it was a rental?"

"Well, he says he can't be sure, but it looked like a rental. You know, a four-door sedan, silver, late-model, with out-of-state plates. Before you ask, no. He didn't get any part of the license number, or even the state. He just noticed it wasn't Iowa."

"Well, it's something," Davis said, knowing it wasn't much. "Was he able to describe this guy?"

"Good news there. The guy came inside to buy a slice of pizza and a Coke. The clerk described him as tall, probably six feet or so, trim, with red hair and a red goatee."

"Red hair?"

"Yep, but don't let that throw you. The clerk also commented on the guy's smile. He said he had the nicest smile, wide, with dimples."

"That's him! My God, Donny was here. Make sure you get the word out to everyone about his change of looks, and get the sketch artist to modify his drawing."

"I've already made the calls," Rooney said. "What did you find?"

Davis smiled for the first time in hours—a thin, tight-lipped smile. "I believe our genius left his thumb print on Madeline's apartment key."

"Well I'll be a frog on fire," Rooney said.

Chapter 20

Tony's mind resisted, but his body wrenched it into conscious-ness with a violent retch. He didn't vomit, but saliva dripped out of his mouth onto his shirt. He immediately was aware of an intense, almost unbearable pain in his left shoulder. He tried to move it but couldn't.

What the hell?

He opened his eyes. Nothing he saw made sense. He had to get... turned... He looked up and realized the source of his pain. His left arm was cuffed to an eye bolt embedded in a concrete wall. His body weight was hanging on that arm. It screamed at him to find relief.

He knew he needed to stand, but he couldn't get his legs to move. The pain was causing him to breathe heavily, and he realized it was clearing his head. He increased the effort, purposefully breathing in as deeply as he could. After a few minutes, he could feel other parts of his body waking, and finally, after what seemed like hours, he was able to maneuver his legs under him. Using the wall to steady himself, he pushed up, sliding against the concrete surface until he was standing. The pain in his shoulder eased a little, allowing him to realize how badly his head was pounding.

Where am I? What happened?

Then, as if someone swept the curtains aside, he could remember. *Caulder. His condo. His security guard. A syringe. Shit. What did they give me? How long have I been out? Where the hell am I?*

He tried to get his eyes to focus and scanned the room. In an instant, his gaze landed on the wooden platform with the disgusting mattress, and a girl. No, not a girl, *the* girl.

"Madeline!" he yelped. There was no response. He pulled on the handcuffs, but he was secured to the wall. "Madeline!"

She didn't stir. "God, please, let her be alive," Tony prayed aloud. Then, fighting to control his emotions, he became as quiet as he could. He stared at her intently. A wave of relief washed over him. He could see she was breathing. They were shallow breaths, and not very regular, but she was alive. That was something.

Tony stood like that for a long time—it was difficult to judge how long—chained to a wall, with nowhere to sit, in a barren room lit by a single lamp, staring at his co-worker, friend, lover. He used the time to think, desperately trying to devise some means of escape, and to pray. He feared others had occupied this same room. It certainly looked as though he and Madeline weren't the first. Those others undoubtedly had prayed to the same God. Tony didn't know if their prayers had been answered or not. He feared they hadn't, but that didn't stop him.

At one point, he inventoried his possessions. It appeared they had taken everything but his clothes. His cell phone, his keys, his wallet, his U of I ring, all were gone. Occasionally, he made another effort to pull free from the wall, but couldn't.

He grew tired and desperately needed to sit, but his butt

couldn't reach the floor, and his shoulder couldn't stand the pain of trying. Then, as the hours passed, he realized his thirst was becoming a bigger problem than either his pain or his exhaustion. There was a sink in the room. It was agonizing to think water might be that close but unattainable. He might as well be in the middle of the Mojave Desert.

He positioned himself in every conceivable position his handcuffs would allow. He stood on one leg, he squatted, he bent at the waist and leaned into the wall, he turned and leaned back against the wall, he flexed his muscles. Everything about his situation was agonizing and infuriating, all exacerbated by his knowledge that Madeline was here, tethered at the ankle, lying on that old mattress. What might be coming was unthinkable. He had to do something!

She stirred, and immediately Tony was rigid, staring at the mattress, willing her to wake. She stirred again, groaned, then suddenly rolled onto her side and vomited onto the floor beside the makeshift bed.

"What the hell?" she moaned.

"Madeline!"

"What? Tony? What the..."

She retched again and sat up, looking first at him, then at the cable attached to her ankle.

"No, no, no, this can't be... Oh, please... No!" Her voice grew louder with each protestation.

"Madeline, I'm sorry," Tony said, tears welling in his eyes.

She inched her legs over the side of the platform, letting them dangle toward the floor.

"Don't try to stand yet. Give it some time," Tony urged.

She nodded.

"Do you remember what happened?"

"Yeah, that bastard Donny was waiting for me in my apartment when I got home from shopping. He had a gun as big as a howitzer. Actually, I don't know what a howitzer looks like. But the name makes it sound like it would be a gun as big as Donny's."

Tony marveled at her ability to think clearly and be sardonic so quickly. She had recovered much faster than he had, and with a lot less effort.

"I spit in his face, and he hit me." She lifted a hand to her cheek. "Then he stuck a needle in me. That's the last I remember before waking up here. Where is 'here' anyhow?"

"No clue," Tony said. "My experience was similar. I found our guy in Kansas City. I was foolish enough to go to his building. His security guard hit me with a similar needle. Whatever they're using is powerful stuff. You were out for hours after I woke up."

"But wait a minute," she said. "If you were in Kansas City, and I was in Orney, we could be..." She thought about all the possibilities and finally said simply, "Anywhere. Oh, Tony." She started to cry. "No one's going to find us here, are they? We're not going to make it, are we? Tony... Tony... I don't want to die."

"Madeline. Stop. Think about it. There're about a thousand really good agents from the DCI, the FBI, and a bunch of other places all looking for us right now. When you didn't show in Des Moines, it had to have created a shitstorm. So we have to have hope."

He thought about it and said, "I bet we can narrow down the possibilities about our location."

"Huh?"

"What time did Donny put you to sleep?"

"It must have been about 6 p.m. Why?"

"Well, they got me before noon. If we assume we got similar doses, then you couldn't have travelled as far as me, because you've been here, passed out in front of me, for a lot of hours. At least I think that logic holds up. In any case, I'm betting we're not that far from home."

"You mean, we might be where Brittany was held before she was killed? That's a great comfort, Mr. Spock."

Tony immediately regretted his comment but had no idea what to say to ease her mind. It could very well be true.

"Are you able to stand now?" he asked.

She gingerly slid off the mattress onto her feet. "Yeah, I feel like I've had a few too many margaritas, but I can manage."

"At the risk of sounding selfish, can you see if you can reach the sink? I'm so thirsty I think I'm going to pass out."

She had no trouble reaching the sink and was relieved to see the water worked. At Tony's urging, she took care of her own thirst first. She cupped her hands under the faucet and gulped down several mouthfuls. She turned to Tony and said, "The bad news is, I don't see any cups or containers."

"We'll manage," he replied. "I'm so desperate I'll settle for anything. Here, take my shoe."

She made a face. "That's disgusting. I have a better idea. Not much better, but maybe it'll work." She pulled her arms inside her sweater, one by one, and slipped them out of her bra. Then she turned it 180 degrees and unfastened it, pulling it from under the sweater. She turned one of the cups upside down under the faucet.

Tony gawked, and she said, "The synthetic liner in the cup might hold water, at least for a bit. If I fill it and race over to you, you should be able to get a couple of swallows from it. Maybe a few trips will do it."

It turned out that racing on weak legs, with one ankle clasped by a metal cable, was a little optimistic. But, after numerous trips clumsily limping back and forth, she had provided Tony with enough water out of her "cup," that his thirst was satisfied.

"You truly are a wonder," he said, motioning to her to come

closer, and then kissing her forehead.

"Well, I'm just sorry the cup isn't bigger... In more ways than one."

They both laughed, then abruptly stopped. No humor would last long in this chamber of horrors.

"Tony, we have to..." she started, just as they heard a metallic sound at the top of the stairs.

"Oh, no," Madeline said, moving away from Tony and retreating to the far corner.

They heard a loud clunk, then saw a pair of legs on the stairs. As he descended, they could see he was a big man. He seemed normal enough, like a farmer or a construction worker, only bigger. He looked at them as he neared, his face oddly expressionless.

He said, "My name's Justin. I don't give a shit what your names are, so just shut up."

Upon hearing the name, Madeline immediately thought of the brutal photographs, of the letters scratched into Brittany's body. She shook and cowered in the corner, trying to press herself through the wall at her back.

Justin stepped toward her. "You're right to be scared, missy. I'm gonna enjoy you 'til there ain't no joy left."

Madeline started to cry, and Tony began yanking on the cuffs again.

Justin looked back at him and said, "Save yourself the trouble. That's solid steel embedded in concrete. It ain't goin' nowhere. And you..." He looked down at Madeline. "Stop whining. At your age, you ain't no virgin. You might even like this big boy." He pushed his crotch up against her, causing her to shriek, then pulled back.

"Sadly, you can relax for today. Ray said I have to wait 'til he gets here. Ain't that a hoot? He wants to watch me do you. Well, he gave you to me for free, so who am I to argue?"

He started to turn away but hesitated. "Course he didn't say nothin' about not having a look." His hand shot out and pulled her sweater up to her neck.

"No bra. Well, that's a nice touch." He reached out and stroked her. "For a grown woman, you sure ain't got much to show for it."

Madeline continued sobbing, dropping to her knees and bending her head to the floor.

"No matter," Justin said. "I'm gonna enjoy every part of you. And you," he said to Tony, "you get to watch."

Tony burned with a hatred beyond anything he had ever experienced.

"You look like you wanna poke me," Justin smiled. "I wish you would. Then I'd have an excuse to break your arm. I'd like to see how well you did, chained to a wall and nursin' a broken bone. Ooh, or maybe a leg. I kin imagine you tryin' to stand with a broken leg. You best behave. I'm likin' the idea more every minute."

He laughed and started up the stairs as Tony called out in desperation.

"Hey, Justin! Wait!"

"Save your breath. You've already heard what I have to say. And there ain't nothin' I kin do to help you, now you seen me and this place."

"But I know something you need to hear," Tony said, trying to sound confident.

"Now just what could that be, smart boy?" Justin backed down the stairs as Tony furiously thought about what he could say that somehow might help.

"You said Ray's coming here?"

"Yeah, so?"

"Think about it, Justin. Think about what you just said to us, about now that we've seen you. You must know Ray feels the same way. He's never let anyone see him. If he comes here for your little party, as you put it, what do you think happens at the end? Do you think he's going to drive away and just leave you here, knowing who he is and what he looks like?"

Justin tried to wave him off, but Tony could tell he had struck a nerve.

"I'm a good client," Justin said, a note of uncertainty leaking into his voice. "He won't let anything happen to me."

"A word to the wise, Justin. That's all. Think about it. Ray has dozens of clients, maybe hundreds. The FBI estimates that he makes millions of the dollars every year. Do you think he cares about one client?"

"The FBI? What about the FBI?"

"Oh, I guess you wouldn't have heard," Tony said. "The FBI is on to Ray. They've been following him. That's how Madeline and I got involved. Our FBI informant told us about Ray, and we're doing a story about him for the paper."

Justin marched up to Tony and shoved him back into the concrete wall. The back of his head slammed against the surface, and suddenly he was seeing stars.

Justin put his huge hand around Tony's throat and said, "Are you fuckin' with me? If you are, I swear I will pound you into sausage meat, then I'll take a razor to your girlfriend here and peel her skin off one spoonful at a time."

Tony shook his head and croaked, "I swear. It's all true. If... If you don't believe me, I know how you can check."

Justin eased his grip and said, "Talk."

***

It was mid-morning Tuesday, and Ben Smalley was having the

worst day of his life. He hadn't slept all night. He was exhausted and scared and angry. *How could I let this happen? What is wrong with me?*

He paced around the newsroom, then sat in his office, then got up and paced. He was in the sixth or seventh cycle of this, returning to the desk, when his phone rang. He didn't want to answer it but knew he should, in case it was the DCI or someone else working on the case.

If this is some old biddy complaining about her paperboy, I'm going to kill myself, he thought, grabbing the receiver and barking, "Smalley."

A man's voice said, "Answer one question right, and Tony gets to live another day. Get it wrong, and he dies."

"Who is this? What are you talking about?"

"Tony said to tell you he 'preciates your advice Sunday mornin'. He said only you and he would know 'bout that."

Ben now was fully alert and using his cell phone to text Rich Davis.

"That's right," he said. "Okay, you've talked to Tony. So what do you want?"

"I din't just talk to Tony, you dumb turd," the voice said. "I *have* Tony. I'm gonna kill him if you don't tell me the truth. Tony said to answer honestly. His life depends upon it."

Ben sucked in a lungful of air. The idea of Tony's life hanging on his words... He couldn't bear it. Was he supposed to be truthful or not?

"So," the man said, "the question is simple. Does the FBI know about Ray?"

Dear God. What am I supposed to say about that? Does Tony really want him to know that? Who is this guy?

"Answer me!" the man shouted.

"I... How can I be sure Tony wants me to tell you the truth? You've put me in a terrible spot here. I feel responsible for him."

"Spare me, Mr. Hot-Shot Editor. Tony said you should be as honest as you was Sunday. That's all I got. Now tell me the truth."

Ben drew another deep breath and said, "Yes. They know about Ray. They're on his trail now." Ben was nearly weeping, hoping he had done the right thing.

"Good man," the voice said, and the line went dead.

Ben's cell phone buzzed. The message read: *Done? Can U talk?*

Ben didn't reply to the text but dialed Davis' number.

"What did you get?" he asked, when Davis answered.

"Well, he called from a burner phone, so we can't trace it back to him."

Ben groaned.

"But," Rich said brightly, "we can tell you the call originated from here."

Ben sat up. "Here? Here as in *here* here?"

"Yes. You did well, Ben. The caller is here in Quincy County. The cell tower is right on the edge of Orney. He's here. Now we just have to find him."

***

Rita's knees were sore. Her back hurt. Her nose was raw from the tissues, needed because it wouldn't stop running. She didn't care. She barely noticed any of it. She fought back another burst of tears and looked up at the crucifix above the altar in Holy Name Cathedral as she moved the next Rosary bead between her fingers... *Hail Mary, full of grace, the Lord is with thee, blessed...*

"Miss?" A soft voice interrupted her tears and her prayer. She looked up to see a priest—she assumed he was a priest because he was wearing a collar and was too young to be a monsignor or bishop —standing in front of her, in the next pew, looking concerned.

"Yes, Father?"

"Are you alright, miss? You've been here for hours. Have you even taken a break? Can I get you some water or something?"

"That's very kind of you, Father, but no. I'm fine."

The priest sat in his pew and turned back so he could look at her eye-to-eye. "You'll forgive me for saying so, but I'm pretty sure you're not fine. Would it help to talk about it? Is there something I can do?"

"No, Father," Rita said, feeling her tears well up again. "I mean, well, you could pray for my brother."

"Ah. Is he sick? Has he been hurt?"

"No, I mean, well, I hope not."

The priest didn't respond. He sat quietly, allowing Rita to decide whether to continue.

"Oh, Father. It's so horrible. He's missing. I mean, these men... There are these men, and they took him. I mean, we know someone has him. They're going to kill him. I *know* they are!" Rita's sobs became a wail that filled the vaulted ceilings of the cathedral.

The priest stood. "Let's take a walk. I'm sure your knees need a break." He held out his hand. "And there's no question God has heard you by now."

Rita stifled her sobs and actually smiled. The whole city of Chicago probably heard her last outburst, so yeah, God probably had too. She took the priest's hand and stood. It felt good. She pulled on her coat, and the two of them walked out into the afternoon sun.

"Won't you need a coat, Father?"

"I'll be fine," he said with a smile. "Let's find a Starbucks."

As they walked, Rita told him what she knew about Tony's

pursuit of a story on human trafficking, the threats he had received, and her resentment of how the threats had turned to her.

"Father, I was so, so selfish. The last time I talked to Tony, I was angry. He could tell I was angry. I know he could. To be honest, I wanted him to feel bad. I wanted him to know how difficult his work... You know, these people he was going after... How difficult it was making my life. It was all about me. Now..." Her voice trailed off. "If he's dead, if they kill him and I never get a chance to talk to him again, to tell him I'm sorry, how will I ever live with that?"

The priest's response was predictable and not very helpful, but Rita still appreciated hearing it. He said, "You're being too hard on yourself. Does Tony know you love him? Of course, he does. Does he know your fears are legitimate? Of course, he does. You just told me he's the one who received your photograph in a package with a severed finger. Dear Lord, he would think you inhuman if you weren't affected by that. You must remember you're not the source of Tony's troubles, these evil people are."

"Well, sure, Father, but I could have been more understanding."

"Oh posh, as my grandmother used to say. Put it out of your mind. The real question is what do you do now? Praying for your brother is important, but you can't stay in my church twenty-four hours a day until they find him."

They reached the Starbucks, and the priest held the door open for her. She ordered a regular coffee, and the priest asked for a caramel brûlée latte. He glanced at her and said, "A priest's guilty pleasure." She smiled weakly, and they found a table.

"So," he said. "Have you thought about what to do besides pray?"

"Yes, I've thought about it, but what can I do? When Dad called this morning, I wanted to jump into my car and drive to Iowa to look for him, but that's just stupid, isn't it? Where would I look? And they aren't even positive he's in Iowa. He was in Kansas City when he disappeared."

She blew on her coffee and took a sip. "I'm supposed to audition tonight. That's one of the reasons I was so pissed at Tony—sorry Father—I haven't been able to concentrate."

"Audition?"

"Yes, I play the cello. There's an opening at the Chicago Symphony. It's a long shot for someone still in grad school, but they agreed to hear me. There's no way I can now. Look at me. I'm a mess. I can't even get my hands to stop shaking. I would have Mozart sounding like screeching cats."

The priest smiled, but reached across the table and gripped Rita's arm tightly.

"I don't know anything about the cello," he said. "I prefer the blues myself. But think about this, Rita. Think about going to that audition. Imagine taking all that emotion you're feeling—your fears, your love for Tony, your pleas to our Heavenly Father—take all of that emotion and put it into your playing. Imagine channeling all that energy into one great performance."

"Oh, Father, that sounds nice, but it's so... Forgive me... It's so naïve. Playing a piece like that requires precision and technique and grace. Do I look like someone who could pull that off in three hours from now?" She held up her watch for the priest to see.

"Yes, Rita, you do." His eyes never wavered from hers. "Ask yourself what Tony would want you to do. I know that sounds like a cliché, but really do that. What will make Tony feel better about the troubles his work has brought to you? Going to your audition or sitting at home, or should I say, kneeling in my church?"

Rita wanted to tell this young priest he was full of it, but she couldn't. The fact was, he was right. *If they find Tony alive, and he finds out I missed my audition because of him, he will feel horrible.*

That simple thought changed everything.

Rita stood, and the priest followed suit. She put her arms around him. "Thank you, Father. Please remember to pray for Tony." She turned and went out the door.

Chapter 21

Madeline and Tony worked on the anchor in the concrete wall. They had no illusions about success; they simply didn't know what else to do. Madeline had been quiet since Justin had left, clearly affected by the intimidation and humiliation she had experienced. Her fear—both their fears—could be felt in the silence between them.

They worked in unison, pushing and pulling, pushing and pulling on the anchor. So far, it had not budged.

Suddenly, Madeline said, "Why did you do that, Tony?"

"Huh? What?"

"Why did you tell Justin the FBI is on to Ray? If he becomes convinced of that, won't he have to kill us and get rid of the bodies before Ray brings the feds here with him?"

"I'm sorry, Madeline. I just reacted, knowing I had to do something to change the status quo. I didn't have time to think it through."

She shook her head, clearly thinking him an idiot, but Tony continued. "Now that I *have* thought about it, I still think it's okay."

"How do you figure that?"

Before Tony could answer, the metal clanking could be heard at the door, and Justin's legs appeared on the stairs. As he emerged into the room, they could see he was carrying a sledgehammer. Tony immediately thought of the crushed skull Brittany's body had suffered. Madeline must have thought the same because she immediately shrunk back into the furthest corner from the door.

Justin sneered. "Looks like you're right, smart guy. That bastard Ray is gonna bring the cops right down on my head. Well, won't they be surprised when they don't find nothin' here?"

Tony responded quickly and firmly. "Don't be an ass, Justin. Think about it. There is no way you can clean this entire room of all traces of us and your other victims. Nowadays, with DNA testing and all, just a single hair in a drain or one of the cracks in the floor will put you away for life. You know you can't run. Look at you. It's not like you can wear a disguise. How long do you think it will take them to find and capture a mountain like you?"

"Shut the hell up!" Justin screamed, lifting the hammer.

"Listen to me," Tony said, fighting to keep his voice from trembling. "There's a way out for you. It's not great, but it's better than life in prison."

Justin walked up and grabbed Tony's shirt with his left hand. He didn't need to raise the sledge in his other hand for Tony to feel the threat. "What? What way out is there for me?" Justin's voice broke, and Tony realized the brute was about to start crying.

"Make a deal," Tony said. "Tell the authorities you'll give them Ray and Donny and the whole cast of characters, if they'll let you plea to something less than murder. Be the guy who rescues us and turns in the really bad guys, and get a break for yourself."

"You're fulla shit," Justin said. "After what I done to girls in here, ain't nobody gonna give me anything." He was almost nose-to-nose with Tony, his face red and his hot breath spilling over

Tony's face.

"It's your best shot," Tony said, trying to sound confident. "Think about it."

"Yeah, I'll think about," he said, backing off a little. "But you're still fulla shit." He suddenly lashed out and hit Tony hard in the stomach.

Tony doubled over and fell to the floor, dangling by the arm affixed to the wall. He groaned in agony.

Justin stomped up the stairs and slammed the metal down onto the opening.

"Dammit!" Tony moaned, climbing to his feet. "I wish people would stop doing that."

Madeline dragged her cable back across the floor and put her arms around him. "You gonna be okay?"

Tony nodded.

"You don't believe what you told him, do you?"

"Of course not," Tony rasped. "Multiple kidnappings, rapes, and murders? No matter what happens, he'll never see the light of day again, once they get him."

"So what were you...?"

"I just want him to make the call. Maybe if he makes the call, they'll trace it. Or they'll lie about a deal. I just want him to reach out, so we have a chance." He gripped her tightly and started to cry. "I just want us to have a chance."

***

Two dozen agents descended on Quincy County Tuesday afternoon. Several began visiting all the stores that sold cell phones. There were a surprising number of them. In addition to the cell phone stores, the big box center at the edge of Orney, the hardware store, and the convenience stores all sold phones. Unregistered pre-paid phones were less common, but the agents agreed they needed to visit all phone outlets to be sure they didn't miss something. The hope—it wasn't quite an assumption—was that the man who had called Ben didn't normally carry a pre-paid phone, and would have had to buy one to make the call.

The remaining agents started interviewing everyone who would talk to them to try to find some anomaly, some hint, about where a person, perhaps two people, might be held captive. The responses they got were discouraging.

The clerk behind the desk at the building supply store said, for example, "Sorry boys, but that's a needle in a haystack problem. You have any idea how many acreages there are 'round here? In addition to the farmsteads, there's dozens, maybe hundreds of places out in the country where people live in remote houses. Ol' Sven Olson died in his house, and no one knew it for almost a month. The postman finally said somethin' to the sheriff when the mailbox got stuffed full. Point is, nobody's got a clue what happens in those houses. And lotsa those places have tornado shelters and cellars. Hell, a few of 'em even got bomb shelters. You know, back in the 60s when the Ruskies was wantin' to blow us to hell, some guys dug some pretty big underground places. If them two reporters yer lookin' for is holed up in one of them, you ain't gonna find 'em."

The agents thanked the clerk for his insights and moved on, leaving their card and asking for a call if he heard or saw anything helpful.

As they climbed back into their car, they looked at each other and nodded grimly, knowing the man had been exactly right.

***

Rita was satisfied. She couldn't be happy. She might never be happy again if Tony wasn't found safe. But she was satisfied she had played her best. It was pretty clear she wasn't going to get hired. The vibe she got from the assistant conductor and first chair cellist was that they were being polite, perhaps doing a favor for her professors, rather than showing any real interest in her.

That was okay. She had known it was unlikely she would get hired. She had played well, maybe the best performance she'd ever given. *Good grief,* she thought, remembering the priest, *I never asked his name.* Regardless, he had been correct. Releasing all that emotion into her performance had made her fingers dance. It wasn't a joyful performance, but it was intense. She was satisfied.

As she lugged her cello out to her car in the parking lot, she noticed a car parked across from hers with the engine running. It was after dark, and its lights were on. A man was standing in front of the driver-side door. Rita glanced around nervously. The FBI had a female agent protecting her. She had been forced to cope with the woman following her everywhere. *Where is she now?*

Rita didn't see the agent anywhere. She was tempted to run, but that would mean leaving the cello behind. There was no way.

Rita was close enough to see that the car was big. It looked expensive, like a Lexus or Mercedes. The man in front of it was tall and distinguished. She thought *elegant* was a better word. As all these thoughts raced through her head, the man spoke.

"Rita, if you're looking for your bodyguard, she's taking a little nap right now."

Rita's breath caught in her throat. She leaned down and eased the cello case to the asphalt.

"Don't run, Rita. I'm here to make you an offer."

The man had a deep, pleasant voice.

Rita stammered a response. "Who are you? What do you

want?"

"Two excellent questions," he smiled. "My name is Ray, and I want to take you to see your brother."

"Tony? What about Tony? Is he okay? How can you...?"

"Easy, Rita." The man was still smiling.

Rita realized she hated it each time he said her name. "So tell me," she said tersely.

Ray said, "Your brother is fine. I know where he is. I'm leaving for Iowa tonight so I can see him tomorrow. I'd like you to come with me."

"You... I... Well, I... You can't be serious," she finally sputtered.

"I'm quite serious, Rita. I know you want to see your brother, and I'm the only person on Earth who can take you to him. You've finished your audition, it's a beautiful night for a drive, and it is a magnificent car we'll be riding in, if you don't mind me saying so."

"You're insane," Rita said. "I'm not stupid. If I get in that car, I may or may not see Tony, but I sure as hell won't see anyone else... ever."

"That's very astute of you. But think about it. If you say no, I drive away, your brother dies, and no one ever finds the body. If you come with me, there's a chance I'll make a mistake, that you'll have an opportunity to put your FBI friends on our trail. It's a long drive to Iowa. You're a clever girl. You're Tony's only chance. Are you really going to say no to that?"

Rita's mind was racing. *The man was right. But could she? Was she brave enough—dumb enough—to get into his car? Could she find some way to save Tony during a six-hour car ride?* She sighed, knowing she really didn't have a choice.

"Okay. You win. Let me put my cello in my car."

"Good girl, Rita. I knew you would do the right thing."

Up yours, mister, she thought. I'm doing the stupidest thing possible.

Rita's hands were shaking, and she had to concentrate to not drop the cello as she placed it in the trunk of her car. With the lid of the trunk blocking the view between Ray and herself, she slipped her left hand into her coat pocket and extracted her phone. She fervently hoped she could get a text off to someone, perhaps her dad, before she joined Ray in his vehicle.

She was startled as the trunk lid descended slowly, brushing her sleeves and forcing her to take a step back. The man called Ray was there, snapping the trunk closed and holding out his hand.

"Your cell phone, please," he said with a smile.

She handed it to him, and he removed the battery and sim card, putting the pieces into his pocket. "We can't have your friends following you, now can we?"

Chapter 22

Many people in Iowa might have described Wednesday morning as glorious. The sun hung in a cloudless blue sky, warming the day into the seventies. The farmers were in the fields, reporting bumper yields, yet, surprisingly, commodity prices were inching up.

None of it mattered to the people whose lives were in the gravity well of evil created by a handful of wicked people.

Rita Harrington had slept fitfully, and now stared at the ceiling of a cheap motel room, somewhere along old Highway 20 in Iowa. Ray had avoided Interstate 80 as well as the new four-lane freeway that served as U.S. 20. He had stopped at a roadside motel in some small town Rita never had heard of, and booked them a room with two beds. She had protested, but in the end, had followed him inside.

Ray had unplugged the telephone and tossed it in a corner while she used the bathroom. He had then handcuffed her wrist to the bed farthest from the window and encouraged her to sleep. He had removed his coat, shoes, and shirt, but had kept on his pants and t-shirt. He had climbed into the other bed and had fallen asleep in minutes.

Rita had tugged at the handcuff, wondering why she had ever agreed to come along. *This is going to end badly. Very badly*, she had thought over and over until sleep finally came. Now it was morning, and their trip was about to resume.

Ray was smiling and pleasant. She wanted to scratch his eyes out.

***

Tony woke to the same steady glow of a single lightbulb, the pain in his shoulder reminding him quickly of his plight. Madeline was snuggled up against him. She had been smart enough to pull the mattress off the wooden platform and drag it over to the wall. By folding it in half, she had created a soft surface just high enough that Tony could sit. His arm still dangled from the anchor above, but at least his body weight wasn't on it. Exhaustion had taken them both.

Tony didn't know if they'd slept two hours or ten, but he was grateful to have slept at all. His stomach was crying out for food, and he knew Madeline must be ravenous as well. People could live a long time with just water, but as the hours passed, the agony of hunger grew.

There was no way to be sure, but Tony's best guess was that it was Wednesday morning by now. Whatever was going to happen was likely to happen today. He tried not to think about it.

Madeline woke soon after Tony. They sat for a time, still holding each other and not saying much. Then she rose and suggested she should return the mattress to its home, so as not to alert Justin to the fact they had devised a small comfort in his absence.

***

Justin Langly was also lying in bed, staring at the ceiling. He had thought hard about calling the cops, but had decided he couldn't do it. He wasn't dumb enough to think they would ever cut him any slack. He had killed those girls. If the cops ever found him, he was toast. So he simply had to hope Ray was smart enough to shake the feds and arrive without the heat. He would tell Ray about Tony's suggestion, and they all would have a good laugh, right before he shoved big daddy inside that bitch. *I'll show her what it means to be "rescued" by me.*

He climbed out of bed and headed for the shower. With any luck, today was going to be fun.

***

Ben had stayed in his office all night. He tried to work but mostly stared at the phone console on his desk, willing it to ring, and begging the universe to align some stars or something to give him a line on how to save the two young people he had let down so completely.

At 8:30, the phone rang. Ben had it to his ear before the first ring had finished. "Yes?"

"Ben, it's Rich Davis. I wanted to call just to let you know we haven't found anything yet, and to bring you up to speed on the preparations at the truck stop to take the guys working there once the money man arrives."

Ben could hear something in Davis' voice. "But...?"

Davis sighed. "But I have more bad news."

Ben sat up straight. "Tell me."

"Rita Harrington is missing."

"What! What happened? I thought you assigned... I thought you had her protected."

"We thought so too. About three this morning, the FBI agent doing protection duty for Rita called in to say she had been assaulted last evening. She was stabbed in the neck and woke up six hours later. Obviously, her attacker used some kind of syringe to inject her with etorphine, a powerful knock-out drug."

"Does he...?"

Davis interrupted, "It's a she, and no, she doesn't have any information that will help. The agent had gone to use the restroom while Rita was in the concert hall for her audition. When she stepped out of the stall, she was attacked from behind. She never saw a thing."

"Jesus Christ! Who are these people?"

"I wish I had answers for you, Ben. I just got off the phone with Charles Harrington, Tony and Rita's dad. I didn't have answers for him, either." Davis sounded completely defeated, and Ben backed off.

"Okay, Rich. Thank you for telling me. I guess now we hope the operation at the truck stop bears some fruit. Maybe the bag man will know something."

"Let's hope." The call ended.

***

"Where are we going?" Rita asked as Ray turned the Mercedes north onto Highway 218.

"We have a stop to make near Cedar Falls," Ray said, smiling. "No, Tony's not there. This will be a very brief stop. Then we'll be on our way to our final destination."

Rita cringed at the sound of that but said nothing. A few minutes later, Ray turned into a long driveway leading to a secluded home in the woods north of the college town. It was a large, two-story brick house with a three-stall garage. A shiny red Maserati sat in the driveway.

"Lenny, you are about as subtle as a roast pig at a Jewish wedding," Ray muttered, more to himself than to Rita.

He turned and looked at her. "Stay here, young lady. There's no point in running away. That just gets Tony killed and ensures no one will ever find him. I won't be long."

"I get it," Rita said, turning away and fuming as she stared out the passenger window.

Ray walked briskly up to the house and rang the bell.

It took a while, but finally Lenny pulled open the door. He was still in his pajamas and a dark maroon robe made of silk.

"Ray? What are you doing here? I haven't been to the truck stop yet, so I don't have the money."

"May I come in?"

"Of course, of course," Lenny said, opening the door wider so his boss could walk past him.

"Beautiful place," Ray said. "I pay you well, but who would have guessed you'd have all this? And that car. My goodness, even I don't drive a Maserati."

"Well, you know my wife? She's a nurse. She pulls down good dough too," he said.

"Really? That's wonderful. Is she here? I'd love to meet her."

"No," Lenny said, his nervousness growing. "She's working her shift in the ER at the hospital in Cedar Falls. Why are you here, Ray? You know, I don't like the possibility the neighbors might see you."

"Good point," Ray said. "I'm not too crazy about that idea either. That's why I came during the day, when they're working. It's just that we have a bit of business to do, and I wanted to take care of it in person."

"Business?"

"Well, yes, Lenny. You see, I'm not the dumb, gullible asshole you apparently think I am. I happen to know you've been skimming."

"No, Ray, I would never..."

"Stuff it, Lenny. I *know*. It wasn't a question. So I'm here to settle your debt."

Lenny seemed to shrink two sizes inside his robe. "Okay, okay. Ray, I'm... I'm sorry. Really. It's just I needed... I mean, please. I can make it right. All of it."

"I know you can, Lenny." Ray pulled his silenced .38 from his inside jacket pocket and shot Lenny in the forehead. The skinny man dropped to the floor like a rock, his blood and hair splattered across the front of the grandfather clock next to the stairs.

Ray didn't even glance at the body. He jogged up the stairs to the second floor, found the master bedroom, and emptied the dresser and vanity of all the jewelry. There wasn't a lot, but a few diamonds, pried from the rings and a pendant, and some gold bracelets, would put a few extra bucks in his coffers. More importantly, it would send the local police looking for a robber rather than a business associate.

Six minutes after he had left Rita sitting in the car, Ray was back and driving south. "Mission accomplished," he said, smiling.

***

At 11:30 a.m., Justin was pacing around his house. He wasn't sure what time Ray or Donny would show up, and the waiting was killing him. He wanted to go to the shelter, but he knew he'd better not. He wanted that girl. He ached to get his hands on her, but he knew he had to wait.

I'm so horny, I'd have sex with a snake if someone'd hold it for me.

It occurred to him he was hungry. He also knew he needed some enticing aromas by which to "encourage" the guests' cooperation.

And he knew it was possible Ray and Donny would be hungry when they arrived. In short, he needed food.

Justin scribbled a note—"Be right back"—on a Post-It and stuck it on the glass of the storm door. He grabbed his keys, went out the door, and jumped in his truck. A quick run to town for food and beer would be better than just waiting around. *This is good*, he thought, as the truck roared out of the lane.

***

"All units report by number," Tabors' voice said over the com in Davis' ear. Then, in order, he heard each unit call in. "Negative. Negative. Negative."

Davis was last, number eight. "Negative," he said. He could hear the frustration in Tabors' voice.

"The girl told us every Wednesday morning, right?"

Davis took a deep breath. "Right."

"It's now after noon," Tabors said. "How many clients are we going to let climb up into that truck before we do something about it?"

"Let's give it thirty more minutes," Davis suggested. "If the skinny guy with the fancy car doesn't show by then, we can move in on the guys who are here." He had that horrible feeling the bastards were a step ahead of them again. He just hoped *something* would come of this operation. Even more urgently, he hoped Emily and the other two girls were still here in that truck, or in the motel, and okay.

***

When Justin returned, driving up the lane and turning past his house, he saw two cars sitting by the barn. One was a tan Ford

Taurus, the other a beautiful silver Mercedes.

The Taurus had made him tense up, immediately thinking *cop car*, but when he noticed the Mercedes, he relaxed. Even the FBI didn't drive Mercedes. Two men stepped out. One was Donny. The other was older, gray, tall and thin, and looked like he was dressed to go to the opera. Justin knew that must be Ray.

Justin climbed out of the truck, carrying four paper bags. He walked over to the two men, apologized for being gone when they arrived, and held out the sacks. "I thought I should grab some food."

Ray glanced down at the logo on the bags, obvious disdain on his face, and said, "Well, you almost did." Donny choked back a laugh.

Justin said, "Well, uh, welcome. This is it. You wanna go in the house, or you wanna see the shelter?"

"Shelter," Ray said. "We have another guest for you."

He opened the back door of the Mercedes, and Rita climbed out. Her eyes were red from crying, but otherwise she looked much as she had when she had stepped out of her audition.

This girl is hot. Justin realized his mouth was watering. She didn't look like the girls in Orney. She had raven-black hair and a tinge of olive in her skin. She looked like a princess from some exotic land.

"Well, hello, sweetheart," Justin said, licking his lips.

"I'm not your sweetheart," she snapped. "Where's my brother?"

"Brother? Oh, the puke in the shelter. He's your brother? Well, I'm happy to take you to him. Let's go." The thought of getting this girl underground and cuffed stirred his most primal desires.

Justin walked over to take her arm with his free hand, but she shied away. "Don't you dare touch me!"

He shrugged and looked at Ray, who nodded. Justin turned and led the way back to the shed where the hidden entrance to the shelter could be found.

***

Madeline was sitting cross-legged near Tony's feet. The two of them had devised a plan. The next time Justin came down the stairs, Madeline would feign being unconscious. Tony would yell at Justin to hurry and help, saying Madeline had passed out, probably from hunger. They had positioned the metal cable so it formed a big loop propped up against Tony's side. When Justin got close and knelt down to check on Madeline, Tony would flip the cable around his neck. Tony knew he wasn't strong enough to take Justin alone, but maybe with the two of them working together, they had a chance.

They heard the door clank open. Madeline gave Tony's legs a quick squeeze, "For luck," she whispered, and assumed her pose on the floor.

Madeline opened her eyes again when she heard Tony groan and mutter, "Get up. I'm sorry."

Justin was followed down the stairs by two other men. The first had to be Donny. Tony recognized him from Madeline's description. The second was older and more distinguished. And then, a woman's legs. Another girl? A female accomplice? A...?

"Rita! Dear God, Rita, what are you doing here?"

His sister bolted across the room and threw her arms around him. "Oh, Tony," she sobbed. "You're alive. You're... Oh, look at what they've done to you. Oh, Tony, I'm so sorry..."

A smorgasbord of emotions erupted from Tony. He was baffled, astonished, scared, and angry. Mostly he was angry. He turned to the men. "What is she doing here? You have me. You don't need her. Get her out of here."

Ray spoke first. "Sorry, Tony. You're right. I don't need her. I don't *need* any of you. But I'm going to enjoy you all. I'm tempted to start with your dear sister, but I think Madeline goes first. She is, after all, the troublemaker. Madeline, I believe you know my recruiter, Donny."

As soon as Ray spoke, Tony knew who it was. He would never forget that voice.

Madeline had slunk back to her corner. Tears erupted once again.

In the back of the room, Justin dropped the bags full of food and said, "Wait, Donny? What about me? I get to do this, right? I've been waiting for days. The bitch is mine!"

Ray turned and stared at him, steely-eyed and irritated. "You're whining, Mr. Langly. I hate whining." Then, as if he had another thought, he said, "Actually, come over here."

Justin approached, and Ray said, "Show me."

"Huh?"

He repeated, impatiently, "Take down your pants and show me your, uh, stuff. Maybe I do want you to go first."

Donny started to object, but Ray held up his hand and stopped him cold.

"Well this is weird," Justin said, "but I got nothin' to hide. Big daddy's been wantin' outta these jeans." He unbuckled his belt and dropped his pants and his underwear to the floor.

"Very impressive. Wouldn't you agree, Donny?"

Tony, Madeline, and Rita were appalled. This was insanity. Ray clearly was completely psychotic.

Ray then proved it, saying, "Well, we can't have someone around who makes my recruiter feel inadequate, can we?"

As Justin started to ask what he meant, Ray pulled out his gun and shot him in the groin.

Justin's scream could be heard by the dead in cemeteries three counties away. He fell to the floor bleeding and screaming, "You fucker! What have you done? You bastard!"

"You're still whining," Ray said, and shot him in the forehead.

Tony and Madeline both screamed. Rita passed out, and Tony caught her just in time to break her fall.

Ray smiled, made a sweeping motion around the room with the gun, and asked, "Anyone else planning to whine?"

***

Ben was in his office, staring at the phone. Davis should have called long ago. Clearly something was wrong. It was too much to bear. Everything they tried came up empty. In the meantime, who knew what horrors his people were suffering? He had never felt so helpless. *Those poor kids.*

He heard raised voices, then actual yelling in the newsroom. He looked up and saw Maggie, the Pizza Hut manager, with her finger in Laurie's face. Laurie was trying to block her way, and Maggie wasn't having it.

"Get outta my way, you little...," Maggie yelled. "I need to see Mr. Smalley now, and I don't need some young whippersnapper getting in my way."

"But you can't just go in there."

Ben stepped out of his door and called across the room, "It's okay, Laurie. Let her come on back."

Maggie rushed to his office, out of breath and talking as she moved. "He did it. He did it again. I know it's him. You were right. He did it again."

What now? Ben wondered. "Slow down, Maggie. Sit. Start at the beginning, and tell me why you're here."

"Mr. Smalley, it's that Langly kid. You know, the one I told you about. Remember, I told you he hadn't been through the burger window drive-up in a while? Well, he was there. After you told me, you know, what he did, I was watchin' for him."

Ben was stern. "Maggie, I did not tell you what he did. In fact, I specifically told you he probably didn't do anything."

"Nonsense," she shot back. "He did. And now we know he did. Your people are missing, and guess what? He's back buying food."

The reference to his missing reporters got Ben's full attention. "Tell me what you mean, Maggie. Just because he bought a hamburger?"

"No, no, no!" she yelled. "He bought four big bags of food. Who buys four big bags of food on a work day, when you live alone?"

"Well, that may be," Ben said, "but he could have been buying for his co-workers or something. Maggie, this is serious stuff. We can't assume..."

She cut him off, looking triumphant. "He wasn't."

"What?"

"I called the co-op. He took the week off. In the middle of the harvest. They didn't sound too happy when they told me he wouldn't be in this week."

"You called the co-op?"

"Well, sure!" She grinned. "I couldn't come chargin' over here not knowin' what I was talkin' about, could I?"

Ben shook his head at the town gossip, but knew he had to take seriously what she was saying. Langly lived on an acreage outside of town. He had taken the week off of work—the same week in which Tony and Madeline had been taken. Then, suddenly, he's back buying fast food in quantities a bachelor wouldn't buy. "Maggie, listen to me."

She still was grinning ear-to-ear. "I figured it out, didn't I, Mr. Smalley? It's Justin Langly. Now you have to get going. Call somebody and save those kids."

Ben was stopped cold. Justin? He realized he had never asked Langly's first name. He had let Tony down again. He had promised to look into Langly, and all he had done was talk to Maggie. He hadn't even asked his first name. He sank into his chair. *What a stupid fucking moron I am. This changes everything.*

He stood up again. "Maggie, please listen. I promise I'm going to follow up on this. In return, you have to promise me you'll go back to work and not say a word to anyone. If you're right, this has to be handled carefully. Do you promise?"

"Course I do," she said. "You know me. I wouldn't say a word to nobody."

***

As Ben raced out the back door of the *Crier* Building, Billy chased him down. "Something going on, chief? Let me grab a camera, and I'll join you."

"Sorry, Billy. No photo ops yet. I'll call you as soon as I can to come join me. Just sit tight."

Billy stopped and stared, then sulked back into the newsroom. He nearly bumped into Maggie as she was leaving. Billy's face lit up.

"Hey, Maggie. I saw you talking to Ben. He left in a pretty big hurry. He said he wanted me to join him, but I couldn't hear the location as he shouted it from the parking lot. Do you know where he's headed?"

Maggie leaned in close and said, "Now don't you go tellin' him you heard it from me, right?" Billy nodded, and she continued. "He's going out to Justin Langly's place. Justin's got your co-workers trapped out there, and your boss is on a rescue mission. Ain't that somethin'?"

Billy agreed that it was.

***

Agents Davis and Tabors were staring at each other glumly over lukewarm coffee in the truck stop cafeteria. The operation in the nearby parking lot and motel had been a bust. When they had finally said go and had swooped in to make arrests and save the girls, they had found nothing. No girls and no evidence of crimes. In the back of the truck, they'd found a man selling watermelons.

"They had to have known we were coming," Davis said. "They had to know."

Tabors didn't argue. Her head hurt, and her stomach ached. She wanted to punch someone. If the waitress had misspoken, she might have taken a swing at her.

Davis was about to ask what they should do next when his phone buzzed. It was Ben Smalley.

"Ben? Did you get another call?"

"No." He sounded out of breath. "But I think we might have found them."

Davis rocketed out of his seat, sloshing coffee on the table. "What!"

"It's an acreage. A young guy lives there. A big brute named Justin Langly. You hear me, Agent Davis? Justin!"

Davis heard a door slam and an engine start. "Ben, where are you? How do you know?"

"It's a long story, but our guy, who lives alone, picked up enough food at McDonald's to host a party at noon today—a Wednesday. He didn't take it to work because he took the week off.

His name is Justin! I think he has them. Even if he doesn't, it's worth a look."

"Ben, it's a great lead. At least it's something, but you know you can't go out there, right? If they're there, you'd be going up against a guy who kills girls for fun. Not to mention the fact we haven't found Donny, so he could be there too. Whether you find them or not, you'll be trespassing. I don't want to have to arrest you on top of everything else."

"Screw that," Ben said. "I'm going. "He could be torturing those kids right now, you know? Right now. At the very least, I can interrupt things until you get there."

"Ben," Davis said with every bit of authority he could muster in his voice, "I am telling you to stand down."

There was no response. Davis looked at his phone and realized Ben had ended the call.

"Shit."

Tabors said, "What was that?"

Davis told her as fast as he could, as he dialed Sheriff Mackey's number.

Chapter 23

"I know the place," Mackey said into his cell phone. He was up and grabbing his jacket, gesturing at two of his deputies to follow him. "And I know the guy. Not well. He keeps to himself. But Smalley is right to call him a brute. He's huge. If it's him... Well, it wouldn't be pretty." As soon as the sheriff spoke, he realized the stupidity of the comment. What was happening to these girls wasn't pretty, no matter who was doing it.

"I'll get Judge Schroeder on the phone and see if I can get a verbal warrant to go onto the property. Extra food is a thin clue, but everybody in this town knows what's at stake here. And with the name matching the one scratched on the dead girl's skin, I think he'll give us what we need. Meanwhile, where are you? Still on I-35?"

"Yes, dammit," Davis said. "We were at the truck stop when Ben called. Even with lights and sirens, we're more than an hour away. This is all on you until we get there."

"Understood," Mackey said. "I'll keep you posted. And Rich, one other thing."

"Yeah?"

"The Langly place is one of those with a bomb shelter. I knew the farmer who lived there when it was a working farm. He was a crazy old goat who was sure the bombs would fall any day. Maybe he wasn't so crazy, after all; we came awful close. In any case, he built himself a one-room shelter near one of the outbuildings on the farm. He tried to keep it a secret, but there ain't many secrets in Orney. You can't hire an excavator and a contractor without half the town knowing it before the first spade of dirt is turned."

The phone was quiet.

"You there?" Mackey asked.

"Yeah, I'm just thinking about the nightmare of trying to roust an armed man or men out of a hole in the ground without getting those kids killed."

"Yeah, no shit. You'd better hurry. I hate getting blood on my uniform, especially when it's mine."

***

Ben was in his 1963 Chevy Fleetside pickup, headed for Justin Langly's place, when he heard the call go out from Sheriff Mackey. He was ordering all cars to Justin's place. That was a good sign.

Ben had a portable police-band radio in his truck. Cops hated it when the media, and even everyday citizens, listened in on their radio traffic, but Ben had found it to be an essential tool for reporting. The newsroom had a desktop unit that never was turned off. Over the years, it had alerted them to more accidents, crimes, and tornadoes than Ben could count. It also alerted them to possible dangers, so his reporters didn't walk into situations they shouldn't. Nowadays, with computer screens in the patrol cars and cell phones, the radios were used less, but officers still relied on them in some situations, such as when they needed to communicate instantly to multiple officers.

In any case, Mackey was on the radio now and what Ben was hearing was the most welcome sound he'd ever heard from that two-inch speaker. It was telling him that Davis had reacted quickly and Mackey was responding.

The bad news was that the Quincy County Sheriff's Department was small. There were a limited number of deputies spread between three shifts. Most day-shift deputies spent their time transporting prisoners, serving summonses, or taking mental health patients across the state to wherever a judge could find an open bed in a psychiatric unit.

Besides Bodke, his chief investigator, Mackey had just two additional deputies available to answer the call. It was clear Ben would arrive at Langly's first. The sheriff and the deputies would follow, but would the cavalry arrive in time?

When the radio traffic died down, Ben pulled out his cell phone and called Mackey.

"Smalley?"

"Sheriff, I'm here. I'm just driving up the lane. Do you know what I'm looking for? Would he have them in the house or the barn? Give me an idea where to start."

"I'll tell you where to start," the sheriff growled. "Start by putting your foot on the brake and waiting right there. We don't need somebody dead or wounded before we even get started."

"Sheriff, I'm going in. Now. There's no point in arguing. Are you going to help me or not?"

The sheriff began to rant again, but Ben cut him off.

"Sheriff, there are three cars parked in back of the house."

"What? Three cars? I never knew Langly to drive anything other than that big pickup. I'm not sure he'd fit in anything else."

"Two of them have out-of-state license plates. One Illinois and one... Let me get closer."

"Dammit, Smalley!"

"The second one is Oregon. They may be rentals or something. Well, actually, the Illinois car doesn't look like a rental. It's a Mercedes S Class sedan. Those things cost a small fortune. I doubt that came from a rental company."

"Okay, that's great, Ben. Note the license number, then get the hell out of there. We're coming hard. It won't be much longer."

"Sorry sheriff, but I'm going to check it out. They're parked in the back by the farm buildings, so they're probably in the barn, or maybe that shed."

"Ben, stop! They're underground. Dammit, they're underground. You can't get to them without alerting them that you're there. You're gonna get yourself killed."

"Maybe, but if they know I'm here, maybe they stop before Tony or Madeline dies." Ben had another thought. "And think about it, sheriff. Maybe Rita Harrington too."

"Huh?"

"Rita was taken in Chicago. Here's a rich guy's car from Illinois. It's possible she's here."

"What the hell kind of party are these bastards throwing down there?"

"No clue," Ben said simply, "but I'm gonna find out."

The sheriff was still yelling when Ben pulled the phone away from his ear. He didn't end the call. Somehow it seemed smart to keep the line open. He moved quickly, and as quietly as he could manage on the gravel, across the open yard to the shed at the back. He decided to check the smaller building first simply because it was smaller. He stayed to the right of the shed's open door as he approached the building. Once up against the side, he lowered himself to a crouch and glanced around the corner into the shed. He immediately spotted the open hatch leading underground. He took a longer look through the door and held his breath, straining to hear.

Someone was crying, and someone was talking. Then someone else. Then a fourth person.

He backed away from the building and whispered into the phone, "Multiple voices inside."

"What?"

"I can hear multiple men talking, and someone is crying."

"Ben, please get out of there. We're almost there."

***

Justin's blood was everywhere. Both bullets had created massive exit wounds. Tony knew it meant the gun was loaded with hollow-points, designed to kill. This was not a gun that created minor wounds.

Having watched it rip Justin to pieces, Tony was terrified of the weapon and of the man who wielded it. However, a corner of his brain was still functioning and realized the beast was dead. And now there were three against two. Maybe, somehow...

Rita stirred at his feet. As consciousness returned, a look of horror crossed her face. Tony knelt down as far as his cuffs would allow, and held her with his free arm. He whispered in her ear, "Rita, hang in there. You can handle this. You're strong. Be ready."

Tony's whisper was masked by Madeline's sobs.

Ray's soft, easygoing voice said, "Okay, Donny. I think you know what to do."

"Do I ever," Donny said. He turned and smirked at Tony. "Enjoy the show, Mr. Harrington." He stepped to the back wall and grabbed Madeline by the hair, dragging her back to the center of the room, where the platform bed was waiting. She screamed in pain and anger, and Tony stiffened.

Ray said, "Make one move to help her, and I put a bullet in that nice young lady on the floor there."

Tony wanted to scream. He pulled at the cuffs but knew it was futile.

***

Outside, Ben heard Madeline's scream. He couldn't wait any longer. All that stopped him from jumping into the gaping stairway was an idea. He turned and ran to his pickup.

He lifted the cell phone to his mouth and said, "Sheriff. Don't talk. Listen. I need your help. Get on the radio and get all your guys talking. Everyone who's on your band."

"What are you...?"

"Listen!" Ben hissed, as he grabbed the police radio from his pickup. Get everyone talking as if they're here. Get them saying they're driving in, they're surrounding the shed, they're in place. You get it? Something bad is happening inside. I need to convince these guys that the troops are here. I've got a radio! Get everyone talking. Now."

Mackey was yelling at Ben to wait for him, but the cell phone call had ended. So he got on the radio and gave everyone instructions.

Ben ran back to the shed, turned up the volume on his radio and tossed it in the door. It slid to a stop at the top of the stairs, then started squawking, "Unit one, this is unit three, we're in position. Roger unit three, get all your men in place by the shed. Unit five, are you and unit four ready? Roger that, unit one. We've got the big guns out. I can hear a girl screaming. We're going in. Roger, unit..."

***

Ray and Donny both spun toward the door. "What the...?" Ray started.

"It's the cops! They're here!" Donny screamed, climbing off the bed where Madeline lay curled into a ball.

As the two men turned their backs to look at the stairway, Tony tried to reach the metal cable laying across the floor. He got his toe under it and was lifting it up so his free hand could reach it.

Madeline saw what he was doing and climbed off the bed in an instant.

However, it was Rita who struck first. She had been curled up on the floor and she simply lashed out with her feet, striking Ray in the back of the legs. He stumbled and tried to regain his balance as his expensive Italian shoes found the pool of blood on the floor and slipped out from under him. In an instant, he was flat on his back.

Madeline didn't hesitate. She jumped on top of Ray's flailing right arm, pushing the hand with the gun into the bloody floor.

Ray was dazed, but only for a moment. Tony couldn't reach him. He was helplessly pinned to the wall. Rita was not. As quickly as Ray had fallen, Rita was on her feet. She kicked him as hard as she could in the side of the head and he went limp.

Donny whipped around at the sound of the commotion, realized what had happened, and scanned the floor.

"Gun!" Tony screamed.

Madeline grabbed for it, but it was slippery from the blood covering most of its surface, and it skittered away toward the back of the room. Madeline and Donny both scrambled for the gun, but as Donny passed, Tony kicked out hard and caught his right knee.

He heard a sharp crack of bone as Donny cried out and fell to the floor.

Rita ran to the stairway and started screaming. "Now! Come now! Come now! Hurry."

Madeline reached the gun, wiped the grip on her sweater, and turned to face Donny, crawling across the floor.

"Come closer, *please*," Madeline said, her voice hoarse.

Tony glanced up at the sound from the stairs. Thundering into the room came...

"Ben?" Tony's jaw fell closer to the floor than it had been in days.

Ben rushed in, trying to grasp what he was seeing. Two bodies on the floor. Well, maybe one body and one man who could be alive. Rita Harrington was standing, and another man crawling on the floor, dragging one leg. Tony handcuffed and Madeline bloody, in a torn sweater, and holding a gun like she meant to use it.

Tony couldn't fathom why he was seeing his boss rather than Davis or Agent Tabors or the sheriff, but he put that aside and called out, "Ben, the red-haired guy there is Donny. He may be armed. Don't let him near Madeline."

Ben rushed across the room as Rita said, "Hit his knee! His right knee is keeping him down."

Ben didn't hesitate. He stomped on Donny's injured knee, causing a shriek of pain to erupt from him.

"If you move an inch, if you even twitch, I'm doing that again, and I won't hold back next time."

Donny went limp. Ben bent down and ran his hands over Donny's clothes. He found no weapon. Then he and everyone turned to look at Madeline as she said through her tears, "I want to kill him." She was still holding the gun in two hands, pointed at Donny on the floor. "He deserves to die. Think about what he has done. The unspeakable suffering he's caused. I *will* kill him."

She was shaking and sobbing. Tony worried that she would fire the gun whether she meant to or not. He started to speak, but Ben stepped forward, putting his body between the gun and Donny.

"Sorry, Madeline, but that's not going to happen. I can't afford to lose my best reporter to a twenty-year prison sentence." He held out his hand. "Give me the gun. Give it to me, and let's prove to Donny there's a difference between animals like him and human beings like us."

Madeline sagged and let Ben take the gun from her.

Ben smiled and pulled his cell phone out with his free hand. When he reached the sheriff, he said, "You need to hurry, but we're secure here for the moment."

"Are they okay? Did you make it in time?"

"Our friends are all safe," Ben said, "But we're gonna need some ambulances and the medical examiner. And send the DCI Crime Lab team."

He looked at Tony, Rita, and Madeline. "Anything else?"

"Food!" Tony and Madeline said in unison.

Chapter 24

Tony ate a sandwich and felt a little better physically. Mentally, however, he was devastated to learn the team had failed to find Emily and capture her slavers.

"They should have been there," he said. "She was sure the money guy was coming Wednesday morning."

They were sitting in a Winnebago motor home in Justin's yard. They didn't want to use the house or any of the outbuildings because all would be carefully inspected for evidence of previous victims. Ben had called in a favor from a friend in town, and the Winnebago had shown up less than 30 minutes later. It wasn't ideal for debriefing, but it was better than standing outside.

Donny was on the way to the hospital, cuffed to his stretcher and chaperoned by an armed deputy. Rita was also headed for the hospital, but as a passenger in a deputy's car. She would get a quick examination, and then would be taken to the Sheriff's Department to make her statement. She had told Tony not to worry about her. She would call and ask mom or dad to come pick her up and take her home.

Justin's body wouldn't be moved until after the Crime Lab team arrived and finished its preliminary work.

Ray had a nasty headache, but Sheriff Mackey had said, "Tough shit" and had put him in the back of a patrol car, hands cuffed behind his back. Except for the complaint about his pain, Ray had refused to say a word to anyone. His wallet and his car, however, had provided a lot of what they needed to know. They had asked him about Emily and the other girls, but he had kept his mouth tightly shut.

Tony glared at Davis. "You know we have to move fast, right?" If his guys get wind of the fact that we have him, they're going to dispose of those girls and disappear."

"You may be right, but I can't make him talk."

"I could." It was Madeline's voice from the back corner of the motor home.

Tony gave a quick shake of his head to discourage Davis from responding and said, "I have an idea. Do you have his cell phone?"

"Sure, but it's password-protected."

"Of course," said Tony. "But he's rich. He uses the latest and greatest. We don't need a password; we just need his face."

Davis knew immediately what Tony meant, and asked Dan Rooney to go get the phone from the evidence locker in the trunk of their car.

Rooney nodded and left. He was gone a long time. It seemed like forever to Tony. The members of the team just stared at each other in silence as they waited.

When Rooney came up the stairs into the motorhome, he said, "Well, that worked like a charm." Tony's eyes widened and Rooney threw him a wink, "He resisted. It was fun." He slid the phone across the table where Tony and Davis could both see the screen. It was open to recent calls. There were multiple numbers, which was to be expected considering Ray's legitimate business as well as his criminal enterprise.

"I don't know where to start," Davis said.

"Wait." Tony pulled the phone closer. "I recognize that number. Why do I know that number?"

"It looks a lot like yours," Davis said. "You sure you're not just seeing the similarities?"

Davis was right. It had the same area code and exchange as Tony's number, which told him it could be local. With cell phones, you couldn't be sure, but it might be. In any case, there was something else about it. Tony was sure he had seen the number before.

"Hey everybody, take a look at the number with the 515 area and the 202 exchange. I'm sure I know that number, but I can't remember. See if you know what it is."

When the phone got to Ben, he took one glance and said, "Well, I'll be damned. This is Billy's phone." He locked eyes with Tony. "We just found our leak."

After rounds of disbelief and rounds of cursing and promises to inflict bodily harm, Tony finally said, "Before we say or do anything to Billy, I think we can use this to find our slavers. Look, Ray took a call from Billy yesterday afternoon. I'll bet that's when Billy told him you were planning a raid on the truck stop. Then look, when that call ended, Ray immediately called this number. I'll bet you anything that's our guys."

"That's pretty good, Tony. Now we go to work. We can find that phone's location, and we can find them. We'll get the team back in place."

"I have a better idea," Tony said, "if you'll trust me."

Tabors said no. Davis was reluctant. Sheriff Mackey said, "After what the kid's been through, and everything he's already delivered, give the little egomaniac a chance."

Tony practiced talking like Ray for a few minutes. When everyone agreed he sounded close, he tapped the number in question. Ray's phone dialed, and a man answered. It sounded like John from the truck stop operation.

Tony mustered his best impression of Ray and said, "Everything go okay?"

"Course it did. What's wrong? Don't you trust me to make a simple move?"

"I didn't say that," Tony replied, trying hard to keep that infuriating, smile-in-the-voice tone Ray liked to use. "I'm calling to tell you I've had to make another change."

"Another change? Like what?"

"I need you to put the girls in the vehicle and bring them to me."

"What, tonight? They're working. They got clients waiting."

"This is important. I have a very special client who's paying six figures for one night with multiple girls. Make excuses to your clients, and bring the girls to me as quickly as you can. There's a major bonus in this for you if you get them here tonight."

"I should hope so. Where are you?"

"I'm in Orney, Iowa. I took care of our little problem. Now I have an acreage I can use for a few days. Bring them here." He gave John the address.

"Jesus, Ray. That's two hours away."

"Don't whine. You know I hate whiners." Tony smiled. "I'll be waiting." He ended the call and handed the phone back to Rooney. "Now we just need to get things ready here so we don't spook them, and they can bring the girls to us." Tony's smile had grown cocky.

"What a dick," Madeline muttered from the corner.

"Well I'll be a frog on fire," Rooney said. "This might work."

***

The slavers arrived in a late model Chevy Suburban, having changed vehicles after learning the FBI/DCI team was looking for the minivan. John was driving, Emily was in the passenger seat, and another four girls were in two sets of rear seats. Sam was in the rear with two of the girls.

It was nearly 10 p.m. when they arrived. Everything had been arranged so that all they saw were the three vehicles by the house, Ray's Mercedes, Donny's Taurus, and Justin's pickup. The lights were on in the house, so the men ushered the girls out of the SUV and started in that direction. Suddenly, they were swarmed by a dozen armed officers. Less than ninety seconds after they arrived, it was over.

John and Sam were face-down in the grass, handcuffed and guarded. The five girls, ranging in ages from thirteen to seventeen, were "contained." Tony disliked the word, and disliked the situation even more. However, he understood that the authorities didn't want one or more of the girls fleeing into a neighboring farm field in the dark. Dressed in jeans and sweaters, all appeared to be terrified. Three were crying at the sight of all the uniforms and guns. They had been told so many times about the horrible consequences that would result from any interaction with authorities, their natural reaction was to flee or fight back. Female officers were among the group, helping to subdue and reassure the girls. One girl kept screaming at them to let her boyfriend go, and calling them pigs and bastards.

It was disturbing to see, but no one was overly surprised. They had been briefed to expect resistance. As with most law enforcement personnel, they knew about the Stockholm Syndrome, in which some victims, after long stints as captives, feel attached to their captors. Some victims have been known to fight aggressively to protect the criminals who have caused them so much pain and despair. Some simply have feared that any alternative to the status quo would be worse. Tony and everyone on the team recognized that recovery for these girls would be a long and difficult process.

Tony was relieved and happy to see Emily was among the group of girls. As he approached her, she shied away, and he realized she didn't know him without the gray hair and moustache.

He said, "Emily, it's me, the guy you punched in the face a few nights ago. My name's Tony."

"You!" she said, clearly recognizing the sound of his voice."

Tony walked up to her, and the deputy gave them a little space. He reached up and touched Emily's cheek and said, "I am so glad you're okay."

"Am I? Am I going to be okay?"

"Emily, in our one conversation, I learned you are smart, brave, and determined. You have survived things no young person should have to see, let alone endure. If you decide right now that you're going to be okay, I have no doubt you can make it come true. All these people are here to help you. Just remember, and don't be afraid to remind them, that you're a victim, not a criminal."

"Okay," she said, tears rolling down her cheeks. "I choose to be okay." She threw her arms around him and said, "Thank you." Tony returned the hug, then the deputy led her away.

Tony wasn't naïve. He knew one conversation on the lawn on a warm October night wasn't going to solve everything for a girl who'd been through hell for three years. But it was a start. Emily and the other girls now had a chance to make it. A chance they didn't have before all these good people had banded together to make it possible.

Madeline had not approached the girls, but was hovering close to Rich Davis. Tony wandered over and realized Madeline was anxiously waiting for the girls' names to be collected. Dan Rooney came across the yard waving a piece of paper. "We don't have them all yet," he said. "The one young lady is more stubborn than a mule on steroids. But we have four of the five."

Madeline snatched the paper from his hand. There it was. Girl number three: Shelly Blaine. Madeline collapsed to the ground, sobbing.

***

The icing on the cake was Billy Campbell. He had used the information supplied by Maggie to find, and sneak onto, Justin's property. He had found a perch in the barn loft and had taken pictures of everything that had occurred in the yard. As the operation was winding down, Billy came trotting across the property, looking smug.

"Hey, everybody, look who's here!" he said brightly, "and guess what I have in here." He flicked on his Canon SLR.

Rich Davis stepped up and said, "Hello, Mr. Campbell. First, why don't you guess what I have back here?" He reached behind his back and pulled out his handcuffs.

Billy looked at him quizzically. The agent then took him by the shoulders, turned him around, pulled the camera out of his hands, and snapped the cuffs on.

As Billy yelped, Davis recited his Miranda Rights and asked if he understood.

"Yes," Billy snapped, "I understand my rights. What I don't understand is..."

"Quiet," Ben barked. "Don't even try. We have the phone history, Billy. We know you were talking to Ray, telling him about our plans. You came this close to getting Tony and Madeline killed, and probably Tony's sister too. How could you, Billy? How could you do that?"

Billy protested loudly, then less loudly after Rooney showed him the call history in Ray's phone. In the end, Billy admitted to calling Ray with updates. But he claimed not to know anything about Ray's operation or the risks he was creating for others.

"He was just a guy who sounded nice on the phone. He paid me a lot of money just to tell him what we were doing. I figured he worked for another newspaper or something. I didn't know. I swear, I didn't know!"

Ben wanted to believe him, but he didn't. Even if Billy had been fooled by Ray at the start, he had to have realized what was happening after Tony and Madeline went missing and the girls were moved from the truck stop. He was just as wicked as the rest of the bastards.

As they put Billy in the back of the sheriff's car, he let his anger overtake his good sense and revealed the truth. He shouted back at Ben, "Maybe I would have been more loyal if you'd included me in some things. Maybe I just got sick of photographing cars at the Chevy lot while Tony-fucking-Harrington was out winning Pulitzers."

Ben simply turned his back on Billy and walked away.

***

Tony and Madeline were taken to the hospital in Orney. Both had visible injuries from their ordeal, but those were minor. After their cuts and bruises were cleaned and dressed, and they were given some mild pain relievers, the Emergency Department doctor discharged them with instructions to rest and follow up soon with a psychologist or psychiatrist.

What they did instead was call Ben and ask for a ride to the *Crier*. They had an article to write and the midnight deadline was approaching. During the short ride from the hospital to the newspaper, the three tried to figure out how to report on a day in which so many major newsworthy events had happened. Writing the story was complicated by the fact they were in the middle of it. Ben normally would have assigned it to someone else, because of his and the reporters' direct involvement. However, in this case, he said there wasn't enough time to explain it all to someone and expect them to have an article ready in time for the press run.

"You two know it best. Go figure it out," he said. They didn't have time for the debates that were inevitable. *What's the lede? Is the rescue most important or the murder? Or maybe the arrests?*

Verb tenses and points of view were also struggles. *Do we write in the first person again? If we want to keep a breaking news tone, how do we handle our roles as captives and witnesses?* Their relationship helped. They trusted each other's judgment, and in the end, turned in an article for the front page with three minutes to spare.

Town Crier

A Day of Rescues, Arrests, and Death

Sex trafficking victims and journalists saved in two emergency operations; Local man dies of gunshot wounds

Tony Harrington and Madeline Mueller, Staff Writers

ORNEY, Iowa – Five teenage girls and three adults were rescued on a rural Orney, Iowa, farm Wednesday night from men believed to be human traffickers, who had abused the girls and had forced them into sexual slavery. Four men were arrested and charged with multiple felonies.

A fifth man, Justin Langly, 31, of rural Orney, was shot to death by Harlan Havercamp, 52, known as "Ray" to his colleagues and his captives, of Chicago, Ill. Havercamp is being investigated as the possible ringleader of a human trafficking and sexual slavery operation that extended across four or more states.

The murder was witnessed by the three adults who were later rescued. Two of the three were Tony Harrington and Madeline Mueller of the *Town Crier* staff, and the authors of this article. They had been held captive for more than two days by Langly, in a former bomb shelter located underground on his farm.

The third adult rescued was the sister of Tony Harrington, who had travelled to Orney in an attempt to find her missing brother. She, too, had been captured and was being held against her will on Langly's farm. The full name of the sister and the names of the underage girls are not being released out of respect for their personal privacy and safety.

The rescues and arrests were spearheaded by the Quincy County Sheriff's Department, with assistance from agents of the Iowa Division of Criminal Investigation and agents from the FBI field office in Chicago. Deputies and officers from other jurisdictions were also involved in various aspects of the investigation and raid of Langly's farm, according to Quincy County Sheriff George Mackey. Also assisting was *Town Crier* Editor and Publisher Ben Smalley, who was first to arrive at the Langly farm after it was learned to be the site where the captives were being held.

"The success we had tonight was the result of true collaboration of multiple people and agencies," Sheriff Mackey said Wednesday night. "By working together, we closed down a truly evil enterprise and released innocent people from slavery as well as from captivity. I'm proud of our success, but I'm saddened to think there are people in the world who would inflict such incredible pain on children and adults."

Mackey said the teenage girls have been turned over to the Department of Human Services for...

Chapter 25

Tony was playing the old upright piano in the back of the Iron Range Tap when Ben walked in. Ben let Tony finish a soulful version of "Summertime," then said, "Buy you a beer?"

"Sure, boss," Tony said, debating whether this would be a good time to have a beer or to stick with his usual. He was driving tonight, so when the waitress asked, he said, "Diet Dr. Pepper."

Ben didn't appear to have anything specific on his mind. They slid into their usual booth, away from the noise of the pool table. The conversation became more of a casual debriefing of the events over the past three weeks. After a few minutes, Ben asked, "You doing okay?"

Tony wasn't sure how to answer. "Physically, I'm pretty good. My shoulder still hurts and may never be the same. And I'm really tired of getting punched in the stomach. But I'm certainly not complaining, considering I would be decomposing in a shallow grave somewhere if not for you."

"Nonsense," Ben said. "I only beat the sheriff there by ten or twelve minutes."

When the room grew quiet again, Tony said, "I know you weren't asking about my shoulder or my stomach. The fact is, I'm okay, but just barely. The relief I feel about Madeline and Rita and those girls being safe is dampened by this unshakable feeling that the evil is lurking out there, just waiting to pounce again."

Ben nodded and took a long draw on his beer.

"We've done good work. Again, you've put the *Crier* on the map. But I know exactly how you feel. You and I both know that if I pulled my laptop out of the pickup and opened it up right now, we could go online and find other girls for sale. Closing down Ray's operation barely puts a dent in the overall problem."

Tony winced. Ben had nailed it exactly. He said, "How is it possible for one human being to do these things to another human being? Who decides one day that their career choice is profiting off of children held in slavery? And the clients... The experts continually point out that the problem exists because there are clients willing to pay. How can men and women who work respectable jobs and go to church on Sunday and maybe volunteer at the Firefighters' Breakfast or the Library Book Sale, go out and pay money to abuse a twelve-year-old kid? It's just unfathomable to me. I feel like my whole concept of humanity—of how the world works—has been knocked off its foundation in the past three weeks."

"I wish I could say something to make it better," Ben said, "but I can't. Except perhaps to urge you to focus on the good people you know. And to keep working to raise awareness of the problem. It's not going away anytime soon, but neither are we."

"Cheers to that," Tony said, holding up his glass of soda.

He tried to keep a smile on his face, but his mention of trafficking clients reminded him of Everett Caulder, who was still living high in his penthouse in Kansas City. Caulder had been arrested, of course, based on the information provided by Emily and Tony. However, he had paid the million-dollar bail in cash and been released the same day. Tony's guts churned whenever he thought about it. After what Caulder had done, he hadn't spent a single night in jail. So far, that is. The bodyguard hadn't fared as well and was still locked up. Apparently Caulder's money wasn't going to be used to help anyone but Caulder.

Tony turned his attention back to Ben. "Have you had this same chat with Madeline?"

He nodded. "Last night."

"How's she doing?"

"About the same. Hard to tell. But haven't you asked her?" Ben seemed surprised.

"We haven't talked much since the incident at Justin's. I made an overture or two, but she shied away. I'm trying to be respectful. If she needs some time, that's okay."

"Makes sense," Ben said. "She seemed pretty good last night, but some of the fire was gone. She never cursed or called me a dick even once."

Tony laughed, then changed the subject. "I heard that the girls —four of the five we rescued— have been accepted into Dorothy's House in Des Moines."

"Yeah, it's a stretch for them to take four at once, but they're going all-out to make it work."

"I'm not surprised," Tony said. "That's an amazing place. I learned about it when I was doing my human trafficking research. A young woman bought two private homes in 2014 and converted one to a residential and treatment facility and the other to a transitional home to help ease these girls back into normal life. The whole operation is supported by private donations and grants, and by a small farm they operate."

"There you go," Ben said. "Another reason to feel better about humanity. There are plenty of evil bastards out there, but there are many more good people who are trying to do the right thing."

"I'll try to remember that." Tony said.

Ben added, "In case you're wondering, the fifth girl, Shelly Blaine, has been returned to the social services people in Missouri. She and her dad have been reunited. Madeline talked to Mr. Blaine, who said the reunion was tearful but wonderful. We all should be very proud of them both."

Tony shifted gears again. "Speaking of proud. Rita's already back at school, plugging away. She's either recovered and doing fine, or she's a great actress and needs to change majors and join the Theater Department. She's not happy about the prospect of testifying against Ray and Donny. She can't really afford to interrupt her life multiple times over the coming year."

"That reminds me," Ben said. "The report this morning is that Rita's account of her trip with Ray allowed the authorities up in Black Hawk County to tie him to the murder of a man there. Apparently, Ray stopped there as they traveled from Chicago to Orney and basically executed a guy."

"Really?" Tony was amazed his sister hadn't mentioned it.

"Don't worry about this one adding to Rita's trauma. She was waiting in the car while Ray went inside the man's home. Rita never even realized a crime had been committed. The DCI put two and two together when they got called in to help with the murder near Cedar Falls."

"I heard some nurse up there found her husband dead. I never dreamed it was Ray."

"Davis thinks the dead guy is the money man who never showed at the truck stop."

Tony's eyes widened, and Ben continued. "He fit the description, and there was a red sports car in the driveway."

"Well, I guess if your boss murders you, that's a pretty good reason to not show up for work."

Ben smiled. "Don't worry. I usually stop short of assassination when disciplining my employees."

"I appreciate it. The less like Ray, the better."

Ben nodded over his beer glass again. "I guess we should stop calling him Ray, now we know his real name."

"Nah," Tony said. "Why make the effort? He's not worth another ounce of mental energy." He remembered something Ben said earlier and changed the subject again. "By the way, you can't get your laptop out of your pickup because you loaned the pickup to me until I get my Explorer back from KC."

Ben smiled. "Good point. When will that be?"

"I'm not sure. I'm really digging driving a '63 Fleetside. I may just leave the Ford down south for a while. And by the way, now that I heard you tell Madeline she's your best reporter, I may just keep the pickup as penance for your sin."

"Yeah, it's funny how the truth slips out during moments of stress." Ben, still smiling, finished his beer and rose. "Just keep my precious truck between the fenceposts," he said and strolled out the back door.

Mention of the loaned pickup reminded Tony of his second vehicle, a classic Ford Mustang Lisa's dad had given him after she'd died. Tony could have gotten it out of storage instead of bothering Ben, but he had just paid to have it prepped and locked away for winter. Ben had insisted it was no trouble to loan him the pickup since he also owned a late model Chrysler 300.

Thoughts of Lisa served to double Tony's melancholy. He still missed her terribly. His time with Madeline was fun and a much-needed step forward in his recovery, but it wasn't the same as having a partner you truly loved and who loved you back.

Tony sighed and stood. Time to go home. Tomorrow, Doug was driving him to KC to pick up his vehicle from the Country Club Plaza parking lot. *I can't wait to see Ben's face when he gets that bill.*

***

The trip to KC with Doug was fun. Time with Doug was always fun. They timed it so they could catch the Saturday evening Royals game before Doug headed home. The playoffs were underway and the Royals had made it into the championship series. Doug had somehow scored tickets for seats above the third base line. The food was greasy, the weather was warm, and the score was close, with the Royals eking out a victory with a two-run double in the bottom of the eighth, and a flawless closing performance by the pitcher in the ninth. In short, it was a perfect evening.

Later, as the friends enjoyed a cold beverage in an overcrowded sports bar, Tony told Doug not to expect him in Orney right away. He had a couple of other stops to make in KC before going home.

"If it involves a casino or a strip club, I'm staying with you," Doug teased.

"Sorry, my friend, but after what I've seen the past three weeks, I'm swearing off all sin."

Doug put on an exaggerated pout. "How can I be friends with someone as boring as that? Can we at least have burgers at Hooters?"

"Nope," Tony said with a smile. "And no R-rated movies or video games either. It's strictly work, exercise, and church for me from now on."

"Well, let me know how that goes," Doug said as Tony climbed out of the booth to go fetch his car. "You can find me in my usual place."

"The county jail, you mean?"

They both laughed, then Tony turned somber and said, "Seriously, Doug. Thanks for everything. I don't know how I could manage all this without a friend like you at my side."

Doug just nodded, finished his beer, and squeezed Tony's arm as he turned to head out the door.

***

Soon after, Tony was back on the barstool in the restaurant in Country Club Plaza.

"Hey, it's the cat burglar," Brenda said, smiling widely. "You're back."

"Yeah, I missed your winks." Tony smiled back. "Pour me your favorite IPA."

She did, then waited on two other customers before wandering back. She eyed Tony for a long time, no longer smiling.

"I'm glad you're okay," she said. "I hate it when my customers get kidnapped and murdered."

Tony grinned. "I guess I'm not so incognito anymore."

"Well, maybe to most of the folks here, but when I read the story in the newspaper about what happened in the rich guy's penthouse, I realized immediately who that Tony Harrington guy was."

"You read newspapers?" Tony said. "I may ask you to marry me."

Brenda chuckled and put on a heavy southern accent. "Careful what you wish for, honeycakes."

"What I'm wishing for at the moment is a chance to punch Caulder in the nose. It burns my butt that the guy who almost got me killed is running around free."

"Running around is right," Brenda acknowledged. "He was in

here last night, acting as if nothing had happened. He's one of those guys who thinks money buys him a free pass. Good thing he didn't come to the bar, 'cause I would have refused to wait on him."

"Good thing he came in last night instead of tonight, or you might have had a mess to clean up," Tony retorted, his anger growing at the thought of Caulder's brazen behavior.

"Woulda been a pleasure," she said. "But I suggest you put it out of your mind. Now everyone knows who he is and what he is, he'll get his due. Fate has a way of settling the score."

"From your lips to God's ears," Tony said quietly.

"From my lips to where?" Brenda grinned, tilting her head and fluttering her eyelashes.

"Nice move. I think I like that even better than the wink. I like you, Brenda. I think I'd better go before I get myself in trouble."

"Damn sorry to hear it. But if you an' that girlfriend part ways, you know where to find me."

He nodded, left cash on the bar, and headed out the door.

***

Debating what to do next, it occurred to him that Caulder's bodyguard was still in jail. *Maybe I should pay our rich friend a visit.* It went against his grain to seek a confrontation with anyone, but the man had, after all, drugged him and shipped him off to be tortured and killed. *I have a gun and a permit to carry it. Maybe I should carry it up the hill to that fancy condo.*

Tony went to the Explorer and got his automatic out of the case in the back. He stuck it in the back of his pants and pulled his jacket on to cover it. He grabbed his gloves from the floor of the back seat and walked up the street toward the condo building.

He walked past the front doors once and confirmed there was

no guard at the front desk. Caulder could have hired someone else by now, but it had only been a few days since the arrests. Even if a guard showed up, it wouldn't be anyone who would recognize him.

Tony walked into the lobby and strode up to the front desk. No one was in sight. He didn't have a key to the door employees used to access the back, so he simply hopped over the desk. He then let himself into the office he had been taken to before. It wasn't locked. The video surveillance and recording system was there. Tony shut everything off. Then he rummaged through a couple of drawers until he found a screwdriver. He removed the hard drive and put it in his jacket pocket.

With any luck, I'm now invisible. Can I really do this? Yes, I can. He set his jaw and walked to the interior service elevator.

When the elevator doors opened, Tony was looking at concrete pillars, a striped floor, and a handful of very expensive cars. He spotted Caulder's hot new Corvette immediately. He walked up to it, pulled the gun out from behind his back, released the safety, and fired all eight bullets into the car's side, front, rear, and dashboard.

"Bastard!" Tony said, placing the gun back in his belt and walking out of the parking garage.

***

At 5:30 the next afternoon, Tony pulled into his drive at the back of his house. He immediately spotted Madeline sitting cross-legged in front of his door under the carport canopy.

"I hope you haven't been there for two days," Tony teased, as he walked up.

"Don't flatter yourself. Ben mentioned you were headed back this afternoon, so I came by a little while ago. When you weren't here yet, I decided I could wait."

"Works for me," Tony said, unlocking the door.

"Yeah, you're not the one with gravel digging into your boney butt."

In the kitchen, Tony asked if she had eaten, offering to make something or take her out—her choice.

"Tony," she said, immediately alerting him to one of *those* conversations. "I can't stay. I just stopped by to tell you I'm leaving."

Tony froze. "Leaving? Leaving what? The *Crier*?"

"Leaving everything: the job, the relationship, the town. I'm going back to Ohio for a while. As dad slows down, mom's gonna need help with him and with the shop."

"Madeline, are you sure? You know, what happened, it's not going to be like that in the future. Life at the *Crier* is usually..."

"Tony! You are such a dick. I'm not running away from the bad guys or the work. You may remember that I asked Ben to let me into the action, and he did. I'm grateful. Nothing else. You and I may very well win some awards for what we did and what we wrote. More importantly, the whole state of Iowa is now talking about the problem of human trafficking. And it may be a little harder for those bastards to operate here, at least for a while. It feels wonderful to be a part of that."

"Then you should stay," Tony said. "We make a good team. There's more to be said about this topic and a lot of other important issues."

"Tony... Have I mentioned you're a dick? It's you, Tony. I'm leaving because of you."

"Me?"

"I like you. I *really* like you. I didn't want that to happen, but it did. Once I realized we—as a couple, I mean—weren't going anywhere, then I knew I couldn't stay. I can't just hang around, getting laid once in a while and pining for something that will never be."

"But how do you know? We're just getting started."

"I know. *I know*, Tony, because I know I cannot compete with Lisa. I hate admitting that. I have a pretty high opinion of myself. I've fought off boys since the seventh grade. But you and I both know Lisa was in a very special category. For you, I mean. She was your *Imzadi*. I can't replace her for you. For me, there's no other answer. I'm leaving because I can't compete with a memory of perfection."

Madeline stood on her tiptoes and kissed him once, lightly. Then she turned and walked out.

Tony dropped into the kitchen chair and stared at the door. He was saddened on many levels. He was losing a friend, a great co-worker, and wonderful partner in the bedroom. He was also saddened because he knew she spoke the truth.

"You're right," he said to the empty room. "You can't compete with Lisa."

Chapter 26

Blaine pushed his soiled clothes into the automatic washer in the basement of his farmhouse and walked naked up the two flights of stairs to the master bathroom. He took a long, hot shower, scrubbing carefully, not wanting any part of his most recent efforts to remain on him. Shelly had been on his mind all day, and he struggled not to cry as he thought about his reunion with her.

Two days ago, he had gone to Manhattan, Kansas, to the West Region offices of the Kansas Department of Children and Families. Shelly had been there, nervously waiting to see her father. She had cried and begged his forgiveness for running away and causing him so much pain and worry. He had cried and told her over and over again that he was grateful she was safe.

The state was keeping Shelly for now, but they had assured him she would be returning home soon. The authorities weren't yet done with their interviews in the criminal investigation, and Shelly needed counseling and treatment before being released. And they had said there would have to be an investigation into her home "situation" to ensure she would be safe. The implication of that had angered Blaine, but he understood. In their eyes, Shelly had run away, even if she had meant to be gone only a short time. They had to ensure there wasn't a reason behind her actions related to something at home.

Blaine had left Manhattan and driven straight to Kansas City. Shelly had told her father enough of the story that he had not hesitated in deciding what to do next. Donny had taken her to that rich guy's penthouse in Kansas City. She had been held there and raped repeatedly for more than a week. Just like Emily, by the time Caulder had finished with her, she was trapped. She was their slave.

As Blaine stood in the shower and thought of Shelly, he thought, *Forgive me, baby. Please. Forgive me for not bein' a better dad. Forgive me for not bein' there when you needed me. And forgive me for today. If you knew what I done, I'd hope you'd understand. A man can't just let it go. He had to pay. Those other bastards are in prison. I may never be able to do nothin' to 'em. But Caulder was easy. And now it's done. Maybe I'll sleep better. Maybe I won't too. But I don't regret it.*

Blaine was still working through how it felt, but he had no worries about being caught. No one had seen him approach Caulder. No one had seen Caulder get into the truck, with a little urging from Blaine's double-barrel shotgun, and no one had seen him since. One advantage to farming over a thousand acres was he had a lot of places to bury the garbage. And he had the digging equipment and chemicals to make sure no dogs, and no people, would ever find the grave. *Caulder won't be pushing up daisies, but he might fertilize a couple of rows of field corn. Serves 'im right to have his nutrients eaten by somebody's pigs.*

***

Town Crier

Accused Kidnapper, Rapist Missing

Ben Smalley, Editor

ORNEY, Iowa – Albert Caulder, the Kansas City electronics entrepreneur and the man arrested a week ago for the kidnapping and rape of a 12-year-old girl, did not appear in U.S. District Court in Kansas City yesterday morning for a scheduled hearing related to charges of human trafficking.

Authorities said it is possible Caulder forfeited the $1 million in bail money and fled the area to avoid prosecution. A nation-wide search is underway, and all international terminals have been notified to watch for the man accused of taking a young girl to his penthouse condo, holding her captive there, and repeatedly raping her over a period of days.

Because of Caulder's association with the human trafficking ring, he is being investigated for possibly

having committed similar crimes against other girls. Caulder is also accused of kidnapping *Town Crier* reporter Tony Harrington and turning him over to a ring of sex traffickers to be held against his will and possibly killed.

Authorities said Caulder has the economic resources to travel anywhere. However, they have suspended his passport and have alerted Interpol.

Kansas City police reported finding Caulder's car, apparently abandoned, in a KC parking lot. They said foul play was a possibility because multiple bullet holes were found in the car's exterior metal panels as well as interior. No blood or any other sign of injury was found.

U.S. District Court Judge...

Ben's article ticked off Tony even more. He knew the bullet holes weren't the result of foul play, which made him certain Caulder had skipped. He couldn't believe it. *Would this bastard really get away?*

His desk phone rang.

"Harrington."

"Mr. Harrington, can I trust ya?"

Dear God, not another one of these.

"Sure," Tony said abruptly, "trust away."

"You sound upset. Could it be you're not happy 'bout Mr. Caulder's disappearance?"

Tony reached for his keyboard, cradling the phone under his chin. "You know something about Albert Caulder?"

"Sorry, Harrington, you first. Can I trust ya?"

"Well, of course, but it depends on what you're asking. I'm not, for example, going to help you let that bastard get away."

The man chuckled softly.

Tony recognized the voice, but he couldn't remember from where. "What's this about?"

"I called because ya seemed like a nice young man. Ya seemed to really care 'bout those missing girls, 'bout what happened to 'em. I didn't want you to think that Caulder guy got away."

"So you're saying he didn't... Where is he, then? Have you called the police? You know you should be helping them find him."

"No, I'm not gonna do that. Mr. Caulder is right where I want 'im. I 'spect he's where you want 'im too. If I can trust ya to never share this with nobody, I can give you a little more."

"Okay," Tony said. "I'm in. Where is he?"

"Well, speakin' plain-like, I'd say he's somewhere he'll never be found, and his soul is burnin' in hell."

"You mean he's..."

The voice interrupted. "Let's just say my ba... I mean, those girls he abused and used as slaves... Let's just say they're not the only ones crying from unknown graves."

The line went dead.

Tony smiled. He remembered the line from Longfellow. Now he also remembered the voice. The farmer was better read than Tony would have guessed. Far more importantly, it appeared fate had indeed caught up with Caulder, and fate's name was Blaine.

Tony knew what Blaine was claiming to have done was wrong. He knew it went against everything he believed, ethically, morally, and spiritually. He also knew hearing it had created only overwhelming feelings of relief and satisfaction. And he knew that no one but Irwin Blaine and Tony Harrington would ever know about it.

Chapter 27

"Is this Grady Aston?"

"Who wants to know?" came the gruff reply.

Tony was using his "Ray" voice, not to imitate Ray, but simply to save himself the trouble of creating a second voice different from his own.

"You can call me John. I'd like to buy some of your merchandise."

"Who is this? I don't do business with strangers over the phone."

"You're worried I'm a cop. Well, Mr. Aston, I'm not. I'm just a lonely man with a lot of money. I heard your daughter's for sale, and I'd like to buy some. I've never had a young girl like that. The idea is, shall we say, intriguing. I'll pay triple your normal rate if I can have her tonight."

Any semblance of caution Aston was expressing disappeared at the mention of the money. "Triple? That'd be like..." He hesitated, and Tony imagined him counting on his fingers. "That'd be fifteen hundred."

Tony assumed Aston was lying, but the amount didn't matter. He said, "Money is no object. I'll pay two thousand if I can have her for the night, and if we do this my way."

"What way is that?" Tony could hear the skepticism in Aston's tone. He also could hear a tinge of excitement. He had him hooked.

"Well, first of all, you deliver her and pick her up at the motor inn on the highway outside of Orney. Second, you make no attempt to find out who I am. Third, you assure me she'll do whatever I ask of her." Tony struggled to maintain the silky, easygoing manner of the Ray voice as he spoke these last despicable words.

Aston said, "I can do that. I always deliver her and pick her up, so that's no problem. I'll send her in to get half the cash in advance. Then I'll leave until she calls me to come pick her up. You won't have to worry about me seeing you or knowing who you are. Lastly, I promise you'll like what you get. This girl could suck rust off a bumper. She knows she has to do whatever you ask, or she pays for it later at home. So go for it. Do every hole twice if you want. Enjoy yourself, mister."

Tony's face was flushed with anger, but he managed to conclude the deal. "Okay. I'll look for her at 7 p.m. Room 14 on the far end of the motel."

When the call ended, Tony shut off the digital recorder, made three copies of the audio recording onto three separate thumb drives, and put them in three envelopes.

Despite his promise to Agent Cunningham, Tony had not shared with anyone what he had learned from Glenda about Trina. He had asked Glenda not to tell anyone else, promising he would find a way to help Trina. Tony was doing this on his own—no Davis, no Ben, no Sheriff Mackey, no FBI. It flew in the face of every relationship he had built. If they found out, neither Davis nor Ben would forgive him. Least of all Ben, in light of the conversation they'd had in Tony's kitchen.

Tony was putting everything on the line for a reason. It had occurred to him that if Aston was caught by the authorities and arrested, Trina would have no chance at an ordinary life. She was an only child. Orney was a small town. Everyone would know what had happened to her. She would be branded at school. The brands would vary—victim, slut, whore—but all would isolate her and rob her of any chance to get free of these horrors in the way she wanted.

Tony had an alternate plan.

***

When Trina arrived at Room 14, the door was ajar, and the lights were on. She knocked and stepped inside. The room was empty. On the desk by the TV was an envelope with a note on it reading: *Take this to Mr. Aston, then return here please.* She did just that. After her father had pulled out of the parking lot, she closed the door to the room and sat on the bed. She ran her fingers through her hair, pulling it forward to cover her face, and looked down.

Tony stepped out of the bathroom, and Trina glanced up. "You!"

Tony smiled and tried to adopt a stance that was as non-threatening as possible.

"No, no, no," the girl said, shaking her head vigorously. "Not you. I thought you were nice. I thought you were..."

"Trina." Tony spoke quietly but firmly. "Stop talking. I didn't ask you here to have sex with you. I'm not going to have sex with you. I'm here to help."

"Help? What do you mean help? Paying my dad to bring me here is helping somehow?"

Tony said it could be if she would cooperate. The scene became a forty-minute rerun of what he had experienced with Emily in the back of the truck. Trina's fear and self-loathing were barriers to convincing her things could be different. Tony kept at it. This time he had all night if he needed it, and he wasn't letting go.

In the end, he convinced her. He painted for her a picture of what life could be like if his plan succeeded, and she decided chasing a glimmer of hope was better than resigning herself to the so-called life in which she had been trapped for nearly five years.

Tony retrieved his digital recorder from a shoulder bag, and Trina told her story—every gruesome, heartbreaking detail. Tony captured some of it on video, using his smartphone, just for the added benefit of being able to say he had it. He was going to need all the leverage he could get.

***

It was 11:45 p.m. when Grady Aston pulled his car up to the end of the motel, in front of the door marked "14." He waited, but not very patiently at that hour. *Christ, I have to work tomorrow. Come on, girl.*

Five minutes later, he was out of the car, prepared to pound on the motel door. However, he noticed it wasn't shut tight. He pushed it open. "Trina? Time to go. Let's get a move on."

The room appeared to be empty. A second envelope was on the desk, identical to the first, with Aston's name on it. It felt too thin, so he ripped it open. A printed note said simply, *If you want your money, close the door and wait there.*

"What the hell?" Aston said, but he kicked the door shut. As soon as it slammed, the telephone in the room rang. Aston grabbed it.

"Yeah?"

"Mr. Aston, this is John."

"Where's my money, you prick? If you're stiffing me, I'll..."

"Mr. Aston," Tony said, his voice syrupy and deep, "I'm doing a lot more than stiffing you. I suggest you sit down and listen to what I have to say."

"Up yours! Where's my money? And where's my daughter?"

"Mr. Aston, there is no more money. In fact, I want you to open your wallet and leave the money there in the room—the money that I already paid you."

"You're crazy, old man! Why would I..."

"And," Tony crooned, "you no longer have a daughter. You might as well start getting used to that right now."

Aston screamed into the phone for a few minutes more. Tony let him vent. When he finally ran out of energy and curses, Tony began explaining that he now had an audio recording of their original conversation in which Aston admitted to delivering his underage daughter to motels for men to abuse in return for cash, two-hour audio and video recordings of his daughter describing everything that had happened to her since she was eleven years old, and a video of him accepting the envelope full of cash in his car earlier that day. Now he had an audio recording of Aston's reaction to not finding the additional money as he'd expected.

Aston screamed and sputtered as Tony described the recordings, but Tony talked through it, concluding with his explanation that he had, or soon would have, three copies of everything, stored in three secure locations where Aston would never find them.

"In short, Mr. Aston, I have you by the balls. You're going to do exactly as I say, or your daughter is going to be turned over to Social Services and these recordings are going to be given to the FBI, the DCI, and the County Attorney's Office. You will spend the next twenty years in prison. In fact, you will spend life in prison because we both know you won't last twenty years. Inmates at the state prison have a special hatred for child molesters. I predict you won't last three months."

At Tony's last remark, Aston finally sat. The bed sagged as he held the phone away from his ear for a moment, stared at it, then said, "What do you want?"

"I want Trina to have a life. That's it. She deserves, and is going to get, a chance to live her high school years as a teenage girl should, free from mental and physical abuse. You, sir, better pray nothing happens to her. If she disappears, or dies, or gets hurt—hell, if she gets a bloody nose—whether it's you or not, these recordings are going to the authorities."

"So I'm supposed to just go home and pretend none of this ever happened? Suddenly I'm going to be dad of the year? How is that supposed to work?"

"No. You and I seem to agree on this point. You and Trina clearly cannot live in the same house. In fact, I'm going to suggest you don't even live in the same town. In any case, you're going to tell people you've decided you can't raise Trina on your own. You have to work, and she needs someone with the time and resources to take care of her. You're going to tell everyone that you're very fortunate a friend of the family, a wonderful man, a retired attorney named Nathan Freed, has agreed to let Trina live with him."

"Freed? You mean that rich guy? The guy with a house that's big enough to host the state fair? I don't even know him."

"Starting tonight, you do. You tell everyone he was a friend of your late wife's. That's true, by the way. Remind people that Freed's daughter Lisa was killed a couple of years ago. You think it's a terrific thing for both him and Trina to have her live there for a while. You and Trina and Mr. Freed will know it's permanent, but you don't have to say that right away."

"And I'll get to see her when?"

Tony raised his voice to nearly double the volume, which wasn't easy in his Ray voice. "You do not. You never again go near her. And, by the way, you never again engage in any activities that bring harm of any kind to any other girls. We'll be watching you. At any hint of your involvement in human trafficking, prostitution, or other sex crimes, the same thing happens. You. Go. To. Prison. Are we clear?"

"Yes," he mumbled. "We're clear as a damn July afternoon."

"Good. Now put my money on the bed and get out of there. Then go home and start looking for work in another town. The sooner you announce your move, the better."

The line went dead. Aston stood, got out his wallet, removed the ten C-notes and threw them on the bed. He never stopped cursing until he got to his car and roared out of the motel's parking lot onto the highway.

About a hundred yards away, Tony and Trina sat in the front of Tony's Explorer. The SUV was parked in the shadows of a trucking company's maintenance garage. As they watched Trina's dad race away, she turned to Tony and asked, "Do you really think this will work?"

"Yes, Trina. I do. Once Nathan agreed to help you, to welcome you into his home, I knew you'd be safe. Your dad knows now he has no choice. Coming after you in any way not only risks his exposure and arrest, but risks crossing paths with one of the most visible and influential leaders in the community."

Tony turned and looked her in the eye. "This is real, Trina. This is the legitimate chance you've been wanting. Now it's up to you to accept Nathan's generosity and support, and use it to create a real life for yourself."

"Wow," she said, sitting back in the seat.

***

When Tony turned into Freed's driveway, the attorney was waiting on the wide, pillared front stoop with both of the house's double front doors standing open and all the lights on.

Nice touch, Tony thought. *Nothing has ever looked more welcoming.*

As the vehicle came to a stop, Trina pulled her gaze away from the mansion and asked, "Tony, how can I ever thank you?"

"Just do what I said. All the thanks I'll ever need is to see you enjoy high school and grow into a strong, successful woman. This won't be easy, even with Nathan's help. But hang in there. Make me proud."

"I will. I swear I will. But Tony..."

She had his full attention.

"You know, Tony, there are lots more girls like me out there. They all need to be saved. And you can't do it. I'm so grateful I'm the one, but you can't save them all."

"I know it," he assured her, smiling ruefully. "But I saved the one. Maybe more than one. That will have to do for now."

She nodded and was gone.

As Trina climbed the steps, Freed also nodded at Tony and waved, but soon turned his attention to Trina. There was an awkward moment of introductions and a handshake. Then Trina threw her arms around Freed and hugged him. Both were smiling through tears as they turned to go inside, pulling the doors closed behind them.

Afterword

As Tony Harrington states in the text of this novel, "Slavery may have been abolished in America, but it hasn't been eliminated." This is the horrifying truth I learned as I began researching the topic of sex trafficking for this, my second novel.

In contemplating a second adventure for Tony and his family and friends, I knew I wanted a big topic. In his first adventure, *Burying the Lede*, he investigates multiple murders and a sinister plot involving the most powerful people in the state. I couldn't imagine following that by involving Tony in a simple "whodunnit."

As a result, human trafficking seemed an obvious topic for him to pursue next. It's a huge problem and an important subject for discussion and action, and it involves a long list of complex legal and social issues. It presented endless opportunities to create a story in which Tony and others would face real challenges, ethical dilemmas, personal dangers, and heroic, if sometimes poorly-advised, efforts to help others.

I must admit, however, there were times during the process—

both in researching and in writing—that I wished I had chosen another topic. Learning about and later writing fictional depictions of despicable acts of violence and sexual abuse was not fun. I told my wife more than once that I was writing a book I didn't want my children to read.

In the end, I have tried to create a story that is reasonably accurate in depicting that world, while not being so graphic that it becomes impossible to enjoy. I also tried to create an upbeat and hopeful ending, while still acknowledging that the problem was not solved, and could not be solved, by one or two successful interventions.

In researching this topic, I read many news accounts and articles about the problem, and I talked to several people with firsthand knowledge about it, including a former Iowa sheriff who said it was the biggest problem he dealt with when serving in law enforcement in rural Iowa.

Most helpful was the woman who founded and directs "Dorothy's House," a shelter and treatment center for young women who have been rescued from the horrors of human trafficking. Dorothy's House is mentioned in the book. It is important to know it is a real place, located in Des Moines and doing outstanding work. As noted in the novel, Dorothy's House operates primarily on the generosity of private donations. If you would like to support this lifesaving ministry, go to www.DorothysHouse.org. It is a not-for-profit organization, and is recognized as such by the Internal Revenue Service.

Another not-for-profit organization in Des Moines devoted to helping women and children recover from the worst circumstances of life—homelessness, abuse, drug addiction, etc.—is the House of Mercy. It has operated for many years in a former nursing home and has a tremendous track record of success in helping women and their children recover and begin new, hope-filled lives. It, too, needs the support of private donations to continue its ministry. You can make a donation at www.MercyOne.org/DesMoinesFoundation.

There are many other excellent organizations working to address this problem nationally, including Ashton Kutcher's and Demi Moore's Thorn organization, and the National Center for Missing and Exploited Children.

Whether or not you choose to donate to one of these important ministries, I hope you will engage in discussing this serious problem and helping to educate others about the importance of doing all we can to end the modern slave trade and sex trafficking industry. I also hope this book adds a tiny drop of awareness to the growing wellspring of determination to address the problem and protect our children and others from these crimes.

Acknowledgements

As noted, I need to thank the director of Dorothy's House for taking time from her busy schedule to educate me about the horrors of human trafficking. In addition to sharing extremely valuable, first-hand information, she took the time to read an early draft of the book and provide extensive comments. Her reactions and insights were very valuable in improving the story and helping to make the book a more realistic depiction of a dark world most people never experience. Any mistakes or misrepresentations about human trafficking are mine alone, and most likely a result of my poor listening skills, or my reluctance to depict that world in its most brutal form. While this book might be described as "dark," she and others would tell you the reality often is worse.

It is important to note that this is a work of fiction. Take to heart the standard disclaimer language: "Names, characters, businesses, places, events, locales, and incidents are either products of my imagination or used in a fictitious manner. Any resemblance to actual persons, living or dead, is purely coincidental."

I also want to thank my wife, Jane, and our six grown children, all of whom have been incredibly supportive of my efforts to be an author.

My appreciation also goes to the crew at Bookpress Publishing. I couldn't ask for a better partner in getting my stories from manuscripts to finished products in readers' hands.

Lastly, we all should thank the men and women who strive every day to keep daily and weekly newspapers, and other forms of news media, alive and available to everyone. The economic and operational challenges of running a high-quality and viable news organization are enormous, and we're fortunate to have people in our communities who are dedicated to the effort.

Thomas Jefferson said democracy cannot exist without a free press. He was right. As a result, we owe our friends in the media a tremendous debt. I hope my tales of Tony Harrington and his friends and co-workers in the world of small-town newspapers pay proper homage to the journalists doing this work in the real world.

Very Special Thanks

Following are the names of people who have gone above and beyond the norm in supporting the Tony Harrington mysteries/ thrillers. I am extremely grateful to each and every reader of my books, and especially to the people listed here:

Jared & Rachel Abel

Terry & Mariann Alcorn

Dan & Harriet Aten

Jill Austin

Lorene Baran

Beaverdale Books

Dean & Nancy Beckman

Craig & Sarah Black

Daniel Bohlke

Lori Bonnstetter

Kendra Breitsprecher

Dr. Matt & Amy Brown

Tessa Burchardt & Meghan Nelson

Alex Carlson

Dennis & Rita Carlson

Tim Coffey

Joyce Dauenbaugh

Dayton Public Library

Patricia Donovan

Dave Elbert

Jim & Pam Feld

Joe & Barb Feld

John & Sue Feld

Paul & Sandi Feld

Leslie Garman

Dr. Brad Hammer

Phil & Janice Harrington

Bob & Betty Hellman

Peggy Taylor Hemness

Gale Hererra

Laura Hollingsworth

Doug Hotchkiss

Kristine Howe

Diane Kinneberg

Rex Bradley & Sandra Kragh

Jackie Frost-Kunnen

Curt Krull

Josh Krull & Emma LeValley

Daniel & Paulette LeValley

David & Chris LeValley

Paul LeValley & Diane Shinn

Kathy Magruder

Kellie Markey

Bob & JoAnn Mason

Perry & Jeri Meyer

Mark Mittelstadt

Aaron Morse

Abby Morse

Andrew Morse

Doug & Ann Morse

Don & Sally Myers

Wade & Joan Nelson

Tim & Diane Neugent

Mary Newbrough

Dr. Andrew & Elizabeth Owens

Warren & Joan Owens

Pageturners Bookstore

Tom Parsons & Beth LeValley

Heath Pattschull

Dr. Anthony Paustian

Abby Pepper

Maureen Powers

Bob & Mary Ritz

Gary Richards

Jason Brandt Schaefer

Maxwell Schaeffer

Bill & Candi Schickel

John Smith

Robin R. Spear

Robin Thompson

Brenda Tsuda

Dave & Nancy Vellinga

Robyn Wilkinson

LaVonne Welch

Lindsley Withey

Ann Zierke

Enjoy Joseph LeValley's other mysteries/thrillers
featuring journalist Tony Harrington

If you haven't read it already, get a copy of the original, award-winning, Tony Harrington adventure, *Burying the Lede.*

Critics Loved It!

- **U.S. Review of Books:** "Don't miss it" – RECOMMENDED
- **Midwest Book Reviews:** "Nearly impossible to put down"
- **Publishers Weekly BookLife Prize (9 of 10):** *"Filled with suspense"*

Get Your Copy Today!

Joseph LeValley's books are available from your Local Bookstore, Amazon, Barnes & Noble, or the author directly at www.josephlevalley.com.

Check the website for author information, public appearances, preview chapters of future books, and much more!

Coming Soon! Two New Tony Harrington Adventures!
The Third Side of Murder and *Performing Murder*